WINGS of GOLD

BOOK II

THE FLYBOYS

T. E. CRUISE

POPULAR LIBRARY

An Imprint of Warner Books, Inc.

A Warner Communications Company

POPULAR LIBRARY EDITION

Popular Library® and the fanciful P design are registered trademarks
of Warner Books, Inc.

Cover design by Mike Stromberg
Cover illustration by Mark Skolsky

Popular Library books are published by
Warner Books, Inc.
666 Fifth Avenue
New York, N.Y. 10103

 A Warner Communications Company

Printed in the United States of America

First Printing: November, 1988

10 9 8 7 6 5 4 3

BOOK I:
1943–1945

FLYBOYS OVER NEW GUINEA—
Massive Bomber Attacks on Jap Strongholds—
Philadelphia Tattler

ALLIED TURBOJET PROJECTS REVEALED—
Brits and Yanks Disclose Their Top-Secret Jet Airplane
Research—

Aviation Industry Weekly

NORMANDY INVASION PRESSES ON—
Nazis Fall Back After Bitter Fighting at 'Omaha Beach'—
Miami Daily Telegraph

JAPS INITIATE AIRBORN SUICIDE ATTACKS AT LEYTE
GULF BATTLE—
Jap Pilots Crash Their Airplanes Into Our Ships—
Call Themselves *Kamikaze*—'Divine Wind'
Boston Times

FDR DEAD—
Vice President Truman Takes Oath of Office—
New York Herald

JAPS VOW TO DEFEND HOMELAND DOWN TO LAST
MAN, WOMAN, CHILD—
Millions Mobilized in Civilian Defense Corps—
Baltimore Globe

HITLER DEAD—
RUSSIANS TAKE BERLIN—
NAZIS SURRENDER—
Washington Star Reporter

AWESOME NEW WEAPON USED AGAINST JAPAN—
Jap City of Hiroshima Leveled by A-Bomb—
Los Angeles Tribune

CHAPTER 1

(One)

**USAAF Advance Air Base
Tobi Point, New Guinea
19 August 1943**

Lieutenant Steven Gold, wearing khaki overalls, his .45 in a shoulder holster beneath his yellow Mae West, settled into the cockpit of his fighter. He pulled his canvas helmet over his close-cropped blonde hair and plugged in his radio earphones, but left the Lockheed Lightning's plexiglass canopy raised against the sweltering tropical heat.

He waited until his ground crew was clear, and then started the P-38's twin liquid-cooled Allison engines. The engines sputtered in complaint for a few moments before wheezing to a roaring fury in a cloud of blue smoke. All along the ready line the fifteen other swallow-tailed, twin-engine P-38 fighters that made up the squadron were adding their voices to the clacking piston chorus.

Lieutenant Gold affectionately patted the P-38's scarred instrument panel. The joke was that his fighter had so many Jap bullet holes in it that the mess hall wanted to requisition it as a noodle strainer. It was true that the mottled green and tan exterior of the P-38 was pocked with patched holes, but it was also true that this mount had taken good care of her previous owner, a captain who'd been rotated out of the squadron after an illustrious twelve-kill career. The twelve scarlet "meatballs" on the fighter's forward fuselage had been painted over. Her new owner would have to rack up his own score.

But there's not much chance of me racking up that score today, Steve brooded as he waited the operations officer's red flag signal to take off.

Today the squadron was flying a bomber escort mission, and Jap fighter resistance was expected to be light. A lot of pilots would have been grateful for that, but Steve thought the situation stunk. As far as he was concerned, multiple opportunities to wax Zeros was the only thing that could make up for being stuck out here in this godforsaken, vermin-infested jungle, literally under the Japs' noses.

Tobi Point was a forward air base tucked in between the emerald wall of vegetation and the indigo Solomon Sea. It was a tent and tin hut village under a camouflage-net ceiling, clustered around a single hard-packed airstrip less than seventy miles down the coast from extensive Jap airdrome complexes. The strategy behind Tobi was that a fighter squadron so near the enemy could, in addition to flying bomber escort, hit and run like a swarm of angry wasps.

Until, of course, the Japs happened to *find* the wasp's nest, Steve thought, and then reminded himself that fighter pilots were like toilet paper: absolutely essential, and totally expendable.

Steve hurriedly turned down the gain as a deafening squawk of radio static filled his headset.

"Big birds approaching, hombres," the squadron's leader, Major Wohl, announced. "Saddle up!"

The major was from Texas, and liked to remind everyone of that fact by peppering his easy drawl with lots of "you-alls" and "hombres" and "buckaroos" and so on.

"We'll be moving out in a few minutes, men," the major continued. "Lieutenant Gold, you-all come in, please. Over."

Steve keyed his throat mike. "Yeah, Major? Over."

"Lieutenant, this time around I want you-all to fly as my wingman, over."

"I don't see why I have to sit on the bench, sir," Steve protested. What a wingman did was watch his leader's back. It was a crucial job, but in combat the wingman hardly ever got a taste of the enemy, unless it was sloppy seconds.

"Lieutenant," Wohl began patiently, "how old are you?" He paused. "Nineteen, I seem to remember."

"Roger, Major."

"And you're already an ace, right? Lieutenant, you-all just lay back today. It's gonna be a long war."

"Roger, Major," Steve repeated, disappointed.

"And don't sound so down in the dumps," Wohl chuckled. "You've only been with us a couple of weeks. You're the new kid on the block. I want to make sure you know the program, how we operate. I run a tighter herd than Cappy Fitzpatrick, that old hombre you *used* to ride with."

"Roger, Major."

"All right, then," Wohl said, sounding satisfied. "Here they come," he told his squadron.

Steve, looking up, saw the bombers. There were twenty of them, flying high and looking like glinting silver crosses stitched in orderly procession against the deep blue sky.

He lowered his canopy, trapping several two-inch, spindly legged mosquitoes inside the cockpit. He idly squished them against the plexiglass with his finger, thinking, *Fortunes of war.* Out on the airstrip's edge the ops officer was waving his red flag.

"All right, let's ride," Wohl said.

Steve opened his throttles, building up rpm's, waiting his turn as the pairs of P-38s moved out onto the airstrip. When it was his turn to roll, he felt a twinge in his knee as he worked the rudder pedals. He ignored the sharp stab of pain. He'd gotten used to it.

Last April he'd been flying combat air patrol out of Guadalcanal, with Major Cappy Fitzpatrick's fighter squadron, when a Jap managed to lock on to his tail, putting a bullet through his leg in the process of chewing up his airplane. Steve had managed to turn the tables on that Jap, knocking him out of the sky. It had been his fifth kill, the one that made him an ace, but at the time he'd had other things on his mind. His fighter was so badly shot up that he was forced to ditch at sea.

Air-sea rescue eventually fished him out of the drink. He'd spent some time convalescing in the hospital, and then had a couple of weeks' R&R, which he spent back home in California with his folks. When he came back on active duty, he was promoted to first lieutenant and assigned to Wohl's outfit at Tobi Point. Since then, he'd flown a few routine patrols, but had not met up with the enemy. Steve was feeling a little anxious about that. He figured that surviving being shot down was like falling off a horse, the idea being to get right back into the thick of it to dispel any self-doubt about courage or competence.

Once all sixteen fighters were airborne the squadron formed into four flights of four each. The bombers dropped down to about twelve thousand feet as the four flights of snarling P-38s rose to meet them. The fighters then took their positions all around the big bird formation—as Wohl would have put it, like cowpokes riding herd.

It would be a short ride to the target, a Jap airdrome on the coast. Once over the target the squadron would fly high cover for the bombers. If enemy fighter resistance turned out to be as light as was expected, the P-38s were to do some mop-up strafing after the bombers were done.

The bombers were light twin-engine airplanes: North American Mitchell B-25s and GAT AC-1s. They were attack bombers: deck-level lawn mowers modified with extra-capacity fuel tanks and a half-dozen .50-caliber machine guns sticking like whiskers out from underneath their chins. The bombers would go in fast and low, strafing the Jap airstrips while dropping parafrags: twenty-five-pound bombs suspended by midget parachutes. The parafrags wafted lazily down from the sky, giving the low-flying bombers plenty of time to get away before they exploded into wicked clouds of shrapnel.

Steve heard a clicking through the static in his headset. "Hey, Lieutenant Gold," somebody said. "Settle an argument some of us had the other day. Aren't you Herman Gold's son? Over."

"Roger," Steve replied wearily, knowing what was coming.

"Hear that, guys? I told you so! Hey, Lieutenant Gold! Your old man owns Gold Aviation and Transport, right? He's got millions! Wasn't it your father's company that built these AC-1 BuzzSaw bombers we're escorting?"

"Roger," Steve muttered as he scanned the clear blue sky and the thick green coastline for signs of the enemy. The P-38's teardrop canopy afforded excellent visibility, if a pilot wasn't too lazy to take advantage of it.

"I guess we better take extra good care of these bombers, else Lieutenant Gold will tell his daddy on us," another pilot cracked.

"Or maybe Gold will just repossess his daddy's bombers. . . ."

Steve forced himself to keep his mouth shut. He knew from past experience that this was a no-win situation. If you too readily joined in the joking, you were a horse's ass; if you complained, you were a sore-ass. Meanwhile, he irritably thought that maybe Major Wohl was more spit and polish than Cappy Fitzpatrick, but at least Cappy knew enough to enforce radio silence en route to a target.

Then Steve realized that there was no point blaming Wohl. What was really pissing him off was having his illustrious father's reputation thrown up to him.

"Hey, Gold," another voice cut in. "How's it feel to be rich? Over."

Steve ignored the remark.

"What's the matter, Lieutenant? Cat got your tongue? Your daddy could always buy you another. . . ."

Steve waited for Wohl to cut in and get him out of this, but he didn't. Steve guessed he was on his own. He still didn't immediately reply. He knew he had to handle this correctly. He was, as Major Wohl had put it, the new kid on the block. If he wanted to fit in, he was going to have to head-on defuse the issue of his famous father's wealth and power.

Come to think of it, maybe Major Wohl had realized that as well, Steve decided. Maybe that was why the major was allowing this hazing to take place.

"It's like this," Steve began, keenly aware that the entire squadron was listening. "Sure, my family is wealthy. We live like royalty back in California. But home might as well be a million miles away. As much money as my old man has, it doeesn't mean much out here. I can't *bribe* the Japs to go down in front of my guns. I've got to *shoot them down*, just like anybody else. That answer your question? Over."

"All right, hombres, palavering time's over," Major Wohl cut in, sounding amused. "We're approaching the target. The bombers are going in. Remember," Wohl counseled, "we stay high while the bombers are on the deck. Lieutenant Gold, you *will* remember to stick close by me. Over and out."

Down below, Gold saw tongues of fire as the Jap antiaircraft ground fire commenced. The first wave of bombers was diving toward the compound of hangars and the network of tan airstrips cut into the dense green jungle. There were plenty of Jap heavy bombers parked in muddy, earth-embankment revetments alongside the runways, but no fighters. With nothing to do, the formations of P-38s cartwheeled in the sky like vultures as the marauding bombers did their on-deck dirty work. Every few moments Steve would break off searching the sky for the enemy in order to watch the lethal, silent aerial ballet unfurling down below.

The bombers went in fast and low, braving the steady stream of antiaircraft tracer and cannon fire arcing up. They strafed a path with their machine guns, and then released their parafrags, which drifted down in a deadly snowfall. The first flurry of parafrags detonated upon contact with the uppermost palm fronds lining the airstrips. The scythelike bursts of shrapnel decapitated the palms, revealing Jap ground personnel and vehicles. Orange fireballs began to rise up out of the denuded jungle as other parafrags touched off fuel depots.

The defensive ground fire had been silenced by the time the second wave of bombers made its pass. The wafting parafrags were disappearing into rolling clouds of oily black smoke.

"Major Wohl," one of the pilots called, "there's no way we can go down on deck through all that smoke."

"Roger that," Wohl replied.

Steve was relieved. He hated going down on deck to strafe, where a fighter pilot's attributes of sharp eyes, sharp flying, and sharp shooting did no good at all.

On deck you had to fly as low as possible so that the defensive machine gunners couldn't track you, but that just made you all the more vulnerable to small-arms fire. On deck you just mashed your trigger, blindly hosing the targets that passed beneath you in a blur, and if your mount was hit, you sure as hell weren't going to get a chance to finesse or bail your way out of a flamer when you were indicating four hundred miles an hour seventy five feet above the ground. Chances were you'd end up plowing your own grave before you knew it.

"Major, we've got to have us *some* action," one of the pilots was complaining. "I'm gonna have me a raging case of the blue balls if I don't get my rocks off shooting *something*."

"Roger that," someone interjected.

Steve was feeling the same way. His neck muscles were aching from all the head-swiveling he'd been doing, looking for the enemy. He scanned his port side and looked away, but then something—hell, if he *knew* what it was, he'd bottle it and sell it to Uncle Sammy—made him do a double take.

"We've still got plenty of gas," another pilot cut in.

Steve continued to stare into that dizzying, boundless curve of blue sky, until he'd reassured himself that what he was seeing weren't just specks floating across his eyeballs. He already knew that what he was seeing wasn't his imagination. A guy with a head full of dreams made for one shitty fighter jock, so he'd trained himself to leave his imagination in the ready room before going out on patrol.

"We could swing out to sea and wax some of those tankers anchored offshore," a pilot suggested.

Steve keyed his throat mike. "Nix that. We've got company. Bogies—a whole slew of 'em—at nine-o'clock level."

Silence, except for the cackle of static and whoosh of white noise coming over Steve's headset, and then: "Bullshit! This is Captain Leeland, and I don't see shit out there.... I—oh, wait a minute. I *do* see them now...." More static, sizzling like bacon frying. "Jesus, Gold! You've got some eyes."

"Roger that," Major Wohl said expansively. "I count twenty." He paused. "How many do *you* count, Lieutenant Gold?"

Steve chuckled. "Twenty, sir. Over."

"Leeland, your flight will escort those bombers home," Wohl commanded. "The rest of you follow me."

The squadron came apart. Leeland and his flight of four broke right, banking out over the sea in order to catch the bombers just now hugging the coastline on their way home. Wohl, with Steve as his wingman, led his remaining twelve fighters on a diagonal to intercept the rapidly approaching Jap fighters.

Steve saw that they were Zekes: Mitsubishi Zero-Sen single-engine fighters. They were more maneuverable than the P-38, but lacked the speed, firepower, and sturdiness of the dual-engined American plane.

The Zeros scattered and began to climb. The P-38s climbed as well. The G-force flattened Steve against his seat back as the twin-engined P-38s rose like rockets, easily gaining the ceiling advantage over the Zeros.

"Break into teams," Wohl ordered. The P-38s broke into six pairs. "You're on your own, hombres. Good hunting," the major said calmly. "Gold, follow me in."

Steve followed as Wohl pushed his P-38 over into an attack dive toward a Zero that did a barrel roll trying to get away. Wohl expertly banked his aircraft in tandem with his target, and needed to fire only a single burst from the 20-millimeter cannon and four .50-caliber machine guns clustered in his fighter's nose to open up the Zero's burnished silver belly. Gutted, the smoking Jap fighter tumbled out of the sky.

"Nice shooting, Major," Steve said, thinking, *When do I get my turn?*

"Just keep watching my back, old son," Wohl murmured.

All around Steve the sky was a hornet's nest of activity as

the P-38s tangled with the Zeros. The deep blue heavens became slashed with bold black brushstrokes of smoke as waxed Jap fighters plummeted to the sea. Steve remained dutifully glued to Wohl as the major went after another target. The Zero corkscrewed as Wohl hosed it down with tracer rounds. An instant later it cracked open like a seed pod blossoming into fire.

Steve glanced into his rear-view mirror, and then craned his neck to check the blind spots behind him. He saw a pair of Zeros angling in. He keyed his throat mike. "Major, we got company—"

"Tell you what, old son, you've been a good boy so far. Why don't you have at 'em? Over."

"Can I have 'em both, Major?" Steve asked eagerly.

Wohl's laughter filled Steve's headset. "Sure, old son." He banked hard left, skidding steeply away as the lead Jap's twin 20-millimeter cannons and a brace of 7.7-millimeter machine guns begin winking fire. "Take two, Lieutenant. They're small."

The brace of Zeros were closing in fast as Steve worked his speed brakes and hauled back on his throttles and stick to roll up and over. The Zeros overshot him, streaking past still flying wing to wing. Steve leveled off and sighted in on the lead plane. He pressed his triggers. The staccato chattering of his quartet of .50s played counterpoint to the thudding of his 20-millimeter cannon. The gunfire reverberated inside his cockpit as his rounds hammered sparks from the silvery wings and fuselage of the Zero. The wounded Jap plane yawed in preparation for a desperate skid to safety, but then Steve's rounds blew off its propeller. The crippled Zero slammed into its companion, and then both disappeared in a crimson fireball.

"Two for the price of one! Well done, Lieutenant," Wohl said. "Now come on back into position as my wingman."

Fuck that, Steve thought. He now had seven kills. There were still a half-dozen Zeros in the sky. With a little luck, he could get three more, to become a double ace. He keyed his throat mike. "Major, your signal is breaking up. Please repeat orders, over."

"I said get back into position as my wingman. Over."

"Major, there must be something wrong with my radio. I'm not receiving."

"Now you listen, you son of a bitch—"

Steve turned down the gain until the major's voice was barely audible. No way was he going to quit now. Maybe it was the fact that this was the first action he'd seen since being shot down, or maybe it was the ribbing from the other guys he'd just taken about how he'd been born with a silver spoon in his mouth. Whatever it was, Steve knew that he just *had* to wax a couple more tails. He realized that he would likely catch hell for it, but he was willing to take the heat later on in exchange for more kills now.

Steve opened up his throttles and pushed his stick forward, chasing after a fleeing Zero skimming low over the sea. He quickly closed the distance between himself and his target. He was less than a hundred feet above and behind the Jap when he began firing, whittling away the Zero's tail. What remained of the Jap fighter tore itself to pieces cartwheeling across the surface of the sea.

"Lieutenant Gold, this is Major Wohl. Return to position. I repeat—"

Steve pulled up and began to climb, on the lookout for fresh meat as Major Wohl's tiny voice continued buzzing in his ear like a baleful conscience. Steve ignored it. It had been a long time since he'd seen combat, and now it felt just too good to stop. A Zero darted across his nose and Steve instinctively kicked rudder to try a difficult deflection shot. He managed to rivet a generous burst into the big red circle painted on the Zero's side, evidently cutting come of the Jap fighter's control cables. The Jap pilot slid back his canopy and bailed out as his fighter fluttered out of control like a flame-singed moth.

"Damn, I never ever saw *anybody* shoot like that," Steve heard Major Wohl blurt out.

He was about to acknowledge the compliment when he remembered that his radio was supposed to be broken. *Next victim*, Steve thought, feeling evil. Just one more and he'd be a double ace.

He looked around for a target, but the dogfight was over. All twelve P-38s were still flying, but the sky was cleared of Zeros. Oh well, being able to paint four "meatballs" on the side of his airplane was better than nothing, Steve thought. The honor of becoming a double ace would have to wait until next time.

"Let's go home," Major Wohl said.

Steve breathed a sigh of relief. The major didn't sound too pissed. Maybe his cutting loose like he did was going to turn out to be okay.

The flight back to Tobi passed quietly. Steve was one of the last to land. As he taxied his P-38 past the palms and sandbagged machine-gun emplacements, he saw Wohl talking to the operations officer, Captain Mader. As his plane approached the hangars, the two officers both paused in their conversation to look in Steve's direction.

Neither man was smiling. Steve guessed that the shit was going to hit the fan after all.

Wohl went stalking off, and Mader was climbing up on Steve's wing even before his props had stopped turning.

"What kind of crazy stunt did you pull up there?" Mader demanded as Steve raised his canopy. "I've never seen Wohl so hot." Mader was a pudgy, moon-faced man with light brown hair and military-issue wire-rimmed eyeglasses.

"The major was just probably beside himself with joy," Steve said. "I just waxed four Zeros."

"No shit? Congratulations, I guess," Mader said reluctantly. "But whatever you did up there, Wohl ain't too happy about it. I'm supposed to check out your radio and get your gun camera film developed. You're to report to his office pronto."

Steve glumly nodded. "I'll just change out of my flight suit."

The sunlight glinted off Mader's specs as he shook his head. "The major said pronto, Lieutenant."

(Two)

Steve Gold stood at rigid attention while Wohl, seated behind his desk, scowled at him. The major's telephone rang. Wohl snatched up the receiver. "Hello? Yeah, Mader! What have you got?"

Major Wohl's office occupied the rear half of a plywood hut with a canvas roof. The walls were painted light green, and were taken up with filing cabinets, silhouette identification charts of enemy planes, and a large map of the Pacific theater of operations. On the wall behind Wohl's beige metal desk was a grouping of framed reproductions of Frederic Remington prints: grizzled, bearded cowpokes were chasing Injuns across the prairie and otherwise generally having themselves a high old time back in the Old West. Steve wished he could join them. That son of a bitch noncom who sat out front shuffling papers for the major had kept Steve waiting while Wohl showered and changed and had himself a bite to eat. Now Steve, tired and hungry, was standing at attention in his sweat-soaked overalls, stinking of gas and cordite fumes, his .45 in its shoulder holster a chafing burden against his ribs, as the major continued talking on the phone.

"Yes, Captain," Wohl said. "I understand. Just as I thought! And what about the gun camera film?"

The major was in his midthirties. He had pale blue eyes and thick brown hair which he wore in a waxed brush cut. His face was colored by the sun, except for where the rays had been blocked by his flight goggles. The pale circles were like a mask around his eyes and made him look like a raccoon.

As the major listened to what Mader had to say, he glanced murderously at Steve, who was careful to keep his eyes front, studying his reflection in the Remington prints' glass.

Standing six feet tall and weighing one-seventy, Steve

knew he was almost too big to fit into a fighter's cramped cockpit. He kept his weight down—and kept himself strong —with calisthenics and by not eating much, which was no big sacrifice considering the quality of front-line chow. There wasn't much he could do about his height, except grin and bear it when he had to fold up like a pocketknife to tuck into his fighter. Fortunately, his concentration was such that he forgot about his discomfort and everything else except waxing the enemy once he was in the air.

He had always been big for his age. His size had always made him seem older than he really was. These days, so did his profession. His blond hair was cropped to brush-cut length, but worn unwaxed so that it fell forward, flat on his skull. His skin had been burnished by the sun, and the long hours spent scanning the sky from his cockpit had etched squint lines on either side of his hawk's nose, at the corners of his narrow slash of mouth, and around his brown eyes.

Steve snuck a glance at Wohl. The major had picked up a pencil and was jotting notes to himself as he sat with the telephone receiver cradled between his shoulder and ear. The beige enamel paint had begun to blister and peel off Wohl's desk due to the tropical heat and humidity. The major was absently picking at the marred finish, stripping off paint curls and dropping them to the muddy plywood floor as he continued talking to Captain Mader.

"Set the projector up. I'll want to view Lieutenant Gold's film. I'll be over in a few minutes." He hung up and glared at Steve. "Mader says there's nothing wrong with your radio."

Steve resisted the urge to shrug. "I guess it got better, Major." He allowed himself a ghost of a smile, just to test the waters.

"You think this is funny, Lieutenant?"

The ghost of a smile took a powder. "No, sir."

The major jerked his thumb over his shoulder toward the Remington prints. "You-all think that you're one of them ornery Old West gunslicks who didn't need nobody? You think you can charm your way out of the fact that you disobeyed my orders in a combat situation?"

"May I speak frankly, sir?"

"Go ahead." Wohl's eyes were just about bulging out of his head, he was so mad. He was scratching at his desk as if it itched.

"What I think, sir, is that since I shot down four Japs, the major ought to be congratulating me and putting me in for a promotion and maybe a medal, not chewing out my ass," Steve concluded, remembering at the last possible instant to add, "sir."

If flashing eyes were machine guns, Wohl would have been scoring direct hits, blowing Steve out of existence. But then the major closed his eyes for a second and took a deep breath. As he exhaled it seemed that the anger and tension went out of him. He gestured toward a straight-back chair against the wall. "Drag that over and sit down, old son."

Steve did as he was told.

"You want a drink?" Wohl asked, opening a desk drawer.

"Anytime, sir."

Wohl brought out a bottle of gin and two glasses. Steve's heart sank. He was a bourbon man, and failing that, rye whiskey or scotch. He hated gin, especially straight up, but there was no way he was going to further antagonize the major by refusing what he figured was a peace offering.

Wohl poured two fingers into each glass, and slid one across the desk toward Steve.

"Thank you, sir," Steve said. As Wohl knocked back his drink, Steve, forcing himself not to gag on the smell of juniper berries, flung the gin against the back of his throat and swallowed it down, shuddering.

"Another?" Wohl asked, reaching for the bottle.

"No, sir! Thank you, sir."

The major nodded and put the bottle away. "Now then, let me run through this with you from the beginning. First off, you-all did shoot down four Jap fighters. Your gun camera film confirms this, and I eyeballed you making that one incredible shot when that bandit crossed your flight path. Congratulations on some fine shooting and flying. Just about the finest I've ever seen."

"Thank you, sir," Steve said. The gin was rolling around like a ball of mercury in his empty belly.

"But I'm still very pissed off with you."

Steve nodded distractedly. That wallop of gin combat-patrolling his gut was making him feel like he was going to upchuck. "Sir? Excuse me, sir. May I smoke?"

"Go ahead," Wohl drawled.

Steve pulled out a rumpled package of Pall Malls and a battered, nickel-plated lighter. He extracted a cigarette, smoothed out the worst of its hooks and bends, and lit it. He inhaled deeply. The tobacco seemed to settle his stomach.

"You suggested that instead of raking your ass over the coals I should put you in for a promotion. No way would I do that, Lieutenant."

"But—"

"Shut up," Wohl said wearily. "Just sit there and smoke your cigarette and listen. You were my wingman. A wingman's sole purpose in life is to sit like a fucking boil on his leader's ass, watching his back while he does the shooting. A wingman needs to be reliable, because if he isn't reliable, he's going to cause his leader to be distracted worrying about him, and a distracted fighter pilot is a dead one. A wingman needs to be disciplined. He's flying so close to his leader that he's got to respond in an instant to his leader's moves. If he doesn't, he's going to get shaken loose from his leader, or worse yet, crack into him. Finally, a wingman has got to have willpower. The willpower to deny himself personal glory on behalf of the greater good. He's got to be able to say to himself, 'Okay, maybe I'm not going to get any kills, but my leader will, and by watching his back I'm serving the greater good of the squadron?'" Wohl paused.

"Major, I don't see what all this has to do with me being denied a promotion. I mean, *okay*, so what if I played the lone wolf up there? I'm alive and well to tell about it, so what's the beef?"

Wohl stared hard at Steve. "You really have no idea what I've been talking about, have you?"

"Sir, with all due respect, maybe what you've been talking about doesn't apply to me. Rules were made to be broken, if you're good enough to get away with it."

"You don't think you have limitations, Lieutenant?"

"Not in dogfighting, sir," Steve grinned. "If you'll pardon me saying so." He was careful to keep his tone respectful so Wohl wouldn't misunderstand. He didn't feel he was being arrogant. Just truthful.

"Reliability, discipline, the will to see beyond one's self-interest to the greater good," Wohl ticked off the attributes on his fingers. "Those are the same qualities an officer needs. By your insubordination today you proved to me that you don't have those qualities, Lieutenant. You've got everything it takes to be a superb fighter pilot. You've got none of what it takes to shoulder the responsibility of being in charge of other men. That is why I will not put you in for a promotion."

Steve struggled to control his temper. He couldn't help thinking that a lot of this was just sour grapes; that the major was merely jealous of his air combat skills. "Sir, I personally don't see it that way, but I'm sorry I've disappointed you. I sincerely apologize for not fulfilling your expectations, sir."

"You just don't get it," Wohl repeated. He looked tired. "Ah, fuck it. I tried, right?" he sighed. "What the hell, you're only nineteen. You probably think you're going to live forever. I was nineteen once, believe it or not, but when I was nineteen I was jerking sodas and trying to wax co-eds, not knock Jap fighters out of the air. . . ." he trailed off, shaking his head.

"Sir, I'm kind of enjoying the war," Steve shrugged. He stubbed out the remains of his cigarette in the tin ashtray on the major's desk. "I guess I'd rather dogfight than anything."

Wohl seemed not to have heard him. "Lieutenant, this was the first chance I've had to see you in action. Now that I have—I'm going to look at your film in a few moments, but it's not going to show me anything I don't already know about you—I want to talk to you about your future."

"Sir?"

"I want to transfer you out of this squadron."

Steve was appalled. "Begging the major's pardon, I said I was sorry for what just happened. Look, I promise that it won't happen again—"

Wohl held up his hand. "Slow down, old son. This isn't a punishment I'm talking about. It's . . . well, I guess you'd have to say that it's a kind of reward. There's a new, elite fighter squadron being formed. It's going to be the only Army Air Force unit based at Santa Belle."

"Where's that, sir?" Steve asked.

Wohl stood up and went to the map on the wall. He pointed to a brown dot near New Georgia Island in the Solomons chain. "Santa Belle is a hot area, Lieutenant. It's only recently been taken from the Japs by the Marines."

"I don't get it, sir," Steve said. "If the webfoots are holding the island, they'll have their own fighter squadrons there."

"Command doesn't explain everything to me, Lieutenant," Wohl scowled. "I do know the Army doesn't like the idea of the Navy and the Marines getting all the limelight for the Solomons campaign. This elite squadron will represent our branch of the service during the push to close the ring around the Jap stronghold of Rabaul."

"Sounds like a public relations stunt to me," Steve scowled.

"I guess it is, in a way," Wohl agreed. "But that's not necessarily a bad thing. For instance, the Army is going to equip this new squadron with its latest fighter, the Republic P-47D Thunderbolt. The 348th at Lae has just gotten some of them," Wohl said. "You might have seen them flying. They're calling the P-47 the Jug."

"I did see them," Steve said excitedly, but then his expression soured. "Gee, I don't know, Major. I've kind of gotten used to the P-38 Lightning."

"She's a good mount, all right," Wohl agreed. "But let's face it: she's no match for the Navy's Hellcats and those gull-winged Marine Corsairs. The Jug is supposed to be faster than the P-38, and carries more firepower. I'd think a red-hot jockey like you would be itching to fly one."

"But I've only been at Tobi Point for a couple of weeks, Major," Steve protested.

"That just makes it easier for you to transfer," Wohl prodded. "It's not like you'll have to leave behind any good buddies."

Steve looked Wohl in the eye. "You really want me to go, don't you, sir?"

Wohl hesitated. "Son, I'll put my cards on the table. After watching you fly and having this palaver with you, I think that you're too rich for my blood, and too rich for the rest of the squadron. You're all raw talent and no cunning," Wohl continued. "My big worry concerning you is that your tremendous talent is going to keep you brash. That it'll get you killed before you get enough experiencee to learn to be in control of your skills, and not the other way around."

Steve frowned. "You mean I let my skills control me?" He paused. "I never really thought about it that way. . . ."

"Roger that," Wohl smiled. "You need seasoning, old son, and the way you *get* seasoned is by watching and emulating more experienced pilots, but before you can *learn* anything from someone else, you've got to *respect* them."

"Sir, I know I was insubordinate," Steve said, getting upset. "But I never meant disrespect—"

"Simmer down. I know that, old son," Wohl snorted. "If I'd thought otherwise I'd be busting you down to noncom, not spending all this time palavering. What you need is to fly with pilots as good as you are. Maybe even get a taste of what it's like to be second best, unlikely as that prospect might seem to you now. The only way that's going to happen is if you get assigned to an elite squadron where *everybody* is a top scorer."

"Well," Steve said, "I guess I'm going."

"I can't force you into a volunteer outfit," Wohl replied. "But speaking man to man, I advise you to take advantage of the opportunity. I think it will build your character. You see, it won't be easy being a member of the sole Army squadron on a Marine-held island. You and the rest of your squadron buddies are going to have to pull together unless you want those webfoots to run you right into the sea. You having to count on others—and knowing that they're counting on you —will be good for you, old son. It'll help you to mature."

"Yes, sir," Steve said evenly, hiding the fact that he thought that what Wohl was handing him was a crock. He was mature enough to get the job done, which was shooting down Japs, right? On the other hand, he probably wouldn't have to put up with any more of this pussy shit that Wohl was trying to hand him in a sharpshooting outfit.

Wohl pondered him. "By the way, I've been saving the best for last. This new squadron is going to be commanded by your old buddy Cappy Fitzpatrick."

"Major Fitzpatrick?" Steve repeated happily. It was a sure bet that Cappy wouldn't try to make him hang back. "That settles it! I'm going!"

Wohl chuckled. "Thought that would close the deal. I'll start the paperwork. You're dismissed, Lieutenant."

Steve got up, came to attention, saluted, and turned to leave the office.

"By the way, Lieutenant," Wohl called out.

"Sir?" Steve asked from the doorway.

"I'm also putting you in for the Air Medal."

"Sir?" Steve asked, mystified. "But I thought . . ."

Wohl waved him quiet. "You're a wild man, Lieutenant Gold, and you're going to have to be tamed if you're to be of any real use to this Army, but that aside, you're presently the goddamned angel of death in a dogfight. For that you deserve recognition, and I intend to see that you get it."

"Thank you, sir!"

"Don't thank me, old son. You earned it," Wohl said wryly. "I guess that this will only be the first in a chestful of medals coming your way." He pasued. "*If* you can develop the self-discipline you'll need to stay alive long enough to collect them."

CHAPTER 2

(One)

**Gold Aviation and Transport
Burbank, California
5 October 1943**

The intercom buzzed. "Mr. Quinn to see you," the secretary said.

Herman Gold pressed the intercom's talk button. "Send him in," he told his secretary, one of the three who sat outside the massive double doors to his large office. While he waited, Gold realized that his heart was pounding and that his throat was dry.

And why shouldn't I be nervous? Gold asked himself. *Teddy must have the XP-4 test results.*

The XP-4 was an experimental turbojet fighter plane prototype, the first jet to be built at GAT. Gold had sunk a lot of time and money into this project.

Gold leaned back in his leather chair, away from the papers littering his long, marble-topped oak desk, as GAT's chief engineer Teddy Quinn appeared in the doorway. Teddy was of average height, with a wiry build. Like Gold, he was in his late forties. He had a shock of black hair seeded with gray, and green eyes magnified by the thick lenses of his tortoise-frame eyeglasses. He was wearing a white lab coat, the front of which was smudged with ashes from the ever-present cigarette stuck in the corner of his mouth.

"XP-4 test results in?" Gold asked, and when Teddy nodded, he demanded, "How'd she do?"

"Shitty," Teddy said simply. "The XP-4 is a bust." The

cigarette bobbed up and down between Teddy's lips as he spoke, and another snowfall of ash littered the front of the lab coat.

Gold swallowed hard against his bitter disappointment. "Son of a bitch. . . ." he muttered beneath his breath.

"Now calm down, Herman—" Teddy warned as he made the long trek from the double doors to Gold's desk.

The office had wall-to-wall, moss-green carpeting and was furnished with sofa and armchair groupings upholstered in supple burgundy leather. Custom-built display cases loaded with mementos highlighting Gold's decades in the aviation business lined the oak-paneled walls beneath ornately framed oil painting landscapes and commissioned oil portraits of successful GAT airplane designs in flight.

Teddy settled himself into one of the armchairs in front of Gold's desk. "It's not the end of the world."

"But it *is* the end of the XP-4," Gold said, his voice cracking with barely repressed fury.

"Herman—"

"Damn it, Teddy!" Gold exploded. "I hate to lose!"

"No wonder," Teddy murmured coolly. "You've had so little practice at it."

"Just get to the bottom line." Gold heard the rude impatience in his tone. "Sorry," he said quietly.

Teddy smiled and nodded. "Don't mention it. Like you said, you hate to lose. Well, flight-stability considerations aside, the bottom line problem is that the XP-4 is too fucking slow. She's no faster than presently existing state-of-the-art piston engine fighters."

"Which makes her obsolete before she's even put into production," Gold mourned.

Teddy nodded. He took a pack of Camels out of the side pocket of his lab coat, lit a new cigarette off the butt of the last, and dropped the butt into the smoking stand beside his armchair.

Gold stood up and went to the windows behind his desk. His office was located on the top floor of the main building. He had a view of the sprawling factory complex's airfields, which were being used as parking lots for hundreds of finished GAT BuzzSaw AC-1 bombers lined up in orderly rows, awaiting their shipping dates to go winging off to war. Beyond the olive drab armada of bombers were the yellow security guard shacks and the high, steel mesh fence topped with barbed wire. Beyond the fence, watching everything with timeless immutability, were the majestic, tawny California hills.

Gold kept his back to his chief engineer as he said, "Thank you for not saying I told you so concerning this mess."

"I knew you'd say it for me," Teddy chuckled.

Gold sourly nodded to himself. He'd been the one to insist upon a conservative design approach for the XP-4, because he'd felt that it would appeal to the likewise conservative military. Teddy had argued against the design, warning that its inherent performance characteristics and capabilities would likely be inadequate for a jet fighter.

Gold turned away from the windows and sat back down behind his desk. "You know what really galls me, Teddy? That I've been thinking like a businessman instead of an engineer. You were *right* when you tried to tell me that I was making a mistake, but I just wouldn't listen."

"Hey, you did listen," Teddy said. "You just didn't agree with me at the time." He shrugged. "You had a good point about sticking to a conservative design to romance the military. Hell, if it had worked out, we would have been sitting pretty."

Gold pointed to his old drafting table and the glass-fronted bookcases filled with technical manuals taking up one corner of the office. "You know what the problem has been, Teddy? I've been away from that drafting table and sitting behind this fucking landing strip of a desk for too long. Goddammit, I've got a hundred bookkeepers working for me! Why should I think like one!"

Teddy grinned. "It comes with the territory, boss. I can afford to sit downstairs and think like an engineer. That's my job." His arms spread wide. "But you're responsible for everything. You've got eighty thousand people working for you around the clock in three shifts. How many AC-1 Buzz-Saw air combat bombers did we build last year?"

"Fuck that," Gold scowled. "Who *can't* sell airplanes to the government during a war?"

"How many?" Teddy persisted.

"Four thousand," Gold said, and found himself grinning.

Teddy laughed knowingly. "Thinking about big sales figures always *did* help you to relax. And the year before, we built two thousand of them, plus a couple of thousand Bear-Claw fighters."

"But the BearClaw orders dried up as newer fighter designs became available from the competition," Gold said quickly, getting upset all over again. "That's what I'm worried about, Teddy! I'm convinced that piston-engine technology has gone as far as it can go. If GAT is going to stay on top, it's going to have to continue to meet the challenge of developing new aviation technology."

Teddy held up his hand like a traffic cop. "Herman, you and me go back, what, over twenty years?"

"Yeah, so?"

"So spare me the stockholder's speech. I'm your best friend. I've been with you from the beginning, put GAT stock at the ground floor. Today, thanks to you, I'm a rich man. You don't have to convince me of anything. Just tell me what you want. Do we try to redesign the XP-4, or—"

"No way," Gold cut him off. "No sense throwing good money after bad. That drafting table over there is calling to me," he continued. "Know what it's saying? Come back to the drawing board. And that's what we're going to do."

"Okay, Herm. I'll get my department started on it." Teddy frowned. "But starting from scratch is going to take time."

"I don't care. At this point, no matter what we do there's no way were going to be first with a viable jet fighter for the military. For instance, my contacts in Washington tell me that Larry Bell's outfit in upstate New York is working on something the government supposedly likes a lot."

"And right here in California, Lockheed is supposed to have a very promising turbojet fighter in the works," Teddy nodded. "Yeah, I see your point."

"And who knows what the other companies have up their sleeves?"

"You're not worried about it?" Teddy asked.

"Sure, I am," Gold said gruffly. "I'm scared shitless that we'll be left behind, but remember one thing, buddy. It's not about being first, it's about being the best!"

Teddy laughed. "I just wanted to hear you say it, Herman."

Gold had to laugh as well. "You do know me, Teddy."

"You bet your ass, I do."

"Our asses are already on the line," Gold reminded him.

"But not for the first time," Teddy countered. "And not for the last."

"But the older they get, the fonder of them we become," Gold pointed out. "So get the hell out of here and design me an airplane."

Gold left instructions to his secretaries to hold all calls. He wanted to clear his desk of some backed-up paperwork, but after a fidgety half hour he threw in the towel, admitting to himself that the XP-4 fiasco had him too upset and depressed to concentrate.

He was feeling jumpy and threatened, he thought as he took off his reading glasses and massaged the bridge of his nose. He wished that he smoked—the advertisements had it that smoking calmed the nerves—but he'd never taken up the habit: tobacco gave him headaches.

He briefly considered taking the rest of the day off and going to the movies, but all the pictures had gung-ho war themes. Watching them would only make him brood about his son, Steven.

Gold had pleaded with his only son to let him use his contacts to get the kid a safe assignment out of combat, but Steve had insisted on front-line combat duty. The boy's determination had caused some hard feelings between father and son in the past, but now, as much as Gold worried about his son risking himself in the war, he had long ago gotten over being angry with the kid about it. He had to admit that he was proud of Steve, who was a fighter ace who'd been shot down and wounded, but who had the guts to go back for more.

Thinking about it, Gold supposed he was also a little envious of his son. He himself had tried to enlist in the Army Air Force after Pearl Harbor, but had been rejected for being too old, too overweight, and for weak eyesight.

Gold sighed. It seemed like only yesterday when he himself was Steven's age, and also a fighter pilot and an ace, flying with Herr Rittmeister Richthofen during World War One.

Feeling restless, he got up from his desk and wandered over to the memento-filled display cases. His smile was wistful as he gazed at the faded black-and-white photograph of himself alongside his barnstorming buddies Hull and Les Stiles. The picture had been taken in 1921, when he'd been a tall and gangly kid, a carrot-topped, freckled-faced scarecrow in high scuffed boots, faded flannel, a brown leather jacket, and a battered gray fedora. He'd only emigrated from Germany a few months before his barnstorming tour across America, flying stunts in Captain Bob's Traveling Air Extravaganza.

Gold moved on to photographs taken of himself a couple of years later, when he and the Stiles brothers and Teddy Quinn were running a fledgling mail, freight, and passenger air transport service out of Los Angeles. How proud that bright-eyed, bushy-headed young Herman Gold looked in his suit and tie! Gold thought ruefully as he ran his fingers through the short curls wreathing his ears and the strawberry-colored fuzz he presently had left up top.

Gold continued his tour of the display cases, letting the memorabilia jog his memories. Gone yellow with age were the framed commendations and the newspaper photos of Gold with Los Angeles politicos; there were pictures of himself and his one-time partner Tim Campbell at the groundbreaking ceremony for the Burbank complex.

In a glass case occupying a place of honor in the office was a large silver-framed photo taken in 1934 of Gold shaking hands with President Roosevelt in the White House Rose Garden. The occasion had been the presentation to Gold of the coveted Ross Trophy, aviation's award for design excellence. Bracketing the photograph was the large, ornate bronze trophy itself and a model of the GAT Monarch airliner that had won him the award.

There were also more recent mementos, leading up to the present. *But what about the future?* Gold found himself wondering.

He paused when he got to the portion of the collection devoted to his wife Erica's accomplishments. Gold had taught his bride to pilot a plane during their honeymoon, and now she could be proud of her own illustrious career in aviation spanning the twenty-one years of their marriage.

There was a photo of Erica when she was a newlywed barely out of her teens, a brown-eyed blonde beautiful enough to be a starlet, waving from the cockpit of a De Havilland DH 4 biplane. There was a photo of her dressed in her flying gear, posing beside her silver-skinned GAT Yellowjacket racer at the National Speed Competitions. The display case held a complete collection of the many magazine covers that featured Erica after she'd stunned the world by becoming a GAT test pilot.

Gold realized that his dark mood had lightened. He was smiling, thanks to thinking about Erica. It had helped to talk things over with Teddy, who was a good friend, but not his best friend. He suddenly knew where he wanted to be for the rest of the afternoon.

Gold went to the intercom on his desk and asked the secretary to call to see if his wife was at home. A few moments later the secretary buzzed back to say that Mrs. Gold was on the line. Gold told his wife that he was on his way, and asked her to stick around.

(Two)

Gold Household
Bel-Air

Gold guided his Cadillac through the wrought-iron entrance to his estate. He was pleasantly surprised by how little time it took to make the drive from Burbank to Bel-Air, but it made sense that midday traffic would be light, considering the gas rationing, and the automobile tire and parts shortages.

Gold knew the right people so that he didn't have to worry about gasoline, and his car was new: a 1942 raven-black Caddy convertible. He had twisted the arm of an aircraft parts supplier in Michigan to get him one of the last of the Caddys off the assembly line before production of civilian vehicles came to a halt.

Gold drove slowly up the hedge-lined, crushed-gravel drive toward the house. It was a rambling English colonial, with a vine-covered, gray stone exterior, black iron casement windows, and a green copper, mansard roof. Behind the house was a four-car garage, broad expanses of rolling lawn, a tennis court, a pool, and stables where the family had kept Shetland ponies when the children were young. A full-time handyman gardener lived above the garage. He'd been with the estate for many years. He kept everything running smoothly. Thank God the man was too old to be drafted.

Gold parked in front of the house. As he went up the front steps, Erica swung open the oak double doors.

"I'm so surprised that you're home at this hour," she said, smiling.

"Good surprised or bad surprised?" Gold teased, putting his arms around her waist.

"Oh, very good," she murmured, kissing him.

Her shoulder-length blonde hair shimmered in the sun. She was wearing no makeup as far as Gold could tell, except for the lightest touch of lipstick. As lovely as Erica had been when she was a young girl, Gold thought her more beautiful now. Time had replaced her dewy radiance with a serene and wise beauty.

Gold closed his eyes, hearing her pleased sigh as he lost himself in her embrace.

"It's usually impossible to tear you away from the office, Herman," Erica said, stepping away to lead him into the house.

"Not today it wasn't," Gold replied as he followed her into the cool, dark front hallway.

She was wearing a green and tan striped wraparound skirt over a black one-piece bathing suit, a tan cotton cardigan sweater over her shoulders, and tan leather open-backed sandals. Around her throat was a slender gold chain, and on her wrist was a gold tank watch on an alligator strap. Her simple gold wedding band was on her left ring finger. Long ago when they'd become engaged Gold had been too poor to buy her a diamond. Since then, despite all the other jewelry she'd accepted from him, she'd refused his attempts to give her an engagement diamond, saying that the wedding band meant everything, and that no diamond could improve upon it.

"You sounded so funny on the phone," she said, turning toward him, her expression concerned. "But I'm so glad that we'll have the rest of the afternoon together," she added, brightening. "First you'll have lunch—"

"I'm not very hungry," Gold said, loosening his black silk knit tie.

"There you are! Something *is* bothering you," Erica frowned.

"Just because I said I wasn't hungry?" Gold asked mildly as he unbuttoned the collar of his light blue cotton shirt.

"*And* because you come home early. It's so unlike you. When Susan found out you'd left the office, she called home, worried sick."

Gold smiled. His daughter, Susan, had moved back in

with them after her husband was killed in action overseas. She had recently gone to work at GAT as a secretary in Teddy Quinn's department. Gold had tried to talk her out of it. He'd felt that her place was here at home, caring for her infant son. Suze, however, had been adamant. She'd argued that these days GAT had more female employees than male —which was true—and that like those women, she wanted to do her part for the war effort. Gold had been convinced when Erica had pointed out that letting Suze go to work might help her to come to terms with her recent widowhood.

"Where's my grandson?" Gold demanded.

"With his nanny. But you can play with Robbie later. Right now I want to know what's bothering you."

Gold nodded. "Tell you what," he said as he shrugged out of his gray linen suit coat. "Let me go upstairs to change, and we'll talk by the pool."

"You've got yourself a date. And I'll have Ramona bring your lunch out to the patio. Lately you've been working too many eighteen-hour days, and skipping too many meals."

"Tell it to my belly," Gold muttered, patting his ever-thickening middle.

"Just more of you to love," Erica said, giving him a pinch. "Go change."

He moved quickly through the house with its high, gilded ceilings and mahogany paneling, going up the central, curved marble staircase and down the long third-floor hall-way to their bedroom suite. In his dressing room he changed into a pair of navy-blue boxer swim trunks, black leather sandals, and a white belted terry-cloth robe. He went back downstairs, and out through the solarium's French doors, to the flagstone patio landscaped with shrubbery and redwood flower boxes. The maid was setting out sandwiches and iced tea on the white enameled table in the patio's screened dining area. Gold ignored the food and went out to the deck chair surrounding the Olympic-sized, rectangular pool.

He stretched out on a duck canvas chaise longue beneath the shade of a eucalyptus tree. He closed his eyes and listened to the birds and the drone of the bees in the rose bushes. A few minutes later he heard Erica come out. He opened his eyes and watched her kick off her sandals and unwrap her skirt, revealing her long, shapely legs. She was tanned all over and her hair looked like burnished gold. The black stretch fabric of the strapless suit fit her curves like a second skin. Gold imagined that it was due to all that tennis and swimming she did, or maybe it was just plain luck, but at forty-three her body was as firm and lithe as when they'd first met. He'd seen her turn the heads of men young enough to be her sons.

Gold felt himself stirring and thickening beneath the thin fabric of his trunks as Erica moved with a she panther's supple rhythm to the edge of the pool, to sweep the surface of the water with her nut-brown toes.

"Ooh," she murmured languidly. "Nice and warm."

"That's some body you got there for a grandma," Gold said.

She cast him a dazzling smile over her shoulder. "It comes from clean living, and a wholesome childhood spent on the farm. I remember all that work I used to do plowing the fields."

"You grew up on a tree farm!" Gold laughed. Erica was the daughter of Carl Schuler, a German American who ran one of the biggest, most prosperous fruit tree nursery operations in the Midwest. "And the only *work* you ever did, as I recall, was work the gearshift on that sports car you used to tear around in."

"That *was* hard work," Erica laughed. "And what about all those long, sleepless nights I spent trying to figure out new ways to spend my daddy's money?"

"Poor baby—"

"And now look how much brain work I put into spending *your* money," she teased.

Gold shook his head. "Our money," he said quietly. "We're a team."

Erica just smiled. "Anyway, all that farm-fresh milk and fresh air must have blessed me with good bone structure." She slapped her haunch. "I guess it holds up all my flab."

"Why don't you come over here and let me hold it up for a while?"

"Speaking of bones . . ."

The way she was looking at his groin—and the way she was smiling at where she was looking—made Gold even harder—it was as if he had a tent pole beneath his navy-blue fabric. "God, I do love you," he told her.

"That's what they all say in your predicament, bub," she wisecracked, but there was no joking in her dark eyes so full of love.

"I really think you should come over here right now," Gold said.

"There is a chance you could get lucky," Erica nodded, coming over, "but first I want to know."

"Know what?" Gold evaded.

"To what do I owe the pleasure of your company?"

Gold moved his legs to give her room to sit at the foot of the chaise longue. "Couldn't it just be my hormones acting up?"

"No," she smiled. "You've got very horny hormones, my love—"

"And I'm going to have to have the GAT metallurgy department whip up a pair of duralumin swim trunks if you keep denying me." Gold tried to interrupt.

"But not even your hormones have ever kept you from your work," Erica continued, becoming serious. "A moment ago you told me that we were a team, and it pleases me so to hear you say that, but now you're going to have to prove it to me by telling me what's wrong."

"Ah, shit," Gold muttered. He could feel his erection going limp. He avoided her stare, gazing up at the shifting light patterns filtering through the lacy green latticework of tree boughs overhead, but he could feel her attention focused upon him. She could, and *would*, wait quietly like this until he gave in and told her.

"Something happened today at work. . . ." He explained about the failure of the XP-4, and his decision to scrap the entire project.

"But Herman," she began tentatively after he was done, "I'm still not sure I understand why you're so upset. Is it the money?"

"Nah," he shrugged. "Not really. Sure we lost a bundle,

but we'll write it off. Uncle Sam will pick up most of the tab."

"So if it's not the money . . . ?" she trailed off.

He took hold of Erica's hand. "Try and understand," he said. "Since the war began I've been pretty much content to just sit back and rest on my laurels."

"You make it sound like you're lazy," Erica laughed. "My God, Herman, nobody we know works as hard as you do."

"But what have I been producing?"

"My love, you've been producing marvelous airplanes for the military!"

"But they're just more of the same," Gold complained. "Don't you see? GAT became the power it is today thanks to *innovation*. Take our Monarch series of airliners—"

"Exactly!" Erica said triumphantly. "You've been constantly improving the Monarch line. The GC-6 and GC-7 versions were among the first airliners in the world with pressurized cabins."

"Honey, listen a minute. . . ."

"No, you listen, Herman!" Erica scolded. "Versions of the Monarch are being flown by virtually every airline in the world. And you've sold millions more to the British and our own military as cargo and troop transports."

"And millions of dinosaurs ruled the earth," Gold cut her off. "Until they suddenly became extinct!"

Erica stared at him a moment. "Now I get it," she said softly.

Gold nodded. "Piston-engined airplanes are fast becoming technological dinosaurs."

Erica shrugged. "So GAT will build jets," she encouraged. "It's as simple as that."

Gold chuckled humorlessly. "As simple, and as complicated." He squeezed her hand. "It's a new technology, Erica. I'm not sure I understand it." He swallowed hard. "I'm not sure that my day hasn't come and gone."

"Failure is always frightening," she said evenly. "You'll get over it. You'll find a way to accomplish your goals. You always have, and you always will."

"It's true I always have in the past," Gold said listlessly.

"But this is the future. There's a lot of fresh young talent out there. Competition that's comfortable with the new technology." He sighed. "I just don't know."

Erica stood up and began to pull him to his feet. "Come on, come in for a swim."

"I don't feel like it."

"Tough. You're coming anyway."

Sighing, Gold got to his feet, stepped out of his sandals, and removed his robe. He followed Erica to the deep end of the pool, and the two of them dived in.

Erica had been right; the water temperature was delightful. She was swimming ahead of him as he broke the surface. She was a superb swimmer, able to move through the water with a minimum of effort and splash.

Gold, treading water as he watched her, felt an idea tugging restlessly at the edges of his mind. Something to do with Erica's swimming.

She slicked her wet hair back behind her ears. "Hey, com'ere, you," she called to him. She was standing at chest depth at the pool's center. Her eyes were bright with mischief as she slicked her wet hair back behind her ears.

Gold swam over to stand next to her. She put one arm around his neck and began to nibble at his mouth. Her other hand slid underwater to the waistband of his trunks.

"What do you think you're doing?" Gold pretended to demand.

"Rebuilding your self-confidence," she said, untying the drawstring and pushing the trunks down past his thighs. "And anyway, I'm horny."

"There must be a Bel-Air ordinance against this sort of thing," Gold said as he stepped out of the trunks and let them drift toward the pool's turquoise cement floor. "You know, 'No running near the edge of the pool. No splashing. No fucking.' "

"You see a lifeguard around?" Erica asked between kisses.

Underwater he was undulating like a serpent, but he began to stiffen as Erica stroked him.

"The maid?" he asked hoarsely.

"Told her under no circumstances to come out here.

You're trapped within my clutches," she said, fondling him.

Gold gave her strapless suit a gentle tug downward, and her breasts popped free. He watched them bob beneath the water, her pink nipples rising and falling as the water beaded and trailed in droplets down her cleavage. He bent to gingerly take one of her nipples between his lips.

Erica threw back her head, cooing softly like a bird. She began to wiggle and squirm, rolling her suit down past her hips. At last she was able to kick one leg free. She pressed against him, spreading her thighs as she guided him home.

Warm as the water was, it was warmer inside her. She wrapped her legs around his waist and began to rock against him. Gold held himself back until her movements began their familiar urgency. Her fingers, pressed lightly into his back, abruptly dug in.

She arched her back and cried out shrilly as she reached orgasm. He growled into her hair, its texture like damp silk against his face, as he came.

He was still shuddering against her as she abruptly came to her senses. Clearly mortified, she glanced around with impossibly large, round eyes. Once she had reassured herself that their act had gone unwitnessed, she begin to giggle.

They were still locked together when Gold shifted his weight and lost his footing. He tumbled backward, and the two of them splashed beneath the surface. They came up sputtering and laughing like children.

"Well, how do you feel *now*?" Erica demanded.

"Much better than I did fifteen minutes ago," Gold admitted. He put his arms around her to give her a kiss.

He froze, staring at her.

"What?" she laughed.

"I was thinking about how you were swimming before." Erica nodded. "So?"

Gold grinned. "So, you've given me an idea about where we might have gone wrong with the XP-4."

"That's not *all* I gave you, bub," Erica smiled. "I mean, I'd always *heard* that men thought with their—"

"It has to do with the angle of the wing," Gold said, more to himself than to Erica. "An airplane meets something like the same resistance in the air that you met when you were swimming. You created a wake—a vee-shaped wake—as you moved through the water. An airplane forms something like a wake—of shock waves—as it moves through the air," he continued, warming to the subject. "The XP-4 had conventional straight wings. Now, if we redesigned the craft around a *swept-back* wing that could fit *inside* those shock waves, drag would be lessened to such an extent that . . ." He paused. "I need a pencil and paper."

He gave Erica a quick peck on the lips, swam over to the edge of the pool, and hoisted himself out.

"Darling?" Erica called out gaily. "Aren't you forgetting something?"

"What?" Gold asked absently, standing by the deck chair. His head was full of sketches he was anxious to get down on paper. "Oh, I'm sorry, honey," he added quickly, focusing on her. "I love you," he called out.

"You're sweet," Erica observed. "You also happen to be bare-assed naked."

Gold looked down at himself. "Oops!"

Grinning foolishly, he grabbed his tangled robe and fumbled into it. Once he was decent he padded barefoot back toward the house. There was a drafting table in his study. The more he thought about the new wing design, the more convinced he became that it just might work.

CHAPTER 3

(One)

Santa Belle Airfield
Solomon Islands
22 October 1943

Lieutenant Steven Gold smoked his first cigarette of the day slowly, meditatively. It was just a little after dawn. Steve was in his tent, freshly washed and shaved and dressed in a fresh set of khakis.

The insects were setting up an unnerving metallic racket in the high grass beyond the base perimeter. The occasional screech of a jungle bird sounded like somebody being tortured. The tent's vent flaps were open, but no breeze was stirring. Steve's cigarette smoke rose straight up through the humid air to collect in a miniature fog against the ridgepole and green canvas. He could feel the temperature rising. His khakis wouldn't be fresh for long.

The day had started out badly an hour earlier, when some goddamned bug had bitten him on the ankle, shocking him out of a sound sleep. He'd rubbed some spit onto the swelling bite as he swore loudly and freely. There was no one around to disturb. The pilot who'd had the tent's other cot had been shipped out with two broken legs after he'd cracked up his airplane.

Steve was sorry the guy had been hurt, but didn't particularly miss him. He didn't mind being alone. He'd been here six weeks, but he hadn't yet made any new buddies, although it had been great to renew his friendship with his squadron commander, Major Sam "Cappy" Fitzpatrick.

What Steve did mind was the boredom of the daily routine on this sweltering hunk of volcanic rock in the middle of the Pacific. Santa Belle was a Marine-held island, which meant that the Marine VMF fighter squadrons got to hog all the action, while the single Army Air squadron on the base had to be content with practicing takeoffs and landings in its shiny new P-47 Thunderbolts.

Steve liked flying his Jug, although he'd reserve final judgment on the airplane until he'd taken it into combat. *If* he ever got to see combat again. He was thinking he'd made the wrong decision when he'd agreed to join this so-called elite fighter squadron. If he was going to be kept out of the fighting, he might as well have gotten himself reassigned to Henderson back on Guadalcanal, where life was at least reasonably comfortable. On Santa Belle he had only the bugs and the stinking hot climate to distract him from his boredom.

The Marines had endured a long, bloody struggle to wrestle away this pesthole of an island from the Japanese. As soon as the shooting had slowed, the Seabees had arrived to clear away the rusting wreckage of enemy fighters and bombers, and repair the ruined runways. The Seabees barely had time to finish laying down steel mesh over the first sandy airstrip when the dark blue, gull-winged Marine Corsairs began landing.

Since then, the Seabees had branded onto the steamy rain forest a half-dozen more interlocking runways, interspersed with oases of palm trees, antiaircraft gun emplacements, and earth-banked protective revetments for parked planes. The bulldozers were still busy. The base would be a work in progress for some time to come. Everybody was still living out of tents. The only relatively substantial buildings were "Polly's Pit," the barracks dive where the off-duty Marine officers did their drinking, and the big, barnlike hangars for the Marine squadrons of Corsairs. Cappy Fitzpatrick's single Army Air Force squadron of P-47 Thunderbolts was making do under open-sided canvas awnings. The squadron's combination operations and ready room was comprised of a couple of Nissen huts shoved together wth the center walls removed.

Steve caught a whiff of freshly brewed coffee. He listened intently, and heard the clatter of pots and pans that meant the squadron's mess was coming to life. The Army pilots and squadron ground personnel were all bivouacked —read that, segregated from Marine personnel—in the same area of the base. The squadron had its own supplies, followed its own rules, and more or less lived in an uneasy truce with the Marines who controlled the island. There'd been a couple of brawls between the webfoot and Army enlisted men, but that was to be expected. Mixing branches of the service was like mixing cats and dogs.

Steve stubbed out his smoke in a sand-filled ration can.

He made sure that his silver first lieutenant's bars were pinned to his shirt collar, and silver wings were affixed just above his left breast pocket flap. He put on his billed, tan cotton flight cap with a first lieutenant's bar pinned to the crown, and grabbed his .45 in its shoulder holster off his footlocker at the end of his cot. There were still Japanese ground forces hiding out in the island's jungle interior, and the base had experienced some trouble with enemy sappers trying to infiltrate by night and snipers during the day. Marines guarded the base perimeter, but all personnel were nevertheless required to carry sidearms.

Steve adjusted the shoulder holster's harness and left his tent, heading for the mess. He hadn't gone more than a few paces before the sweat began rolling out of him, soaking his shirt. He stopped to remove his cap and mop his brow with his handkerchief, and that's when he saw it.

It was a large canvas tarp stretched like a billboard between two poles at the entrance to the Army encampment. Neatly painted in bright white paint on the olive green tarp was:

> *Here by the lair of Army Air*
> *On patrol their Jugs make loud dins;*
> *But when it comes to a bout,*
> *These guys never put out;*
> *Marines call them the Vigilant Virgins.*

Several of the pilots and a bunch of the squadron's ground personnel were all staring up at the thing, grumbling about it, as Steve walked over. Lousy rhyming aside, this was one hell of an insult to the squadron, Steve thought furiously.

And it hurt all the more because it was true.

The insult was painted on both sides of the tarp so that everyone could see it. It must have gone up sometime during the night. Steve hadn't noticed it earlier on his way to the latrine, but he'd been pretty much walking in his sleep.

"Anyone know if the major's seen this?" Steve asked.

"I don't think so," one of the other pilots said. He was a captain named Crawford.

Steve nodded and turned to a corporal. "You go get the major."

"Jeez, Lieutenant, you know how the major likes to sleep late," the corporal complained.

"Get him, dammit!" Steve exploded.

"Okay, Lieutenant, calm down," the corporal said as he took off. "*I* didn't put the thing up."

"Take it easy, Lieutenant," Crawford said.

A group of Marines were passing by. They were on their way to guard duty. They were wearing helmets, camouflage-printed jungle suits, and carrying M-1 carbines, Garands, and Thompson submachine guns. The Marines paused to read the tarp and made a point of laughing as loudly as they could, before sauntering on.

Steve waited until the webfoots were out of earshot and then turned to Crawford. "See that, Captain? The Marines think we're shit!" He turned to a couple of enlisted men. "You two get this tarp down, and burn it."

"Just hold on there."

Steve turned around. "But Cappy—"

"But nothing, Steve," Major Sam "Cappy" Fitzpatrick mumbled sleepily.

He was in his thirties and short, but broad-shouldered and muscular. He had curly black hair, a mustache, and dark eyes. Just now those eyes were bloodshot, and he needed a shave. His olive-drab T-shirt had large, dark sweat rings under the arms, and his khaki shorts were grimy. He was wearing a cotton, peaked bill cap displaying his gold oak leaf, and a revolver slung on his hip in a tan leather, gold-tooled western-style rig that matched his cowboy boots.

"Cappy, let's get that thing down!" Steve insisted.

"I told him not to get so upset," Crawford announced smugly.

"Everybody shut up and let me think," Cappy sighed. He looked around, bellowing, "Where's my coffee!"

"Here, sir!" The corporal who Steve had sent to fetch Cappy was hurrying toward the major, carrying a tin mug.

Cappy took the mug, sipped at it, and winced. "I

wouldn't half mind this goddamned war if I could at least have a cup of decent coffee. Who's got a smoke?"

Crawford leapt forward, a pack of Luckys appearing like magic in his hand. Cappy plucked a cigarette out of the pack and allowed Crawford to light it for him.

"That's better," Cappy said to no one in particular. He took another sip of coffee. "Now then, Steve, what's got you so hot under the collar?"

"I don't like being insulted like this," Steve replied. "I'm fed up with taking shit from these Marines."

"Did you ever stop to think that by blowing your stack you're giving the Marines exactly what they want?" Cappy asked.

"I hear what you're saying. They want a reaction and I'm supplying it." Steve shrugged. "I guess I don't care. It's all just getting to me. I'm fed up with not getting the chance to prove to these webfoots that they're wrong about Army Air. And I'm fed up with not being able to shoot at anything other than a towed target. We were sent here to underscore the fact these sailors and Marines aren't single-handedly winning the war in the Pacific. Well, if Army Air is gonna be in on it, we'd better start doing our part."

"Soon as *I* think we're ready," Cappy declared. "I'm the one who makes that decision, and I'm not about to let a bunch of wisecracking Marines goad me into making that decision prematurely."

"You're making it sound like we're a green squadron," Steve complained.

"We *are* green," Cappy said.

"Every one of us is an ace!" Steve exploded. "Hell, some of us are double or triple aces—"

"But with the exception of you and me, none of us have flown together," Cappy pointed out. "And all of us have gotten our experience in different airplanes. I'm not risking this unit in combat until every one of us is up to speed with his Jug and with the other men."

"Yes, sir." Steve sighed.

Cappy looked at him and grinned. "Don't worry, Steve.

Don't be so impatient. Trust me, this squadron is going to wax Tojo like he ain't never been waxed before. Okay?"

"Yes, sir."

"And don't worry so much about what other people think," Cappy added. "You're an ace. You should have proven yourself to *yourself* by now."

"Okay, Cappy." Steve felt uncomfortable having Cappy say stuff like that to him with other guys listening.

Cappy must have sensed his embarrassment. "Good." He nodded and then abruptly turned away to study the tarp. "Vigilant Virgins they called us, huh?" he chuckled heartily. "I kind of like it."

"That insult?" Steve asked in disbelief.

Cappy nodded. "You know what? I believe that we're gonna leave that up."

"You can't be serious." Steve was appalled.

"I'm never serious, kiddo, but I always mean what I say. Vigilant Virgins . . . Vee Vee . . . the Vee Vees— No!" Cappy snapped his fingers. "The *Double* Vees. . . ." He grinned triumphantly. "I like it." He looked around. "Anyone seen Sergeant Wallis this morning?"

"Sir, I saw him in the mess when I went to get your coffee," the corporal volunteered.

Cappy nodded. "See if he's still there. Tell him I want to see him pronto."

"What do you want with Wallis?" Steve asked. Sergeant Wallis was Captain Crawford's crew chief. He was a burly, balding guy who was always chewing on the butt end of an unlit stogie.

"He worked in an automobile body shop before the war," Cappy said. "He knows about painting vehicles and stuff like that. He and I have been knocking around a few ideas for a squadron insignia, but we haven't been able to come up with anything good." He paused. "Until now."

Steve's eyes flicked to the tarp and then back to Cappy. "Oh, no. . . ." he murmured sorrowfully.

"The Double Vees, the Vigilant Virgins," Cappy repeated. "Yeah. . . . Thanks to our web-footed friends, I think we've finally found our squadron insignia."

"Aw, Cappy," Steve implored.

"Hey, Wallis!" Cappy yelled as the sergeant approached. "I finally figured out what I want for a squadron nose marking!" The major sketched his ideas in the air for Walli's benefit. "Picture this: we paint the cowling a solid color. On both sides we put a sort of shield shape with a big vee in the upper left- and a big vee in the lower right-hand corners. In between the vees, going on a diagonal from upper left to lower right, I want a lightning bolt. Got that?"

Wallis nodded. "Whatcha want for colors, Major?"

Cappy shrugged. "I haven't gotten that far." He glanced at Steve. "You once told me about how your old man was a German ace during the last war. What'd you say his colors were?"

Steve stalled. "Cappy, don't you have to get group's approval for something like this?" he asked hopefully.

"Group will go along with anything I fucking well say," Cappy replied impatiently. "If they don't, I'll take it up with wing, or Hap Arnold, or fucking FDR if I have to. Got it, Lieutenant?"

"Got it, Major," Steve replied quickly. Cappy may have looked like a black sheep, but he was a bona fide war hero. He had twenty-seven confirmed kills, for which he'd been awarded a Silver Star and the Distinguished Service Cross. The brass had already sent Cappy home to take part in a highly publicized cross-country war bond tour. Cappy had friends in high places, and had earned himself a shitload of favors when he'd agreed to head up this squadron.

"My pop's personal colors were turquoise and yellow," Steve said. "But all the airplanes in his squadron had to incorporate some of Richthofen's signature scarlet into their markings."

"Hey, if it was good enough for the fucking Red Baron, it's good enough for us," Cappy said. He turned to Wallis. "Paint the nose cowlings yellow. Make the shields turquoise. The vees and lightning bolts are scarlet. Got it?"

"Whatever you say, Major," Wallis replied. "The design ain't too complicated. I'll start on it right away. The job should be done in a couple of days."

"Cappy, at least take down the fucking tarp," Steve fumed.

"Nope, it's staying up."

"But they're laughing at us."

"Let them," Cappy said. "Pretty soon these webfoots are gonna realize that what they've given us is a flag of honor, and then the laugh will be on them. Like I said before, you're too thin-skinned, Steve. It's a bad trait to have generally, but it's especially bad in our trade. You want to survive, you're going to have to learn to be cool and collected under pressure."

"Cappy, you know that I don't lose my nerve when the chips are down," Steve said hotly.

Cappy laughed, shaking his head. "You're proving my point right now by not listening to me, kiddo. What I'm saying is that courage and grace under pressure are two different things. You were born with balls, Steve, but grace is something everybody has to *learn*." The major studied him a second and then turned back to Wallis. "Tell you what, Sarge. You *hand paint* Lieutenant Gold's airplane first thing."

Wallis nodded. "Like a sample, huh? No problem, Major."

Steve winced. "Cappy, give me a break."

"Someday you'll thank me for this," Cappy said. "Then again, maybe not. . . ." His grin was evil. "Sarge, I want the lieutenant's plane done in time for this afternoon's practice."

"Yes, sir!" Wallis hurried away, muttering to himself.

Cappy looked around. "Who's got a smoke?"

(Two)

That afternoon Steve's freshly painted airplane was waiting for him as he left the ready room. He was wearing his Mae West and pistol over his khaki uniform. His goggles and rubber oxygen mask were dangling around his neck, and he was carrying his helmet.

Sergeant Wallis was standing in front of Steve's Jug, chatting with Steve's crew. Wallis looked proud as a new papa. He was obviously hanging around in order to get Steve's reaction to his handiwork.

"What do you think, Lieutenant?" Wallis demanded. "Looks good, huh? And she's all dry. I had one of the spare Jugs backed into position and kept its engine going so that the prop wash could help dry the paint."

"It looks good, all right," Steve said grudgingly. Wallis looked crestfallen at his reaction. *Fuck,* Steve thought. *The guy worked his ass off to get it done, and get it done right.*

"Sarge, you did a great job." He forced the enthusiasm into his voice. "And I'm proud of the fact that my old man's colors are going to grace the squadron." The vibrant hues of yellow, turquoise, and scarlet did look swell against the Thunderbolt's burnished silver skin.

"The shields turned out real sharp on both sides of the cowling, I think," Wallis said. "They're so bold and ballsy they suit this big mother."

Steve nodded. The Jug *was* big. She had a forty-foot wingspan, but it was her thirty-six-foot-long, fifteen-foot-high fuselage that won her the title as the biggest single-engine fighter. The Thunderbolt was nicknamed the Jug because of its profile. Most fighters had a streamlined, sharklike fuselage, but the Thunderbolt's nose was stubby, rounded, and blunt, like that of a sperm whale.

Wallis's eyes were narrowed. "Lieutenant, I gotta ask. Is there something about the paint job that's bothering you?"

"Nothing, Sarge," Steve sighed. He reached up to pat the turquoise shield embossed with those scarlet vees and the lightning bolt. No way anyone could miss those shields on both sides of the cowling which framed the ram scoop air intake for the high-altitude turbosupercharger. *If only the vees stood for something other than Vigilant Virgins.* "Like I said, you did great." He clapped Wallis on the shoulder. "I gotta get airborn."

Steve climbed up onto the wing, and then hoisted himself into the spacious cockpit. What a pleasure! Every other fighter that Steve had flown had a tiny, cramped cockpit that made him feel like a pretzel, but the Jug's fuselage was so deep that even a six-footer had room to stretch his legs.

He waited for his crew to stand clear, and then started up the air-cooled, 2,100 horsepower Pratt & Whitney. The four yellow tips of the twelve-foot-diameter paddle-blade prop began to spin. Steve tested out his oxygen mask as he waited for the ops officer to signal him takeoff permission. Once he'd received it, he lowered the electrically operated teardrop canopy, locked it down, and moved the Jug out.

The heavy Thunderbolt needed a lot of runway to get off the ground. As he was rolling along, building up speed, he passed a group of Marines in the midst of a softball game on an unused airstrip. The webfoots broke off playing to point and laugh at Steve's gaudy Jug as it rumbled past.

Fuck them, Steve thought savagely. Grace under pressure, Cappy had said. The Marines would eat crow once the Double Vee Squadron had proven themselves in battle.

He pulled back on the stick, luxuriating in that special instant when his wheels left the ground. He retracted his landing gear as he climbed, his spirits lifting along with his airplane. Any day spent flying was a wonderful day.

Steve was especially pleased with the Thunderbolt's performance. He thought the Jug was an outstanding airplane. A lot of the pilots in the squadron didn't agree with him, but they were pilots who'd gained their experience flying much smaller fighters. The chief complaint was that the Jug handled like a truck. Next on the list of gripes was the fact that the Jug was so big. The concern among many of the guys was not how *they* were going to shoot down the enemy, but how the Japs could ever miss *them*.

It was true that it took a steady hand to show the musclebound Thunderbolt who was boss. Steve guessed that it made sense that a pilot would feel nervous riding such a headstrong mount into battle if all his experience had been in lighter, more nimble fighters like the Bell Aircobra or the BearClaw fighter designed and built by his father's company. Steve wasn't worried about the Jug's size or its lack of maneuverability, but then he'd been happy flying his twin-engined, twin-boomed P-38 Lightning, which was even bigger than the Jug, and also something of a truck. Also, he'd found that what counted over maneuverability was speed, stability, the ability to deliver a knockout blow, and if need be, to take a few punches in return.

The Jug could do all that, in spades. She had an outstanding top speed, and a 42,000-foot ceiling. It was true that she presented the enemy with a big target, but her air-cooled engine allowed her to shrug off the kinds of hits that might sever the coolant line of a liquid-cooled power plant, causing it to overheat and seize up. When it came time to hit back, the Jug's eight .50-caliber guns could literally blow out of existence Tojo's lightweight, unarmored airplanes.

Not that the Jug was perfect, Steve thought as he and the rest of the squadron slowly followed Cappy Fitzpatrick up to thirty thousand feet. She gulped fuel, making her an extremely short-range airplane unless she was equipped with drop tanks. It was a good thing she could absorb hits, because she sure as hell was going to take some. At high speeds and high altitudes she was unbeatable, but the Japs liked to fight low. Dropping the Jug down below fifteen thousand feet, or letting her air speed fall below 250 miles per hour turned her into one sleepy babe. Steve found this especially irksome since his last mount, the twin-engined P-38 Lightning, could climb like an angel and dive like a submarine at any altitude. Finally, like a typical heavyweight, the muscle-bound Jug had spindly legs. Her weak landing gear could snap on you if you set her down too hard.

"All right, you *Virgins*—"

Steve cringed as Cappy's voice crackled through his headset. Thankfully the Marine fighter squadrons used a different radio frequency, so they couldn't eavesdrop. Then he remembered that it was the webfoots who'd christened the squadron in the first place: one look and the Marines would know exactly what those double vees stood for.

"Find your positions," Cappy ordered.

The squadron broke into three flights of four, each flying in box formation. Steve was in the last box, in the rear starboard corner, flying as flight leader Captain Crawford's wingman. Cappy had assigned flight positions according to an officer's rank and the number of his kills. Steve was only a first lieutenant, and his nine kills might have been hot stuff in some other squadron, but here his score was relatively low. Crawford, for instance, had twelve kills. Steve's position in the extreme rear outside corner of the last squadron was an especially dangerous one because he'd be the first guy to be jumped in an ambush, but because of his excellent eyesight and ability to spot the enemy, Cappy had figured Steve could handle it. Steve considered Cappy's confidence in his ability an honor.

"Remember our procedure," Cappy was saying. "We fly high. We spot Tojo, and we power-dive on him like a ton of bricks."

Ton of bricks was right, Steve chuckled to himself. The Jug, empty, weighed maybe three times what the Zero did loaded.

The squadron was flying just off the coast of Santa Belle. There had been no enemy air activity in the area for weeks, but Steve constantly swiveled his head, searching for the enemy against the infinite pale blue sky banded with wispy high-altitude cirrus clouds. He didn't expect to see any Japs, but he had long ago trained himself into the routine of knowing what was happening in the sky around him. It was a habit he didn't want to break.

"—The idea is to destroy your target in a single pass,' Cappy was lecturing the squadron. "Hit and kill him before he even knows what's happened. With eight guns, you've got the firepower to do it."

Something caught Steve's eye on his starboard side, and his heart began to pound with that scary, giddy jolt of combat anticipation. As the specks closed on the squadron Steve saw that they were Marine Corsairs. He relaxed, and as his pulse slowed, he wryly noted his undeniable sense of disappointment.

"You get yourself into a turning fight with Tojo and you'll find yourself spiraling downward," Cappy was warning. "Then, before you know it, you'll be beneath the Jug's optimum operational altitude, and Tojo will be flying rings around you."

Steve waited for Cappy to finish and then clicked his throat mike. "This is Gold. We've got company. A finger four formation of webfoots coming at us three o'clock level."

"I see them," Cappy said. "Just ignore them."

"That's gonna be hard to do, Cappy," Steve replied as the gull-winged, dark blue Corsairs surrounded him.

"Lieutenant Gold, this is Captain Crawford. You've got a darned webfoot coming up between us."

Steve had to smile. Crawford had been a grammar school teacher before the war, and couldn't ever bring himself to swear.

"He's trying to cut you out of the box," Crawford continued. "Tighten up, tighten up, Lieutenant."

The Marine pilots were good. They were operating almost at ceiling, but they still managed to slice Steve out of the flight's box formation. Before he knew it he was neatly corralled by the four Marine fighters. They were close enough for Steve to see the pilots' faces. They were pointing to the double-vee shield insignias on his cowling. *They were laughing.*

"Cappy, this is Steve!" he snarled furiously into his throat mike. "I told you they'd make fun of us! They're laughing at this fucking shield you've got me branded with!"

"Steve, calm down," Cappy ordered. "All right, everyone, listen up: follow me up to thirty-eight thousand feet. Steve, you just climb right out of their box. Those bluebirds can't fly much higher than present altitude."

"At thirty-eight thousand any meaningful flight practice is going to be spoiled," Crawford cut in. "We'll never really see combat at that altitude. The Japs are willing to concede the heavens to their honorable ancestors."

"Don't bust my balls, Captain," Cappy muttered.

"I hate running away from these bullies," Steve grumbled.

"I hate it, too," Cappy said. "But we can't shoot them down because Uncle Sammy wouldn't like it, and anyway, we're guests on their fucking webfoot island, and we're going to behave like guests, God help us. Just do as I say:

follow me up to thirty-eight thousand and leave them behind."

"But what are we going to do up there?" another pilot cut in. "Just wait them out?"

"I guess," Cappy said helplessly. "Maybe they'll get bored and go away."

"Or maybe they'll hang around and wait for us to come back down," Steve said. "Like the damn bullies they are."

"You got any better ideas, Steve?" Cappy demanded fiercely.

"Maybe I do," Steve said. "You can't run from bullies, Cappy. You've got to stand up to them! Do I have your permission to try?"

"Try what, Steve?" Cappy asked, sounding apprehensive.

"I have to demonstrate, Major," Steve replied, and before Cappy could stop him, he orchestrated his throttle and ram scoop turbo supercharger to abruptly rise up out of the Marines' box formation like a pigeon out of the bush. He next popped his flaps to abruptly slow down, causing the surprised Marines to shoot past. Steve had no problem dropping down onto theirs tails.

He saw Captain Crawford turn his head to see what he was doing, and thought the captain gave him a friendly wave of acknowledgment, but that might have been wishful thinking. As the formation of Corsairs broke apart to escape, Steve picked out one bluebird and went after it. As he did, he wondered how long it would take Cappy Fitzpatrick to realize what he had planned, and stop him from doing it.

The Corsair's pilot had chosen to make a flat-out run. *Bad choice,* Steve thought gleefully.

The Corsair was a good mount, but at this altitude she was straining for breath, while the Jug was happy as a pig in shit this high in the sky with room to gallop. For ten deliciously long seconds Steve stayed glued to the Corsair's tail, waxing the webfoot soundly. He'd made sure his guns were on safety, and then activated his gun camera to record the rout.

"Lieutenant Gold," Cappy's voice suddenly exploded in Steve's headset, "what the fuck do you think you're doing?"

Steve smiled. He'd known the major long enough to recognize when Cappy was truly pissed and when he was just acting like he was.

"Aw, come on, Cappy," Steve cajoled affectionately. "Can't you just pretend you don't see me for a little while longer?"

There was a moment of static, and then Cappy said, "Don't . . . see . . . *who*?"

Thank you, Steve thought, as just ahead the desperate Marine went into a dive to escape. Steve dived right after him, waxing the bluebird for five seconds longer. He thought, *If this were real, I'd be a double ace right now.*

And then Steve had to break away.

The pursuit and power dive had cost him ten thousand feet, and the Jug wasn't happy about it. Above his own excited breathing into his rubber oxygen mask he could hear the difference in his engine: the liquid growl had dropped in pitch to a harsh rumble. As he pulled back on the stick and worked his rudder pedals, he felt the Jug's sluggish response. There was no problem, and no danger. It was just that the lower the Jug flew, the more dimwitted she got. The altimeter was presently indicating sixteen thousand feet. Drop her down another few thousand and she'd turn into a goddamned railroad locomotive: just as dependable and rock steady as a choo-choo, but a little less responsive and agile.

He climbed slowly; it took him a couple of minutes to regain the ten thousand feet he'd lost in only a few seconds. While the Jug was huffing and puffing up the ladder, Steve had plenty of time to search the sky. The Corsair he'd waxed was heading for home. The remaining three bluebirds were a couple of miles away, at two-o'clock high. They were *coming toward him to intercept.*

Steve smiled broadly. He would have had no hope of catching up to the three Corsairs if they'd chosen to escape, but he knew that they wouldn't—*couldn't*—run. He'd already blistered one of their brothers-in-arms. As far as they were concerned, the fucking honor of the fucking Marine Corps was now at stake.

Cappy's voice came over his headset, singing, "Oh where, oh where could my little Jug be . . . ?"

"Cappy, this is Steve. Do I have permission to continue upholding the honor of the squadron awhile longer?"

"What squadron would that be, kiddo?" Cappy demanded.

"The . . . Double Vee Squadron, sir."

"The *what*?" Cappy persisted.

Steve had to swallow hard before he could bring himself to say it. "The Vigilant Virgin Squadron, sir—"

"Good enough," Cappy laughed. "You've got my permission to show those webfoots what it means when a virgin says no!"

"Roger that, Cappy," Steve said.

Now that the Jug was back up to 22,000 feet, she was again feeling her oats. There was a little less than a mile separating Steve from the Corsairs, which had come around to approach him head-on. He didn't expect them to break; it was three against one, after all. He knew what they expected *him* to do: break sharply, either to port or starboard, and then they'd have him broadside in their sights. In real life he'd be a tough deflection shot for the Marines, but since this was a mock dogfight, all three webfoots would simply run their gun cameras and claim a "likely victory," one that would counter the embarrassment they suffered over the waxing Steve had inflicted on the other Corsair.

The webfoots were expecting Steve to break, because that was all a typical airplane was capable of doing, but the Double Vees' Thunderbolts weren't typical. They had been factory equipped with an emergency water injection system that shot water into the engine cylinders, temporarily—*very temporarily*—increasing horsepower from 2,100 to 2,800, increasing the Jug's top speed to about 470 miles per hour. The Corsairs were due to be fitted with the water injection system, but Steve was pretty sure that hadn't yet happened; otherwise the pilot he'd just waxed would have used the system to try and save his tail.

Steve and the Corsairs—still rushing toward each other —had closed the gap between them to about a quarter mile.

Again, if this had been a real fight, both sides would have begun firing by now, but gun cameras would have a problem clearly filming a head-on airplane at this distance. Steve still had a few seconds before the Marines could claim victory.

He cut in the Jug's turbosupercharger as he dropped into a shallow dive, offsetting the Jug to one side by banking hard, beginning his turn virtually beneath the Corsair's noses. He held full throttle as he continued what amounted to an aerial U-turn. The Jug's bones groaned in protest, and Steve's vision dimmed as the G-force flattened him, but the maneuver worked. The Corsairs badly overshot him. The Marine pilots were sparing their bodies and their airplanes as they began a leisurely turn to come after him. They were obviously confident that in a tight dogfight their Corsairs were more than a match for the Jug.

Surprise, surprise, Steve thought as he came out of his U-turn well behind the tail of the last Corsair. Steve kept his throttle wide open as he activated the water injection system. The Jug howled like a goosed dame, and then the great silver airplane leapt forward. Steve glanced at his air speed indicator: 475 miles per hour! His pulse was zinging just as fast. He was going at least 50 miles an hour faster than what the Corsairs were capable of doing. He barely had time to activate his gun camera before he overtook the first bluebird. He shot past it and got the next webfoot on film for a good five seconds before it broke away. He didn't chase it, but went after the last plane; he wanted all four. Four fucking Marines waxed by one Army airman—he was going to be famous, assuming he wasn't court-martialed.

Steve's finger was reaching to activate his camera on the last Corsair when "Break! Break!" filled his headset. He reacted automatically, veering off sharply, giving up the pursuit.

Break. It was the signal from a fellow pilot that the enemy was on your tail, that at any instant gunfire might be rattling through your cockpit. A fighter jock was trained to react instinctively to the warning. He couldn't afford to think about it, because the time it took to think might be all the time the enemy needed to kill him.

It had taken Steve less than a second to almost involuntarily react. By the time his consciousness had caught up to remind him that this was a mock dogfight and that there could be no enemy behind him, the Corsair was long gone, and in hot pursuit was the son of a bitch Thunderbolt pilot who had issued the phony warning. As the Jug flashed past, Steve had barely enough time to read the Pilot's personal name for his airplane plastered beneath the canopy, written in yellow script against a blue background: *Miss Bessie.*

You bastard! Steve cursed the pilot who had ruined his perfect run against the Marines. *You bastard, you stole my kill!*

It was the oldest asshole's trick in the book: the asshole waited for a fellow pilot to do all the hard work of lining up, hammering, and hamstringing an enemy. Then, at the last possible second, the asshole yells, "Break!" The rightful pilot takes evasive action, allowing the asshole to move in, put a short burst into the falling enemy, and in that way get to claim false credit for the kill.

Steve clicked his throat mike. "Hey, Miss Bessie, you son of a bitch! You stole my kill."

"Steve, this is Cappy. Calm down."

"Cappy, did you see what that son of a bitch did?"

"We all saw it. But this is just a mock dogfight, Lieutenant. Don't take it so seriously."

"Well, I *do* take it seriously, Cappy!" Steve protested. "I've got three of them on film. I was about to wax the last one, and then that bastard goes and pulls a dirty stunt like that. Who the fuck *is* he, anyway?"

A new voice cut into the conversation. "Lieutenant Gold, the name's Detkin. Lieutenant Ben Detkin."

Steve mentally ran through the members of the squadron. He knew the name, of course, but he just couldn't attach it to a face. "Detkin, just wait till I get my hands on you."

"Gold, you're talking to a fellow officer," Detkin chuckled. "You'd better watch your tone."

"Oh, yeah, Detkin, I'll watch it. And *you* can watch *me*

shove those louie's bars of yours right up your fucking, deceitful ass."

"That's enough!" Cappy cut in sharply. "Benny, you were wrong to cry wolf the way you did. And as for you, Steve, come on! Lighten up, for chrissake. You got three of those webfoots, and you ought to be satisfied with that. We're going home. I want to get your gun camera film developed. I can't wait to send it over to the Marine group commandant, along with some pillows for his pilots to sit on."

Steve was tempted to go after Detkin and wax *his* tail, but by now the water squirted into the engine had been used up. He could inject water again, of course, but he couldn't see straining his Jug that way in a noncombat situation. The Jug's power plant was already sounding rough—complaining about the abuse. Anyway, his fuel supply was low, and the loss of altitude was further hampering his performance.

"Cappy, this is Steve. I'm returning to base." He put the Jug into a gentle coasting turn back toward Santa Belle.

Detkin—I'll wax your tail on the ground.

(Three)

Santa Belle Airfield

Steve had the Jug's canopy up while he was still taxiing toward the hangar area. He cut his engine, coasting to where he wanted the Jug to stop with just a feather touch on the brakes. He was out of his plane the instant the wheels stopped turning.

"Get my gun camera film into the lab," Steve ordered his mystified crew chief as he strode past the man without stopping, heading for the squadron's ops-ready room.

Most of the pilots—Cappy excluded—were already there as Steve banged through the double screen doors. They froze in front of their lockers in their various states of undress, staring back at Steve as he stood with his hands on his hips, glaring into the room. One wall was taken up with a bank of narrow dark green metal lockers and long wooden benches, where the pilots could change into their flying gear. The other side of the room had folding wooden chairs haphazardly arranged in front of a low, raised platform. Attached to the wall behind the platform were a large rectangular blackboard, a duty roster, and a set of roll-down maps. The squadron's ops officer had his desk and file cabinets next to the podium. Next to him was where the radio operator sat in front of his equipment. In the hut's far corner a bar had been set up for the use of the officers.

"Detkin!" Steve roared.

"Take it easy, Steve. That's an order," Captain Crawford said as he stowed his gear.

Steve, pissed off, ignored him, despite the fact that he was a superior officer. When Cappy wasn't around, Crawford or any of the other three captains in the squadron were in charge, but a guy who pulled his weight in a combat unit could get away with a certain amount of insubordination. Anyway, Steve disliked schoolteachers telling him what to do.

"Detkin!" he repeated. "You in here? Or are you too chickenshit to show yourself?"

"I'm Detkin," a pilot Steve's age, or maybe a couple of years older, replied softly, stepping away from the others. He was barefoot and wearing just his boxer shorts. He was about five feet ten inches tall. Like all the pilots, he was built thick through his shoulders and arms, thanks to the effort it took to work a fighter plane's controls at high speed. "You ought to know your squadron mates by now," he mocked.

"I'll know you from now on," Steve said. He stripped off his Mae West and shoulder holster, threw his gear into his locker, and advanced on Detkin.

"Lieutenant Gold," Crawford was sputtering, "I swear to God, I'll have you up on charges if you don't cool off."

"Don't worry about it, Captain," Detkin said. "I can handle this *putz* okay by myself."

"You think so?" Steve demanded.

"I know so," Detkin replied.

"Your tricks can't help you now," Steve said.

"Face to face I don't need tricks." Detkin had stepped in close to spit the words into Steve's face.

He was swarthy, one of those guys who always looked like they needed a shave. He had heavy-lidded brown eyes that gave him a sleepy look, a broad, flat nose, and a strong jawline. He wore his glossy black hair cut short in the back and on the sides, but in thick tousled curls on top.

Steve knew that Detkin had to be a good pilot and an ace or else he wouldn't be in the squadron, but beyond that he drew a blank, although he had been able to connect the man with his name as soon as he'd identified himself. During the time the squadron had been together, Detkin had been flying as a wingman in one of the other flight formations.

"I believe you think you have a score to settle with me?" Detkin was smiling.

"Goddman right I do," Steve said. "You stole my kill by using one of the lowest tricks in the book."

Detkin shrugged. "It worked, didn't it?"

"Sure it worked!"

"So what's your problem, pal?" Detkin chuckled. "Come on, it was just a joke. Are you pissed at me for fooling you? Or are you pissed at yourself for being fooled?"

The other pilots were smiling in agreement, Steve noticed. That made him angrier. "Detkin, I consider you the lowest of the low."

Detkin stopped smiling. "I couldn't care less what you consider. Number one"—he poked Steve's chest with a rigid forefinger—"*don't* come crying to me because you fell for a sucker play. Number two"—he poked Steve a second time—"*don't* call me an asshole. And number three—"

He tried to poke Steve's chest again, but this time Steve slapped away his hand. "You got the balls to take that attitude with me after what you pulled?" Steve asked harshly.

"I got more balls than you could ever dream of, pal," Detkin sneered. "Anyway," he laughed, "like I said, you're making too big a deal out of this, you *schmuck*." He began to turn away.

"Let's see how seriously *you* take *this*, Lieutenant." Steve clenched his hand into a fist and delivered a short, stiff uppercut to the side of Detkin's jaw. The punch took the man totally by surprise. His head rocked sideways, and he lost his balance, tumbling over a bench. He landed sprawled on his hands and knees on the wood planking of the floor.

Shit, that was a sucker punch, Steve realized belatedly. His anger had vanished the instant he'd hit Detkin. He was sorry he'd done it. The other pilots were all staring at him accusingly, like he'd just shit in the mess hall. Steve tried to look them in the eye, but he couldn't. Hell, he knew he'd done wrong by overreacting that way. *Grace under pressure had to be learned,* Cappy had said. Steve guessed he had a lot to learn after all.

Some of the other guys were helping Detkin to his feet. "I'm all right, I'm all right," he told them as he sat down on the bench. He looked up at Steve, who could read nothing in Detkin's brown stare.

"Maybe I deserved that," he mumbled thickly, rubbing his jaw.

"Maybe I think you did, too, Benny," Cappy Fitzpatrick said from the doorway before Steve could reply.

Steve whirled around. "Cappy," he said, surprised. "How long were you—?"

"Long enough to see you strike an officer," Cappy muttered.

"I gave Gold a direct order to calm down—" Crawford began.

"Stow it, Captain, will you please?" Cappy said wearily as he studied Detkin, who was still rubbing his jaw. "Lieutenant, you need medical attention?"

Detkin experimentally moved his jaw from side to side. "From a little love tap like that from a *nebech* like him? No way, Major."

"What did you call me, you son of a bitch?" Steve demanded.

"*Nebech* means 'jerk' in Yiddish," Detkin said. "Get it? You're a—"

"Stow it, both of you," Cappy ordered, cutting off Detkin. "Now then, I'm not interested in putting anybody on report unless I'm forced to. Benny, you deserved that sock on the jaw for the stunt you pulled on Gold. That was wrong."

"It ain't wrong if you get away with it," Detkin said under his breath.

Cappy glared at him and he shut up. "Steve, you took your poke at Benny for the trick he pulled. Hopefully you got everything out of your system. So now both you guys are even with each other, right? I want you to shake hands so we can forget about this."

"Sure, no problem, Cappy," Detkin said evenly.

He extended his hand to Steve, who shook it. Steve knew that nothing had really been resolved between them by their confrontation or this forced handshake. He guessed that Detkin knew it as well.

"Come on, Benny, get dressed and we'll have a drink," Crawford said.

The other pilots were already moving toward the bar. Steve noticed that nobody was inviting him. *Fine,* he thought. *Who needs them, anyway?* He grabbed his gun rig out of his locker and left the building.

"Steve, wait up!" Cappy called out.

Steve turned around to see Cappy step out through the screen door toward him. "Yes, sir?"

Cappy jerked his thumb over his shoulder. "I stuck up for you back there because I thought you had a legitimate beef," Cappy said quietly. "But we both know that taking a swing at Detkin was uncalled for, considering the circumstances. When those Marines butted into our practice flight you wanted to indulge in a little horseplay."

"For which I asked permission," Steve pointed out.

Cappy nodded. "Right, and I gave permission. Then Detkin horns in, and you react by getting fired up and punching out the guy's lights, just because he wanted a little part of the action—"

"*My* action." Steve interrupted.

"The *squadron's* action!" Cappy declared, for the first time sounding really angry. "Remember this, Steve: whatever you do reflects on the squadron, and whatever the squadron does reflects on you!"

"Understood, sir."

Cappy stared at him. "Steve," he began, his voice softer, "you've got to learn how to fit in with the others. How to get with the program, become part of the team."

"I've heard that before," Steve sighed.

"Because it's true," Cappy nodded. "Why haven't you made any friends here?"

Steve looked away, shrugging. "I guess it's the same old bullshit," he said tiredly. "I guess it's hard for people to see me for who I am instead of being Herman Gold's son."

Cappy looked dubious. "You mean the fact that your old man is loaded?"

"Right," Steve said. "I get my father's reputation thrown up at me all the time, Cappy. I'm just fed up with making excuses for who I am."

Cappy hesitated. "Steve, I've known you a long time, and I'm probably your best friend, so I've got to tell you that from where I'm sitting, your problem has nothing to do with your father."

"What are you saying?"

"Face it," Cappy said. "You've been acting like an asshole. You've been arrogant, stubborn, selfish, a wise guy."

"Gee, thanks," Steve scowled. "And you're my best friend, did you say?"

"But you *could* change."

"Cappy, spare me this psychological bullshit!" Steve snapped.

Damn, I shouldn't have said that, Steve thought. The way Cappy was staring at him now was making him feel as bad as when he'd lost it and socked Detkin.

"Yeah, I'm done," Cappy said. "And I was wrong. I apologize." He shouldered past Steve. "You don't *act* like an asshole. I think you really *are* one." He paused. "And I'll tell you something else. I don't care how well you fly, or how many Japs you shoot down. I'm not putting you in for a promotion until you start showing me some responsibility and maturity!"

"Cappy, you can't do that to me!" Steven said angrily, thinking that his old buddy had turned out to be worse than his previous commander, "Spit and Polish" Wohl.

"Just watch me!" Cappy nodded.

"It's not fair!"

"Life isn't fair," Cappy said, walking away. "I hope you enjoyed your promotion from shavetail to lieutenant, because if you don't grow up, you're going to be wearing that single silver bar for the duration."

CHAPTER 4

(One)

**London, England
22 March 1944**

It was very early on a chilly, drizzly morning when Herman Gold got into the garnet-red MG parked in the alley behind his hotel. The MG's black leather bucket seat felt icy as he ground the starter until the engine caught. He let the car warm up for a few minutes and then pulled away.

The MG's clutch needed work, and its shifter was balky. Every time Gold came to a traffic light he had to rev the engine to keep it from stalling. The heater seemed to be taking forever to warm up. Gold shivered despite his wool-lined trench coat, his fedora, and his calfskin gloves as he drove slowly, in unison with the stop-and-go traffic, along the twisty cow paths that passed for streets in London.

He passed whole blocks that were nothing but bombed-out ruins. Seeing the destruction jolted him into a new awareness of the war. He was actually *here,* not simply reading headlines about the Nazi bombing raids against valiant London from the safety and comfort of his California home.

An angry horn blared at him. A lorry was coming at him head-on. *What the hell is wrong with that driver?* Gold thought as the truck driver frantically waved at Gold, waving him to the left.

Shit! Gold thought, panicked, realizing he had drifted over to the right-hand, wrong side of the road. He jerked the steering wheel, swerving to the correct, left-hand side.

"Learn to drive, you bloody fool!" the lorry driver yelled at him as the truck rumbled past.

Gold, his nerves rattled, pulled over to the curb and stopped to calm down. He hated not knowing his way around, and not feeling comfortable with the rules of the road. He wouldn't have been driving at all, but he'd been told that if he chose to accept the invitation he would have to come alone, and that a car would be put at his disposal.

Sighing, he put the car in gear, checked carefully to make sure that he was not cutting anyone off, and pulled away.

It began to rain harder once he'd left the outskirts of London. The MG's convertible top, ballooning in the wind, began to leak. Gold was looking for a place called Wattham, a village in Hertfordshire just northwest of London. He couldn't wait to get there and come back, but he didn't dare drive any faster, considering the weather. By now the MG's heater was going full blast, but it was a miserable, puny thing that did little more than roast his left foot.

The MG's rubber wiper blades needed replacing; they were doing little more than smearing the rain across the windshield. Gold strained to read the road signs through the impenetrably gray curtain of rain and fog.

What I wouldn't give to be back home, Gold sighed, wiping the condensation that was his own breath from the inside glass of his windshield. He hadn't felt comfortable since he'd arrived in England two days ago.

He'd been flown over by the Army Air Force, along with other top executives from the United States aircraft industry, to take part in a secret USAAF-RAF joint conference on Allied progress to date in the development of jet aircraft. The conference was held at Bentley Priory, an abandoned girls' school to the northwest of London that was now being used as RAF Fighter Command.

Gold had almost refused the invitation. He thought the whole idea of holding the conference around London was stupid.

For one thing, he didn't consider London to be safe. The Eighth Army Air Force and the RAF were crowing about how the Luftwaffe was beaten; that whatever was left of it after the ill-fated Battle of Britain and the Russian offensive, was now being shredded as Allied air power took the war home to Germany.

Gold happened to believe that such declarations of victory were premature. Just last week the Luftwaffe had launched a night raid. It was true that the enemy planes had been stopped at the coast, but the attack was evidence that the Nazis were still capable of delivering an air strike against England.

The road had narrowed to a serpentine two-lane blacktop with lots of little hills. Gold had to constantly upshift and downshift, and each time he did, the transmission protested a bit more loudly. He wondered how many more shifts the gearbox had in it. That's all he needed, to be broken down out here where he had no desire to be in the first place.

There was another, more personal reason why Gold had considered refusing the invitation to the conference—sour grapes. Why should he come when he had nothing to crow about?

With GAT's XP-4 project a total failure, and Gold's concepts for a new swept-wing jet fighter design still nothing more tangible than a heap of drawings on Teddy Quinn's drafting table, he'd had to sit quietly in that drafty, cold conference room, suffering in humiliation while the others crowed about their advances in jet technology.

The people from Lockheed had announced that they had an order from the United States military for five thousand of their recently unveiled Shooting Star jet fighters. Hugh Luddy, an old friend and the representative from the premier British aviation firm of Stoat-Black, had proudly announced that the first of his company's Sky Terrier turbojet fighters would be delivered to the RAF by early summer. There had been additional boastings of grand things from Bell, Republic, and Grumman.

Gold had to listen to it all, gritting his teeth in envy and frustration. When it came time for Gold to speak, he had to put out a lot of red-faced double-talk, all the while knowing that news traveled fast along the industry grapevine, and that his huey was fooling no one. Everybody knew that GAT had failed.

When at last his period of agony at the podium had ended and he was able to return to his seat, he'd reminded himself that the only reason he'd decided to show up was because GAT's absence from these proceedings would have been the greatest admission of failure of all.

Gold slowed down the MG. Ahead, a sheepherder in a bright yellow slicker and thigh-high black rubber waders was taking his time guiding his muddy flock across the roadway. Gold waited, goosing the idling engine to keep it from stalling, impatiently tapping the steering wheel as he listened to the rhythmic groans of the impotent wipers. The sheep were sauntering along single file, for chrissake. He glanced at his wristwatch. According to the directions he'd been given over the telephone, he should have been there by now, he thought sourly, wondering if he was lost.

The road cleared and he continued driving, slowing down at every intersection to check the signs. He saw the sign for his turnoff—*Crowell Lane*—as he was about to pass it. He quickly checked his rear-view mirror to make sure that there was no one behind him and then double-clutched a downshift as he threw the little car into a hard right turn. The MG seemed to go over on its two right wheels for an instant, and then its rear end fishtailed, spraying mud and gravel. Gold steered into the skid, straightened out, and continued on, ignoring the sign that announced the road was closed.

He drove for another two miles along the curving lane. It was only one car wide, and the thick, high hedges on both sides made the road even more claustrophobic. Gold felt like he was traveling through an undulating trench. It was enough to make even an old ex–fighter pilot carsick. He hoped he didn't run into anybody coming from the opposite direction, because he wasn't about to back up.

The road widened as he came to a high barbed-wire gate across the lane, guarded by a pair of sodden-looking British soldiers armed with Sten submachine guns. Gold came to a stop and unsnapped the MG's side curtain as one of the soldiers came around.

"Sorry, sir, but you'll have to turn around," the soldier began. "This is a restricted area."

"My name's Herman Gold. Would you check with Hugh Luddy, please? I'm expected."

The soldier nodded. "Yes, Mr. Gold. We were told to expect you. Might I see some identification, sir?" the soldier asked politely.

"Uh, sure." Gold unbuttoned his trench coat and reached for his passport in the left inside breast pocket of his suit coast. As he made the movement, he noticed that the second guard was casually lowering the barrel of his Sten gun in the direction of the MG's windshield.

"Very good, sir," the first soldier said, glancing at Gold's passport and then handing it back. The second guard began opening the gate. "Welcome to the Stoat-Black Experimental Works," the first guard continued. "If you'll just drive through the gate and continue on for about a quarter mile, you'll come to a low clapboard-sided building painted light green. That will be HQ, sir." The soldier paused and smiled sardonically. "You'll find *Sir* Hugh there."

Gold winced as he put the car in gear and drove through the opened gate. He felt like kicking himself for forgetting that Luddy had recently been knighted in appreciation for his work in the national interest. Gold had chatted with Luddy a number of times at the conference, but had yet to offer the man his congratulations on his knighthood.

The road had become a single, paved ribbon through a sea of muddy pastureland. The compound reminded him of the Hoovervilles—the slummy campsites—that had dotted California during the depression. Crowding both sides of the road were parked cars and canvas-sided lorries. Set back were a number of metal trailers—caravans, the British called them. The trailers were painted dark green, but in this damp climate nothing metal lasted for long. The trailers were blotched with rust. They all had gray smoke pouring out of their stovepipe chimneys. The smoke was mixing with the steady rain to form a suffocating haze.

Now and then Gold glimpsed a face at a trailer's curtained window, but with the rain falling, the only people he saw outdoors were the armed guards patrolling with leashed attack dogs that went into a lunging, fang-baring frenzy as the MG rolled past.

He pulled up in front of the only building in the compound that fitted the guard's description, and got out of the MG. Off in the distance, behind the sprawling, pale green HQ, he could see a number of windowless hangars clustered at the head of a single, concrete airstrip. The airstrip was empty, but then this wasn't flying weather.

Gold went up the steps and tried the front door. It was open. He stepped inside a small anteroom with a worn red linoleum floor and dingy white walls. The room was crowded with wooden office furniture and dark green metal filing cabinets, and smelled of coal smoke and wet wool. A young, rather horse-faced woman with dark brown hair was seated behind a desk. She looked up at Gold and smiled.

"I'm Herman Gold, here to see Sir Hugh."

"Welcome, Mr. Gold," she said brightly, standing up. She was wearing a rust-colored tweed skirt suit, white knee socks, and low-heeled oxfords. She had wonderfully huge breasts that were inflating the front of her ruffled white blouse. "May I take your coat and hat?" As she reached for them, Gold glimpsed the butt of a pistol in a shoulder holster underneath her tweed jacket.

The woman caught him staring at her chest. "I do hope it's my gun that has captured your eye?" she said primly, but with a hint of amusement.

"I've always been an admirer of massive firepower."

She laughed as she placed his coat and hat in a closet. "If you'll follow me, I'll take you to Sir Hugh's office."

Gold followed her down a winding, narrow hallway lit by naked bulbs that had been hastily strung along the ceiling. The building was a warren of doorless cubbyhole-sized offices. Behind a few of the desks were men and women in RAF uniforms, but most of the people were in civvies. Gold wondered if everyone in here was carrying a gun. Maybe that was the secret to staying warm in England: packing heat. Nobody looked cold, damn them, while Gold could see his own breath. He was wearing a dark blue cashmere turtleneck sweater and a heavy wool gray suit over long underwear. Even his black rubber-soled shoes were fleece lined, but his nose was running, his fingers and toes were numb, and it was all he could do to keep his teeth from chattering.

The woman stopped in front of a plain wooden door, knocked once, and then opened it, standing aside to let Gold enter. It was a large room and slightly warmer, thanks to the ticking coal stove tucked in one corner. There was a braided oval rug taking up most of the scuffed wooden floor, and, against the walls, freestanding steel shelving haphazardly piled with papers and books.

Luddy was seated behind an oak desk with his back to the room's single window with its view of the airstrip. On the desk was a telephone, a single, large manila folder, and a fat black cat reclining like a sphinx as it looked at Gold with disinterested, mustard-yellow eyes.

"Hello, old chap," Luddy said, standing up. "Thanks so much for coming."

Luddy was bandy-legged like a bulldog, and like a bull-dog, gave the impression of being shorter than he was wide. He had a closely trimmed auburn beard and a matching corona of shoulder-length brown curls around a high, bald dome. You could take Luddy just as he looked—except maybe exchange his heather tweeds and knee-high cordovan walking boots for Elizabethan-period tights and a doublet—and he'd be just right to play Falstaff.

"Hugh, or I guess I should say, *Sir* Hugh, I haven't had a chance to congratulate you on your knighthood."

"One does that kneeling on one knee," Luddy observed quietly.

"Pardon?"

Luddy laughed richly, holding up his hand and shaking his head. "Just indulging in a giggle, lad. Pay it no mind." He glanced behind him as the wind rattled the window in its frame. The glass was being pelted by rain. "The weather is so dreadful, Herman! Was it *very* terrible finding your way here?" he sighed sympathetically, rolling his blue eyes.

"It was certainly inconvenient, Hugh," Gold nodded. "What's with all the soldiers and guns and guard dogs? What do you *do* out here in the middle of nowhere?"

"This is where we did all of the important work on our Sky Terrier jet fighter," Luddy explained. "We want to stay well out of the public eye to guard against the possibility of Jerry seeking us out for a bombing raid. There's a strict no-visitors policy in effect here. You'll never know how many arms I had to twist to allow *you* to visit. That's why you had to do your own driving, dear man. If we had sent around an official car, it might have been noticed by the others at the conference who are staying at the same hotel. There would have been questions, and perhaps jealous complaints about what courtesies Stoat-Black was extending to you but denying the others. And, of course, having a cab bring you out here was out of the question. The local police have been quite cooperative about enforcing the no-trespassing laws. The public has learned to give the area a wide berth. We'd rather not have a cabbie spoil the status quo with blather about what he'd discovered at the far end of Crowell Lane, inciting the adventurous to come see for themselves.

"But why all the secrecy in the first place, Hugh?" Gold

asked. "Why couldn't we have met at the Stoat-Black offices in town?"

"As I said, we'd rather the other Yanks who are attending the conference not know about this little tête-à-tête. They would be very jealous, Herman. It would certainly weaken Stoat-Black's working relationships with those firms in the future. You'll understand why in a moment."

"Okay, so what's this all about?" Herman demanded.

"Our respective futures, dear lad, and the future of commercial aviation."

Luddy opened his blue eyes wide to emphasize his melodramatic statement. The cat watched approvingly. *Probably taking notes on technique*, Gold thought.

"Stoat-Black believes it has something very special in the works," Luddy continued. "Something GAT will want to become involved with on the ground floor, as it were."

"Another joint effort between Stoat-Black and GAT. . . ." Gold nodded, his interest piqued. "Well, we've certainly done well by each other in the past."

Gold had first met Luddy back in 1936, when Gold had been in England unsuccessfully trying to sell the British airlines on the GAT Monarch GC-3 airliner. The British airline executives had wanted to buy, but for political reasons they were wedded to their own British-built airplanes, despite the fact that they were slower and more expensive to operate than GAT's GC series. Gold had found a way around the problem by subcontracting to Stoat-Black the assembly of GAT airliners for British and European markets. The association had turned out to be both pleasant and profitable for both sides. Since then, the two companies had successfully collaborated on a seaplane project for the RAF's Coastal Command, and a single-engine fighter that had been dubbed the Supershark in England, and the BearClaw in America.

"Come around beside me," Luddy said, shooing away the cat in order to spread wide the manila folder on the desk. "I want to show you the plans for a new airliner, one that will shrink the globe, and in the process render every other commercial airliner obsolete—including your commendable Monarch GC series."

Gold scanned the blueprints and then turned his attention to an artist's rendering of a large, streamlined airliner with four engine pods—*jet* engine pods—built right into the wings for maximum aerodynamic efficiency.

"My God, she's lovely," Gold breathed.

"Aye, lad, that she is," Luddy chuckled appreciatively. "You're looking at the SB-100 Starstreak, the big bird that will carry Stoat-Black to preeminence in the world of aviation. She'll carry thirty-two passengers and a crew of six at a cruising speed of five hundred miles an hour, with a range of seventeen hundred miles, and she'll do it all as quietly as I'm whispering to you now, lad."

Gold nodded. "Because she's jet propelled there'll be less engine noise, and no numbing vibration the way there is with piston-engine liners. But I don't see how you can expect that kind of range from those jet engines. How could she every carry enough fuel to feed four thirsty engines for that amount of time?"

Luddy chuckled. "The secret's in getting the engines to operate at high altitudes. Every sort of engine operates the same way: by burning a mixture of air and fuel. Up high—let's say thirty thousand feet or better—the air is thin. Thin air means the engines burn less fuel—"

"And while the engines might be producing less power at high altitudes, it won't matter," Gold noted quickly. "Because it takes less power to move an airplane through thin air!"

"There you have it, lad," Luddy said.

"It's a swell solution to the fuel consumption problem, all right," Gold said, "but it brings with it a whole new slew of problems. For example, no pressurized cabin has ever had to withstand the stresses of cruising at those altitudes."

"Every problem has a solution."

"You're ready to build this?" Gold demanded. *"Now?"*

"No, not now," Luddy said. "But we have the basic technology, thanks to what we've learned putting together the Sky Terrier."

"Who would build your engines?"

"Layten-Reese," Luddy replied. "The same firm that built the Terrier's engines."

"What's your projected schedule?"

"Right now all our resources are tied up in the Sky Terrier. As we begin to see profits, we'll siphon the money into the Starstreak. From start-up we figure two years of research and development."

"Two years alone spent on R&D!" Gold laughed.

"Maybe longer," Luddy shrugged. He took a bent-stemmed briar pipe and a brown leather tobacco pouch out of the patch pocket of his tweed suit coat. "We don't want to rush this, Herman. We don't want any mistakes. This is to be a commercial airliner—a *passenger* plane—utilizing new, not completely understood technology. We want to make very sure that all the bugs are ironed out of our prototypes before the actual plane is put into service. We don't want any doubts on the part of the public concerning safety and reliability."

"Of course," Gold said, thinking back to 1925 and the crash of his German-built, Spatz F-5a airliner. That crash killed ten people and the attendant bad publicity almost killed his fledgling air transport company. And then there was the 1931 Fokker Trimotor crash that killed Knute Rockne, among others, and caused the grounding of all Fokkers, and a tremendous, thankfully temporary, public backlash against air travel.

"We intend to overbuild the Starstreak," Luddy said, tamping his pipe. "We want to promote her as the most vigorously tested aircraft in history. Obviously that's going to require tremendous financial resources. The British government will help with that to some degree, but we'd very much like GAT assisting."

"You're looking for investment capital?" Gold asked.

"We do want your money," Luddy began, "but we also want your expertise." He paused to strike a match and get his pipe going. "Virtually all of Stoat-Black's design experience has been in building military aircraft. We've learned a great deal during the time we spent assembling your Monarchs, but we don't pretend to have GAT's experience in constructing commercial airliners," he finished, exhaling smoke.

Gold nodded, trying hard not to let it show that he was smarting over the fact that Luddy was lauding GAT's talent at *constructing*, not *designing* airliners. "I need some time to go over these specs before I can give you an answer about whether GAT wants to buy in. And I'll need to bring other people into the decision-making process. Teddy Quinn, for example."

"Of course, Herman," Luddy said. He closed the manila folder, removed a large brown clasp envelope from a desk drawer, and slipped the folder inside. "This set of plans is yours to take home with you to California." He handed it to Herman. "Study it at your leisure. I'll be looking forward to hearing from you. I only ask that you, and any of your staff you may consult with, respect our secrecy concerning the Starstreak project."

"I understand," Gold said. "Thank you for offering GAT the opportunity to consider coming into a partnership with you," Gold said.

"No thanks are necessary, Herman. GAT helped put Stoat-Black on the map, and now it's time for us to return the favor."

Meaning you think GAT is a has-been, Gold thought. Luddy, wreathed in an aromatic, blue pipe smoke, was grinning like a Cheshire cat. "I'll think very seriously about this," Gold told him.

"You do that, lad. But just so there's no misunderstanding, let me say one last thing." Luddy grew very serious. "It would be grand to have your experts—and funding—but we mean to proceed with the Starstreak, with or without your help."

"I understand the situation."

"Do you?" Luddy persisted, looking quizzical. "We're old friends, so I know you won't take it amiss when I say that it's no secret that GAT has fallen flat with its own jet fighter project," Luddy confided as he walked Gold to the door.

"Hugh, it's a temporary setback—" Gold started to protest.

"Herman! You don't need to trot out the excuses for me!" Luddy patronized. "It's a natural law, you see! What comes up must come down! GAT has been enjoying grand success for many years now, but no one can forever remain king of the mountain. Now it looks as if it's going to be Stoat-Black's turn to enjoy the view," Luddy said smugly, patting Gold's shoulder. "Lad, you grab on to our coattails while you can."

(Two)

On his way back to London Gold stopped at a roadside pub for a bite to eat. Inside, the pub was all dark mahogany and polished brass. Gold found a small table near the roaring fire and ordered a plowman's lunch and a pint of ale.

He watched a dart game in progress between the locals while he ate. He tried to put it out of his mind, but he couldn't help thinking about what Luddy had intimated.

"You've fallen flat on your face. . . . Your day has passed. . . . GAT had better grab on to Stoat-Black's coattails while it can. . . ."

At one time in the not very distant past, Luddy's condescension would have infuriated him, but not these days. Truth was, Gold found himself agreeing with Luddy. GAT *was* falling fast. His organization seemed to have run out of creativity, and ideas were the lifeblood of flourishing business. How long had it been since he'd felt the enthusiasm— the *fire*—that had been in Luddy's eyes when he'd been talking about the Starstreak?

Gold couldn't help thinking that the way things looked now, it was only a matter of time until GAT did scrape bottom, unless this Starstreak deal served to somewhat break the fall.

And that wasn't just *his* opinion. . . .

Gold nursed what remained of his ale as he thought about

the last letter he and Erica had received from Steven. The kid was doing really well. In the past few months, Steven's squadron had taken part in the invasions of Bougainville and the Green Islands, helping the Navy and the Marines to close the ring around Rabaul. Steven was now better than a double ace, with twelve kills to his credit. Hell, three more and he'd be a *triple*, Gold thought, proud of his son.

He wondered if Steven was destined to best his own score in the First World War? Gold had twenty confirmed kills to his credit. He hoped Steven did better. *Let him stay alive to best me*, Gold thought, rapping his knuckles against the worn, varnished tabletop to insure Steven's good luck. It could only be a pleasure to have his record broken by his son.

Thinking about it, it puzzled Gold that with such a high score, Steven was still only a first lieutenant. He'd heard that promotions came fast to successful combat pilots. Gold also wondered why his son never mentioned any buddies he might have made.

But then, his son had always been a loner, Gold mused. A certain amount of that was good—it showed independence—but too much was bad. A fighter pilot needed friends to protect his back during combat, and to help him blow off tension between the battles.

What most stuck in Gold's mind from his son's last letter home was how Steven had raved about his Thunderbolt fighter. The kid had written that he'd wished Gold could fly the plane in order to experience its raw power. In his letter Steven had wondered why GAT wasn't building them like that.

Gold had hidden it from Erica, but God, how it had hurt to have his own son ask such a thing. Gold could read between the lines. What Steven was saying was that he thought GAT *couldn't* build a fighter that good.

Gold paid his bill and left the pub. He got back into the MG and continued on to London. He felt listless and discouraged, sick at heart and almost unwilling to try anymore for fear of suffering further humiliating failure. There was a knack to success. Gold couldn't shake the gnawing suspicion that his knack had been lost.

Gold was going to have to face the reality of his situation. GAT might well survive the immediate future by hanging on to Stoat-Black's coattails, but it looked as if times had changed.

It looked as if times had passed him by.

CHAPTER 5

(One)

Santa Belle Airfield
Solomon Islands
22 June 1944

It was around nine that night when Steven Gold, feeling restless, left his tent to go for a walk. It was a beautiful evening. A refreshing sea breeze had blown away the gnats and banished the clouds, revealing a vast array of stars flying escort for a fat crescent of pink moon.

There were no runway lights on Santa Belle, and the carriage-mounted searchlights set up to guide AA fire in case of a Jap air attack had never been used. The occasional lantern spilled lemony light through a partially open tent flap, and here and there a passerby's cigarette tip glowed cherry red, but mostly there was only the silvery starlight and the pastel glow of the tropical moon.

As Steve walked, he thought back on all the action the squadron had seen. Months ago he'd celebrated his twentieth birthday by shooting down a "Val" dive bomber off Bougainville. That had been his tenth kill. Since then he'd shot down two more Japs—both of them Zekes—during the struggle to conquer the peripheral island enemy bases that ringed the main Jap base at Rabaul. That enemy stronghold had been isolated, making an actual invasion unnecessary. Word had come down from the brass that the stranded enemy forces on Rabaul would be left to wither on the vine.

Around March, things had begun to quiet down. The daily air patrols had become milk runs. The opinion was that the Japs bottled up on Rabaul and the other pestholes in this part of the world had no airplanes left, and that the fighter squadrons on Santa Belle were just marking time until the brass decided what to do with them.

Steve hoped that the brass would decide soon. He needed action; needed it the way a hophead needed dope. Combat absorbed all of his energy and concentration. It made his problems go away.

He stopped walking, to listen to the distant, soothing crash of waves against the shore and the rhythmic sawing of the nocturnal insects. The sounds of nature played counterpoint to the low murmur of voices punctuated by bursts of laughter carrying across the quiet dark compound.

The noise was coming from Cappy's big tent, where the squadron's nightly poker game was going on. Steve approached the tent, and watched silently from the shadows just beyond the outer reach of the light spilling out from the gathering. The tent looked crowded, as if all the pilots were in there. The men's silhouettes loomed larger than life through the lit canvas interior.

He backed off, away from the circle of light, and continued walking beyond the Army encampment, into the larger Marine portion of the base. He walked with his shoulders hunched, his hands in his pockets, a lit cigarette stuck between his lips.

He'd guessed that it was that stupid confrontation with Detkin that was to blame. He'd replayed that damn October day countless times while lying on his cot, tossing and turning his way through the sweltering, sleepless nights. Right now, as he listened to the waves, he could again taste the sweet triumph of chasing down those four Marine Corsairs, and his bitter anger as he watched Detkin steal his last "kill."

Later that same day, Steve and the rest of the squadron had assembled in the ops-ready room to view his—and Detkin's—gun camera film. Everyone had enjoyed a good laugh over the way Steve had waxed the three Corsairs, and Cappy had promised to send the film over to Marine Group HQ, just to rub a little salt into the webfoots' blistered tails.

The guys in the squadron had gone through the motions of congratulating Steve, but by then the news about how Steve had slugged Detkin had gotten around. Maybe if he'd taken the lecture Cappy had given him to heart and apologized to Detkin right away things would have turned out differently, but at the same time Steve was still all puffed up with righteous rage over the "theft" of his kill.

So he'd never apologized, and the breach with the rest of the squadron was never properly healed. Now that breach was like the scar tissue puckered around that old bullet wound in his leg: it would always be slightly painful to the touch, and it would never completely go away.

Steve lit another cigarette, amused and a little disturbed by the way his fingers were trembling as he brought up his lighter. Hell, by now he ought to be used to being a loner. What the hell did he need friends for? Friends were just a liability in his line of work.

"*Back off, you guys—*"

"*Fuck you, pal! You're not going anywhere!*"

The angry shouts distracted Steve from his brooding thoughts. They were coming from behind Polly's Pit, the Marine officers' club. A bunch of Marines were congregated out in front, drinking and making a lot of noise on their own, but the shouts that had caught Steve's attention were coming from around the back, where it was dark. Steve thought he could see some people milling around back there among the shadows and the garbage cans, but he was too far away to make out anything more than vague shapes in the dark.

He sure as hell wasn't going any closer. It was one thing to take a stroll around the base, something else entirely to try and barge into a webfoot watering hole. Cappy had put the club off-limits—needlessly, because any Army man with half a brain knew enough to give the Pit a wide berth. Steve was turning to head back the way he'd come when the shouting began again.

"I said take your hands of me, you *putz!*"

Putz? Steve stopped in his tracks.

"What the fuck did you just call me?" another voice demanded from behind the building. "And what are you gonna do about it anyway if I *don't* get my hands off you, you asshole?"

"I'll kick your Marine ass right now."

Steve, crouched low, began to move toward the confrontation. As he got closer he could see four guys—by their uniforms he could tell that they were Marine pilots—in a semicircle around one guy who had his back up against the wall. The cornered guy was rocking on the balls of his feet, nervously shifting his position as if he was considering trying to make a run for it, which was a smart idea, considering the odds he was facing. A shaft of moonlight fell on the guy's face.

It was Detkin, all right.

What the hell do I do now? Steve wondered. He was only a few feet away, but he was hidden by the darkness. He was crouched behind a parked truck, peering over the hood like Kilroy in the drawing.

He wasn't wearing his gun. The island had been cleared of Japanese some time ago, so the general order requiring Army personnel to wear sidearms had been lifted. Not that he would have flashed a pistol if he'd had one. The Marines and the Army were *supposed* to be on the same side, for chrissake.

Steve watched as Detkin abruptly tried to run. One of the Marines stepped into his path and punched him in the stomach.

Oh shit, Steve thought. He heard the air whooshing out of Detkin and watched the guy's knees sag as he bent over double. Detkin might have crumpled to the ground, but two of the Marine pilots grabbed him under his arms, hauling him up to straighten him, and then slammed him against the wall.

"That's enough," Steve said firmly, standing up.

The Marines turned to stare as he stepped out from behind the truck. Detkin tried to make another break for it, but one of the Marines put a hand against his throat, shoving him back up against the wall and pinning him there.

The other webfoots, looking around, began to smile. "That's it?" one of them grinned. "Just you?"

Steve nodded. He gestured toward Detkin. "He didn't do anything to you, did he?"

"He walked into the Pit like he owned the place," the Marine pilot said. "It's our territory and he invaded it. Marines aren't in the habit of allowing the enemy to make a beachhead."

"All right, so he's a jerk," Steve laughed, trying to make a joke out of the whole thing. "You proved your point. Now let him go, and you can watch him run."

"No, pal, I don't think so," the pilot said. "We're gonna keep him, *and* you."

Two Marines remained where they were, bracketing Detkin, while two came toward Steve. One was kind of pudgy and had a nervous look about him. The other guy looked hard as nails. He had a flattened nose and scar tissue around his eyes. Probably the kind of guy who laughed when he felt pain, Steve thought, feeling sick to his stomach.

"Hey, fellas . . ." Steve forced a grin. "Come on, let's talk about it—we're all on the same side, right?"

"Against the Japs? Sure," scar tissue said, "but right now I don't see any Japs around, do you, dogface?"

"Just wait a minute!" Steve brought up both his hands, palms out, as if in surrender. Both Marines were distracted by the movement. Steve used the opportunity to kick pudgy in the balls. The webfoot opened his mouth to scream, but no sound came out. He bent over, clutching his groin, and began to vomit. The smell of sour beer filled the sultry night.

Out of the corner of his eye Steve saw Detkin take a

swing at one of *his* two Marines. Detkin was fast and light on his feet, and managed to get in a couple of good shots, but up against that wall he didn't have anywhere to go. One of the webfoots hit him in the kidneys, taking the fight right out of him.

Steve took a wild swing at scar tissue, who expertly dodged with a minimum of movement. He let Steve's momentum carry him around, and then delivered a crisp right, catching Steve just beneath the ribs. Steve gasped, letting his hands drop for a second. The Marine stepped in fast, snapping out a pair of jabs to the face that rocked Steve. His ears began to ring, and hot, salty blood began to fill his mouth. He backpedaled, desperately windmilling his fists, trying to hold off the guy.

Can't fall down, Steve thought groggily. *If I fall down they'll stomp the shit out of me.*

He caught a glimpse of Detkin taking a punch in the face, but right now he had his own problems. The pudgy webfoot he'd kicked in the balls had straightened up and was coming toward Steve on bowed legs, scuttling like a crab. The guy definitely looked like he wanted to get even. Steve lashed out a backhand left that caught pudgy on the nose, but it didn't slow him down.

Steve saw Detkin topple sideways into the garbage cans, knocking them over. The cans rolled back and forth as Detkin lay still. The two Marines were standing over him, looking satisfied.

Pudgy got behind Steve and made a grab at Steve's shirt collar, trying to lock him in a bear hug. Steve drove his elbow into the man's gut and twisted away—directly into scar tissue's solid right cross.

The punch caught Steve on the side of his neck, sending an electric jolt down his spine that turned his arms and legs to rubber. He closed his eyes as a reddish haze descended and all sound seemed to recede. His head lolled forward until his chin touched his chest. Steve felt himself falling. It seemed to take a long time to hit bottom.

"That's enough," one of the Marines said, from what sounded like a great distance.

"You guys had enough, huh?" Steve mumbled thickly. The cool ground pressing against his face felt as inviting as a mattress.

"What'd he say?"

"Who knows? He's out cold and he doesn't even now it. Let's get out of here."

Steve struggled to open one eye and saw several pairs of black shoes walking quickly away.

"Detkin?" he murmured into the dirt. He planted his palms against the earth and did a push-up that rolled him onto his side. *Good enough*, he thought as he closed his eyes, curling up into a fetal position. "Detkin . . . you alive?"

"Yeah, Gold." Steve heard the hollow, metallic clanking of a toppled garbage can being rolled away. "Can you get up?"

"Maybe later," Steve muttered. "Now I just want to lay here and bleed."

"You mean lie."

"What?"

"Lie, not lay," Detkin reiterated, grunting as he stood up and stumbled over. He sank down to the ground next to Gold and patted him on the shoulder. "The Marines laid you out, but you're *lying* there."

"Son of a bitch," Steve laughed weakly. "Oh, my ribs—" he gasped. "I can't believe I saved you, you son of a bitch."

"Some save," Detkin said.

"You're just lucky I was here. Otherwise they would have stomped you once they knocked you out, you pussy," Steve said.

"What luck? And who's a pussy?" Detkin bristled. "You never heard of playing possum, you *putz*?"

"Oh, I can't believe I saved you." Steve opened his eyes and looked up at Detkin. "Christ, you're a mess!" Detkin's right eye was swelling shut, his nose was dripping blood, and his lower lip was split. Steve wrinkled his nose. "Plus you smell like garbage."

"I was lying in garbage, so what should I smell like?" Detkin said, sounding disgusted. "Anyway, you think *I* look bad, you should see what they did to you."

"I believe you." His jaw felt like he'd been slugged with a baseball bat. His side ached each time he took a breath, and his mouth kept filling up with blood. He ran his tongue around the inside of his mouth. At least he hadn't lost any teeth.

"Hey," Detkin began, and then paused. "Why *did* you help me, anyway?"

Steve thought about it. "I'm not sure. I mean, it never occurred to me not to help. I mean, Army oughta stick together, right?"

"Sure," Detkin murmured. "Listen, if you can walk, I think we should get out of here."

"All right. Okay." Steve tentatively began to get to his feet. His ribs were still killing him. He took a few hobbling steps and began to get dizzy.

"Lean on me," Detkin said, moving quickly to put a supporting arm around Steve.

"Ow! Watch out for my side, Detkin!"

"Call me Benny."

"Yeah, sure," Steve nodded. "Anything to keep your big mitts off my ribs. Go slow, Benny," he cautioned. "Or I'm not gonna make it—"

"Like I said, lean on me."

With Benny Detkin's help, Steve made it to the Army encampment. They went directly to the latrine, where they cleaned themselves up.

It was a little after eleven by the time the two of them began slowly and painfully toward their tents. Their hair was still wet from the showers. They were wearing just their boxer shorts, T-shirts, and service caps. Their unlaced boots were flapping around their ankles, and their soiled, bloody khakis were rolled up and tucked under their arms.

"Maybe you should have a doctor take a look at those ribs," Benny suggested.

"Nah, I don't want any medics poking at me, and maybe grounding me," Steve said. "I'm on the roster to fly patrol tomorrow."

"Yeah, me too," Benny said.

"Anyway, I'm feeling better now that I'm up and around." Steve glanced at Benny. "But you don't sound so good. You're talking funny. You think maybe your nose is broken?"

"Nah, it's just my sinus condition," Benny muttered. "I've got adenoids, allergies—you name it, I got it. I've been to the top nose-and-throat men in New York, but they couldn't do a thing for me." He sounded as if he was boasting.

"You probably didn't shut up long enough to give them the chance," Steve said wearily. "I'm surprised they took you into the Army in the first place, considering all your health problems."

"They took me because I never told them, and believe me, those horse doctors who looked me over, they didn't ask." Benny gingerly massaged his nose. "That poke in the *shnoz* I took from those Marines didn't help matters any."

"*Shnoz* is more of that Yiddish, right?" Steve asked. When Benny nodded, he said, "Jimmy Durante is always saying *shnoz*. I guess that's how I know it."

"So you really *don't* know Yiddish?" Benny shook his head. "I'm surprised. I seem to remember reading that your father is a Jew."

"He is," Steve shrugged. "But I guess he's not religious."

"You guess?" Benny asked, amused. "Your own *father* and you have to guess if he's religious?"

"We're just not that close," Steve said evasively.

"But he is German, right? I mean a lot of Yiddish is based on German, so I'd think that you—"

"I don't know any German either, okay?" Steve interrupted, feeling angry and uncomfortable at the way Detkin was trying to corner him. "And my father is American; that's what he is. And we speak English in our house, okay? Anyway, I don't want to talk about my dad anymore."

"Yeah, sure," Benny said warily. "Sorry . . . I didn't mean to pry."

"You don't have to be sorry. Just drop it," Steve crossly muttered.

There were a few seconds of awkward silence.

"Anyway," Steve began, "you asked for that punch in the *shnoz* by sticking it where it didn't belong in the first place."

"I'm in the habit of going where people tell me I don't belong," Benny replied. "I've been doing it all my life. You weren't raised as a Jew, so you don't know."

"I guess," Steve remarked.

"That's right. You guess, but I know," Benny said. "I grew up in a small factory town in New Jersey. We were stuck in that town until after the worst of the depression. Jobs were hard to come by, and my old man had a steady one there, so we stayed. No matter where I went in that damn burg—the school, the library, the corner store—it was always the same. Somebody would call me a name, and I'd get into a fight. Pretty soon I went out of my way to get into a fight, just to show I couldn't be intimidated."

"Like tonight?" Steve asked.

Benny didn't say anything for a moment. "Yeah, I guess," he finally sighed. "I don't know why I do it. Stupid, huh?"

"Having all those brawls, I would have figured that by now you would have picked up some decent boxing techniques," Steve chuckled.

"I did pick up a boxing technique." Benny laughed. "I learned how to take a dive, remember?"

"Yeah, right," Steve nodded, smiling. "I'm surprised you lived long enough to grow up."

"I probably wouldn't have," Benny replied. "But when the economy got better my dad got a job in Brooklyn, so we moved there into a Jewish neighborhood, thank God. Things there were okay, as long as you didn't wander too far off your own turf." He scowled. "Just like this goddamned base."

"Roger that," Steve said.

"From then on, I was lucky," Benny continued. "I didn't run into any anti-Semitism at college or law school."

"I might have known," Steve grumbled disdainfully. "You're a college boy!"

"It so happens I went on scholarship, but I dropped out after my first year of law school in order to enlist. I didn't want to get drafted into the infantry. I wanted a crack at the Air Force."

"Law school," Steve said, disgruntled. "How old are you anyway?"

"I'm going to be twenty-three," Benny replied. "Hey, why does my having been to college bother you so much?" he asked, sounding mystified.

"Who says it bothers me?"

"The expression on your face says it," Benny declared. "I said I was in college, not prison. What's your gripe?"

"No gripe at all," Steve shrugged, brooding that it wasn't fair that the guy should be an ace fighter pilot *and* good in school. Steve had never got better than C's on his report cards, and then he'd defied his father by quitting school and running away from home. Up until that time there had been an unending series of battles with his father over his education. He knew that his father still had high hopes that Steve would go to college after the war.

"I was thinking about going to college. . . ." Steve glared at Benny, as if daring him to contradict. Steve knew that there wasn't much chance of that happening. He'd barely managed to pass his high school equivalency exam during flight school. "So the college boy wanted to fly, huh?"

"Yeah, it so happens I did," Benny declared. "I like vehicles, see? Cars, airplanes, stuff like that."

"Me too," Steve grudgingly admitted.

"Well, hallelujah. Common ground at last," Benny said gently.

Steve glanced at Benny and smiled.

"My old man could never afford a car," Benny confided. "I figured learning to be a fighter pilot would put me one up on all those rich bastards who were always driving while I had to walk."

"Well, when you finish law school you'll be able to buy yourself a real nice car," Steve couldn't help saying.

"I can see this is a sore point with you, so let's change the subject," Benny said. "Cappy once mentioned that you flew with him in China back in '41," he coaxed. "With the Flying Tigers?"

"Yeah . . . I did," Steve said quietly.

"And that you shot down five planes?" Benny persisted.

"Yeah," Steve sighed. "But I'd joined up with the Tigers under an alias, and lied about my age. When the Tigers found out, they sent me home and wiped my record so that my kills with them don't count officially."

"That's a raw deal," Benny said. "I'd sure hate it if any of Miss Bessie's nine kills didn't count."

"Miss Bessie. . . ." Steve chuckled. "You guys with your names for the fighters really crack me up. An airplane is an airplane. Some are better than others, but they're all just machines and nothing to get sentimental about. It's the man in the cockpit that makes the difference. Who's Miss Bessie, anyway? Your girlfriend?"

"My *bubbeh*."

"Your buddy?"

Benny chuckled. "*Bubbeh*—it rhymes with 'tubby.' *Bubbeh* means grandmother," Benny explained. "Bessie was the name of my maternal grandmother in the Old Country."

They were at Steve's tent. "Hey, how about a drink?" Steve asked. "I got a bottle of genuine sour mash stashed away. My old man sent it to me for my birthday."

Benny looked uncomfortable. "I don't drink."

"Oh." Steve shrugged.

"Hey, thanks again for helping me with those Marines," Benny said earnestly.

"No problem," Steve replied awkwardly. "I would have done it for anyone." *Stupid thing to say,* he thought as Benny flinched.

"Yeah, right." Benny was smiling thinly. "Well . . ." He held out his hand to Steve, who shook it. "Maybe someday I can repay the favor."

"Yeah, sure."

"You take care of those ribs," Benny cautioned.

"The only medicine I need is a stiff drink," Steve replied.

He watched Benny walk away, and then stepped inside his tent, where he tossed his soiled uniform onto the vacant cot. He lit the lantern and rummaged through his footlocker until he found the fifth of bourbon and pulled the cork. He took a swig off the bottle. The cuts in his mouth burned like hell from the alcohol, but at least the bleeding had stopped.

He stepped out of his unlaced boots and gingerly lowered himself onto his own cot. He took a couple more sips off the bottle. He had his cigarettes rolled up in the sleeve of his T-shirt. He took them out, shook a smoke from the pack, and lit it. It hurt his ribs to inhale, but it was worth it.

What I should have said was that I wanted to help Benny out of that scrape to make up for what happened between us back in October, he thought, and sighed. *Yeah, that's what I should have said.* Wasn't it just like him to think of the right thing to say when it was too late?

He took another long pull off the bottle, recorked it, and got up to put it away. He ground out his cigarette and turned down the lantern. He was asleep thirty seconds after his head hit the pillow.

(Two)

The next morning Steve woke up at six A.M., feeling like he'd been run over by a Seabees bulldozer. His back and side muscles were as stiff as a board, and his face was one big purple bruise. He got dressed and hobbled over to the mess, where he managed to choke down some breakfast and coffee. He saw Benny Detkin coming into the mess as he was going out. Detkin looked even worse than he did: he had a black eye, and his swollen split lip was scabbed over.

By eight, Steve was in the ops-ready room along with the three other pilots scheduled to fly patrol.

"Golly," Captain Crawford said disapprovingly. "First

Benny comes in looking like death warmed over, and now you." He was frowning in his best schoolmaster's style.

Before Steve could think of a suitable reply, Cappy came in to deliver his briefing.

"Good morning," Cappy began, scanning the room. "Who's got a smoke?" He stopped in his tracks as he looked at Steve, and then saw Benny Detkin over on the other side of the room. "Holy shit!" Cappy said, and whistled. "Kerrr-ist, you two guys look like dog meat. Did you two do that to each other?" he demanded.

"No, sir!" Benny said. "You see, Cappy, last night I got into a little scrape with some Marines, and the lieutenant there was wandering by and was good enough to help me out, and . . ."

Cappy held up his hands. "I changed my mind. I *don't* want to hear about it, okay? Just tell me one thing, are you fit to fly today?"

"Yes, sir," Benny said.

Cappy turned toward Steve. "What about you? You fit to fly?"

"Yes, sir."

Cappy nodded. "Case closed," he said as he made his way up to the podium. "By the way, anybody got a smoke?"

An hour and a half later, the patrol was in the air over Buka, a tiny clot of emerald jungle just northwest of Bougainville. The four Thunderbolts were arranged into two pairs. Steve was in the rear flight and, as usual, was flying wingman position for Captain Crawford. Up ahead, Benny Detkin was flying as wingman for a captain named Williams.

A couple of months ago the squadron's Jugs had been fitted with drop tanks, so now almost all of the Solomon chain was within the Double Vees' reach. This morning the patrol would sweep as far as Emirau, north of New Ireland, and then swing around to head home.

The patrol was veering for a pass over Rabaul when Cappy Fitzpatrick's voice came rattling over the headsets. "The Marines here have picked up an SOS call from a cargo supply ship in your vicinity," Cappy said. "It's the damnedest strange thing. The ship claims it's being attacked by some Jap planes."

What bullshit, Steve thought as Cappy relayed the ship's coordinates. It was just off the Green Islands, about a hundred miles east of Rabaul.

"It sounds unlikely, but *something* has got to be spooking that ship," Cappy said. "The Marines don't have any CAPs in the area. They're putting up a patrol, but in the meantime they've asked us to check it out," Cappy finished. "Over and out."

"Let's go have ourselves a look." It was Captain Williams.

"Roger," Captain Crawford transmitted. "We're right behind you on this wild-goose chase."

The patrol cranked their throttles, and less than fifteen minutes later the ship came into view, riding the waves with stately grace, the way the big ones always seemed to do when viewed from the air.

"Well, I'll be darned," Crawford said.

"Roger that, Captain," Steve muttered softly.

The ship was doing its best to fend off a trio of "Jill" Nakajima-built single-engine torpedo bombers, mixed in with a half-dozen Kawasaki "Tony" single-engine fighters.

The Jills were painted lime green, with olive-colored engine cowlings. They were big red "meatballs" on their fuselage sides and on their wings. Steve knew that each Jill had two fixed-position 7.7-millimeter guns firing forward and a sting in its tail—a rear-mounted 7.7 gun—but its ship-killing ability came from the single shiny silver tin fish slung beneath its belly.

The Tonys were wearing green and tan camouflage paint. In profile the enemy fighters looked something like British Spitfires, except for their Rising Sun insignia. The Tonys were well armed with a pair of 20-millimeter cannons and twin 7.7-millimeter machine guns.

"I count ten bogies," Captain Williams breathed over the radio. "Where the fuck did they come from?"

"There's a lot of jungle on these islands. More than

enough to hide an airstrip," Benny Detkin replied. "We already know that the Japs can hide out and survive anywhere. Look how long they held out in the swamps of Santa Belle."

"This really sucks eggs," Captain Williams was fretting. "Those Jills are going to hug the waterline in order to release their fish. Our Jugs are gonna fly like bricks at that low altitude, and that's when those Tonys will have at us."

Steve shared Williams's concern. The Tony was not a great fighter, but at low altitudes it was a lot more nimble than the Jug. Normally that wouldn't matter, but the squadron was going to have to abandon its bounce-and-run tactics and engage in some down-and-dirty dogfighting in order to stay in the immediate area and protect the ship.

Being a cargo vessel, the ship was lightly armed. Steve could see scattered tracer fire reaching out toward the Jap planes from the handful of .50-caliber machine guns mounted on the upper decks. The ship also had the canvas shroud off its single-barreled 20-millimeter cannon mounted on the forward deck. The cannon kept swiveling around, firing in rapid bursts, spewing white smoke and flame. The gun crew was wearing glinting steel helmets and bright orange life jackets. They were stripping fresh clips of cannon rounds into their gun as the expended shell casings littered the deck around their feet.

"Where the fuck are those Marine Corsairs?" Williams wondered out loud.

"At least another twenty minutes away," Crawford replied.

"That's Navy down there," Williams argued. "Marines are Navy. This is their mess. Why not leave it to them?"

"You know we can't do that," Crawford replied calmly.

Atta boy, Teach, Steve thought. He was beginning to feel a new respect for Crawford.

"We'll start out doing it by the book," Crawford continued. "Bounce as many of them into the sea as we can on the first pass. If whatever's left of them runs, great. If they stay, well, so will we."

"I still don't like it," Williams said.

"Williams, we don't have time to debate," Steve cut in.

"Lieutenant Gold, you stay out of this!" Williams shouted. "Your superior officers will make the decision."

"Yeah, right," Steve said. "Well, if you guys don't decide something soon, it won't matter. That ship doesn't have near enough guns to set up the defensive cones of fire necessary to knock down those Jills before they release their fish."

"Okay," Crawford said. "Steve and I will make the first pass. Williams, you and Detkin stay high and try to keep those Tonys off our backs."

"Roger that," Williams said, sounding relieved.

"Hey, Benny, it looks like you get pussy patrol," Steve cracked.

"Hey, Steve, let's hope you can shoot better than you use your fists," Benny taunted in return.

"Okay, cut the chatter," Crawford said, sounding the way he probably did when he'd been quieting unruly classrooms back home. "Everyone, drop tanks. Lieutenant Gold, follow me in."

"Yes, Teach," Steve joked as he punched loose his exterior fuel tank.

"Just stick with me, or you'll stay after school," Crawford muttered as he began his attack dive. "I'm going after those Jills setting up for their runs."

A pair of Jills had come around and dropped down low to skim over the waves on a torpedo-launching attack toward the cargo ship. The ship's gun crews were blasting away, but they lacked both the skill and the firepower to set up a defensive curtain of lead to stop planes that were coming at them head-on at wave height.

Crawford and Steve dropped down just behind the Jills. The Jills' rear gunners opened up with their machine guns, but didn't seem to be hitting anything. Meanwhile, a couple of Tonys had dropped down to try and spoil Crawford's aim, but Williams and Detkin bounced them, chasing them away.

Steve watched out for more Tonys as Crawford opened up on a Jill with his eight .50-calibers, and it was suddenly raining lead against the surface of the ocean all around the Jill. Some of Crawford's rounds hit the Jill's long plexiglass canopy, sending shards flying and abruptly silencing the rear mounted gun. The Jill began leaking gray smoke. It dipped one lime-green wing into the azure sea and then cartwheeled across the surface, breaking herself into fiery pieces.

"Nice shooting, Teach," Steve said, all the while using his rear-view mirror and swiveling his head to make sure that Williams and Detkin were keeping the Tonys busy.

"I'm going after that second Jill," Crawford replied, just as the Jap torpedo bomber released her fish and began to bank out of her attack approach. "I'm right on her," Crawford said excitedly.

The launched torpedo was streaking a white wake toward the ship, which was coming around in a desperate evasive attempt. The Jill was still banking. As she exposed her vulnerable belly to her prey, the ship's .50-calibers, and the 20-millimeters cannon tracked her, firing steadily. Steve watched, horrified, as Crawford's Jug banked along with the Jill, less than two hundred feet behind her tail.

"Crawford! You're too close!" Steve called. "You could be hit by defensive fire coming from the ship."

"Just another second," Crawford muttered. He began firing short bursts at the fleeing Jill.

"Break! Break!" Steve called. He was just a little behind Crawford, and the tracer fire coming from the ship seemed to be angling right toward them. As he was pulling up and away, the torpedo struck the vessel toward the stern, sending up a geyser of water. Steve saw the ship's superstructure tremble as it took the hit. Then there was a second explosion, one that sent pieces of the deck and cargo flying. The ship began to list, spilling spiraling plumes of oily black smoke.

Those gun crews still at their posts on the crippled ship kept firing as the Jill streaked past, followed closely by Crawford, who hammered the enemy plane until he'd knocked her out of the sky.

"Got her, Steve!" Crawford yelled triumphantly. "I'm coming around."

Steve watched Crawford begin to pull up out of the

gauntlet of defensive fire, but then a stray machine-gun burst from the ship sprayed Crawford's canopy. Crawford must have pulled back on his stick as he was hit. The Jug's nose lifted up, and then she stalled, her prop pointing up toward the sun. The Jug hung in the sky for an instant, and then began to tumble. As she hit the water, she exploded in a cloud of fire and smoke that flared out over the surface of the sea.

"Did he get out?" Williams was yelling, sounding panicked. "Gold! Did you see him get out?"

"He never had the chance," Steve muttered. "He probably never knew what hit him."

Below Steve, the last Jap torpedo bomber was coming in to take a crack at the crippled ship. The deck cannon crew and machine gunners began gamely firing.

Steve struggled to bring his reluctant Jug around in pursuit of the Jill beginning its run. *This one's for you, Captain. Schoolteacher or not, you had a lot of balls.*

He bounced the Jill hard, hosing her from nose to tail with his guns. Her own torpedo exploded while still lashed to her belly. The Jill vanished in a cloud of orange fire.

"Gold, this is Captain Williams. Join up with us. We're getting out of here."

"What?" Steve blurted. He looked up and saw Williams and Detkin disengaging from the Tonys. "What are you doing?" Steve demanded.

"We're out of here. The Jills are all gone."

"Yeah, but the Tonys are still here. If those sailors have to abandon ship, those fighters will strafe their lifeboats."

"The Marine Corsairs will be here in a few minutes. Let them handle this. This is no win for us. It's bad enough that our Jugs can't decently dogfight at this altitude. Now we've got to contend with being knocked out of the sky by friendly fire."

"Come on, Captain, you can't blame those sailors for what happened," Steve argued. "They're scared shitless. How would you react if you were inexperienced in combat, serving on a goddamned helpless cargo ship in an area that was supposed to be secured, and you were suddenly attacked by a swarm of Japs?"

"Gold, they're sailors. We're going to let the webfoots handle it," Williams decreed.

"Sailors or not, they're our guys," Steve said. "We can't leave them to the Tonys."

"I'm giving you an order—"

"Fuck you and your orders," Steve cut Williams off. He brought his sluggish Jug up and around and toward the six Tonys converging on the crippled ship.

"Gold, listen to me." Williams was shouting.

"No! You listen! I said I'm not leaving those poor bastards to the Japs, not while I still have ammo and I still see targets. Killing enemy planes is what I do. You and Benny want to run, you do it. I'm going in."

"Gold, I'm warning you," Williams snarled. "You do this, you're gonna be all alone."

"What else is new?" Steve laughed grimly. "Over and out."

There were fires sprouting all over the ship. With the crew busy fire fighting, Steve guessed that a lot of the gun positions had been abandoned.

Meanwhile the six Tonys had stacked themselves into three staggered flights in leader-wingman formation, so Steve immediately comprehended their strategy. The Jap pairs would strafe the ship in rotation. One pair would rake the length of the ship with cannon and machine-gun fire and then lift off as another pair took its place.

Steve skidded his Jug across the sky in a dive on the closest pair of Tonys. He lined the wingman up in his sights, reminded himself that if he intended on dropping all six fighters he had to conserve his ammo, and squeezed off three short bursts.

The Tony dropped away, leaking blue smoke. As it was plowing into the sea, he shifted his attention to the lead Tony, now diving to escape. Steve followed it down, hammering it until it broke apart.

Up above, Steve saw the highest pair of Tonys banking like vultures. Steve struggled to bring up the lumbering

Jug's nose and began his slow but steady climb toward the Japs.

The middle pair of Tonys surprised Steve by coming at him from out of the sun. The Japs had Steve broadside in their sights for a few moments, and Steve felt the Jug shudder as it took some hits.

At least I've decoyed them away from the ship, Steve thought. He hunched his shoulders, flinching as bullets punched holes in his canopy. *Where the fuck are those Corsairs?* It looked like he was going to need help, after all.

He opened up on one of the Tonys above him, stitching a line of holes along its belly. As the Tony blew up, its partner banked, dropped its nose, and attacked.

The Tony's guns were spitting fire at Steve. A 20-millimeter cannon round punched into his wing, and suddenly Steve was fighting for control of his airplane.

The Jap fighter shot past him. Steve kicked rudder and went after it, locking on to its tail and firing short bursts into it, ignoring the two other Tonys converging on him.

The Tony he was pursuing began to trail smoke. Steve moved in for the kill.

"Break! Break!" It was Benny Detkin's voice coming in over Steve's headset.

"Benny, what are you doing here?" Steve yelled into his mike. "And fuck you, anyway!" he added, still firing at his target. "I'm not falling for that trick again."

An instant later Steve heard the clacking rattle of bullets pelting his airplane. He glanced in his rear-view mirror to see a pair of Tonys—their guns winking—on his tail.

And Benny Detkin, bless his soul, on the *Japs'* tail.

Steve broke off his attack, banking sharply just as Benny began firing on the lead Jap, knocking him down. Benny shifted his guns to the second Tony and cut it in two with a steady stream of bullets.

"Thanks, Benny," Steve said, as he came around to renew his pursuit of the lone remaining, fleeing Tony, which was still leaking smoke.

"Hey, I owed you one," Benny chuckled. "Now, I bet I get to that joker before you do."

"Bet you don't—"

Steve opened up his throttle and activated the water injection system. Evidently Benny did the same. The two Jugs simultaneously converged on the Tony. Steve locked on to the smoking Jap plane's tail. Benny was up above him, preparing to bounce.

"On the count of three?" Benny asked.

"Roger that," Steve chuckled, lining up his sights.

Benny began to count, "One, two—"

"Three!" Steve crowed, mashing his trigger.

The two Jugs began firing at the same moment. Their combined guns poured lead into the unarmored Tony at the rate of two hundred rounds per second.

The Tony came apart like a fly hit by a cherry bomb. At one moment it was there, and at the next, there was nothing but a dispersing cloud of smoke and a fine rain of debris wafting slowly toward the ocean.

"Holy shit. . . ." Steve murmured, awestruck.

"That's teamwork," Benny said, sounding satisfied.

Steve shifted his attention to the cargo vessel. It was still listing, but it didn't appear to be sinking, and it looked as if all the fires had been put out. As Steve and Benny flew past, the sailors lining the deck waved to them with their hats and shirts.

"Look who's here, six-o'clock level." Benny laughed.

Eight dark blue Marine Corsairs were coming in fast and low, looking for a fight that Army Air had already finished.

"Let's go home," Steve said.

(Three)

"That was some good shooting you did watching my back," Steve complimented Benny. They were back at Santa Belle, still in their flight clothes, sitting at a table near the bar in the ops-ready room. Benny was sipping a Coca-Cola. Steve was nursing a beer.

Benny smiled. "Know my secret? I pretend those Japs are

Nazis." He was chattering a mile a minute, obviously still high on nervous energy. "I was very disappointed when I was assigned to the Pacific. I didn't feel like the war here was my fight. I mean, I know the Japs are our enemies, but with me, it's nothing personal with them, the way I feel toward Nazis. I really wanted to go to Europe to kill as many of them as I could. As far as I'm concerned the only good German is a dead German."

Steve didn't know how to take that. "My dad is a German."

"You know what I mean," Benny complained. "And for chrissake, we've been all through this. Your old man is a Jew."

"Yeah, but he's still a German."

"Let's drop it," Benny muttered.

"Hey, it's not like I don't understand what you're saying about those Nazis," Steve persisted. "After all, I'm half Jewish, remember?"

"No, you're not, either," Benny snapped. "You're a Gentile! Your mother is a Gentile, which makes you one. It doesn't matter if your father is a Jew. Judaism passes through the mother."

"Yeah, right." Steve scowled. "Excuse me, okay? I didn't realize it was such an exclusive club, like one of those fraternities you probably belonged to, college boy."

"Oh, yeah, all the fraternity boys couldn't wait to get their hands on me," Benny laughed sourly. "Why don't we just drop this entire conversation, okay?"

"Sure," Steve muttered.

"It's my mistake," Benny added. "I thought I could have a friendly conversation with you, but I was wrong."

"Who said this isn't friendly?" Steve muttered.

"Huh?" Benny looked blank.

"You heard me," Steve glowered.

"Forget it, we've got bigger problems," Benny said, looking past Steve. "Cappy just came in. He's heading this way."

"Gentlemen." Cappy nodded to Steve and Benny.

"Major," Steve said respectfully. He tried to read Cappy's

expression in order to guess how badly he was going to get reamed, but couldn't. Cappy wasn't a world-class poker player for nothing.

"Captain Williams has filled me in on what happened out there," Cappy said. "I've also received a detailed account from the captain of that cargo vessel. He radioed in his report to Marine HQ, who forwarded it to me. Lieutenant Gold, would you mind stepping outside with me for a little stroll? I'd like to have a talk with you."

"Yes, sir. Of course, sir." As he stood up, Steve glanced at Benny, who gave him the tiniest commiserating shrug.

"Lieutenant Detkin, please remain here," Cappy said. "I'll be back to talk to *you* in a moment."

Cappy was silent until they got outside. "So you shot down four planes today?" he began.

"Four and a half," Steve replied, and then went on to explain how he and Benny had both blasted the last Tony. "And Cappy, please don't forget to add to the record that Captain Crawford bagged a Jill before he augered in."

Cappy nodded. "I'll remember, son. I always do. Now, then, as for your actions today—"

Steve held up his hand. "Cappy, excuse me, but I know what you're going to say."

Cappy stared at him. "You do, huh?"

"Yes, sir. I know that I was insubordinate to Captain Williams. I know that was wrong, and I'm prepared to take my licks for that. I have no defense for disobeying a direct order from a superior officer. All I can say is that I just couldn't bring myself to leave that crippled ship to the mercy of those Japs. I'm sorry, but I just couldn't do it." Steve paused. "It seemed to me then—and it does now, sir—that letting those sailors get killed would have made Crawford's death meaningless."

"You really cared about Crawford, huh?" Cappy asked sarcastically.

Steve stared down at the ground. "No, sir. I can't say that I gave one flying fuck for the captain—until I saw him buy it today, and then I *did* care about him. When he went down, it was like a little piece of me went down with him." Steve paused. "I can't explain it any better than that. I've never felt that way before, sir."

Cappy nodded. "It's how I always feel when we lose a man."

"I guess it's like what you told me a long time ago," Steve said. "Whatever diminishes the squadron diminishes me. And I know I further diminished the squadron with my behavior," he added quickly. "I don't know how to apologize for it, Cappy." He shrugged. "I can't even say that if I had it to do over I'd do it differently."

"Uh-huh. . . ." Cappy was staring at him.

"So," Steve hesitated. "What happens next?"

Cappy showed no expression. "Well, son, I can't promise you, but I think that if I use all of my pull with the brass . . ." He paused.

"Yes, sir?" Steve asked, feeling faint.

Cappy broke into a disconcerting, wide grin. "I think I can get you the Distinguished Flying Cross," he said. "The goddamned Navy will probably also want to decorate you for saving their ship, and I tell you now, as one Army airman to another, I probably won't be able to spare you the indignity of that, either."

"I—I don't get it?"

"Of course you don't," Cappy said mildly, clapping Steve on the back. "You were a hero today. And like the genuine article, you needed somebody else to tell you about it. Come on, let's go back inside. I need to talk to Benny."

As Steve followed Cappy back into the ops-ready room, he couldn't help feeling a pang of disappointment over the fact that while Cappy was willing to recommend him for a medal, he was evidently not ready to put him in for a promotion in rank. Steve wasn't about to bring it up. He didn't see what was so heroic about just doing his job, but he guessed he was lucky Cappy wasn't planning on having him court-martialed.

Benny was still seated at the table. When he looked up as Cappy and Steve appeared in the doorway, his expression was that of a man seeing the sun rise on the day of his execution.

"Lieutenant Detkin," Cappy began. "First the good news. For your courageous actions today I'm putting you in for a promotion to captain."

Lucky son of a gun, Steve thought. Benny was being promoted and he was not. "Benny, congratulations," he said, and was a little astonished to realize that he meant it.

"Now for the bad news," Cappy continued. "Steve here is going to fill Crawford's slot as the new flight leader."

"Huh?" Steve stared at Cappy. "Major, you never said anything about that."

Cappy ignored Steve and continued addressing Benny. "Captain Williams is understandably upset with the way you deserted him in order to back up Steve this afternoon. I think it would make things go smoother if I transferred you to Steve's flight, and made you his wingman."

Benny looked at Steve. "What do you have to say about that?"

Steve stared down at his shoes. "I think that would be good." He risked a glance up at Benny and was relieved to see his smile. "Benny, you really won't mind flying wingman for a guy you're gonna outrank?"

"Oh, yeah, that's right. . . ." Cappy said. He winked at Benny, then shook Steve's hand. "Ah, hell. God help the Army. I guess I'm gonna have to make you a captain, as well."

CHAPTER 6

(One)

Hotel Leeland
Downtown Los Angeles, California
28 April 1945

It was a little after three o'clock on a sunny Friday afternoon when Herman Gold entered the hotel through its main entrance on Olive Street, near Pershing Square. Gold tucked his tortoiseshell sunglasses into the breast pocket of his tan silk-weave sports jacket as he crossed the bustling, marbled lobby to the elevators. His destination, the Tap Room Lounge, was tucked away up on the mezzanine.

The lounge was windowless and dimly lit. Gold stood in the doorway, waiting for his eyes to adjust. Just by the entrance was a redwood and brass bar. Three steps led up to a raised, carpeted seating area. Black leather booths and banquettes ringed the paneled walls beneath electric sconces wired to flicker like candles.

Gold stood with his back to the bar to survey the room. The lounge was busy and noisy. Piped-in, sultry jazz swirled in the background along with cigarette smoke, the clinking of ice cubes, and the murmur of talk and laughter. He was not surprised by the number of people having a drink, or their gaiety so early in the day.

There was a general air of giddy high spirits all over the city now that it looked as if the end of the war in Europe was at hand. The Russians were slowly tightening their "iron ring" around Berlin, and yesterday Russian and American forces had linked up on the Elbe. Last night's late radio bulletins from overseas had also brought the news that Goering had been dismissed as Commander of the Luftwaffe. It made Gold feel great to see the Nazis at each other's throats in their rage and frustration over what was now their inevitable defeat. He also took personal satisfaction that Goering, his old nemesis from the First World War, was finally beginning to experience his long overdue comedown.

America had needed the steady good news coming out of Europe to help the country get over the shock concerning President Roosevelt's sudden death. It had been an awful couple of weeks since the President had passed away, a time of national self-doubt and a crisis of confidence. Whether you had loved or hated FDR, he had been President for so long that it had seemed as if he would always be in the Oval

Office. There had been the inevitable worry that Vice President Truman was not up to the job of leading the nation as President and Commander in Chief, but the little guy certainly seemed to be rising to the occasion. From his very first radio address his rational, down-to-earth plain speaking had begun to soothe the panicked country.

"Can I get you something, sir?" the barman asked as Gold was looking around.

"No, thank you," Gold replied as he climbed the steps to the seating area. "I'm meeting someone."

"Mr. Gold!"

A tall, thin man had slid out of a corner booth and was now waving at him. Gold went over and shook hands, saying, "You must be Jack Horton. I hope you weren't waiting long? As usual, the traffic from Burbank was awful."

"I just got here a few minutes ago," Horton said. "Please, sit down. And thank you for agreeing to meet me at such short notice, Mr. Gold."

"I'm always looking for an excuse to play hooky from the office," Gold joked as he slid into the booth across from Horton.

Horton was nodding earnestly. He looked to be about thirty-five. He had short, dark hair parted on the side, and black horn-rimmed glasses. He was wearing a gray gabardine suit, white shirt, and a black knit tie. He had a military-issue, stainless-steel watch on an olive-green canvas strap around his left wrist.

Gold thought Horton looked like a monkish young college professor or an accountant. He certainly didn't look like who he was.

"Anyway, Mr. Horton," Gold continued. "When Reggie Sutherland called me this morning long-distance from Washington, asking me to meet with you, there was no way I could refuse him. He's done a few favors for me in the past."

Horton was still nodding. "Yes, sir. And General Sutherland was very kind to make the call on our behalf. But then, he was always been very helpful to the OSS."

"OSS," Gold murmured. "That stands for Office of Strategic Services."

"Yes, sir."

"That's something like Army Intelligence, I seem to remember Reggie saying."

"We work closely with them, yes, sir," Horton replied. He paused as a waitress came over and placed a bowl of pretzels on the table.

"A club soda, thank you," Gold told the waitress.

"And a scotch and soda for me," Horton said.

Hmm, not such a monk, after all, Gold thought, nibbling on a pretzel. "I was very intrigued by the air of mystery surrounding Reggie's call," Gold said once the waitress had gone. "I'm not very well versed in matters requiring a cloak and dagger."

Horton smiled politely. He produced a pack of Chesterfields, offered it first to Gold, who shook his head, and then lit one for himself with the book of matches in the ashtray.

"Reggie mentioned something about an operation you were working on overseas, but he was vague," Gold continued. "What exactly can I do for you and your organization, Mr. Horton?"

"Sir, your company has been instrumental in the war effort. I'd like to talk to you about helping us win another, *secret* war that we're presently fighting. It's a war, ironically, with one of our allies, Russia."

"You boys in intelligence don't trust our comrades-in-arms, the Soviets?" Gold asked, amused.

"No, sir. Do you?"

Gold shrugged. "I've only known one Red in my time. You see, last year my company was authorized to supply some airplane parts to the Russians. I got to be quite friendly with the Russians' representative when he came to visit for a tour of our factories." He grinned. "You should have seen that guy in L.A. He was like a kid in a candy store." He paused. "I guess what I'm saying is that I don't see how the Reds can do us much harm. They may have the brawn, but we've got the brains."

"We do at the moment," Horton agreed. "But what if the Reds got themselves some instant—German—brains?"

Gold frowned. "I'm not sure I follow you."

"Sir, the Nazis located most of their aircraft industry in the east, to put it out of reach of our joint bombing operations with the British. With the Soviet advance, all of that German aeronautical technology is falling intact into Russian hands."

"I thought we had some kind of deal with the Reds about sharing that stuff?" Gold asked as the waitress arrived with their drinks.

Horton waited until the waitress had served them and left. "We did, but last summer we found out the hard way that the Russians don't intend to honor their agreement. Ever hear of Blizna?"

"Doesn't ring a bell," Gold said.

"Last summer the Reds overran Blizna, a German rocket-launching site in Poland, but when our boys and the British demanded our right to share in the secrets, the Reds stalled. By the time we got in, the Russians had stripped the place."

"That's their style, all right, I guess," Gold commiserated.

Horton nodded glumly. "When we realized that was how the Russians wanted to play, we initiated 'Operation Rustler,' as in cattle rustling. We intend to rustle away as many as we can of those German brains *before* the Reds can brand them with the hammer and sickle. We *don't* intend to let Russia leapfrog us in rocket, or airplane design, technology. We've got scouts in Germany seeking out and recruiting German talent, and helping those scientists to evade the Russians until our forces can get to them."

"But I still don't understand where I fit into this," Gold continued.

"You fit into it because of Heiner Froehlig," Horton replied.

"Froehlig!" Gold blurted, shocked.

Horton was studying him. "Heiner Froehlig—Air Minister Hermann Goering's deputy in charge of aviation research and development—was a friend of yours, was he not, Mr. Gold?"

Gold was appalled. "Sure, we were friends during the war—the *first* war," he quickly added. "But that was over twenty-five years ago, when I was a fighter pilot and Froehlig was the maintenance crew chief for my airplane."

"But you *were* good friends?" Horton patiently repeated.

"What is this, an interrogation? Horton, you're starting to get me angry," Gold warned. "What the hell is going on here? What are you implying? I happen to be an American citizen! I've never had anything to do with those American Nazi organizations that were sprouting like weeds before the war."

Horton held up his hands. "Please, sir, I didn't mean any disrespect, and I certainly didn't mean to impugn your patriotism. Your reputation is spotless."

Gold leaned back. "Okay, then, I'm sorry for the outburst, but you'd jump to conclusions, too, if you were in my shoes, Mr. Horton. I've been raked over the coals more than once concerning my German heritage."

"Yes, sir."

"I am a Jew, you know?"

"Yes, sir, I do know that."

"All right, then. So you can imagine how I've felt in the past when I've been subjected to that kind of dim-witted bullshit."

"Yes, sir."

"As long as we understand each other," Gold grumbled, mollified. "Now then, getting back to the matter at hand, I haven't seen Heiner Froehlig since—"

"Since 1938, at the Moden International Seaplane Competition held in Venice, Italy," Horton said, expressionless. "Yes, sir, we do know that, as well."

Gold took a sip of his club soda. It was a funny, almost queasy feeling to be sitting across from someone who evidently had gone through your past with a fine-tooth comb. "Well, Horton, if you know *that* much, then you also ought to know that Froehlig and I didn't part on friendly terms."

Horton was nodding. "You mean when Froehlig, in his

capacity as a Nazi big shot, unsuccessfully tried to convince you to return to Germany in order to design and build airplanes for the Reich?"

Gold stared. "How *could* you have found out about that?" he harshly demanded. "*Nobody* knows about that. I didn't even tell my wife." He shook his head. "No matter how thorough your investigation, how could you have known?"

"Sir, if you'll let me explain— Froehlig told us. Several days ago one of our operatives made contact with Froehlig at the German Air Ministry in Berlin. The city—or what's left of it—is in chaos right now. Nobody is getting in or out. The Krauts—" Horton stopped, blushing. "Sorry, sir. No offense meant."

"Just get on with it," Gold grumbled.

"Yes, sir. Well, the crux of the matter is that Froehlig wants to cut a deal to come over to our side."

Gold scowled. "What do you want him for? He's not a scientist."

"We know that, and so does Froehlig," Horton said. "In order to sweeten the pot, he's offering us a package deal. He's got a half dozen of the Reich's top aviation engineers in tow. We take Froehlig, and we get the cream of the crop of German jet designers. There's an agreement that Roosevelt made with the Soviets that we would hang back and let them take Berlin. When that happens, Froehlig and his scientists are going to go into hiding in the city until we can get them out."

"It's going to be tricky getting them past the Russians," Gold mused.

"We know that, and so does Froehlig." Horton nodded. "That's why he wants you to come and get him, Mr. Gold."

"Me?" Gold laughed weakly. "Is this a joke?"

"No, sir. Froehlig says that you're the only American he knows and trusts."

"What the hell do I know about shepherding some fugitive Nazis past the Russians?" Gold complained.

"You can leave the details of the operation to us, sir," Horton said quickly.

"What operation?" Gold demanded. "You've got some kind of plan to accomplish this?"

"I think that it would be best if we handled this on a need-to-know basis, sir. That's for your own protection, in case there's a problem with the Soviets."

"In other words, in case this top secret plan of yours falls apart and the Reds grill me before shipping me to Siberia for the rest of my life?"

"Sir, we think that we have a good plan, but there is always an element of risk in endeavors of this nature," Horton admitted. "Let me just add that I myself would be with you every step of the way."

"That's very reassuring, Mr. Horton," Gold said dryly. "But the prospect of you being my roommate in a Soviet work camp does not sweeten the deal."

Horton frowned. "I'm going to level with you, Mr. Gold. Your country wouldn't ask this of you if it weren't absolutely necessary. Either due to your past friendship back in the good old days fighting for the Kaiser, or for some other reason, Froehlig has fixated on you as the only hero who can ride to his rescue. He's made it clear that if you can't—or won't—bring him out, he'll cut a deal with the Reds."

Gold was about to turn Horton down, but then it occurred to him that maybe he could get something out of this for GAT.

Last year Gold had presented GAT's R&D people with Stoat-Black's Starstreak commercial jet airliner coventure proposal. Teddy Quinn and his staff had studied the specs, and then nixed the deal, citing their serious reservations about aspects of Stoat-Black's proposed design for the Starstreak's pressurized cabin. Gold had then tried to get Stoat-Black to modify the design by incorporating Teddy's suggestions, but he'd received the brush-off from Hugh Luddy. It seemed that despite all of Luddy's talk about mutual cooperation, Stoat-Black expected GAT to come in as a silent partner or not at all. Gold was disappointed, but without input, there was no way he would invest a fortune and what was left of GAT's credibility into Stoat-Black's project. He'd walked away.

Meanwhile, little progress had been made at GAT in designing a new swept-wing jet fighter. It seemed that Gold and Teddy and all the rest of GAT's R&D talent were up against a corporate mental block. What was needed, Gold had long ago decided, was a healthy dose of fresh, new talent into GAT's idea pool. To that end, Gold had unsuccessfully tried to raid the R&D staffs of his industry rivals. He'd had no other idea of where to get new, experienced talent.

Until now.

"Okay, Horton," Gold began. "I'll do this for you, but I want something back in return."

"Sir?" Horton asked warily. "What would that be?"

"I want Froehlig's boys to work exclusively through GAT. My firm would be the middleman between them and the U.S. military."

Horton laughed uneasily. "You're joking, right?"

"Do I look like I'm joking?"

"Mr. Gold . . . sir—" Horton was shaking his head. "It's impossible."

"Nothing's impossible," Gold smiled. "It just has to be negotiated, is all. Now then, you want something from me: to go fetch these guys out of Berlin. According to you I'm the only guy in the whole wide world who can do it for you. Okay. All I'm asking for in return is the opportunity to more efficiently put them to work by personally harnessing their creativity. They design jet planes, and GAT will build them for Uncle Sam."

"You mean, *sell* them to Uncle Sam, don't you, sir?" Horton asked wryly.

"Of course, sell them," Gold said impatiently. "That's the difference between us and the commies, isn't it, Horton? We live in a free-market capitalist society."

"Mr. Gold, with all due respect, this is an outrageous request."

"What's so outrageous?"

"What would your competitors think?"

Gold shrugged. "You never heard of 'finders keepers, losers weepers'?"

"Sir?"

"I'm finding these scientists for you, so I should get to reap the benefits of their labors. If you're so worried about what my competitors might think, go ask *them* to risk their skins sneaking Germans out from underneath Soviet guns."

"But there are logistics to be considered once the Germans are here," Horton argued. "These men will be prisoners of war. They must be kept under guard on a military post."

"We have military posts in California," Gold replied, shrugging. "Basically, I don't care where you keep them, as long as GAT gets first crack at their work."

"I'll have to think about this, Mr. Gold."

"Think all you want," Gold said reasonably. "Think about taking it or leaving it," he added, standing up, "because that's your real choice."

Horton frowned. "I'll need to talk to my superiors."

"Okay, I understand that," Gold nodded before walking away. "Think, and talk, and decide with your superiors whether you want to take it or leave it. If you decide the former, give me a call. . . ."

(Two)

Tempelhof Airfield
Berlin, Germany
24 May 1945

Herman Gold was jolted awake as the MT-37 cargo plane touched down on the runway. He'd been dozing on a hammock strung between two trucks in the MT-37's cavernous hold.

"Herman, we're here." Horton was climbing down from the cab of one of the trucks. He had on his black horn-rims and his government-issue watch, but instead of a suit and tie he was dressed in the field uniform of an officer in the

United States Army. It had turned out that Horton was an Army major, on loan to the OSS.

"Easy flight," Horton said, putting on his steel helmet and buckling around his waist a webbed belt holding several spare magazine pouches for his M-1 carbine.

"Told you it would be," Gold replied, standing up and stretching. Some air turbulence had been forecast when they'd left the American-held airfield near Frankfurt, but the good old MT-37—the military transport version of the GAT Monarch GC-10—had smoothed out the ride. "Gold Aviation and Transport builds good planes, Jack, my boy," Gold said jovially.

Horton put a finger to his lips as a soldier came over to unsling the hammock from the trucks. "Remember," he whispered to Gold, "as far as the men are concerned, you're a real major general."

Gold nodded, reaching up to check that the dual silver stars indicating his bogus rank were still pinned to his field cap. Gold's shirt and tie were pale brown beneath his olive drab, waist-length "Ike jacket." His trousers matched the jacket and were tucked into shiny black boots. He was "armed" with a Colt .45 automatic in a russet leather shoulder holster.

Horton had assured him that the unloaded Colt was just for show, which was fine with Gold. He hadn't fired a handgun since he'd been involved in a certain bootlegging incident some twenty years ago, and he'd been a lousy pistol shot back then.

The soldier was finishing folding up the hammock as the MT-37 slowed down and began to taxi. The soldier tucked the folded hammock under his arm, and then came to attention and saluted Gold. Gold awkwardly nodded to the soldier. "You're . . . um—dismissed!"

Horton was grinning as the soldier crisply turned on his heel and marched away. "You carry that uniform well. If you can fool our own guys, you'll fool the Soviets with no problem at all."

The MT-37 came to a halt. There was a loud clanging of gears kicking in, and then a hydraulic whine began to reverberate inside the hold. Daylight flooded the interior of the cargo plane as the rear ramp descended.

"Time to go," Horton said, leading Gold to a jeep parked at the top of the ramp.

Horton slid in behind the wheel, setting his carbine between himself and Gold, who was checking to make sure that his black leather briefcase was where he'd left it beneath the jeep's front passenger seat. Gold looked behind him as a corporal in combat gear got into the rear of the jeep to man the pedestal-mounted .50-caliber machine gun.

Horton started up the jeep's engine. Behind it, the two olive drab trucks roared to life. They were Dodge, 1½-ton six-wheel-drive rigs with high, fat tires and canvas sides rolled halfway down the truck beds' hooped frames. Each truck carried two men in the cab, and six more sitting on the benches running along both sides of the truck bed. All the man were wearing field jackets, helmets, and armed with carbines or Thompson submachine guns.

"Let's move out," Horton said. He put the jeep in gear and led the way down the ramp, out onto the tarmac.

It was a blustery day. A little cool. The sun was playing peekaboo between the clouds, painting rapidly changing patterns of light and dark upon the strange-looking airplanes and vehicles emblazoned with red stars parked around the compound.

"Sure are a lot of Russians here," Gold muttered. The Soviets in their high-collared wool tunics were stopping what they were doing to stare at the American convoy as it rolled past.

Still not too late to back out of this, Gold thought to himself. *You're too old to play the hero.*

It was scary as hell to leave the protection of the airplane, which was sort of like an embassy. Even now U.S. armed guards were taking up positions beside the ramp to insure that the Soviets respected United States sovereignty.

"Herman, from now on, I'll be referring to you as 'General Gold,' or 'sir,'" Horton said quietly so that the gunner riding behind them couldn't overhear.

"Huh? Yeah, sure, Jack," Gold said, feeling distracted

and a little light-headed. *I'm back in Germany. Back in Berlin. I'm home.*

"And you should be referring to me as Major Horton."

Gold nodded absently. "Yeah, okay . . . major." He glanced at Horton. "It's really happening, isn't it? I mean, all that planning during the last month. But now it's really happening."

"Yeah." Horton was peering at him, looking worried. "Are you going to be okay?"

"I won't let you down," Gold declared. He reached down to touch the briefcase beneath his seat, just to reassure himself.

"I wish you'd tell me what the hell you have in there?" Horton complained.

"A little insurance, in case the Soviets give us a hard time."

"But what exactly?"

"Need to know, Jack," Gold winked. "And call me General."

Horton chuckled. "Yes, sir!" But his smile faded as they approached the Soviet half-track blocking the road.

The big, boxy vehicle was painted green. It's star insignia was bright red outlined in white. The half-track had tires in the front and tank treads in the back. Its green nicked and dented armor plating made it look like some kind of prehistoric monster in their path.

The half-track's top turret gunner was watching them approach over the heavy barrel of his rail-mounted machine gun. Horton brought the convoy to a halt as a uniformed Soviet officer wearing a pistol belt stepped out of a tent erected on the road's shoulder.

Gold guessed that the Russian was no more than twenty-five years old. He had dark blonde hair curling out from beneath his visored cap. A black patch covered his left eye. A glistening, pink and white burn scar began underneath the patch. It splashed down the length of the left side of his face and neck, before disappearing beneath his tunic's standing collar. The Russian's good right eye was startlingly blue.

Horton produced some papers and began speaking Russian to the frowning officer. Gold didn't understand Russian, but he knew from all the endless stateside planning sessions and rehearsals what Horton was saying: that the major general was a deputy of Eisenhower's here to make a survey of the city for the Allied Commander. To that end, the convoy had a one-day pass to enter Berlin issued from the office of the Russian military commander Marshal Georgy Zhukov.

The part about the pass was true. A few weeks ago Zhukov had planned a grand reception to welcome Eisenhower to Berlin, but then Stalin reneged on his original agreement to immediately allow American forces to occupy the city. Zhukov, embarrassed over being forced to turn away Eisenhower, had been anxious to make amends. Horton and his OSS and AI buddies had seized the opportunity to go through channels to get Zhukov's office to issue this one-day pass as a goodwill gesture toward Eisenhower.

Horton and the Soviet officer were still jabbering at each other in Russian. Gold began to worry. In rehearsal the exchange had never taken this long.

"What's the problem here, Major?" Gold interrupted, trying his best to sound gruff and angry instead of frightened. In rehearsal Gold had been coached that an authentic senior officer would react aggressively and in frustration to any delay caused by the Russians.

"The colonel here seems to think that three vehicles are too many to be covered by one pass," Horton muttered. "He wants us to leave one truck behind."

Gold nodded. Some petty bullshit from the Russians had been expected. The Russians knew that the United States Army had been hamstrung by President Truman. The new President, preoccupied with domestic policies and the ongoing war with Japan, was not prepared to face down Stalin. Despite that, it had never occurred to the stateside planners that the Reds would try and cut down the convoy's *size*. Both trucks were needed if the convoy was to have enough room for Froehlig and his six scientists.

Gold glared at the Russian officer as he spoke to Horton. "Major, you tell this fella that these stars I'm wearing means that I'm an important *United States Army* officer, and that I don't even go to the *fucking latrine* without an escort this size."

As Gold had hoped, he saw a flicker of a smile cross the Russian's face. The guy may not have known proper English, but he'd picked up on Gold's indignant tone and his use of the obscenity. No matter where you were born or what language you spoke, you had to understand that only a VIP could take such imperious liberties.

The colonel listened as Horton conveyed Gold's message. Meanwhile, Gold was hoping that the Russian officer would realize that he had overplayed his hand, that an ill-tempered United States two-star general could not be stripped of his retinue without causing an international incident.

The Soviet colonel was nodding. He briefly said something in Russian as he handed back the papers to Horton.

"The colonel has agreed to let us pass, sir," Horton told Gold.

The Russian yelled a command toward the half-track. The armored vehicle started up. Its tank treads churned mud as it backed away, clearing the road.

Horton put the jeep in gear and drove on. The trucks followed.

"Nice improvisation," Horton softly told Gold.

"I just figured that since our pass is valid, the colonel was only authorized to push us until we resisted and then back off. I'm just glad it worked."

"I guess it did," Horton said, sounding uncertain as he glanced in his side rear-view mirror. "He's just standing there, watching us."

"To hell with him—we're past him," Gold said firmly. He paused. "Although it is a bad omen that he tried that bullshit with us."

Horton shrugged. "No point in worrying about it now. Let's just hope somebody else is on duty when we come back," he sighed.

Gold shook his head. "I never count on luck." He patted the briefcase, which he had removed from beneath his seat and put on his lap. "I—"

Gold's words died in his throat as they left the Russian-held airfield behind, moving into the urban battleground that had once been a thriving city. *My God,* Gold thought. *What has been done here?*

The devastation was unbelievable. High dunes of rubble lined both sides of the road, and the stench of raw sewage filled the air. Overhead, black, cawing scavenger birds wheeled and danced like furies.

As the convoy turned onto the Mehringdamm, it had to slow down in order to snake its way through a narrow canyon cut through the high walls of rubble. Gold had plenty of time to study the gaunt women and children dressed in filthy scarecrow rags. The people were moving like zombies as they picked what they could out of the garbage. The soldiers in the trucks who had been chatting and laughing became subdued as the convoy passed the women with their silent, staring children. Gold wondered what the men were thinking as they made this journey through this city of the dead.

The convoy drove across a bridge spanning the trash-strewn, oily waters of the Spree. Mounded rubble was everywhere, with the occasional standing, skeletal remains of a building jutting against the sky, framing bright rectangles of blue within the confines of its gutted windows.

Horton led the convoy around the desolate city for a couple of hours. He wanted to kill time and to discover whether the Reds had graced the convoy with a tail. If there was a tail, the meandering route would hopefully convince the snoops that the convoy really was on a mission to survey Berlin.

They were driving through the Tiergarten when Horton glanced at his watch and said, "Okay. It's time." He quietly asked Gold, "Can you get us back to the Friedrichstrasse?"

Gold didn't answer, too overwhelmed by the fact that the Tiergarten, the lovely park that had been the emerald in the center of Berlin, was ruined. Where there had been trees and lawns there were now just clusters of jagged stumps rising up from the scarred earth like the stumps of amputated limbs. In the distance, surrounded by killed trees lying on the muddy, littered ground, the twisted gazebos creaked in the wind. The carousel sat silent and rusting, as if in mourning over its intricately carved wooden horses splintered by shrapnel.

"Herman? I'm lost," Horton was muttering. "You remember Berlin, don't you?"

"Remember is the right word," Gold said despondently.

"Come on, help me out here." Horton pointed to a small map clipped to the jeep's dashboard. "I'm looking for the Friedrichstrasse."

"Street names don't mean much around here anymore. . . ."

"What's your problem?" Horton hissed.

"How can you ask that? Just look around!"

"Hey," Horton said, eyeing him, "don't go soft on me, all right? Sure, what happened here is terrible, just like it was terrible what happened to London during the blitz."

Gold shook his head. "It's not the same. I've *lived* in Berlin. Germany was my *home*. . . ."

"Yeah," Horton said, lowering his voice even further. "But let me remind you that you're a Jew, my friend. If you'd stayed here, this very same city you're currently feeling sorry for would have shipped you off to a—"

"Okay, you've made your point," Gold said sharply, cutting him off.

Horton nodded. "You're all mixed up inside. I can understand that. Being here can't be easy for you."

"It's not," Gold said gruffly as he busied himself studying the map. He looked around for some kind of landmark to tell him where he was. "Take this next right," he said. "And then your first left."

They traveled another couple of miles, and then Horton, consulting his map, turned left onto an unmarked side street. He pulled up in front of a bomb-crumpled building. The trucks ground to a halt behind the jeep. From what was left of the sign over the door, Gold knew that the building's ground floor had once been a butcher shop.

"This shop has a meat locker in its basement," Horton confided, unable to suppress a grin.

"What's so funny about that?" Gold demanded.

"Don't you get it?" Horton demanded, grabbing his carbine as he got out of the jeep. "That's where we've got Froehlig and his boys stashed, in the meat locker."

"Very funny," Gold grumbled.

"All right, sarge!" Horton was shouting at the NCO who was climbing down out of the cab of the first truck. "You've got your orders. Let's move it."

Soldiers were moving down the street to keep watch for Russian patrols as Gold got out of the jeep. He followed Horton around into the alleyway alongside the partially collapsed shop building.

"Watch your step," Horton called over his shoulder. "These cobblestones are slick with some kind of grease."

Gold nodded. The alleyway was dark and narrow. It was littered with garbage and reeked of rotting meat. Gold shuddered as movement in the dark shadows caught his eye. *Rats,* he thought, as he heard the scrabble of claws scratching against the cobblestones and a dark shape skittered across his path almost under his feet.

Horton used the snout of his weapon to push away the debris blocking the cellar's wooden bulkhead door. A cloud of flies rose up out of the cellar's entrance as Horton hauled the door open. Horton took a flashlight out of his field jacket pocket, switched it on, and began moving down the dark cellar steps. Gold followed him down.

The stench was even worse inside the musty, windowless cellar. Horton played his flashlight around the small room, illuminating a double sink with a dribbling faucet standing next to a dirty chopping block. There was a wall of shelves laden with rolls of butcher's paper and twine and dented or broken cans of lard. The meat locker's wooden door was against the far wall.

"This way," Horton muttered. "Watch yourself—"

A rat's eyes glowed red in the flashlight beam. The rat backed away, humping its back and spitting against the light.

The meat locker door suddenly swung open on squeaking hinges. The rat darted past Gold to hide beneath the staircase as a flashlight beam stabbed out from the locker's interior.

"Wer ist es?" a man cried out weakly. "Who? Who is it?"

Gold heard a metallic *click!* echo against the stone walls.

"Get down!" Horton hissed sharply. "That sounded like a gun being cocked!"

Gold was afraid to drop to the ground—a rat might jump at his face—but he didn't want to get shot. He went into a semicrouch, his shoulders hunched and his eyes squeezed shut against the impending bullet. "Heiner! Heiner Froehlig!" he called out. "*Ich heisse* Herman Gold! I've come to take you to America!" he continued in German. "It's all right, put down your guns."

"*Ja! Natürlich!*" a voice called out from the locker.

There came a rasp, and then the tiny flare of a match. The Germans were lighting candles. The wavering flames cast flickering, ghoulish shadows against the cinder block. A thin, sickly-looking young man with a month's worth of beard staggered out of the meat locker. He was dressed in a stained, dingy suit. A Luger pistol dangled limply in his hand. Horton moved quickly to take away the gun.

The man pointed back at the meat locker. "Herr Froehlig izt in zere," he said in thickly accented English. It seemed as if the mere effort of walking and speaking had exhausted him. Horton caught him as he began to sag to the basement floor.

"Get the medics down here," Horton ordered as soldiers with flashlights began tramping down the stairs. Some of the men were carrying duffel bags that had been stowed under the benches in the trucks.

Gold tried not to gag from the smell of excrement as he walked into the meat locker. Inside, amid the garbage and rusted pails of God knew what else, Heiner Froehlig and five others were sitting huddled in the far corner of the chamber.

Froehlig was in his sixties, but he looked a hundred years old. He was barefoot, dressed only in a dingy gray undershirt and a pair of torn trousers. He was coated with grime, and his head was wrapped in a filthy, bloodstained bandage. Some of the blood had run down to crust his scraggly, ivory-colored growth of beard.

"Hermann," Froehlig began, *"danke schön. Ich bin sehr dankbar—"*

"English!" Gold said sharply. "We'll speak English!"

He would not speak his native tongue. He was *afraid* to speak it here in the Fatherland with his one-time friend. Gold needed to speak English in order to latch on to some familiar, present reality that would keep him from being swept away into a past as suffocating as the fetid air in this nightmare cellar.

"Yes, English it shall be, Herman," Froehlig said. "Thank you," he repeated. "I am very grateful you came...." He smiled weakly, revealing a mouthful of green-tinged teeth. "Forgive me for not standing up, Herman, but I don't think I can."

"Let's go! Let's go!" Horton was urging his men as they unzipped the duffels, pulling out canteens, soap, and towels, folded U.S. Army uniforms, helmets, and boots. "Get these guys cleaned up and dressed, and help them to the trucks."

Horton turned to Gold. "I don't think this is going to work," he muttered.

"Hell of a time to tell me." Gold glared.

"We had no idea these guys would look so bad," Horton complained. "We knew that we'd have to hide the old guy Froehlig, but we thought these younger guys would be able to pass as GIs."

"We haf been down here since der Russians *kommen*," one of the Germans volunteered in faltering English. He was wearing a pair of wire-rimmed spectacles with one of the lenses cracked. He lay limp as a rag doll while two soldiers wiped the worst of the dirt from his face and dressed him as if he were a child. "Almost a month *im Dunkein* . . . in the dark." The German broke off in a fit of coughing.

"Is that not funny, Herman?" Froehlig demanded as one of the medics attended to him. "Is that not ironic?" He began to cackle. "Heiner Froehlig, Göring's deputy, and all these bright young scientists, the cream of Germany's manhood, reduced to hiding in the dark for weeks and weeks like vermin. Like Jews—" Froehlig abruptly froze, eyeing Gold fearfully. "Herman, forgive me. I am delirious."

"Shut up," Gold said, turning away.

"I'm a sick old man who doesn't know what he's saying," Froehlig continued babbling, offering a horrendous smile.

"Just shut up!" Gold shouted, whirling around. His fists were clenched as he advanced on Froehlig. "Damn you! Look what you have brought upon yourself! Upon Germany! Aren't you yet satisfied? Can't you just shut up?"

Horton put a restraining hand on Gold's shoulder. Froehlig, mewling in fear, was curled in the corner of the locker with his hands held up as if to ward off a blow. The soldiers were all staring. Gold could feel himself shaking in anger and grief.

And guilt—

What was a Jew doing rescuing these people? To hell with them, and with GAT, if need be. These Nazi bastards were criminals who ought to be turned over to the Russians to be hung.

But the Russians would not hang these men, Gold reminded himself. The Russians would put them to work at drafting tables and aircraft factories, just the way the United States intended to put them to use.

Remember that Froehlig had nothing to do with the crime against the Jews, Gold told himself. *Froehlig was just a pencil pusher in the Air Ministry. He built airplanes. All these men here built airplanes. That's all they did.*

"You okay?" Horton was asking him.

"Sure," Gold sighed. "I'm okay." *I'm an intelligent man,* he added to himself. *I can rationalize my way out of anything. So I'll always be okay.*

"Yes, Herman, I will shut up," Froehlig was whining meekly. "I will do anything you say—"

Gold leaned close to Froehlig so that only he could hear. "What you're going to do is work for *me*, designing jets for America," Gold fiercely whispered.

But Froehlig seemed not to hear. He was looking past Gold and had a dog's grin of supplication on his face. "We will all do what everyone says, *ja*?" Froehlig whimpered like the vanquished and broken man he was. "And you will take us to America, *ja*?"

"That old guy's the last one, sir," the sergeant told Horton.

"Dress him up and get him loaded," Horton replied. He came over to Gold and whispered, "Like I said, no way are they going to pass for GIs."

Gold shrugged. "It was a long shot, anyway," he said calmly.

Horton watched dolefully as Froehlig, swimming in his U.S. Army clothing, was carried out of the basement. "Sarge, have the men put up the canvas siding on the trucks," Horton ordered. "And remember to stash these Germans way in the back. All right, let's get out of here!"

Gold felt calm during most of the ride back, until the convoy began the last stretch of the Mehringdamm before Tempelhof airfield. Suddenly Gold was finding it hard to swallow. He realized that he was sweating, that his hands were trembling.

God, he was scared! The realization amused him. Oddly, he welcomed and was relishing his fear. It had been so long since he'd felt the adrenaline rush that put the coppery taste in your mouth and sharpened your senses, reminding you that you were alive. Over the years he'd experienced more than his rightful share of love and elation, and plenty of anger and frustration as well, but he'd not been visited by fear's needle-sharp flutters for over two decades.

Not since he'd ridden into the sky to do battle from the cockpit of his Fokker triplane.

Gold smiled. Back in those days Heiner Froehlig had also been present, working for Gold as a mechanic. Soon Froehlig would be working for him again. . . .

The convoy was approaching the airfield entrance checkpoint. "That half-track is still blocking the road," Horton said.

"Honk the horn," Gold said forcefully. "Take the offensive."

"Huh?"

"There's three rules to dogfighting: hit first, hit hard, and get the hell out."

"What are you talking about?" Horton demanded, perplexed.

Gold winked at him. "I'm talking about acing this. Trust me, I've got a feeling this is going to work out okay."

Horton shook his head. "I'm glad you're feeling so confident," he grumbled. "Because there's good old scarface still waiting for us."

The Soviet colonel was standing with his hands on his hips and a stern expression on his ruined face. He began speaking Russian to Horton as soon as the jeep pulled up.

"He wants to know why the siding is up on the trucks," Horton relayed to Gold.

"Tell him because we *wanted* it up," Gold snapped, pretending to sound peeved.

The Soviet colonel cocked his head like a parrot to fix his one good eye on Gold.

"Take it easy," Horton cautioned Gold. His voice was light, and he had a big smile plastered across his face, but Gold could read the concern in Horton's eyes.

But Gold had to proceed according to his own instincts, which were that generals did not take shit from colonels.

"You tell the colonel that these happen to be goddamn *American* trucks, and in case he's forgotten, I happen to be an *American* major general," he continued forcefully, keeping his eyes on the Soviet. "That makes them *my* trucks, so I can do whatever I goddamn well *please* with them."

The colonel began to walk away toward the trucks. Gold paused, rattled. "Hey, *you* there!" he called after the Soviet officer, who ignored him.

"Major Horton," Gold said loudly. "Tell that man to come back here. I wasn't finished addressing him."

"The fucker's going to check out the trucks," Horton worried softly.

The colonel walked to the rear of the first truck and stared in. He moved to the second and looked into that one, and then returned to the jeep, where he rattled off a query to Horton.

"He wants to know why there are suddenly so many more soldiers in the convoy," Horton said.

"Tell him he must be mistaken," Gold replied. "Tell him, how could we have more soldiers—?"

The Russian resumed speaking before Horton could relay the message. Horton, shaking his head, said something in reply. The Russian spoke again, this time sounding more emphatic.

Horton, looking bleak, said, "He says that he doesn't think he's mistaken. He wants our men to leave the trucks and line up so that he can look them over."

"Tell him no way does he interrogate American soldiers," Gold said calmly.

"I did," Horton replied. "But he insists."

The Russian turned away from the jeep to issue an order to the gunner on top of the half-track. The man swung his heavy-caliber machine gun around to aim at the convoy. The colonel than turned to stare at Gold and waited.

"Corporal," Horton addressed the man at the .50 mounted in the back of the jeep. "You may chamber a round."

"Yes, sir!" The click of the .50-caliber machine gun's bolt sounded awfully loud in the sudden, tense stillness. Gold listened as Horton said something to the Russian colonel.

"I explained to him that what we've got here is a Mexican standoff," Horton told Gold. "That unless he's prepared to open fire on us and take fire in return, it would be best if he got that Moscow-made tin can out of our way."

The colonel said something.

"He's worried," Horton confided to Gold. "He says this is a difficult situation."

"Tell him only if he wishes to make it so," Gold said. *Come on, sucker, back down,* he thought as Horton relayed his words. Down underneath the jeep's dashboard, where the Russian couldn't see, Gold had his fingers crossed.

The colonel was shaking his head as he spoke to Horton,

who sighed as he translated for Gold. "He offers many apologies to the comrade general, but the convoy must remain here while he contacts his superiors for instructions on how to proceed concerning this situation."

Fuck that, Gold thought. He reached down to haul his briefcase out from under the seat. "Ask the colonel if there is someplace private we can talk."

Horton hesitated. "I don't know what you have in mind."

"Do it, Major!" Gold ordered sharply.

"Yes, sir!" Horton said loudly, his eyes shooting daggers at Gold. "You'd better know what you're doing," he added under his breath.

The Russian looked surprised as Gold's request was relayed. He looked inquiringly at Gold as he gestured toward the tent by the side of the road.

"Tell him the tent is fine," Gold said. "Come with me, Major," he instructed Horton as he got out of the jeep, taking his briefcase with him.

"What are you planning?" Horton quietly demanded as they followed the Russian to the tent. "Herman, dammit— what's in that thing?"

"You'll see. For now, just hope it works," Gold whispered.

Just before he ducked inside the tent, he paused to gaze wistfully beyond the half-track, toward the MT-37 cargo plane parked on the tarmac a mere couple of hundred yards away. *So near and yet so far,* Gold sighed to himself. *Well, here goes nothing,* he thought as he entered the tent.

Inside the tent there was only a table and two wooden chairs. The interior light was diffused and golden from the daylight penetrating the thin, sun-bleached canvas. Gold sat down in one of the chairs without waiting to be asked. He was a general, after all. He watched as the Russian reluctantly sat down across from him. Horton stood by Gold's side.

Gold put the briefcase on the table. The Russian stared at it warily, and then stared back and forth between Gold and Horton.

"Offer him a smoke," Gold told Horton. "That Russian

who visited me in L.A. couldn't get enough American tobacco."

Horton took a fresh pack of Chesterfields and a battered Zippo lighter from his pocket. He held the cigarettes out to the Russian, who stared at the pack with obvious hunger.

"Give him the pack and tell him to keep it," Gold said. Horton did so. The colonel looked grateful. "Give him your lighter. Tell him to keep it, as well."

Horton looked reluctant. "But that's my lucky lighter—"

"Do it!" Gold commanded. As he waited for Horton to explain that the lighter was a gift, he thought that the kid might be a terrific spy, but he didn't know shit about negotiating a business deal.

"Now, then," Gold began calmly, "tell him that both sides have guns, but the last thing either of us wants is to start shooting."

The Russian listened to Horton as he tore the cellophane from the cigarette pack and used Horton's Zippo to light up a smoke. The expression on his face as he inhaled was that of a man having sex. He continued to listen to what Horton had to say, and then said something in reply, meanwhile smiling at Gold.

"He agrees that comrades do not shoot each other," Horton said cynically.

"That's right, Colonel," Gold smiled broadly, nodding vigorously at the Russian. "Comrades don't shoot each other. They cooperate. As victorious comrades it is now our duty to do all we can to foster friendship between our peoples."

As Horton relayed the message, Gold unsnapped the locks on the briefcase, opened it, and turned it around to display its contents to the Russian. As Gold had hoped, the colonel's one good eye almost popped out of its socket as he stared at the the two dozen Mickey Mouse wristwatches on pigskin straps. The light glinted off the shiny nickel-plated cases. The gaudy yellow, red, and black Mickey Mouses painted on the watch faces glowed like jewels beneath the sparkling crystals.

The Russian reached tentatively to touch one of the watches. He breathed a query.

"He wants to know if they're bona fide American," Horton chuckled softly.

"Tell him that's Mickey Mouse looking up at him, isn't it?" Gold demanded. "And then tell him that a smart fellow like himself could peddle these watches to his comrades for a fortune in occupation currency."

The Russian, listening as Horton translated Gold's words, seemed overwhelmed. He just kept nodding and staring down at the watches.

"Tell the colonel that we are now prepared to leave this tent, leaving those watches behind. All he has to do is tell the half-track to move out of our way, and we'll get on our plane and be out of here. That'll be the end of it, and he can start thinking about how he's going to enjoy his newfound wealth."

The Russian, listening as Horton translated, looked sad. He began to shake his head.

"Of course, there's the alternative," Gold said, his tone growing cold. "He can dig in his heels and contact his superiors, and I can close up this briefcase and put it back in my jeep. What happens next is anyone's guess, but it won't be nearly as pleasant as receiving these watches."

The Soviet, listening to Horton, nodded. He was quiet for a moment, smoking his cigarette down to a nub before reluctantly grinding it out against the tabletop. He looked at Gold, who could see by the expression on the Russian's war-ravaged face that he was weighing his decision.

Gold forced himself to look relaxed and unconcerned. Let the Russian think that he was offering this bribe merely to avoid the nuisance of a long delay.

The Russian addressed Horton.

"He wants to know if he can keep the briefcase," Horton said, not quite able to keep the note of triumph out of his voice.

Gold bit down hard on his tongue to keep from laughing.

"Tell him he drives a hard bargain, but sure, we'll throw in the briefcase."

Horton told him. The colonel quickly stood up. He ushered Gold and Horton from the tent, stuck his head through the flap, and called out an order to the half-track. It started up and was backed out of the way by the time Gold and Horton were back in their jeep.

"Move out before scarface changes his mind," Gold quietly said.

Horton put the jeep in gear and rolled away. The trucks were right behind.

"That was brilliant," Horton complimented Gold.

Sighing, Gold leaned back against the seat. "Remember that Russian I told you about?" he said expansively. "The one who visited me in L.A.? He couldn't get enough crap: cigarette lighters, fountain pens...but *especially* wristwatches." He winked at Horton. "The gaudier, the better."

"Just fucking brilliant," Horton repeated in admiration.

Gold cracked a wide grin. "You know what? I think I just made the second greatest deal in history."

"How so?" Horton asked.

Ahead, the MT-37's ramp was looming. Horton beeped his horn. The cargo plane's engines fired up, squirting blue smoke. Its props begun to turn as the aircrew prepared for a quick takeoff. The U.S. Army guards saluted as the convoy roared up the cargo plane's ramp, into the sanctuary of the hold.

"Remember how the Dutch bought Manhattan Island from the Indians for a few bucks' worth of glass?" Gold asked Horton.

"Yeah?"

"Well, don't tell this to Froehlig or any of those scientists," Gold laughed. "It'd upset their precious Teutonic egos if they learned that I just bought myself the cream of Germany's aviation science establishment for a handful of five-and-dime trinkets."

CHAPTER 7

(One)

United States Army Air Force Base
Iwo Jima
6 August 1945

Captain Steven Gold was standing at the crowded bar in the officers' club. He was smoking a cigarette, staring into his bourbon on the rocks.

He was doing his best to ignore the fact that the club was a madhouse of celebration.

Somebody had commandeered the club's phonograph and kept playing a scratchy copy of "You'd Be So Nice To Come Home To." All around Steve men were singing and dancing, laughing and babbling in a drunken tumult. Normally staid officers were spilling booze on their uniforms in the rush to deliver toasts to each other, and to the large, hastily scrawled banner strung across the room:

GOD BLESS TRUMAN AND THE ADAM BOMB

It had been midmorning when Steve had heard about the B-29 that had dropped some kind of new bomb on the Japanese city of Hiroshima. The rumor had been that this Adam bomb (Adam supposedly being the name of the guy who'd invented it) had totally wiped out the city. That it was going to end the war and make an invasion of the Japanese mainland unnecessary.

At first Steve had been skeptical, but as the details kept coming in throughout the day, he'd gradually accepted the news as the truth. So did the brass, evidently. They usually put the kabosh on these kinds of rumors, claiming that they were bad for morale. So far, though, they'd kept mum.

A pilot from the squadron bumped into Steve and toasted him. Steve toasted the guy back. Steve was polite whenever tonight's celebration touched him, but mostly he let it just swirl around him, the way frothing water moves around a stolid gray boulder plunked down in the middle of a rushing stream. He was able to shut out the happy commotion by mentally reliving all the action the Double Vees had seen since leaving Santa Belle last summer.

The squadron had been all over the Pacific this last year, and the hunting had been good. Steve and his wingman, Captain Benny Detkin, had made an unbeatable team. In the spring the squadron had been assigned to Iwo Jima, and been equipped with new fighter planes: North American– built P-51 Mustangs. Steve thought he'd died and gone to heaven flying his Mustang for the first time. She was fast, potent, and in the right hands—*his* hands—nimble at any altitude. The Double Vees' Mustangs were equipped with drop tanks. The squadron's new assignment was to fly long-range fighter escort for the B-29s making bombing runs over Japan. They'd been doing it ever since.

Steve had initially thought that helping to take the war home to the Japs would be satisfying, but he'd found the missions to be depressing. The enemy had been able to send up only a few antiquated airplanes to counter the bombing strikes which were laying smoldering waste to the Japanese cities built of wood and paper. Soon even that pitiful enemy fighter resistance had ceased. The missions had become pretty much milk runs.

About that time it became obvious that the war was winding down. Lately it had become a pale imitation of itself, the way a love affair paled once passions cooled.

But in war, like in love, every crummy action beat nothing at all, Steve thought, taking a sip of bourbon.

He felt a hand on his shoulder and turned. Benny Detkin was smiling at him.

"Steve, why the long face?" Benny asked loudly above the noise of the party. "Isn't this bomb stuff great news?"

"Yeah, sure...." Steve attempted a smile as Benny shouldered his way next to Steve at the crowded bar. He managed to get the harried bartender's attention, and ordered a ginger ale.

"Come on, we've been flying together a long time," Benny said. "You can't bullshit me. What's eating you?"

There were angry complaints by the phonograph as somebody bumped into it, sending the needle skidding across the record. A few moments later the song again began warbling through the room, sounding like the crooner was being accompanied by a frying pan full of bacon.

"You want the truth, Benny?" Steve muttered. "I haven't felt so glum since Roosevelt died. I've always known in the back of my mind that the war couldn't last forever, but—" He paused, feeling ashamed for what he was about to say. "Benny, I don't want it to stop."

"Huh?" Benny was eyeing him.

"I don't want the war to end."

"I can't believe you," Benny said, sounding angry. "How can *anyone* mourn the end of a war? Don't you *care* about all the suffering?"

"Of course I care," Steve replied, annoyed. "But I don't *worry* about it. I mean, I didn't start this war, but I did grow up with it. One way or the other, I've been flying a fighter since I was seventeen. It's been the only real job I've ever had, but now it looks like I'm about to be put out of work."

"Hey, Steve, snap out of it!" Benny laughed. "Take a look at yourself! You're selling yourself short! You're a captain with a chest full of medals and nineteen kills to your credit. Let's see a little of that confidence you've shown in the cockpit."

That's just it, Steve thought glumly. *What confidence out of the cockpit?*

"There's plenty of stuff you can do!" Benny was saying.

"Like what?"

"Well," Benny hesitated, "you could go back to school. Go to college, like you're always threatening to do!"

Steve nodded, but he knew he would never willingly put himself back in a classroom. He was no student. His sister, Susan, was the kid in the family who'd been born with those kinds of smarts. She'd always been the A student, and outstanding in music, dance, swimming, horseback riding; anything and everything she'd ever tried.

"Is that what you're planning to do, Benny?" Steve asked. "You going back to law school?"

"Yeah, I'm thinking about it," Benny said.

"You should," Steve said firmly. "You've got the brains, and you've got the gift of gab. You were born to make a swell lawyer."

"Thanks, I guess...." Benny chuckled. "But what about you?" he demanded, growing serious. "What were *you* born for?"

"What are you getting at?" Steve asked. "Flying a fighter was what I was born to do. That's my gift, such as it is."

"Steve, you're Herman Gold's son," Benny said impatiently. "Your father has a huge company."

"I don't want to hear this, Benny—"

"It's your duty to help your father run GAT," Benny insisted. "It's your fate—" Benny paused, thinking hard. "Just like when a prince takes over from the king!" he finished triumphantly.

"I'm no prince," Steve laughed. "And take it from me, my pop's no king."

"You're too close to look objectively at the situation," Benny said, "or you'd realize that with your aptitude, working with your father is exactly what you should do."

"You're wrong." Steve said.

"Okay, *be* that way," Benny said, sounding angry. "*Be* stubborn! But you and I both know that you're only trying to spite yor father."

"That's not it," Steve said quickly. "I'm *not* being stubborn or spiteful—*really*, I'm not." He shrugged. "Maybe it started out that way, but that's not the way it is anymore."

"Bullshit." Benny began to turn away.

"Listen to me," Steve urged. "If I could, I'd have things different. I *swear* I would. You don't know how often I daydream about going to work with my pop," he said wistfully. "In my head I imagine how everyone sits up and takes notice of me as I lead the company my old man built to even greater heights."

"You could do it," Benny encouraged.

"No, I can't do it," Steve replied dully. "I *wish* I could sit behind an executive desk and know what to do, the way I know how to win while sitting in a fighter's cockpit." He shook his head. "But I don't. I can't. . . ." he trailed off.

"Well, why don't you tell your father all this?" Benny quietly suggested. "And then *try*?"

"Because it's just a pipe dream!" Steve snapped. "I'm a damned sharp fighter jock, nothing more and nothing less. Sure, I could tell my pop, and I guess he'd be kind to me. He'd find me a spot in the executive suite. But let's face the facts, Benny. Without nepotism I wouldn't survive a day at GAT anywhere but in the mailroom or on the assembly lines."

"You're being too tough on yourself."

"No." Steve looked Benny in the eye. "I'm just being honest. Try and understand. I don't want my life to become a bad joke, with the punch line being a nudge and a knowing snicker when they think I can't hear: *'His qualifications for the job? Why, he's Herman Gold's son.'*"

Benny shrugged, obviously for once in his life at a loss for words. He gestured toward Steve's empty glass. "Can I buy you another drink?"

"No, thanks." Steve smiled. "Getting drunk is the *second* best thing I do. Lately I've been doing it a lot, but I've decided that I'm not going to get drunk anymore. Becoming a booze hound isn't the answer."

Benny, smiling, said, "You do know that you're my best friend? And if there's anything I can ever do for you?" He paused, looking embarrassed.

Steve chuckled. "I guess I'll miss you *almost* as much as I'm going to miss my fighter."

"Thanks a fucking heap."

Benny was frowning, pretending to be pissed, but Steve saw the pleased look in his buddy's eyes.

"I'll see you later, huh?" Steve said, gathering up his cigarettes.

"Where you going?" Benny asked.

"Just for a walk," Steve said, lighting a smoke. "I've got to think things through."

Steve pushed his way through the crowded club and out into the warm night. As he walked, he wondered: *What's to become of a guy born to be a warrior once the shooting stops?*

BOOK II:
1945–1953

NATIONAL SECURITY ACT SIGNED INTO LAW—
Air Force Made Independent Branch of Service—
Philadelphia Bulletin-Journal

AIR FORCE BOMBS CAPITOL HILL—
Defends Controversial B-45 Bomber Program at Senate
Hearings—
Washington Star Reporter

ZIONISTS DEFY ARAB THREAT OF HOLY WAR TO
DECLARE INDEPENDENT STATE OF ISRAEL—
Baltimore Globe

REDS BLOCKADE BERLIN!
U.S. Vows Not to Be Intimidated—
Air Force Responds With Airlift—
New York Gazette

BROADSWORD'S HIDDEN TALENTS HELP FIGHT
THE COLD WAR—
Modified GAT XP-90 Jet Fighter Flies Surveillance Over
Russia—
Aviation Trade Magazine

COMMUNIST TRIUMPH IN CHINA—
Mao Tse-tung Establishes People's Republic—
San Francisco Post

REDS CROSS 39TH PARALLEL—
INVADE REPUBLIC OF KOREA—
North Korea, Backed by Russia, Pushes Toward Seoul—

President Truman and United Nations Vow Swift
Retaliation—

Boston Times

KOREAN WAR HERO'S EXCLUSIVE—
My Story: How I Captured "Yalu Charlie"—
by Lt. Colonel Steven Gold—

PhotoWeek Magazine

CHAPTER 8

(One)

Caucus Room
Senate Office Building
Washington, D.C.
12 October 1947

Steven Gold was bored as hell.

It was a warm Friday afternoon. Indian summer in Washington. The Senate hearings being held to explore the advisability of continued funding for the Air Force's hair-raisingly expensive B-45 bomber program had been running six hours a day for the past week. For the past hour an assistant to the Secretary of the Air Force had been droning into the microphone.

Steve restlessly shifted in his hard-backed folding chair, trying to get comfortable. He was seated in the next to the last row, way back near the caucus room's main exit. From where he was sitting he could hear footsteps and soft chatter echoing in the corridor outside.

Must be office workers leaving to get an early start on the weekend, Steve thought enviously. He stared up at the four enormous crystal chandeliers illuminating the marble-paneled room. During the past week he'd already amused himself counting the light bulbs in each fixture. Twice.

"Now then, Mr. Chairman . . ." The witness paused to nervously clear his throat. The microphone amplified it into a lion's roar. "Allow me to bring you up to date concerning what the Secretary has been doing since July 26 of this year, when President Truman signed the National Security Act which brought into being the United States Air Force as an independent branch."

A wave of restlessness moved through the crowded gallery. The hearing's chairman, Senator Hill, rapped his gavel in warning.

A photographer, shaking his head, got up and left. His camera bag jingled loudly as he walked to the exit.

Lucky bastard, Steve thought enviously as the photographer passed him on the way out. Steve couldn't leave. He had orders to attend the hearings from gavel to gavel.

"The witness may proceed," Senator Hill intoned. He and the other senators seated up at the front of the room looked as sleepy as Steve felt.

"Thank you, Senator. Now then, when President Truman signed Executive Order 9877, which defined the roles of the three services . . ."

Steve glanced at his watch. Just another couple of hours until adjournment for the weekend. His attention shifted to the couple seated up front.

They'd come in about a half hour ago. They guy was average, but the dame with him, a brunette with curly shoulder-length hair, was a knockout. She was wearing a light green silk suit and a soft black hat that looked like a beret. Thanks to all the coverage that guy Dior had been getting in the photo weeklies, Steve knew enough to realize that what she was wearing was the latest out of Paris, and had to have cost plenty.

The brunette was looking around in that politely bored, languid, aristocratic way that reminded Steve of some of his mother's woman friends. He watched as she discreetly arched her back, stretching like a purebred feline.

Wonder what it would take to get her to purr? Steve grinned. No question it would be worth the effort.

Steve also wondered for the countless time if the bookish-looking guy next to her was her husband. Somehow he didn't think so. She just didn't look married. But then, the really classy ladies in his parents' social circle never did, Steve reminded himself. Not even when they were grandmothers.

The official at the witness table was continuing his testimony.

"The Air Force's first step on the road to the development of postwar U.S. air power was the decision to create a force with global capabilities, the Strategic Air Command, which came into being in March of last year. SAC reorganized air power into three Commands: Strategic, Tactical, and Air Defense. The theory behind SAC is that a bomber delivering atomic weapons can handle any situation where diplomacy proves ineffective. Predictably, a certain branch of the service lobbied hard against this point of view—"

"Excuse me," one of the subcommittee members, Senator Tabworth, broke in. "I presume the witness is referring to the Navy?"

"I am," the Air Force official said stiffly.

This ought to be good, Steve thought, perking up. The Appropriations Subcommittee Chairman, Senator Hill, was solidly behind the Air Force, but Tabworth, who'd served on a battleship in World War One, was the subcommittee's chief proponent of the Navy point of view. He'd publicly vowed to do all he could to help the Navy scuttle the B-45 and get the millions earmarked for the bomber project reallocated for the development of a larger class of aircraft carrier capable of launching airplanes carrying atomic weapons.

At the front of the room Senator Tabworth was gearing up to make a speech. "May I remind the witness that the proud United States Navy, which has over a hundred and seventy year history of defending this great nation against—"

Hill rapped his gavel. "Would the senator please make his point?" he asked wearily.

"I will, if the chairman shall allow it. . . ." Tabworth huffed.

Steve found it amusing that these two guys, who for the past week had been bickering like Abbott and Costello, looked so much alike. They were both in their sixties and built slender, except for their potbellies. Both favored three-piece suits and bow ties, wore wire-rimmed specs, and had about five strands of hair apiece, which they wore plastered across their scalps.

"If the last war has taught us anything," Tabworth was orating, "it is that the common foot soldier is necessary to get the job done."

"Except in Japan," the Air Force official at the witness table quipped.

Good for you, Steve thought as an appreciative chuckle erupted across the room.

"Atomic weapons will be important," Tabworth agreed, "But such weapons will never replace troops, and that means Navy transports will be necessary to get the troops to where they are going, and that means Navy *carriers* will be necessary to *supply* those troops with air support—"

"Thank you, Senator Tabworth," Hill determinedly interrupted. "Now then, the witness may continue."

"If I may address Senator Tabworth's point," the witness began. "The Air Force views the strategic bomber carrying atomic bombs as the single decisive factor in any future conflict with our likeliest adversary: the Soviet Union. Troop involvement in a conflict with the Russians would be minimal, if at all." The witness paused to glance down at his notes. "Concerning this topic, I would like to quote the Air Force's Chief of Staff, General Carl Spaatz: 'We will not have to plod laboriously and bloodily along the Minsk–Smolensk–Moscow road in order to strike at Russia's vitals. Hence the war may be concluded within weeks and perhaps days.'"

Nice rebuttal, Steve thought to himself. Behind him he heard the door opening and closing.

"This seat taken, Captain?" a man whispered as he sidled into the row and sat down next to Steve.

Steve glanced up. It had been so long that it took him a moment to recognize the face. "Uncle Tim?" he whispered.

"Long time, no see, Stevie." Tim Campbell grinned, the laugh lines deepening around his wide-set, dark eyes.

Campbell was in his late forties. He was short and stocky and wore a rust-colored double-breasted suit. A diamond stickpin winked at Steve from Campbell's yellow and red polka-dot tie, and the big chunk of gold that was his wristwatch looked heavy enough to sink a battleship.

"How you been, Stevie?" Campbell kept his voice pitched low so as not to disrupt the hearings. His gray-tinged auburn hair, slicked down and parted in the middle, glistened under the lights.

"Fine, Uncle Tim," Steve murmured, even though Campbell wasn't really his uncle.

Tim Campbell had once been a close friend and business partner of Steve's father, back when Skyworld Airlines was still a part of GAT, but at some point Campbell and Steve's father had suffered a falling-out. Steve didn't know the details. He'd been a little kid when it had happened, and neither his father nor Campbell would talk about it. Whatever had caused the disagreement, its result had been a split in the company as the two men went their separate ways. Steve's father had retained control of the aviation design and construction portions of the GAT empire, while Campbell had taken control of the airline.

"I guess I haven't seen you since you came back to the West Coast for a visit," Campbell said. "That must have been almost two years ago, just after the war ended."

"I've been home since then to see my folks, but only for short trips," Steve said apologetically. "I guess I should have called."

"Hey, don't worry about it," Campbell said. "I know it can get awkward."

Steve nodded. His father and Tim Campbell professed to still be friends, but Steve thought they behaved more like friendly adversaries. After all these years there was still some sort of mysterious game of financial one-upmanship going on between them, but again, neither man would talk about it. Campbell and Steve's father were cordial with each other when chance brought them together, but neither man went out of his way to look the other up.

Whatever Campbell's relationship with Steve's father, Campbell had remained a presence in Steve and his sister Susan's lives. Uncle Tim had never forgotten their birthdays. Even during the war, no matter where Steve was stationed, around the time of his birthday a card from Campbell and a small token—a bottle of booze or a box of cigars—had always managed to find their way to him.

"You're looking great, Stevie," Campbell murmured. "And I like that uniform! So that's the new Air Force blue, huh?"

"They call it 'sky blue,'" Steve smiled. "They were just issued last month."

Campbell, nodding, gestured toward Steve's decorations grouped above the left breast pocket of his jacket, below his silver pilot's wings. "Pretty impressive helping of fruit salad you have there."

"Yeah, I guess. . . ." It always embarrassed Steve when people made a big deal over his decorations. As far as he was concerned, he'd only been doing his job, a job he'd loved.

There was a moment of silence between the two men. Both shifted their attention to the amplified testimony coming from the front of the room.

"In conclusion, allow me to make the point that to the best of our knowledge the Soviet Union has not yet developed an atomic bomb. Its ground forces, however, greatly outnumber ours and present a formidable threat to most of continental Europe. There can be little debate concerning the Soviets' ability to overrun Europe, and our inability to stem that scarlet tide. Accordingly, our best hope to halt Soviet drive into Europe is in strategic bombing."

"Say," Campbell whispered, "I guess you were pretty lucky to be allowed to stay in the service. The Air Force has really cut back."

"Yes, sir . . . I guess."

Up at the front of the room, Senator Hill was saying, "Let the record show that we extend our thanks to the gentleman from the Office of the Secretary of the Air Force for his valuable testimony."

The Air Force official gathered up his papers and left the witness table.

"So what are you doing here at this hearing?" Campbell asked. "Are you scheduled to testify?"

"No," Steve chuckled. "I'm a fighter jock—or, at least I was," he shrugged. "Anyway, I don't know beans about bombers. I'm assigned to the Air Force's Public Relations Department."

"Ah, now I get it!" Campbell said knowingly. "What better spot for a handsome young ace?"

Steve didn't answer that. "You know the Navy is doing its best to get the B-45 thrown onto the scrap heap?"

"I do," Campbell said. "They'd like to get their mitts on the money being spent on the B-45."

"Yes, sir," Steve said. "Well, my superiors felt that my being present might do our side some good against our web-footed friends."

Campbell grinned. "Smart move on their part, sending an Air Force pilot who single-handedly rescued a Navy ship."

"I'm supposed to lend moral support to the witnesses and get my picture taken. . . ." Steve trailed off, blushing.

"Well, why not?" Campbell chuckled. "You're a war hero, right?" He winked. "So you've got an office at the Pentagon?"

"More like a closet than an office, Uncle Tim."

"Don't worry, the big office will come," he said knowingly. "You're in a pretty darn good spot for a twenty-three-year-old captain. Public relations is going to be *the* front line for the military during peacetime. I'm telling you, Stevie, it looks like you've got it made." Campbell winked again. "I've got a feeling I'm talking to a future Air Force Chief of Staff."

"Yes, Uncle Tim," Steve said, embarrassed. "But what brings you here?"

"Me? I'm here to fight for my baby," Campbell said.

"I don't get it?"

"Amalgamated-Landis is building the B-45 for the Air Force," Campbell explained.

"I know that," Steve said. A-L, like GAT, was one of the giant companies that made up California's aircraft industry.

"Well, did you know that I'm on Amalgamated's board of directors?" Campbell asked.

"No!"

Campbell nodded. "I put money into A-L years ago, but when I got an advance tip-off about the company being awarded a contract to build the B-45, I doubled my stake, buying myself a seat on the board. When the Navy started giving the B-45 program a hard time, I took over the execution of A-L's counterattack. I know something about public relations myself, Stevie, my boy. . . ."

"That I knew, Uncle Tim," Steve smiled. His father had often admitted that if it hadn't been for Campbell's masterful handling of GAT's advertising and public relations, the company would never have survived its early, difficult days.

Senator Hill was rapping his gavel. "The committee now calls Donald Harrison—"

"It was my idea to have Don testify," Campbell boasted to Steve. "He's A-L's chief engineer. The B-45 was his brainchild."

Steve watched as the bookish-looking guy sitting with the knockout brunette stood up. Steve's heart sank when he saw the brunette give Harrison a winning smile as he carried his big briefcase over to the witness table.

Harrison was in his late twenties, Steve guessed. He was tall and broad-shouldered, but he looked a little pudgy, soft around the edges. He was wearing a lightweight blue suit, white shirt, and a red knit tie. His thinning dark blonde hair was slicked straight back from his high expanse of forehead.

"This is going to be good," Campbell whispered to Tim. "Harrison is a real go-getter. He reminds me a lot of your father in his younger days."

"First I'd like to thank the committee for this opportunity to speak on behalf of the B-45," Harrison said, sounding relaxed. He adjusted the mike to suit him, and then opened up his briefcase and began shuffling through his papers. "Let me begin by outlining to you the B-45's projected capabilities." He took a pair of tan, round-framed eyeglasses from the breast pocket of his suit jacket, perched them on the tip of his nose, and began to read. "The B-45 was created to meet the challenge posed by this country's need for a long-range bomber capable of delivering a substantial payload to a target seven thousand miles away. The B-45, powered by six thirty-five-hundred-horsepower pusher-prop engines, augmented by four, auxiliary turbojet engines paired in pods mounted beneath the wings, amply answers that challenge. . . ."

For the next half hour Harrison painted a glowing word picture of the B-45 as a superbomber capable of policing the world on behalf of democracy.

"What did I tell you?" Campbell nudged Steve. "Harrison is demolishing the opposition."

It was true, Steve thought in admiration. Harrison was a skilled and sophisticated public speaker.

". . . The B-45 will carry a maximum eighty-five-thousand-pound bomb load." Harrison paused to whip off his eyeglasses in a dramatic flourish. "Eighty-five-thousand pounds of bombs. . . . Gentlemen, let me remind you that eighty-five-thousand pounds is almost twice what a fully loaded B-17 weighs in its entirety."

"A perfect quote," Campbell pointed out to Steve. "Just look at those news hounds scribbling away."

Steve, nodding absently, found that his eyes kept being drawn to the brunette who'd come in with Harrison. She had to be romantically involved with the engineer, he decided. She was listening to him speak with rapt concentration. But then, so was everybody.

Steve wanted to ask Campbell if the woman was Harrison's wife or sweetheart, but he held back. Questions like that had landed Steve in hot water more than once in his life.

". . . And for those reasons, Senators, it is clear that the B-45 will rightfully take its place as the keystone in the United States' arsenal," Harrison continued. "It will force our enemies to think twice before attacking us, and ultimately persuade them not to attack us at all."

Harrison paused to fix the senators facing him with an intense stare. "Gentlemen, when I designed the B-45, I had in mind the creation of an airplane so awesome in its capabilities that its mere existence would guarantee peace. It was and is my goal to give my country the same sense of reassurance against threat that the average American householder feels knowing he's got a shotgun behind the door. The B-45 is America's shotgun. You cannot—must not—take it away. Thank you."

Scattered applause swept the room.

"Order, please. I'll have order," Senator Hill demanded, rapping his gavel. Senator Tabworth looked fit to bust.

"What did I tell you?" Campbell chuckled to Steve. "Your old man could sway an audience like that in his day."

"Mr. Harrison," Tabworth began as the applause died down. "Isn't it true that you scientists believe that the United States cannot indefinitely retain its monopoly on the atomic bomb? That sooner or later the Soviets will have an atomic bomb of their own?"

"Well, sir, I'm an engineer," Harrison smiled. "Your question addresses a topic out of my bailiwick."

"Nice parry," Campbell observed, nudging Steve. "He's showing that he's not one to shoot his mouth off, and that makes what he *does* say sound all the more important."

"Come, come, Mr. Harrison." Tabworth was scowling. "Surely you've given this matter some thought? You have likened your multimillion-dollar bomber to a shotgun," he scoffed. "If that is so, isn't the atomic bomb like the ammunition loaded into that shotgun?"

"Yes, I suppose it is," Harrison replied.

Tabworth smiled. "Have you ever hunted waterfowl, Mr. Harrison?"

"No, Senator, I can't say that I have."

"Well, young fellow, I have, many times," Tabworth loudly announced. "And from practical experience I can tell you that a shotgun is only as good as the ammunition loaded into it. Do you mean to tell this subcommittee that you have never considered the possibility that the Soviets will one day possess the same atomic ammunition as we for their 'shotguns'?"

"Senator, if you're asking for my personal opinion, I believe that the Russians will, by hook or crook, eventually have their own atomic bomb."

"Thank you for your honesty, Mr. Harrison," Tabworth replied triumphantly. "But you have just demolished your own argument on behalf of the B-45."

"On the contrary, it has just been strengthened," Harrison replied.

"How so?" Tabworth demanded. "What good is your 'shotgun behind the door' if the intruders are similarly armed?"

"Ouch!" Steve said softly. He glanced at Campbell. "Looks like Tabworth has Harrison boxed in."

Campbell was smiling. "Listen and learn, Steve...."

"Senator Tabworth, I suggest that no intruder in his right mind will attack a household if he knows for sure that injury will be his only reward," Harrison declared. "In other words it is clear that the only viable *defense* against adversaries armed with atomic weapons is the promise of our inevitable strong *offense*. Deterrence is the strategy of the future. We must secure our nation by developing and maintaining those weapons, forces, and techniques required to pose this warning to our enemies: If you attack us, expect a devastating counterattack in return."

"But what does any of that have to do with the B-45?" Tabworth asked, frowning.

"Senator, you said you were a veteran waterfowl hunter. Isn't it true that no matter how good your ammunition, you'll never get yourself a duck dinner hunting with a short-barreled shotgun? Don't you need a long-sighting plane for the long-range shooting you'll be doing?"

"Well, yes . . . I suppose that's right," Tabworth admitted. "Say, I thought you said you didn't hunt?"

"Senators," Harrison continued addressing the entire subcommittee, "I can't help but think of our great heavy-weight boxing champion, Joe Louis. Louis—coincidentally dubbed the 'Brown Bomber' by the sporting press—is blessed with what we might say are 'atomic fists.' But what good would his knockout punch be if the champ neglected to straighten his legs, thereby lacking the ability to deliver that decisive blow to his opponent?"

Off came Harrison's eyeglasses as he paused meaningfully. "Senators, I put to you the proposition that the atomic bomb has become modern warfare's knockout punch, but it will prove useless to us, and a meaningless threat to our enemies, if we do not develop the certain means to deliver it. *The B-45 is that means.* Without the B-45, we are as our champion Joe Louis would be if he were forced to defend his title in the ring while strapped into a wheelchair!"

Laughter, followed by applause, filled the room. "Order, order please," Senator Hill called out in vain, pounding his gavel.

"I have no further questions," Senator Tabworth muttered into his microphone.

"What did I tell you?" Campbell elbowed Steve's ribs. "Talk about your knockout punch!"

"This is useless," Senator Hill was declaring. "The hearing will adjourn until Monday morning, when the witness will continue his testimony."

"Come on, I'll introduce you to the man of the hour," Campbell told Steve as the hearing broke up.

Flashbulbs popped as photographers and shouting reporters jostled with one another to get close to Harrison. When the young engineer saw Campbell, he excused himself from the newspaper people and came over. The brunette joined them at the same time.

"Miss Linda Forrest, may I introduce you to Captain Steven Gold," Campbell said.

"How do you do, Captain," the brunette smiled.

Well, at least she isn't Harrison's wife, Steve thought as she offered him her hand. *But is she his girlfriend?*

Steve was reluctant to let go of her fingers. She was a knockout, all right, even better close up than she was from a distance. She had a wide, sensual mouth, and swell, bright blue eyes, just like that kid Elizabeth Taylor in that movie about the racing horse. But unlike Elizabeth Taylor, Linda Forrest was all grown up. As a matter of fact, now that Steve was close to her, she looked older than he'd initially thought. She looked closer to Harrison's age, in her late twenties.

"And this is Donald Harrison," Campbell said.

"Congratulations," Steve said, tearing himself away from Linda Forrest in order to shake hands with Harrison. "You really mopped the floor with Tabworth."

"Well, I was captain of my debating team in college," Harrison laughed. "And it helps when you truly believe in your argument the way I believe in the B-45," he firmly added.

Campbell put his arm around Steve's shoulder. "Don, Stevie here is Herman Gold's son."

"Well!" Harrison smiled. "I have to tell you that your father is something of a hero of mine."

Linda Forrest laughed. "Looking at all those decorations on the captain's chest, I'd say that he's something of a hero in his own right. What do all those pretty ribbons mean, Captain?"

"Stevie," Campbell cut in, "show them which one represents the Distinguished Flying Cross you got for single-handedly rescuing that Navy cargo ship from the Japs."

"It wasn't single-handed," Steve began, glancing at the others. "I had help. A buddy of mine saved my skin when he—"

"Sure, Stevie," Campbell cut him off. He poked at the ribbons on Steve's chest. "But which one is it?"

Steve glanced at Linda Forrest. She smiled, rolling her big baby blues in commiseration. He smiled back as he pointed to the deep blue bar vertically edged in red and white.

"That's lovely," Linda Forrest said. "I suppose you did something terribly brave to receive it."

"You know, that medal is just one grade below the Medal of Honor," Campbell announced before Steve could stop him. "I happen to think they should have given the kid the Medal of Honor," he added sourly.

"I guess they call 'em the way they see 'em," Steve replied modestly. Linda Forrest was still smiling at him as if there were nobody else around. He wondered if Harrison was getting steamed? Basking in a smile like that, he didn't care.

"Stevie, Stevie." Campbell was shaking his head. "You're never going to get anywhere unless you're willing to blow your own horn."

Linda Forrest was laughing. "I do believe the captain is blushing."

"And which is the decoration the Navy lobbied so hard for you to get?" Campbell asked.

"You mean the Legion of Merit," Steve said, wishing Uncle Tim would let up. He pointed out the purplish-red bar vertically edged in white.

"Well, they're all very impressive," Linda Forrest told Steve. She cocked her head to one side, a slight smile playing at the corners of her delicious mouth as she looked him over appraisingly. "Someday I'd love to see the actual medals."

"Uh . . . yeah, sure. . . ." Steve mumbled, wondering what the hell she meant by that. He glanced uncertainly at Harrison, who seemed unperturbed.

"Well, you'll have to excuse us, Stevie," Campbell was saying. "We've got a drink date with a very important fellow on the House of Representatives Military Appropriations Committee."

"Sure . . . of course." Steve glanced longingly at Linda Forrest. "Very nice to have met you . . . and you, too, Mr. Harrison," he added quickly.

"Same here," Harrison said as Campbell began to shepherd them along.

"Good-bye, Captain Gold," Linda Forrest smiled, looking back at Steve.

He watched as she took Harrison's arm. *So she is his girlfriend after all,* Steve told himself, feeling sad as he watched her walk away out of his life. *Good-bye forever, Baby Blue Eyes.*

He spent a few seconds chatting with a senator's aide he knew, and then left the hearing room, passing through the building's octagonal marble rotunda and out the main doors. A cab was just pulling away as Steve ambled down the steps. He thought he glimpsed Linda Forrest looking back at him through the cab's rear window, but he wasn't sure.

He paused to light a Pall Mall, and then began walking in the warm blaze of the dying afternoon down Constitution Avenue. The offices had let out. Steve smiled to himself as he watched the young secretaries in their summery frocks on their way home from work.

He had plans for the evening: he was going to meet some friends at the Siam Club, a dining and dancing spot. The friends were bringing along a blind date for him, a girl they thought he might like. And tomorrow night he had a date with a cute redhead in his office's secretarial pool.

Maybe tonight's blind date would be a dish like Linda Forrest.

She would have to be *something* pretty swell to help him get those big baby blues out of his system. . . .

(Two)

The Siam Club
Washington, D.C.

That evening a little after eight o'clock, Steve Gold was at the bar at the Siam Club, waiting for his friends to arrive. He was sipping a Rob Roy. (He'd switched from bourbon to scotch about a year ago.) While he was waiting he listened to the dance band play an Irving Berlin tune, "You Keep Coming Back Like an Old Song."

The Siam Club was Steve's favorite nightspot. It was located on 16th Street, near the White House and the city's ritziest hotels. The nightclub was pretty ritzy itself. Dreamy, dramatic murals portraying in luminous colors scenes from a fantasy Siamese kingdom lined the walls above red velvet draperies. The central chandelier and wall sconces cast romantic light on the linen-covered tables ringing the dance floor.

While Steve was waiting, he thought about the long letter from Benny Detkin that had been waiting for him in the mail when he'd gotten back to his apartment that afternoon. Benny was still single. He'd graduated from Columbia Law

School at the top of his class last summer, and now he was working as an associate at some hotshot New York firm.

Benny and Steve had remained close. Steve still considered Benny his best friend. They visited with each other a couple of times a year, and wrote to each other regularly. At least Benny wrote regularly, Steve reminded himself, feeling guilty. He hated to write, and usually tried to get by with a hastily scrawled postcard.

Steve patted the pockets of his charcoal-gray, double-breasted suit for his cigarettes, and then remembered that he'd smoked the last one on the drive to the club. He glimpsed one of the cigarette girls passing by in the backlit mirror behind the bar, and swiveled around on his stool to signal her. As he did, he noticed Don Harrison and Linda Forrest being shown to a table.

Steve flipped the cigarette girl half a buck for a package of Pall Malls and told her to keep the change. As he tore the cellophane wrapping off the scarlet pack he thought about how happy his superior officer at the Pentagon had been when he'd telephoned in his report on how Harrison had bested Senator Tabworth at today's hearings. Harrison was definitely a VIP as far as the Air Force was concerned.

Steve saw a waiter gliding by carrying a champagne setup. It gave him an idea. "I'd like to send a bottle of champagne over to a table," Steve told the bartender who came over to light Steve's cigarette.

"Yes, sir!" The bartender presented Steve with the wine card, and then snapped his fingers to summon a waiter.

Steve didn't know much about wine. He wished that he did as he randomly selected a pricey bottle of Bollinger near the top of the list. People who knew about wine and the finer things moved easily through the capital city. Steve wanted to be like them because they had the right skills to survive and win. They were the fighter aces of this place and time.

He had a running tab here, so he signed for the champagne, adding a tip for both the bartender and the waiter. He instructed the waiter on which table to present the bottle with his compliments, and then sat back, feeling very pleased with himself. He looked forward to telling his superior officer about his gesture on Monday morning. It was, after all, a public relations kind of thing to do, and his superior had been after him to get with the department's program.

Getting with the program had been hard for Steve these past two years. His superior officer, a real nice guy even if he had flown a desk all through the war, had once sat Steve down and explained to him that public relations was the art of granting favors and then asking for favors in return. The whole concept was alien to Steve. He hated small talk and beating around the bush, but he really did want to get with the program and advance his military career.

The only enjoyable part of the job was his expense account. He'd have to remember to file an expense report for the cost of the champagne on Monday.

"Excuse me, sir—"

Steve turned to see the waiter who'd delivered the champagne standing beside him.

"The gentleman thanks you, and asks that you join them for a drink."

Don Harrison stood up to shake hands as Steve approached the table. Harrison was dressed in a conservative dark blue double-breasted suit with a barely visible chalk stripe, a white shirt, and a muted tie.

"Thanks for the bubbly, Captain," Harrison said.

"My pleasure," Steve said. "After the way you championed the B-45 it's the least I could do. But it's after hours, I'm off duty, and dressed in civies," he assed, "so please drop the formalities and call me Steve."

"Okay!" Harrison smiled. "And I'm Don."

"Please sit down, Steve," Linda Forrest said as the waiter appeared with a chair, which he placed at the table beside the champagne in its silver ice-bucket stand.

Steve feasted his eyes on Linda as the waiter busied himself opening the champagne. She had her hair up and was wearing black suede gloves and a low-cut black satin evening dress that revealed the tops of her breasts. Steve had a difficult time preventing himself from staring at her luscious cleavage. She was wearing very little jewelry—just a strand of pearls and matching earrings—but she didn't need much in the way of extra ornaments.

Steve picked up his filled champagne glass and toasted Harrison. "To you, and to your B-45 bomber. It's number one on the Air Force's wish list, and thanks to you, it looks as if this wish is going to come true."

"You're embarrassing me," Harrison chuckled as he sipped his champagne.

"He's as modest as you about his professional accomplishments, Steve," Linda Forrest remarked as she took a tortoiseshell cigarette case from her evening bag. You should have seen him blush when I gave him today's pages to review."

"Pages of what?" Steve asked, producing his lighter and leaning toward her to light her cigarette.

"Of the personality profile that I'm writing. I'm a freelance journalist who often specializes in the same line of work as you: public relations. Don's company, Amalgamated-Landis, has hired me to do an in-depth profile on Don."

"You mean you two are working together?" Steve asked, trying hard not to sound *too* elated.

Harrison nodded. "What's the latest title of the thing?" he scowled. "Oh, yeah. Get this, Steve: 'Don Harrison: Unsung Hero of America's Freedom Crusade.'"

"Get *him*," Linda Forrest laughed. "He's such a phony! Secretly, he loves the fuss everyone is making over him."

"Well, maybe I do, a little," Harrison admitted reluctantly, winking at Steve. "Just imagine this mug of mine plastered across all the Sunday supplements in America. I'll get my chance to be the hero, just like you, Steve. You know, I never did get to join the military during the war. They kept me out on account of the work I was doing designing airplanes."

"Hey, guys like you designed and built the airplanes that guys like me flew," Steve said. "Couldn't have had one without the other. I guess it took both kinds to win the war."

"Spoken like a true gentleman," Linda Forrest laughed.

She stubbed out the remains of her cigarette in the ashtray. "I think I'd like to see if you move as gracefully as you verbally extricate yourself from tight corners," she smiled.

"Pardon?"

"She's asking you to dance." Harrison said gently.

"Well," Steve said uncertainly, "if you don't mind."

Harrison shook his head.

The band was kicking into "Almost Like Being In Love" from the hit Broadway musical of the year, *Brigadoon*, as Steve stood up and escorted Linda Forrest to the dance floor. Steve noticed guys watching enviously as she held on to his arm. *Well, why not?* he thought as they began to dance. She was the prettiest girl in the club.

"I bet the idea for the puff piece you're doing on Don came from Tim Campbell, Miss Forrest," Steve said as he led her around the dance floor.

"That's a bet you win," she said. "But don't you think you should call a girl by her first name when you're looking down her dress?"

"Oh! I–I'm sorry!" Steve stuttered, feeling sick that she'd caught him.

Linda laughed. "Don't be sorry. I think I like it. If I didn't like it I wouldn't let you do it. Get it?"

Steve tried to regain his composure. She was a new kind of dame for him. Somehow she'd put herself in the driver's seat, but what ruffled Steve's feathers was not so much that she'd done it, but that somehow she was making him like it.

"Just how old are you, Cap'n Steve?"

"Twenty-three."

"Hmmm. . . ."

"What's 'hmmm' supposed to mean?" Steve demanded, laughing.

"Just, hmmm. . . ." Her eyes were sparkling sapphires. She used them like weapons. She'd moved closer to him, gently drawing his arm tightly around her waist. Her body felt strong and sleek beneath her snug-waisted satin dress. As she pressed against him, the scent of her perfume seemed to rise up from her cleavage, enveloping him in a fragrant cloud that made him feel giddy, as if he were dancing on air.

"How old are *you*?" Steve asked as the soaring music twirled them triumphantly around the dance floor.

"You're twenty-three, all right," Linda chuckled ruefully.

"What's that supposed to mean?"

"It means that you've got a lot to learn about women if you can ask a question like that."

"Please! Turn down those baby blues before I go blind!"

She laughed. "Maybe I *like* to blind men."

"Maybe you don't like to play fair!"

"Maybe you're a fast learner, after all, Cap'n Steve." She pressed her head against his chest as they danced.

It was like being in a dogfight with a master ace, Steve thought as he lightly rested his chin in her hair. He was fascinated, even as he felt stung by the way she seemed to effortlessly fly bewitching rings around him.

He desperately wanted to ask if there was anything besides business between Harrison and her, but he didn't know how to bring it up without risking putting his foot in his mouth. He liked her a lot, but he wasn't ready to show her *all* his cards.

And then the music stopped and their time alone was over. Was it his imagination, or did her arms linger an instant around his neck before releasing him?

As Steve reluctantly escorted her back to the table, he glanced over to the bar and saw that his friends had arrived. There was a blonde waiting with them. He didn't know her. Obviously she was his blind date. She was pretty. She looked okay.

Franks and beans are okay as well, but not when you've just had yourself a taste of filet mignon, he thought to himself. What he wouldn't give to spend the rest of the evening in Linda Forrest's company!

"Do you work on Saturdays?" Linda suddenly murmured.

"No, why?"

"This is my first visit to Washington, but Don is going to be tied up with dreary appointments all day tomorrow. Could I impose upon you to show me the sights?"

"Uh, sure. . . ."

"That's if you're free," Linda added quickly.

"Oh! I'm free!" Steve instantly replied. "Why don't I pick you up at your hotel," he suggested as they approached the table. "Where are you staying?"

"Very near here, at the Mayflower."

"How about eleven?"

She nodded, smiling. "I'll be waiting in the lobby. Oh, I know we'll have *such* fun together. . . ."

(Three)

Mayflower Hotel
Washington, D.C.
13 October 1947

There was a cop pounding the pavement on the corner of Desales Street and Connecticut Avenue as Steve Gold pulled up in front of the hotel's main entrance. The Mayflower was the oldest hotel in Washington, and the largest, with something like one thousand rooms and suites. It was always bustling, and there was never a place close by to park, so Steve tucked the Buick Roadmaster into the only available space: in front of a fire hydrant.

He had no time to find a legal parking spot. He was already fifteen minutes late.

Once last night's blonde was gone, he'd dressed quickly. It was a beautiful day, but a lot cooler than the day before— normal October weather. Steve had pulled on a light blue turtleneck sweater, dark green pleated slacks, tan buck moccasins, and a dark brown horsehide, double-breasted, belted car coat. By quarter of eleven he was in the Roadmaster and on his way, but when he hit the snarl of Saturday morning traffic going into Washington on the Mount Vernon Highway, he knew he was done for. The nine-mile drive took half an hour.

The cop who'd been on the corner looked grim as he came over to the fire hydrant, but before he could say anything, Steve flipped down the passenger side sun visor to reveal the U.S. AIR FORCE OFFICIAL BUSINESS placard he'd swiped from the office.

The cop nodded respectfully and continued on his way. Steve grinned. You weren't supposed to use the placard for personal business, let alone personal cars, but what the hell, it sure made parking a snap.

He jumped out of the car and hurried into the hotel. The lobby was busy. It took him a second to spot Linda. She was standing by the newsstand, reading the various headlines. She was wearing a loden-green suede leather jacket over a white blouse that was tucked into a brown tweed skirt.

"Hi, I'm sorry I'm so late," Steve said, coming up to her.

"It's okay." She looked at him then did a double take. "What are you grinning at?"

"At you," Steve said, unable to wipe the shit-eating grin off his face. "I guess I forgot what you looked like."

"What?" she laughed. "I'd hoped I'd made more of an impression on you than *that* last night."

"I mean, I remembered what you looked like, but not how good."

"Quit right there," she smiled.

"While I'm ahead, you mean," he nodded, chuckling. "I guess I will. If you're ready, I'm parked just out front."

"Just a sec." She scooped up a half-dozen different newspapers, and paid for them, along with a package of Chesterfields.

"Something happen in the news I'm not aware of?" Steve asked her as they left the hotel.

"Oh, these?" She looked at the thick bundle of papers. "I like to keep up with current events. I've worked on a couple of newspapers."

"Well, hand them over and I'll put them in the trunk to keep them from blowing around," Steve said as they walked over to the car.

"Wow! Swell car!" Linda said as she ran her hand over the gleaming, cream and maroon paint of the four-door Roadmaster. "It must have cost a mint. Just what *is* my government paying Air Force captains these days?"

Steve laughed. "Not enough to buy one of these, that's for sure."

"Oh!" Linda snapped her fingers. "But you're Herman Gold's son," she said knowingly.

"I don't take money from my father," Steve said coldly, stung by her assumption that he did.

"Hey," she began softly. "Sorry. . . ."

Steve, forcing a smile, shook his head. "No, I should be the one to apologize. My father is a touchy subject with me."

"Oh, really?" she asked playfully. "I think I smell a story here."

"But I know better than to talk about it to a journalist," Steve said. "To change the subject—which I intend to do," he added firmly, "my maternal grandfather was a wealthy man. When he passed away he left each of his grandchildren a trust fund."

"So you're independently wealthy?"

Steve shrugged. "I can indulge myself when it comes to a nice car and sharp clothes. The Air Force takes care of the rest." He came around to the passenger side of the Buick to open Linda's door. "Now, then, if the lady is ready for her guided tour of our fair city?"

"I place myself in your hands," she said demurely, sliding into the car.

Steve pretended to leer. "The lady knows not what she says."

Linda winked at him. "The lady is a writer, remember? Words are her business."

They spent the next several hours on a whirlwind tour of Washington. The speed at which they zoomed around Pennsylvania and Constitution avenues in the Roadmaster, parking wherever they wanted thanks to the Air Force official-business placard, became their private joke.

They strolled the Mall all the way from the Lincoln Memorial to the Capitol. Then, around three, they hopped back into the car and made a circuit around Union Station, and then down First Street, past the Supreme Court and the Library of Congress, ending up at the Tidal Basin.

There they grabbed a much needed snack of red hots and sodas from a sidewalk vendor near the Jefferson Memorial.

"You've seen a lot," Steve told her as they finished their late lunch. "If you don't mind, I think we should leave the tour of the Smithsonian and the National Gallery for another day."

"You don't have to twist my arm," Linda laughed. "You've been very kind. A marvelous guide."

"It was my pleasure," Steve said. "It was a lot of fun. It let me see this beautiful city through fresh eyes." He paused, looking at her intently. "Very beautiful *baby-blue* eyes, I might add."

Linda blushed and looked away. "As I was saying, you've been a marvelous guide, except that you've neglected to show me one very important sight."

"Which is?" Steve asked, frowning.

"Your apartment," she said, smiling shyly. "It'd be *s-o-o-o* nice to kick off my shoes, put my feet up, and have a drink."

Okay! he thought happily. "Then let's go."

The traffic was light driving back across the Potomac into Alexandria. In ten minutes Steve was pulling up in front of his apartment house on Prince Street.

"Oh, it's lovely," Linda said, gazing at the tall, narrow brick-and-clapboard town house with its green shutters. Do you know its history?"

Steve shrugged indifferently. "Only that it once belonged to a famous Civil War general whose name escapes me. It was turned into apartments sometime during World War One."

He got out of the car and came around to the passenger's side to open the door for Linda. "Hope you don't mind stairs. My apartment's on the top floor."

The apartment—a small kitchen, living room, bedroom, and bath—was in the rear of the building, overlooking a brick-walled garden. Steve unlocked the door for Linda and stepped aside to let her enter.

"It's very nice," Linda said, looking around. "But..."

she faltered, turning to stare at him, "how long have you been here?"

"Two years. Why do you ask?" Steve said as he helped her out of her suede jacket and hung it in the hall closet, along with his own coat.

"Well," Linda began, frowning, and then she burst out laughing. "Where's your furniture?"

Steve shrugged, looking around. The blue-carpeted living room had brick walls painted white. The room was bare except for some large pillows on the floor that were bracketed by a pair of orange crates holding lamps and ashtrays swiped from various nightclubs. Against one wall, on shelving built out of cinder blocks and planking, was a portable phonograph and a radio, along with a small collection of LPs.

"Well, furniture is kind of boring, you know?" Steve said. "I mean, you can't drive it or wear it. . . ."

Linda was laughing and shaking her head. He watched her cross the living room to the bedroom and peek in. He kept his fingers crossed as he came up behind her.

Yes! The bed—a big double mattress resting on a box spring—was freshly made, which meant that he'd changed the sheets. He confidently expected that he'd be changing them again before the day was over. . . .

Next to the bed was another orange crate, this one laden with another lamp, a swiped ashtray, and his alarm clock. Against the wall, between the closet and the bathroom door, was a maple lowboy he'd picked up secondhand at a shop on King Street. (It had been a bitch getting it upstairs, but he'd needed *someplace* to stick his clothes.) On the dresser was the telephone, and next to it, a local directory. Steve could see the cover of his little black book sticking out from beneath the directory, but he didn't think Linda would notice it.

"I've got to see the kitchen," she said.

Steve showed it to her.

"Just as I thought," she laughed, opening the pantry cupboards in the galley kitchen. Steve watched her discover an extensive selection of liquor and mixers, some glasses and coffee cups, two dinner plates, and no food or cooking equipment at all.

"I can make coffee," Steve said, "but most of the time I eat out."

"I'd pretty much guessed that about you, Cap'n," she said merrily. "Umm, I'd love a scotch and soda on the rocks."

"Two scotch and sodas coming up."

He fixed the drinks and brought them into the living room, where Linda was reclining on the stacked pillows. She'd kicked off her shoes and was smoking a cigarette. Steve set her drink on the orange crate, and settled down beside her with his own drink in his hand.

"Well," she said, picking up her drink and toasting him, "here's to a lovely day. Thanks again."

Steve sipped his scotch and soda as he watched her take a big swallow of her own drink. He wondered if she was trying to drink some courage. Was now the time to make his move?

He put his glass down and slid closer to her. She watched him as he took her drink out of her hand and kissed her lightly on the lips.

She kissed him back. Her lips were smoky from the scotch and cool from the ice cubes.

"Is this part of the tour?" she asked, feigning innocence.

"I did place myself at your service. . . ."

"And I did place myself in your hands. . . ."

Uh-huh, Steve thought. "Then I think we should continue this in the bedroom," he confided, standing up. "It's your kind of room."

"You mean it has some furniture?" Linda murmured, getting to her feet.

"All the furniture we'll need," Steve replied.

She grabbed her handbag. Steve picked up the drinks and led the way.

In the bedroom she said, "Let me just pop into the bathroom for a moment." As soon as she'd stepped inside, she began to laugh.

"What's so funny?" Steve called.

"Come in and see for yourself, Cap'n."

Steve went in. "Oh, no. . . ." he moaned, turning white as snow and then apple red.

On the medicine chest's mirrored door, outlined in scarlet lipstick, was a large heart. Scrawled within it was: *"I had a wonderful time last night. Call me! XXX Doreen."*

Steve tried to think fast. "Oops," he sighed helplessly, thinking sorrowfully of how last night's blonde had used the facilities just as her cab had arrived.

Linda pushed him out of the bathroom and closed the door. A minute or so later she came out. "Okay, Cap'n, let's see if you've got any gas left."

He undressed quickly. She needn't have worried about gas, he thought as he stepped out of his trousers and shucked off his briefs. His erection was bobbing as he watched her unbutton and remove her white blouse, then unzip and step out of her tweed skirt. She was wearing a pale blue brassiere and matching gartered panty girdle. His erection began to throb as she reached around to work the clasp that liberated her fabulous breasts, then bent at the waist in a pinup pose to unclasp her nylons and roll them down her shapely gams.

She smiled at him as she worked the zipper on her girdle, and then danced in place, wiggling out of the undergarment's binding confines. He grinned back. Watching them shimmy out of their girdles was a favorite part: kind of like the delicious wait while a present was shorn of its ornate wrappings on Christmas morning.

She'd wrestled the girdle past her thighs. Her curvy, pantied rump bounced free as she stepped out of it. Her panties were pink, trimmed with white lace. The colors reminded Steve of a strawberry ice cream sundae frothed with whipped cream. He knew where the cherry was.

Linda was about to skim off the panties. "Leave them on a minute" he suggested slyly.

"Oh, *ho!*" Linda smirked. "And you, an all-American war hero!" she pretended to scold.

Steve stretched out his arms. She ran, her lush breasts bobbing, into his embrace. Together they flopped onto the bed.

From the start he knew that sex with this one was going

to be different. He knew it from the way she didn't just lie back and let him have his way with her, like all the others. From the start Linda was his partner in passion, but she was also his opponent. She scratched and tussled right along with him, giving as good as she got as they rolled and turned on the big double bed.

When he had her good and ready for him, he reached into the bedside orange crate, where he kept his supply of foil packets of protection. She rolled the condom onto him, and then settled back on the mattress and spread her legs, guiding him into her. As they rocked together, they stared into each other's eyes, giggling in wonderment and awe, and maybe just a little fear.

When she reached her orgasm, she clutched at him, her arms around his neck and her thighs clasped around his waist. Her body went rigid and her back arched with incredible strength, lifting up all one hundred and seventy pounds of him. The roller-coaster ride she gave him brought on his own climax. He came moaning and growling, drowning in sensation, like a swimmer riding a wave that suddenly overpowers him. As he kicked and bucked, she was there for him, whispering endearments, assuring him that she could happily take all that he had to give.

After, for long ticks of the bedside clock, neither spoke a word. It was Linda, lying sweat-drenched in the crook of his arm, her short hair a damp, dark mop on his chest, who broke the silence.

"Tell me everything about you," she languidly commanded, her fingers idly trailing down the hard, flat plane of his belly to tangle themselves in his moist pubic hair. "Tell me everything from the moment you were born."

"The moment I was born was the day I learned how to fly," Steve said.

"You really love the Air Force, huh?"

Steve thought about it. "Love the Air Force? I don't know. For me the Air Force is home. It's family. I mean, it's like how somebody might feel about his *real* family. Sometimes you love your folks, and sometimes you hate them, but the bottom line is that you belong to them and they to you. I guess that's how I feel about the military. When the war ended, I decided that I wanted to make the Air Force my career. I tried to get assigned to a fighter squadron, but that didn't come through. Instead they offered me this desk job I've got now." He hesitated, blushing. "They said the fact that I'm supposed to be a war hero—"

"Not supposed to be," Linda interrupted. "You *are*."

"Well anyway, they offered me this public relations job, I guess, so they could trot me out as a propaganda weapon in the battle with the Navy over control of the nation's air power."

"Come on, you're too hard on yourself," Linda chided him, tousling his short cut, thick blonde hair. "I'm sure you do a great job."

"No," Steve sighed, shaking his head. "The truth is I haven't got the faintest idea what I'm doing. Not that they ask all that much of me," he added cynically.

"But they've kept you at it for two years now," Linda argued.

"Sure, but I'm still a captain, same rank as when the war ended," Steve pointed out. "Nope, I told you what I am. A propaganda weapon. Once in a while there's a hearing like the one presently going on. When that happens, I'm trotted out like a champion hunting dog, except that now the hunt's over." He sighed. "Basically I'm living off my past."

She smiled. "Sounds like you miss the war."

"Can I tell you a secret?"

"Yes, Cap'n."

"Promise not to tell?"

She lightly crossed her left breast. "Cross my heart."

"Here, let me do that." He rolled on top of her and used his tongue to trace a wet X across her breast. Her dark brown nipple, glistened by his saliva, swelled to meet his lips.

"Hmmm," she sighed. "That feels good, but I'm waiting for your secret."

Steve lifted his head to look into her eyes. "The war was the finest time of my life," he said. "Okay, so now you know. You being a woman, you're probably horrified."

She shook her head.

"Come on," Steve scoffed. "Even my best buddy during the war thought I was nuts when I told him."

"Well, I don't you're nuts at all," she said adamantly. "Fact is, I feel the same way as you."

"You feel the same way as me?"

She nodded. "This puff piece I'm writing for Amalgamated is easy work, and it pays a mint, but I don't intend to spend my life writing this sort of fluff."

"What do you want to write? A novel?"

Linda chuckled. "No. I told you that I've worked on newspapers? Well, what I really want to do is be a journalist." Her voice grew dreamy. "Maybe a foreign correspondent for an important newspaper. I had a little taste of it during the war. Thanks to the draft and the civilian man-power shortage, I got the chance to do some hard reporting. I don't mean society-page stuff," she added. "I mean *real journalism*." She signed. "Of course, when the war ended and the boys came home, I got demoted back to the garden club beat. I wasn't interested in that, so I quit."

"So you want to be a correspondent, huh?" Steve said doubtfully.

"Yeah." She stretched to reach over the edge of the bed for her purse. She rummaged through it for her cigarettes.

"You mean kind of like Lois Lane?"

"Yeah," she laughed.

"I dunno," Steve said.

"And why don't you?" she demanded as she lit up one of her Chesterfields.

"I just can't imagine reading a woman reporter's writing and thinking that she knew what she was talking about," Steve said. "I mean, because she's a woman," he added innocently. "No offense."

"Hmmm, no offense, eh?" Linda growled with eyes narrowed as she exhaled smoke. "Don't bother me. I'm counting to ten, *slowly*."

Steve reached out to fondle her breasts. She pulled away, but teasingly. Steve knew she wasn't really mad. "Aw, come on," he cajoled. "Baby Blue Eyes."

"What?" she pouted.

Steve took the cigarette from her and took a puff. "Are you Don Harrison's girl?"

She seemed startled by the question. "No . . . I'm my own girl, Cap'n Steve." She grinned. "Hey, you big lug, did you think that Don and I had something between us?"

"I was afraid that you did, but now I'm relieved," Steve smoothly said.

But he was lying. He wasn't relieved at all.

What he'd felt with Linda had been frightening in its intensity. Sure, it had thrilled him, but it had also scared the crap out of him. He was used to loving 'em and leaving 'em, but this one . . . Well, if he wasn't careful, she was going to leave her mark on him.

"Don is a great guy," Linda said. "He's a gentleman and all, but he's a little too cerebral for me."

"Huh?" Steve had been brooding and was too preoccupied to listen.

"Nothing," she chuckled. "All I was saying is that Don isn't my type."

"No? Who is?"

"You is, Cap'n." She chucked him under the chin as she plucked the cigarette he'd swiped from her from between his lips. "You're my type, all right." She took a puff off the smoke, dropped it into the ashtray, and then stretched out full-length on top of him and began to kiss him.

This is going to be trouble, Steve realized. He was going to have to figure out a way to give her the brushoff. He wasn't ready to fall in love, no matter how good it felt.

She was nibbling on his lower lip. Her breasts were pressing against his chest. He palmed the firm cheeks of her wiggly rump as she rubbed herself against his groin.

Later, he thought he felt himself swelling into the warm, wet fur between her thighs. *I can always give her the brushoff later. . . .*

It was a little after five in the afternoon. Steve was wearing a terry-cloth robe. His hair was still wet from the shower, and his groin was aching pleasurably. He was on the telephone, calling around, trying to get a dinner reservation for this evening. So far he'd called three places, but they were all booked. He wanted to take Linda somewhere that was tops, but it wasn't easy booking a table someplace like that at the last minute on a Saturday night.

Saturday night, Steve thought, wincing. The redhead from the office. He'd totally forgotten about it, but he already had a date for tonight!

He glanced at the closed bathroom door. Linda was taking a shower. He could hear the water still running.

Thank God.

He hauled out his little black book and riffled through the pages until he found the redhead's number. He dialed it. *Please, please be home,* he thought.

She answered. He immediately began coughing and wheezing as he launched into a bullshit story about a sudden cold and how sorry he was about breaking their date at the last moment.

The redhead sounded icy, but he thought that she bought his cock-and-bull story. As he was hanging up, he heard Linda say from behind him, "You really shouldn't have done that."

He whirled around. She was wrapped in a towel, standing in the bathroom doorway. The shower was still running, but she didn't look as if she'd gotten wet.

"How much of that did you hear?" Steve asked weakly.

"All of it. I was about to step into the shower when I realized that I'd left my purse with my hairbrush out here."

"Well," he shrugged, grinning sheepisly. "It's done. Now we can spend the evening together."

Linda shook her head. "I'm sorry, Cap'n, but, you see, I already have a date for tonight."

That hit him like a ton of bricks. "But—I thought after dinner tonight we could come back here for a brandy, and..." He trailed off, gesturing to the telephone. *"You* could suddenly catch a cold as well." He tried to make a joke out of it. "There's a lot of that going around."

"I can't. I'm really sorry, Cap'n, but I can't."

Steve stared at her. *I don't believe this,* he thought, stung and feeling foolish. *She's giving me the brush-off.*

She saw his upset look. "Look, what we had this afternoon was swell, but I don't want you to start carrying a torch for me. I mean, you're a nice boy—"

"Stop it!" he abruptly shouted.

"Stop what?" she asked, looking mystified.

"Calling me a boy! You keep doing it, and I don't like it!"

Linda smiled slightly. Her eyes searched his. "Honey, how old do you think I am?"

Steve pondered it. Women were touchy about this sort of crap. "Twenty-five?"

She shook her head, laughing. "You are a very sweet b—Oops! I mean, a very sweet *man,* but I'm thirty years old."

Wow, Steve thought, shaken. She was even older than his big sister, and Suze had already been married and had herself a toddler.

He kept staring at Linda in disbelief. He didn't know what to say.

Her laughter faded. "Well, the water's running. I'll go take my shower."

Steve was dressed and waiting when she came out of the bathroom wrapped in a towel. Her skin glowed from the hot shower spray. She'd put her hair up to keep it dry, but a few dampened tendrils had escaped to frame her lovely face.

"I'll drive you back to the hotel," he said as she began to get dressed.

"No, thanks. I'll take a cab," she replied.

He nodded. "A drink before you go?"

"I don't think so."

He nodded again, and went to the telephone. The cab company said that a car would be there in a few minutes.

Steve watched her finish dressing. They were both quiet.

He wondered if she felt as awkward as he felt. The doorbell, when it rang, made them both jump.

"Well," Linda said brightly.

"This date you've got tonight . . ." Steve began gruffly.

She held up her hand to stop him. "It's with a California newspaper editor in Washington for the hearings. Tim Campbell introduced me to him the other day."

"Is it strictly business, or . . . is it pleasure?"

"A little of both, I'd say," Linda replied evenly. "He might offer me a job."

"On his newspaper?"

"Yes."

"And you'd probably sleep with him to get it, wouldn't you?" Steve accused. He instantly regretted his words. He'd just met her. Who was he to act so jealous?

Linda glared at him. "Who the hell do you think you are to say that to me, you bastard! That's a terrible thing to say!"

"But is it true?"

"Go to hell!" she spat at him, her eyes flashing blue flame. "And what if I *did* sleep with him for a job! What of it? I know what I want for myself in this man's world, and I intend to get it, and if sometimes being a woman is a disadvantage and sometimes it's an advantage, *what of it?*"

"You're such a wiseacre," Steve sulked.

"Don't give me too much credit for brains," she muttered, grabbing her purse and lighting a cigarette. "I said *you* were my type, didn't I?"

"Dammit! I don't want you to go!"

She nodded. "I know. And part of *me* doesn't want me to go. That's the major reason why I'm going."

"I don't get that," he complained angrily.

"Yeah, you do," she said quietly, exhaling smoke.

Steve glanced at her. "Well, maybe I do." Looking at her, he couldn't suppress a smile. "You're one tough dame."

"Tough as nails," Linda agreed. She winked at him. "Tough as you, and that's no lie."

The doorbell jangled insistently. On her way out she

paused to kiss Steve on the cheek. "See you in the funny pages, Cap'n."

"'Bye, Baby Blue Eyes."

She left the bedroom. Steve listened to her cross the apartment and open the closet to fetch her coat. Then he heard the click of the front door as she let herself out.

"Wow," he told the empty room.

He was on his way out of the bedroom when he happened to glance into the bathroom. He laughed out loud.

Linda had used her lipstick to cross out Doreen's name and insert her own. After *"Call Me"* Linda has inserted her Los Angeles telephone number.

Steve fetched his little black book and carefully copied the number down. He knew he'd be calling it one of these days.

"Tough as nails," she'd bragged to him. *"Tough as you."*

An older woman . . . son of a bitch.

CHAPTER 9

(One)

Gold Household
Bel-Air, California
4 August 1948

"Son, I'd hoped that you would have come to your senses by now," Herman Gold murmured into the telephone.

"Why do you look at it that way, Pop?" Gold could clearly hear Steven's angry tone above the hiss and crackle of the transcontinental telephone wire. "Why do you insist on viewing my decision to make a career in the Air Force as some form of temporary insanity on my part?"

"Because I know where you belong—" Gold began.

"Oh, is that right?" Steve demanded, sounding sarcastic. "*You* know where *I* belong? And where's that? As your office boy?"

Gold struggled not to lose patience with his son. Anger only made things worse between them. "I would never have you be an office boy, and you know it. I'd give you a good position at GAT. A responsible, respectable job—"

"As your lackey," Steven cut him off.

"No! As my assistant!" Gold said, his voice rising.

"Oh, sure," Steven laughed. "Assisting you in *what*? Answer me this, Pop. If I wasn't your son, and my résumé came across your desk, would you hire me *then*?"

"But—but *you are* my son." Gold evaded.

"That's what I thought," Steve said, sounding weary. "Thanks, Pop, but no thanks."

"Okay," Gold sighed. "Have it your way. But you yourself have told me how unsatisfied you are stuck in Air Force public relations."

"Pop, I'm working on something for myself," Steve said.

"A promotion?" Gold asked eagerly. "You've been a captain a long time now, son."

"I *know* that."

Gold heard the cold, flat tone. *He's feeling bad enough about his stalled career. He doesn't need his father rubbing salt in the wound.* "Don't get me wrong," Gold said hastily, trying to repair the damage. "You'll always be tops in my book."

Gold was gratified to hear Steven chuckle. *Damn*, Gold thought sadly. *When he was a little boy it was always a snap for me to get him to laugh.*

"Pop, don't sweat it. Like I said, I'm working on something. . . ." He trailed off.

"Can't you tell me what you have in mind?" Gold asked, intrigued.

"It's going to take some time," Steven said evasively. "I don't want to tell you any more about it right now."

"Okay. All right," Gold said, disappointed. "But I don't understand why you have to expend so much energy working on *creating* something for yourself when everything you could want is right here waiting for you."

"Pop, I've got to hang up now."

"Yeah, sure," Gold said softly. "Stevie," he hesitated. "I . . ."

"Talk to you soon, Pop."

". . . love you—" Gold told the dial tone. As usual, a hundred different things to tell his son flooded into Gold's mind. Why couldn't he ever think of the damned things while Steve was still on the line?

He hung up the telephone and lay back on the big circular bed, to stare up at the cherubs cavorting across the bedroom's painted ceiling. It was just seven in the morning. What with the time difference between the coasts, Steven found it most convenient to call home early.

The bedroom Gold shared his wife reflected her tastes. The French doors leading out to the balcony were framed in draperies of embroidered, emerald satin. Mirrors gilded in honey gold reflected ebony wall paneling inlaid with floral bouquets carved from ivory and rosewood. The room's scrolled, gilt-bronze furniture reposed on lion's paws upon the plush ivy-green carpeting.

What Erica had spent down through the years just on interior decorating this house was more than they had paid in total for their first home, Gold thought. But what the hell; they had the money.

He thought about how Steven liked to make all of his long-distance calls from his Pentagon office in order to save money. *He wouldn't have to worry about finances if he came to work at GAT,* Gold brooded. *And I wouldn't have to worry about our estrangement.*

Father and son had traveled a rocky road since Steven had entered manhood. The battle over the boy's destiny had begun back when Steve was still in high school. Gold had insisted that his son pursue the goal of a college education, but Steve had defied him by running away from home when he was barely seventeen. Gold had hired private detectives to track his son, but the gumshoes had lost the kid when he'd lied about his age and used a phony name to volunteer for service with the Flying Tigers in China. Gold had managed to find Steve and bring him home, and there'd been a reconciliation between them when Gold had accepted the fact that his son intended to serve as a fighter pilot. That uneasy truce had ended with the war. Gold had assumed that when the fighting ended his son would settle down into a career at GAT.

He'd assumed wrong. Gold had never been so disappointed as on that day back in the fall of 1945 when Steve had informed him that he'd decided to make a career of the Air Force. Since then, Gold tried to understand that Steve wanted to be his own man, but he could not totally suppress his bitterness over the way his only son had so harshly and easily rejected everything he'd spent his life building.

Gold got out of bed and headed for the shower. As he passed a mirror, he stopped to gaze at himself. He looked drawn and tired standing there sleepy-eyed in his rumpled pajamas. There were deep lines etched into his face. His day-old beard and what was left of his red hair were flecked with white.

Fifty years old, he thought. *Old enough to stop kidding myself; to know that I'm not going to be here forever.*

Old enough to accept the fact that Steve was not going to come into the business. Gold had no other sons. He had to wonder who would carry on as leader of GAT. What was the point of all his hard work if control of GAT was destined to pass into some other man's—a stranger's—hands?

Gold showered and shaved and dressed for the office in a gray linen double-breasted suit, black leather loafers, maize cotton shirt, and a maroon and yellow foulard-patterned silk tie. He went downstairs to find his wife and daughter just finishing breakfast in the screened veranda off the kitchen.

Large potted palms stood guard in the corners of the veranda's gray slate floor. A slowly revolving fan suspended from the teak ceiling stirred the morning breeze. The veranda looked out on a fragrant flower garden. The splashing pink marble fountain was framed by a whitewashed arbor draped with purple wisteria.

Erica was sipping her coffee as Gold came into the room.

She was wearing a plum-colored satin dressing gown. Her blonde hair was down around her shoulders.

"Good morning, darling," she murmured as Gold came around the table to give her a kiss. "I thought Steve sounded good this morning, didn't you?"

"Hmm," Gold grunted noncommittally. Erica had always sided with Steve against him. He loved his wife dearly, but sometimes it got on his nerves the way she persisted in the crazy notion that their son was right in resisting Gold's efforts to bring him into the business.

"Hi, Daddy," Gold's daughter, Susan, greeted him. Suzy was twenty-six. Like her brother, she had Erica's coloring. This morning her blonde hair was twisted up into a bun. She was dressed for work in a gray skirt and white blouse.

"Hi, Grandpa!" Gold's grandson, Robert, was on the floor peeking out from beneath the table beside Erica's chair.

"Hi, kiddo!" Gold stooped down to give Robert a hug and a kiss. The boy was barefoot, wearing blue shorts and a white polo shirt. "Where's your shoes?" he asked jovially.

"Don't need 'em!" the boy boasted. Almost six years old, Robert was the spitting image of his late father—handsome, with eyes the color of emeralds, and thick coal-black hair. "I'm goin' to the beach, Grandpa!"

"Wish I could go," Gold moped exaggeratedly.

"Why can't ya?" Robert demanded, his face scrunching up in concern.

"Grandpa has to go to work," Susan answered absently. "Just like Mommy," she murmured, her brown eyes intently scanning the sports page of the morning newspaper.

As Gold straightened up from his grandson in order to give his daughter a good-morning peck on the cheek, he glanced at the sports headlines. They were all about the upcoming summer Olympics in London, the first such games since Jesse Owens's 1936 triumph in Berlin.

As usual, the news and business sections of the paper were by Gold's place setting. He scanned them as the new girl they'd hired to assist Ramona, the housekeeper, came out of the kitchen to pour him coffee.

The front page had stories on the continuing political

mess that was the presidential campaign, the turmoil in the Mideast as the fledgling state of Israel skirmished with the Egyptians in the desert, and the ongoing Berlin airlift. The business section had an in-depth article concerning where the presidential challengers—the Republican Thomas Dewey, the States' Rights Dixiecrat candidate Strom Thurmond, and the Progressive Party's Henry Wallace—stood on the Taft-Hartley union-busting law. In the article all the candidates took the opportunity to attack the incumbent Truman, who was in the midst of a valiant but probably doomed whistle-stop campaign to save his presidency. Truman's strategy so far in the election was to blast the Republican Congress for doing nothing, and to attack Taft-Hartley as a setback for the American working man.

There was also an article in the business section on the windfall profits being enjoyed by various companies leasing transport equipment to the military for the duration of the airlift. GAT, for example, had leased some MT-37 cargo planes to the Air Force. Accordingly, Gold had been interviewed for the article.

Gold was happy to see that the reporter who'd written the article had kept her promise to treat GAT kindly. He had initially been reluctant to cooperate with the reporter. From past experience he'd learned to be wary of the media, and in this specific instance he'd worried that it might put GAT in a bad light if the public knew the company was profiting from the Berlin crisis. He'd agreed to the interview only as a favor to Steve. It seemed that his son was close friends with the wire service correspondent, a young woman named Linda Forrest. According to Steve, Miss Forrest was just beginning a new job at World Press. Steve felt getting an exclusive with Herman Gold would be just the boost this particular assignment—and her career—needed.

"Daddy, I'm going to drive my own car to work this morning," Susan said as the nanny came in to collect Robert. "I've got a lot of work piled up on my desk, and I want to tackle it before the phones start ringing."

Gold watched admiringly as his daughter scooped up

Robert, lifting the giggling boy high in the air before giving him a kiss good-bye. His daughter was a big, strong girl.

"Remember," Susan warned the nanny as she set down her son. "Not too much sun for him today. I don't want him coming home red as a lobster, like last time."

"Yes, Mrs. Greene," the nanny said.

"Good-bye, Mommy, good-bye, Grampa, good-bye, Gramma," Robert called gaily as the nanny carried him out of the room.

"Another fifteen years and *he* can come into the business," Gold muttered.

Both Erica and Suzy burst out laughing. Gold immediately blushed. He hadn't realized that he'd been thinking out loud.

"Poor Daddy!" Susan said sympathetically. "I'm so sorry that your talks with Steven upset you so."

Gold, frowning, waited until Suzy had left the veranda. "Working all day and taking those art courses at UCLA at night . . . I don't think she's spending enough time with Robert."

"Oh, Herman," Erica chided affectionately, "we've been through all this countless times."

"I know," Gold moped as Ramona, the matronly servant who ran the household, came in with his bacon and eggs. His mood momentarily lightened. Ramona was the only person in the world who could cook eggs just the way he liked them. A few months ago, with his pants getting tight in the waist, he'd put himself on a diet: bacon and eggs for breakfast only every third day, fruit and wheat toast the rest of the week. Normally he looked forward to his big breakfasts, but this morning he had no appetite.

He stared at his wife. "I still think you're defending Suzy because it was your idea that she go to work."

"I just thought that if Suzy began to get out and around, meeting new people—*new men*," Erica emphasized, "she would come out of her shell."

"I know, I know. You meant well, and I agreed with you at the time," Gold admitted.

Suzy and the baby had moved back in with them in December 1942, just after her husband, Blaize Greene, an RAF fighter ace, was killed in action. Blaize and Susan had been married just over a year, and his death had left her emotionally shattered. If it hadn't been for the baby, Suzy might have gone completely to pieces, but the responsibilities of motherhood helped her to pull herself together. About a year later, Erica came up with the bright idea that Gold should offer Suzy a job at GAT.

Suzy had been enthusiastic when Gold had offered her a position. Like a lot of women, she'd felt that going to work during wartime in a defense-oriented industry was the patriotic thing to do. Suzy had some secretarial skills from finishing school, so Gold put her to work as a secretary in Teddy Quinn's Engineering Research and Design Department. Eventually she'd moved up in the department to become Teddy's personal secretary.

"I've started to think your strategy has backfired," Gold complained to Erica as he picked at his breakfast. "I asked her the other day why a beautiful girl like her wasn't dating when there were so many eligible men around. You know what she told me? That with work and school she didn't have the time!"

Erica frowned. "You think that she's using the job and her night school courses as an excuse to keep men at arm's length?"

"That's right," Gold replied. "She keeps herself busy, and that way she doesn't have to think about the fact that she's determined to be a widow for the rest of her life."

Erica shook her head. "I still think she has a better chance of running into the man who might snap her out of it by being out and around, instead of staying home with Robert all day."

"And what about Robert?" Gold demanded irritably. "Is *he* better off?"

Erica shrugged off his question. "What about *you*?" she countered, quietly scrutinizing him.

"Huh? What do you mean?"

"You know as well as I do that Robert is doing just fine. The question is, what has put *you* in this foul mood?"

"Who says I'm in a foul mood?" Gold said defiantly.

"For one thing, you haven't stopped growling like a bear since you came downstairs. For another, it's bacon-and-eggs day, but you're not eating."

Gold looked down at his plate. He'd nibbled most of the bacon, but the two untouched sunny-side-up eggs were staring back at him accusingly. He pushed away the plate. "Okay, okay, so maybe I'm not in such a great mood today."

"What's wrong?" Erica paused. "Suzy was right, wasn't she? It *was* your conversation with Steve, wasn't it? Did you two get into another argument once I was off the line?"

Gold shrugged. "Not another argument, the *same* argument." He paused while the new maid came in to pour them both more coffee and take away his plate. "Every time it's the same thing. I swear to myself that I'm not going to bring up the matter of his coming into the business, that I'll leave the entire subject alone and keep the peace." He shook his head sorrowfully. "But then, while we're talking, my mind starts to play tricks on me. I want so badly for him to change his mind that I start to think I'm hearing that he *has* changed his mind, but that he's too proud to tell me. *Then* I think that if I make the offer again, this time he'll *accept*." He sighed. "But, of course, he doesn't accept, and I hear that sarcastic tone in his voice, and it pushes my buttons, and then we're off and running."

"All I can tell you is that it's the same thing from his side," Erica said. "He doesn't want to fight with you, but he's just as helpless as you to avoid the arguments."

"How do you know that?" Gold asked sharply.

"He tells me."

"Great," Gold muttered. "You'd think he'd tell me something once in a while," he trailed off, shaking his head.

"This is a difficult time for him, too, you know," Erica said. "We both can read between the lines, Herman. We know it's not all peaches and cream for him in the Air Force. He's not happy stuck where he is."

Gold nodded. "He said he's working on something for himself, but he was vague." He eyed his wife. "Did he tell *you* about it?"

Erica shook her head. "Only that he wants it to be a surprise."

"Maybe it's a big promotion," Gold fantasized. "Or maybe he's going to be reassigned as an aide to a general. A couple of years doing something like *that* would give him the confidence he needs to come to work at GAT," he added wistfully.

"Herman," Erica said in warning.

"Okay, okay," Gold surrendered. "You know, as much as I want him working with *me*, at least I'm grateful that he's safe and sound at a desk job in Washington, and not risking his neck flying fighters."

Erica laughed. "You make it sound like we're still at war."

"Well, look at what's going on in Berlin," Gold pointed out. "You don't think our SAC interceptor squadrons in Europe aren't on alert in case the Reds try something? And even in peacetime fighter squadrons fly practice maneuvers, you know. And accidents happen."

"Stop!" Erica complained. "Herman, you *are* in a black mood talking like that! I swear, if this keeps up I'm not going to *let* you talk to Steven anymore."

"It's not just Steven," Gold said, shrugging.

"Then what?"

"Ah . . ." He made a face. "I've got a luncheon meeting with some big shots from Air Force Procurement today. They've flown in for a few days to meet with the various contractors. Maybe I'm a little worried about it."

"Is it about the BroadSword?"

Gold shook his head. "It's about a new design for a bomber we've come up with. These guys have had our proposal for months, but we haven't heard a thing from them."

"I'm sure they're going to buy lots of your bombers, darling."

Gold chuckled. "You know, you're pretty cute when you talk like that." He glanced at his watch. "I'd better get going," he said, standing up. "I've got a ton of things to do at the office."

"Just remember," Erica smiled, "you had butterflies in

your belly the day you pitched your first airplane, and you probably always will."

"Hmm, you're so smart," Gold murmured, coming around to kiss her.

"Hmm, I know," Erica said, kissing him back. "Go sell your airplanes, and then come home to me and we'll celebrate."

"Champagne?" Gold asked.

"Uh-huh."

"Caviar?"

"But of course."

"Wanton lovemaking?"

Erica pretended to ponder. "It depends on how large an order the Air Force gives you."

"Then it shall be for a vast air armada," Gold declared.

"Don't make promises you can't keep," Erica laughed.

"Whose fleets shall darken the skies."

"You'd better call before you leave for home tonight, so I can turn down the covers and put on perfume."

"Just make sure you perfume all of my favorite places."

"And where, pray tell, might those be?"

Gold winked at her. "How big a bottle of that stuff have you got?"

It was a sunny morning, so Gold put the top down on the scarlet, Cadillac Series 62 convertible for the drive to Burbank. With its 150-horsepower V-8 engine, the convertible wasn't the biggest or most expensive Caddy out of Detroit, but it was the only one the company made.

He'd bought the car last year, as soon as the '47s had come out, and had it shipped directly from the showroom to the company that did the interiors for his airliners. He'd had them gut the Caddy's interior along with its bench seating for six, and install new carpeting, burled walnut inserts for the dashboard and inside door panels, and a single pair of custom-built, thronelike bucket seats upholstered in cream-colored leather—the same kind used in the first-class sections of his Monarch GC series. The customized interior made the Caddy a better car, but it was still not a great car.

Nevertheless, Gold figured to stick with it until somebody somewhere began selling a vehicle designed for serious driving.

Gold usually enjoyed threading in and out of traffic, giving the Caddy a workout as he made a game out of trying to get to the office in the shortest possible time, but this morning he was content to motor sedately with the stop-and-go traffic. He figured he was going to need all of his energy and competitiveness for his upcoming lunchtime encounter with the tightfisted skeptics from Air Force Procurement.

Gold thought about his exchange with Erica just before he'd left. He wished that he felt as confident about selling his new bomber as he'd pretended.

Gold rapped the Caddy's walnut dashboard. *Knock on wood the deal making today goes as smoothly as the negotiations went concerning the BroadSword....*

For the past few years GAT research and design had been advancing on two separate fronts. The first front concerned the development of a jet fighter.

Back in 1945, the grateful United States government had kept to its part of the bargain in exchange for Gold's having rescued Heiner Froehlig and his six aeronautical wunderkinder from the Russians. Directly after the Germans had been reunited stateside with their families who had been brought out of the Allied-held sectors of Berlin, they'd been hidden away in a top-secret compound at Muroc Air Base in the Mojave Desert about seventy miles northeast of Los Angeles.

Once settled, the Germans were instructed to cooperate with GAT in its USAF-authorized and -funded preliminary research for a jet fighter. Gold's chief engineer, Teddy Quinn, and a hand-picked team practically moved in with the Germans to expedite the work. Gold held down the fort at GAT, and began the laborious process of translating from German into English the wealth of microfilmed research data concerning the aerodynamics of high-speed flight that Froehlig had brought with him out of the Berlin Air Ministry.

For the next sixteen months the American-German team

worked on Gold's original swept-wing design: essentially the concept that Gold had conceived while watching his wife swimming in their pool back in '43. A swept-wing model, dubbed the Experimental-Pursuit (XP) 90, was built. Wind tunnel tests proved that the swept-wing concept was fast. Unfortunately, the new concept created an equally new and frustrating problem. The tests revealed that swept wings were unstable at *low* speeds; an airplane so equipped would have a totally unacceptable tendency to stall.

Froehlig's people were familiar with the problem, and had previously warned the Americans about it. They had encountered the low-speed instability phenomenon during their R&D on the legendary World War II Messerschmitt 262 jet fighter. The Germans had, in fact, abandoned their hopes for a fully swept-wing Me 262 because they could find no workable solution to the problem.

Things were looking bleak at GAT the winter of 1946. The Air Force had placed large orders for Lockheed's P-80 Shooting Star, and the Navy was going with Grumman's proposed Panther jet fighter bomber. Because neither plane was a swept-wing design, there was a lot of self-doubt at GAT, a lot of talk of abandoning what looked like yet another dead-end concept.

Gold, however, was adamant that swept wing was the way to go. While the German-American team collectively tore out its hair, Gold spent his days administrating at GAT, his evenings locked in his study at home, translating Froehlig's smuggled documents. It was while he was translating an almost overlooked appendix to some research on the Me 262 that he came across a hastily scrawled sketch for a slat, or movable surface, that could be set into a swept wing's *leading* edge. The sketch had a brief, scribbled notation suggesting that when the plane was moving at low speeds, the slat would open to give more lift to the wing. As speed picked up, the slat would retract.

The drawing was unsigned. Neither Froehlig nor any of the other Germans recognized it. It was little more than a doodle in a margin, but something about it appealed to Gold. It was just the kind of quick sketch that he'd used to make back when he was a young man and a blank sheet of drafting paper had seemed a glorious challenge, not fraught with peril and the threat of failure.

The Germans warned Gold that the Me 262's wings had been equipped with a version of this leading-edge slat, and the results had been mixed. They were doubtful that the slat concept would lead to anything, but Gold had a hunch. He ordered that time and money be expended on the idea.

And so GAT had picked up where the Germans had left off. A German may have conceived the idea, but it took good old American know-how to turn the concept's potential into reality. Teddy Quinn and his band of crew-cut, slide-rule-wielding sorcerer's apprentices captured the dream on graph paper. GAT's production line built a working sample.

By New Year's Day 1947, a new XP-90 model equipped with leading-edge wing slats proved itself a winner in wind tunnel tests, thanks in part to a kid on the production line who earned himself a bonus and a big promotion by suggesting a new approach to dive brakes. Instead of trying to fit them onto the already overburdened wings, the kid came up with the bright idea of doors which could be fanned out from the lower side of the jet's rear fuselage. The brakes seemed to work perfectly on the model, promising to afford the XP-90 the ability to stop on the proverbial dime.

GAT had gone as far as it could go with models. It was time to build a full-scale prototype. Gold took his test data to the Air Force, which was impressed and authorized the necessary funding to build three airplanes.

GAT's labs and assembly lines went to work around the clock. As always, the prototypes were built around a power plant supplied by the San Diego–based engine-producing firm of Rogers & Simpson. It was an improved version of the nose air intake jet engine that had powered the XP-4, GAT's early, ill-fated first attempt at a jet fighter. Gold had always believed that the problems with the XP-4 had been due to its aeronautical design, not its reliable R&S engine.

The prototypes rolled off the assembly lines in May 1947. On May 12 at Muroc, GAT's senior test pilot took the first prototype up for the first time.

Gold and Erica had been there, squinting up into the blazing California sun, nervously watching along with a hundred skeptical pairs of eyes from Air Force Procurement as the XP-90 soared over the dried-up lake beds and Joshua trees of the desert.

The XP-90 flew for an hour. For Gold it had been a nerve-racking ordeal. Erica had held his hand, keeping him calm by amusing him with memories of how it had been back on that day in November 1926 when *she* had flown the first ever GAT airplane prototype, the open-cockpit G-1 Yellowjacket mail plane. She reminded him how she had flown that test flight in order to convince the purchasing agents from the post office that the G-1 was so good that "even a woman" could fly it. The stunt had worked. The post office had bought hundreds of G-1s. It was that bonanza influx of revenue which became the financial bedrock on which Gold had built his company.

Now, as the Caddy crept along with the rest of the traffic past the industrial complexes and tract housing developments of Burbank, Gold's mind skipped across the decades from the Yellowjacket's test flight to that sunlit morning on May 12, 1947, when he'd listened to the XP-90's banshee howl and watched it streak like a silver arrow across the pale blue desert sky.

How bittersweet to remember Erica in her oversized shearling flying suit. How triumphantly she had waved to Gold from the Yellowjacket's open cockpit.

Those days are long gone, Gold thought as he joined the back end of a line of cars waiting for a traffic light to change. The complexity of the XP-90's instrument panel stood in mute witness to the fact that the time had long since passed since either Gold or his wife had the technical expertise to pilot the planes his company built.

A blaring horn snapped Gold out of his reveries. The traffic light had changed. The guy behind him in a dark green Studebaker stuck his head out the window and yelled, "Move it, mac!" Gold put the Caddy in gear and stepped on the gas.

For three months the XP-90 prototypes were flown by

military test pilots, all of whom gave the airplane glowing evaluations. Convinced, the Air Force ordered an initial fifty. Gold dubbed his fighter the BroadSword, due to its stubby, snub-nosed configuration and, hopefully, in anticipation of its battle prowess.

Meanwhile, Rogers & Simpson made further assembly line modifications on the engines they were shipping to GAT. The new engine had almost twice as much thrust as the power plant used in the XP prototype, giving the Broad-Sword a top speed approaching seven hundred miles per hour.

The first batch of production line BroadSwords had been delivered to the Air Force in June. The airplanes had been redesignated as F-90s to comply with the Air Force's new regulation replacing P for "pursuit" with F for "fighter."

Since then, the Air Force had ordered two hundred more BroadSwords. That was just the first of many such orders, Gold knew, and when the international climate was right, he was certain that the United States would license the sale of the BroadSword to friendly governments all over the world.

Gold had felt it in his bones from the day Teddy Quinn had unscrolled the initial blueprints for the XP-90: the airplane was a winner.

Gold had been right when he'd told his disheartened design team not to fret over the fact that the United States military had placed large orders for fighters with GAT's competitors. The old rule he'd learned through a lifetime spent in this business still held. It was not important to be first, but to be the best.

That same rule was guiding Gold concerning GAT's second front: the endeavor to enter the market with a viable commercial jet airliner.

The dawning of the jet age had turned the airlines jittery. They were all behaving like horny virgins: impatient to spread their legs, but at the same time reluctant, afraid of the possible consequences of risking their money and reputations on unproven jet designs that might prove costly to maintain and dangerous to fly.

Gold had to give credit to Stoat-Black. The British firm

had from the very first been aware of the airline industry's timid mind-set. Hugh Luddy, SB's chief engineer, had taken even longer on research and design than the two years he'd projected when the bearded Scot had first told Gold about the SB-100 Starstreak jetliner back in '44. Today, Stoat-Black's painstaking testing program was the talk of the industry. The Starstreak, not even scheduled to begin rolling off the production lines until 1950, was benefiting from advance promotion as the most efficient and fail-safe airplane —jet or piston powered—in aviation history.

The European airlines had been convinced, and had lined up to place their advance orders for the Starstreak, provided, of course, that the jetliner lived up to its advance billing. So far, the American airlines had resisted, adopting a wait-and-see attitude, but Stoat-Black was indifferent to the cool reception on this side of the Atlantic. Once the production lines were tooled, it was going to take the company several years just to fill its European back orders.

As a matter of fact, Hugh Luddy had recently contacted Gold to gloatingly suggest that GAT might want to make a bid on a subcontract to manufacture the Starstreak for the American market. Left unsaid in the exchange had been Luddy's clear opinion that Gold had been a fool not to come into the project as an equal partner when he'd had the chance.

It's not about being the first, but being the best, Gold reminded himself. But on some days, the rule was harder to believe than on others.

The BroadSword's success was a tremendous load off Gold's mind, but if GAT was to remain an industry leader, it needed to reestablish its mastery in the commercial aviation field. GAT had long ago grown too fat to thrive on military business alone.

There was still time for GAT to compete with Stoat-Black, at least for the American market. A lot would depend on Gold's luncheon meeting with the boys in blue from Air Force Procurement.

As the BroadSword's costly and lengthy genesis had proven, the time had passed when even a company as enormously wealthy as GAT could afford to bankroll its own R&D. The postwar costs of sheparding a new airplane from the drafting table to the prototype had vastly increased. Jets required pioneering research on metallurgy, more complex electronics, and advanced noise supression. It all cost big, big money.

The BroadSword had taken three years, and had cost over six million dollars to bring into existence. GAT—keeping in mind its duty to its stockholders—could never have gambled so much on a single roll of the dice without mitigating its risk by receiving advance USAF funding. At present cost levels, the expense of developing a single airplane could bankrupt a company if that airplane turned out to be unsuccessful.

Stoat-Black, for example, had spent almost ten million dollars on the Starstreak, and SB's own cost projections were predicting that the total would be closer to fifteen million before the first SB-100 rolled off the assembly lines almost a decade after the project's beginning. Stoat-Black could never have made the commitment without being bankrolled by the British government, which had also promised a bailout should the project end up a failure.

Unfortunately, things weren't so cushy here in America, where commercial aviation ventures were expected to be bankrolled by private investment. Traditionally, the airlines had been the commercial aviation industry's bankers, but these days the airlines were arguing that it cost too much and took too long to develop a new airplane. They could no longer be expected to wait so many years for a return on such a huge investment, especially since they were now operating on increasingly thin profit margins.

The Air Force had no such money worries. It was receiving close to five billion a year in appropriations, more than either the Army or the Navy. The hitch was that the Air Force would only bankroll military aviation projects.

About a year ago Gold had come up with what he hoped was a strategy around that hitch. The idea had come to him while contemplating the success of his MT-37 military cargo transports. Those big prop-driven beasts of burden had evolved from GAT's largest commercial liner, the Monarch GC-10.

Why not reverse the evolutionary process? Gold had wondered. Why not go from an Air Force funded military project (say, a multi—jet engined bomber), to a commercial airliner?

Accordingly, fourteen months ago, once the BroadSword prototypes were in the hands of the Air Force test pilots, and the lion's share of R&D work on the project was done, Gold had put Teddy Quinn and his crack team to work on coming up with a long-range jet bomber. At the same time he contacted Rogers & Simpson, and had them begin R&D on a new turbojet engine powerful enough in tandem to power such a bomber.

As Teddy liked to put it, the R&D on this baby took place in Oz.

The engineering department ransacked the GAT cupboards, putting together the wings, tail, fuselage, and landing gear from various aircraft in the GC and MT series in order to come up with a frame from which to hang Rogers & Simpson's "hypothetical" half-dozen turbojet engines. The completed blueprint for the proposed heavy intercontinental bomber was titled GAT Multi-Jet Bomber Number One.

In April of this year Gold began his hard sell of the GAT/MJB-1 to the Air Force. There were others in the race. GAT was in competition for Air Force dollars with such proven winners in the bomber-building business as Convair, Boeing, and, of course, Amalgamated-Landis, whose controversial prop-driven B-45 intercontinental was now scheduled to begin flying in 1950.

For the last few months, trying to get some feedback from the Air Force had been like pulling teeth, but a couple of weeks ago Air Force Procurement had contacted Gold. An evaluation team was making a trip to California. Would Gold care to have lunch?

He'd subsequently made some phone calls to his contacts in the military and in Washington. They'd been able to confirm that a decison on the GAT/MJB had been reached, but not what that decision was.

Now, as Gold steered the Caddy onto the access road to the plant, he tried not to brood. *Are the Air Force officials here to authorize appropriations or to ax the GAT/MJB?*

The lunch was called for one o'clock, Gold comforted himself as the Caddy rolled past the uniformed security guards on duty at GAT's front gates.

Gold would know the fate of his bomber in just a few hours.

(Two)

The Top Hat Grill
Los Angeles

It was a little after one o'clock when Gold pulled up in front of the Top Hat on Wilshire Boulevard near the Ambassador Hotel. He turned his Caddy over to the parking valet and went inside. The girl behind the counter in the cloakroom took his hat. Gold paused to shake hands with the tuxedoed maître d' who stood guard at the entrance to the dining room.

"A pleasure to see you, Mr. G," the maître d' smiled. "Your guests are already seated." He gestured expansively. "They're in the corner booth, just as you asked."

"Thanks, Victor." Gold's discreetly folded ten spot disappeared in the man's palm.

"Enjoy your lunch, Mr. G—"

I hope I do, Gold thought as he made his way into the dining room. *I hope I do.*

His guests saw him coming and waved. Gold had known both men for years. Howard Simon was a brigadier general in his fifties. He had a thick shock of snow-white hair and bright blue eyes. Howie was a blunt man. Sometimes his childlike, painful honesty could wound, but Gold liked him a lot. The other Air Force officer, William Burnett, was a lieutenant colonel in his late thirties, but his thinning auburn hair and wispy mustache made him seem older. Billy Burnett had a fussy style about him; he went strictly by the book and liked to pinch pennies. They'd probably had Billy Burnett in mind when they'd coined that bit about not being able to see the forest for the trees. For all of that, Gold thought Billy was okay; just occasionally something of a fuddy-duddy pain in the ass.

Gold thought that both men looked odd out of uniform. Gold's prior dealings with them had always taken place at the Air Force's R&D center at Patterson Air Base, just outside of Dayton, Ohio. This was the first time Simon and Burnett had come out west. They were probably wearing civvies in hopes of blending in with the crowd here at the Top Hat.

No such luck, Gold thought to himself, stifling a smile. Their pasty complexions, dark blue suits, white shirts, and muted ties gave them away amid all the California chic like a pair of starlings trying to crash a parakeets' convention.

The Top Hat Grill was a favorite L.A. watering hole of the rich and famous. The place regularly showed up in the gossip columns. The dining room was a mix of formality and casualness. The staff all wore tuxes, and Gold could only wish that his airplanes might someday soar as high as the prices on the menu. Meanwhile, the tables and chairs crowded into the room's center and the red leather booths along the walls were straight out of a corner malt shop. The dining room's walls were covered with autographed photos of movie stars. One wall, nicknamed the "milk bar," was plastered with photos of Hollywood starlets in their most risqué cheesecake poses.

Gold enjoyed coming to the Top Hat when he was entertaining business prospects from out of town. The place was undeniably the essence of moviedom glamour; the Top Hat's sizzle was what sold its steaks. When Gold had telephoned his visitors from Dayton to suggest the restaurant for lunch, he'd heard the excited intake of breath at the other end of the line.

"Herman, good to see you," General Simon said, standing up as Gold reached the booth.

"Howard, Billy," Gold nodded in turn as he shook hands with both men.

Billy Burnett sidled up close. "Is that who I think it is?" he whispered, pointing at a nearby table.

"John Wayne?" Gold said, amused. "Why, yes it is."

"Holy shit," Burnett breathed, shaking his head. "You don't *know* him, do you, Herman?"

"As a matter of fact, I *have* met him. GAT had occasion to lease some airplanes to the studio for one of his war pictures."

"Damn. . . ." Burnett sighed.

"Would you like to meet him?" Gold asked.

"Uh—" Burnett blushed bright red. "Maybe later. He looks like he's busy talking right now."

"Dammit, Billy, show some gumption," Howard Simon laughed, shaking his head. "You're a *real* airman. He's just *played* them in the pictures."

Gold chuckled as he slid into the booth, and all three men sat down.

"I could understand a man getting the shakes over meeting Ava Gardner," Simon continued to rib his junior officer, and then he perked up. "Say, Herman—*she's* not around, is she?"

"Doesn't seem to be, Howie."

"Too bad. . . ." Simon winked.

"Have you had a drink yet?" Gold asked.

"Well, I'd rather have Ava Gardner," Simon persisted. "But a drink will do."

"Why don't I order champagne?" Gold smiled brightly as he flagged a waiter. "I trust we *are* here to celebrate the Air Force's acquisition of its latest bomber?"

Simon and Burnett exchanged dark glances. *Uh-oh*, Gold thought, but when the waiter came he ordered the champagne anyway.

They caught up on old times while they were waiting for the wine to be served. Gold wanted to steer the conversation back to his bomber, but he figured that Howie Simon would get around to it in his own good time.

The waiter appeared with the wine. "Congratulations on

the BroadSword breaking the record," Simon said, lifting his glass once champagne had been poured all around.

"Thanks," Gold grinned. He sipped at his champagne. "This bubbly is sweet, but not as sweet as breaking that record."

In July, an F-90 BroadSword at Muroc had broken Mach One in a shallow dive, to become the fastest combat aircraft in the Air Force. A few days later a successful attempt on the world speed record had been made, and the BroadSword had entered the record books as the fastest combat aircraft in the world.

"You know, I got a whole stack of congratulatory telegrams when the BroadSword entered the record books," Gold confided. "It felt really good to get the recognition from the industry after all the years of setbacks trying to come up with a viable jet fighter." He grinned. "It shows that if you can just hold on long enough, things always get better."

"Well, that's a good way to look at it," Billy Burnett seemed to pounce. "Win a few, lose a few." He laughed nervously. "Sometimes you're on top, and sometimes you're on the bottom. You know how pleased the Air Force is with the BroadSword. We've done business with you in the past, and you know that we'll be doing business with you again in the future."

Gold stared blankly as Howard Simon held up his hand to silence Burnett. "What he's trying to say is that your bomber is a bust."

"I see," Gold muttered. He felt numb with disappointment as the waiter arrived to present them with menus, and then went away.

"There're a number of things we don't like about the airplane," Burnett said, setting his menu aside. "The bottom line is that we're sticking with Boeing. We're very pleased with their progress to date on the XB-47."

Gold nodded. He knew from the industry grapevine that Boeing had some time ago come up with a lovely swept-wing design for a jet bomber, and a little birdy had told him a bit about the XB-47's specs. "She's a fine airplane, all right, but she hasn't got intercontinental range—"

"How did *you* know that?" Simon asked sharply.

"Howie," Gold chided affectionately, "these things get around."

"Well," Simon grumbled, "they've submitted a proposal for a larger intercontinental bomber—"

"General . . . sir. . . ." Burnett said in warning.

"Um, I guess that's all I can say about it, Herman," Simon shrugged. "Bottom line, Boeing is offering us a better airplane than what you came up with."

Gold didn't say anything. He guessed that he should be arguing on behalf of GAT's design, but his mind was a blank. Anyway, what was the point? The decision had been made.

"GAT has proven itself to be a leader when it comes to building fighter aircraft," Simon was saying. "But Boeing has far more experience building bombers."

"I hear you," Gold replied.

"Now, then, Herman," Simon smiled, holding up his menu, "do we still get lunch?"

"Howie," Gold began, deadpan, "if I were as ugly an old coot as you, I'd sure as hell work on my personality."

Simon laughed. "Just for that, I'm ordering me a lobster salad!"

Chuckling, Gold signaled the waiter. They ordered the lobster all around. "What the hell, might as well give the GAT/MJB-1 a Viking's funeral," Gold joked. "Maybe I should send this lunch tab to Boeing."

"They're going to be able to afford it," Burnett replied. "Just between us, Herman, their XB-47 is one outstanding airplane. If it weren't limited in range, it would be ideal. As it is, it's going to put us ahead of the Soviets for some time to come."

Limited range, Gold thought. He knew that the SAC's chief prided himself on his organization's long reach. That meant Boeing's new bomber would have to refuel in flight.

The idea, when it came to Gold, was so totally, outrageously audacious that it gave him a chill.

He took a deep breath. "Okay, so you don't want our bomber. But what about our proposal for the tanker?"

Simon glanced inquiringly at Burnett. Burnett shrugged.

"What tanker?" Simon asked.

"The GAT AeroTanker," Gold said, and then smiled. "Come *on*, Howie. Quit kidding around. You're making me nervous."

"Herman, I don't recall a tanker proposal from you," Simon said, his brow furrowing.

"The AT-909," Gold insisted, making up a designation on the spur of the moment, as he had the entire airplane. "We sent you the proposal for it along with our bomber specs." He struggled to look convincing as General Simon stared at him.

"Um, Herman..." Billy Burnett was nervously fingering his mustache. "I don't seem to recall a GAT proposal for a tanker."

"Shut up, Billy," Simon muttered. "Herman, what are you trying to pull?"

"Pull? Me? I'm not trying to *pull* anything," Gold declared, trying to sound insulted. "Look, if you guys lost my proposal, just say so."

"We didn't lose your proposal," Simon began.

"Um, we never got it," Burnett said. "We don't know what you're talking about." The fact that he sounded apologetic inspired Gold to push on.

"Well..." Gold tried to sound aggrieved. "My people are going to hit the roof, but *I guess* I can put together another set of specs and rush them over to your hotel."

"How big of you." Simon was scowling.

"You're going to be in town for what," Gold persisted, "another three days?"

"Two days," Simon replied. "Herman, all kidding aside. We're not looking for a new tanker."

"Come on, you guys *need* a new tanker," Gold said, talking fast. "Sure, Amalgamated-Landis is promising you delivery of its B-45 long-range bomber next year, but you yourself just admitted to me that the only decent *jet* bomber that's even *close* to going into production is the XB-47.

There's no way that she's going to be able to reach Moscow without in-flight refueling."

"We've got tankers," Billy Burnett objected.

"Sure, KC series airplanes," Gold replied. "But they're prop driven, right?"

"Yes, but—"

"But nothing!" Gold overrode Burnett. "No way are those prop-driven clunkers going to be able to keep up with jets. You know what's going to happen? Your brand-new, shiny jet bombers are going to find themselves very close to stalling when they try to creep along slow enough to fly nose to tail to those KCs. SAC won't need a war to lose bombers. Routine in-flight maneuvers will do your bombers in long before the Soviets get their chance."

"Well, actually we were thinking about a new tanker," Billy Burnett began to hedge. "Somewhere down the road. . . ." he trailed off.

Now it was Gold's turn to pounce. "Ah-hah! Down the road! But GAT already *has* a proposal put together for the jet tanker you're going to need to support your jet bombers.' Gold shook his head sadly. "If only you guys hadn't lost it."

"But we didn't lose it!" Burnett complained. "We never got it."

"Sure, Billy." Gold looked disgusted.

"Well . . . maybe you *could* send us over another set of specs," Billy began. He glanced at Simon. "That is, if the general is agreeable?"

"What the hell," Simon shrugged as the waiter appeared with their lunch. "It's highly unusual, but seeing as how we *lost* the first set—" he scoffed merrily.

"You understand that all we can do is present it?" Burnett warned.

"Of course." Gold was nodding so hard he thought his head was going to snap off and land in his plate.

"Why don't you tell us more about your tanker proposal that we lost?" Simon suggested gleefully as he dug into his lobster.

"Well, um . . ." Gold hedged. "It's been awhile since I 'ooked those specs over, you understand."

Simon cackled. "Tell you what, Herm—" He snapped his fingers to signal the waiter. "This lobster is delicious, but I'm gonna need a whole lot of wine to wash down this proposal of yours. You'd better order another bottle of champagne."

Gold smiled at the waiter. "You heard the man."

By the end of lunch—and a second bottle of wine—Gold had managed to persuade Simon to allow GAT the full forty-eight hours "to assemble and collate another set of specs." Gold would have a courier waiting at the airport with the proposal when the two officers arrived for their flight back to Dayton. Gold also got Billy Burnett to outline all of the Air Force's objections to GAT's bomber proposal.

They were lingering over their coffee when Billy Burnett excused himself in order to use the men's room. General Simon, puffing contentedly on a cigar, waited until his junior officer was gone, and then demanded, "All right, Herman, what's this crap about?"

Gold struggled to look innocent. "What do you mean?"

"Don't bullshit me any more than you already have, which is a substantial amount. Admit it, you ain't got a tanker."

"What I have is forty-eight hours," Gold said steadily. "Right?"

"Sure, sure. Forty-eight hours," Simon snorted. "What you going to do? Backdate the blueprints?"

Gold allowed himself a thin smile. "You really want to know?"

Simon, studying the tip of his cigar, sighed and shook his head.

Gold shrugged. "Then don't ask."

"All right, Herman. But you know we're going to be objective," Simon cautioned. "Forty-eight hours or forty-eight months, the specs will move through channels just like any other proposal."

"That's all I ask."

"One more thing," Simon said. "We'd better not let Billy in on this." His bright blue eyes glinted as he grinned around his cigar. "Old Billy would bust himself a new asshole if he ever found out."

(Three)

GAT
Burbank

The Caddy's tires squealed in protest as Gold skidded into the parking lot and then thrust the big car into its space like a dagger into a sheath. He'd made the drive back to the plant in record time. His heart was pounding and he felt giddy.

Forty-eight hours to come up with a new airplane design from scratch. If GAT pulled this off, it would become legend!

He ignored the astonished stares from his employees as he dashed into the building with his coattails flapping and his necktie streaming over his shoulder like an aviator's silk scarf. He pounded the elevator's call button. When it arrived, its passengers were stupefied as he commandeered it, ordering the operator to take him directly to the floor where Teddy Quinn's R&D engineering department was located.

In the design studio, the young engineers in their shirtsleeves and loosened ties stopped what they were doing to gape, their mouths open, as Gold stampeded past the rows of desks and drafting tables on his way to Teddy's corner office.

Gold's daughter Susan looked up, startled, from her desk outside Teddy's door as he approached. "Daddy? Are you all right?" she asked, sounding flustered.

"Of course I am!" Gold said.

"Are you *sure*?" she asked uncertainly. "You look— *strange*."

"I'm fine," Gold replied impatiently. "Teddy in?"

"Yes, Daddy—"

Gold barged past her and into Teddy's office.

"Hi, Herman. Where's the fire?" Teddy asked mildly, not

looking up from the papers on his lap. He was sitting slouched in his chair behind his desk, where he was almost hidden by a precariously balanced wall of stacked folders. The folders threatened to topple into the automobile hubcap overflowing with butts that Teddy used as an ashtray. He had his shoes off, and his stockinged feet—one sock was blue and the other was brown—were propped on an open desk drawer. He was wearing an open-necked green and red plaid sport shirt, tan corduroy pants, and a white lab coat. As usual, the lab coat was smudged with the accumulation of ash that had fallen from the smoldering cigarette stuck between his lips.

"God, Teddy," Gold scowled. He personally needed a tidy workplace, but Teddy was one of those who seemed to thrive creatively amid chaos. The office was a mess. Balled-up papers littered the carpet, and haphazard drifts of folders and rolled-up blueprints blanketed Teddy's drafting table and every stick of furniture. The only oasis of neatness was the glass display case that took up one whole wall. The case held scale models of the entire GAT family of aircraft, including the latest, the BroadSword.

"I'll be with you in a minute. . . ." Teddy murmured. His tortoiseshell eyeglasses were perched on the tip of his nose as he studied the work perched on his lap. He had a pen in one hand, and in the other a half-empty bottle of Coca-Cola from which a bent straw bobbed.

Gold wrinkled his nose. "It smells like week-old sweat socks in here."

"I resent that insinuation." Teddy wiggled his stockinged toes. He jotted a quick note on the top sheet of the papers on his lap and then tossed them aside. He swung his feet off the desk drawer and sat up. "How'd it go with our bomber at lunch?" he asked.

"Fuck the bomber," Gold said. "We're building them a tanker."

Teddy didn't say anything for a moment. He just stared at Gold, his green eyes magnified by the thick lenses. Then he said, "What?"

"A tanker," Gold repeated.

Teddy ran his fingers through his thick, dark hair, salted with gray. "Herm, I'm your chief engineer, right?"

"Of course," Gold said distractedly.

"Well, unless you've got some *other* chief engineer stashed away around here someplace, I'm pretty sure we haven't designed a tanker."

"I know that! We've got forty-eight hours to come up with one."

"Forty-eight hours?" Teddy echoed weakly.

"Right."

The cigarette between Teddy's lips had burned down to almost nothing. Teddy pinched the inch-long butt between thumb and nicotine-stained index finger, took a final drag, and then shook loose a fresh cigarette from the pack of Camels on his desk. He lit it off the butt.

"You smoke too much," Gold said.

"That's because I work for you." Teddy exhaled a perfect smoke ring and then flicked the butt through it. It arced, trailing smoke like a crippled fighter before nose-diving into the hubcab. He gestured toward the folder-laden armchair in front of his desk. "Herman, throw some of that crap on the floor, sit down, and tell me what the fuck you're talking about."

Gold filled him in on what had taken place at lunch. "So I think Howie is on to us," he concluded. "But I'm pretty sure Billy Burnett hasn't caught on."

Teddy frowned. "I don't get something. If the general knows that you were bullshitting, why would he go along?"

Gold laughed. "I think Howie thinks the whole idea is a pisser. If I know him—and I do—I'd wager that he's willing to go along just to see if we can do it."

"Okay," Teddy nodded. "Now I understand."

"Good!" Gold jumped to his feet. "Now we haven't got any time to waste! Let's get everyone together in the conference room and—"

Teddy held up his hand. "Herm, I understand, but I don't want to do it."

Gold wanted to shout, but he forced himself to remain

calm. After all, he wouldn't have lost his temper with Howie Simon or Billy Burnett. It was hard to be as diplomatic with friends as he could be with business acquaintances.

"You have to do it, Teddy," he replied softly, sitting back down. "You said so yourself. You're my chief engineer."

Teddy took off his eyeglasses to rub the bridge of his nose. "I'm still exhausted from the BroadSword project. We went for weeks at a time with little sleep and bad food." He shook his head. "I'm fifty-three years old. I'm just not as young as I used to be," he laughed weakly.

"Hey," Gold shrugged. "Who is?"

"You're missing the point—" Teddy began.

"No," Gold cut him off. "*You* are. GAT has got to come up with a jet airliner. We've *got* to. Sales of our prop-powered Monarch GC series have been steadily tapering off as the airlines look ahead. Teddy, we have grown *used* to those revenues. If we want to survive, we are going to have to come up with an airplane we can sell in place of those Monarchs. If *we* don't, someone else *will*, and GAT will become an also-ran."

"But, Herman," Teddy was pleading, "you can't expect us to come up with an airplane in forty-eight hours?"

"That's all I could get," Gold replied. "General Simon is bending over backward just to give us that much time."

"But we spent months working on the bomber proposal, and the Air Force shot it down."

"Yeah, but Billy Burnett told me what they didn't like about it," Gold enthused. "So all we have to do is design out those flaws. And anyway, we were up against everyone in the business in the bomber competition, but we've got a head start concerning the tanker, and the Air Force *needs* a jet tanker fast enough to keep up with a jet bomber, so they're going to be more willing to buy."

Teddy sighed. "I guess the airlines *will* feel a whole lot better about investing in a jet airplane that has already met the Air Force's high standards."

"*That's* the Teddy I know and love. Whatever we come up with has to be able to also serve as a commercial transport with only minor changes. Once we put this airplane into production we're going to be able to save a lot of money if we can easily divert the product to either the commercial or military markets."

"You sound awfully confident," Teddy chided.

"We're winners," Gold declared. "Winners *win*."

"Forty-eight hours," Teddy mused, chuckling. "Everybody is going to have to fucking sleep here."

"Suzy!" Gold yelled.

A second later she stuck her head inside the office. "Daddy!" she scolded. "There's an intercom buried somewhere on Teddy's desk, so you don't have to yell like some crazy person."

"Honey!" Teddy put his fingers to his lips. "Be quiet, and listen. I want you to order some folding cots and have them delivered ASAP."

"But not too many," Gold cautioned. He glanced at Teddy. "We want them sleeping in shifts. While some sleep others should be working. And we'll keep an eye on all of them," he elaborated. "The best ones won't *want* to sleep. They'll be too afraid that they might miss something." He glanced back at his daughter. "Call the cafeteria in this building. I want the place open around the clock for the next forty-eight hours."

"Daddy, what's going on?" Suzy demanded. When Gold was done telling her, she said, "It sounds exciting, Daddy. I'd like to stay as well. It'd be my chance to really contribute something to GAT."

Gold looked at Teddy, who said, "She's the best secretary I've ever had. She'd be useful to us."

"Okay," Gold shrugged, smiling at Suzy. He pulled his leather-bound note pad out of his pocket and handed it to her. "You can start by typing up the notes I took during lunch."

"Yes, sir!" Suzy said, leaving the office.

"And make lots of carbons!" Gold called after her. He sighed. "I'd better telephone home and break the news to Erica."

Teddy laughed. "That's what you get for being a family man," he teased.

"Wise guy," Gold muttered. Teddy had once been married, but the marriage hadn't worked out and had ended, childless, years ago. Teddy had been a bachelor ever since.

"Actually, I'm jealous," Teddy said.

Gold was hardly listening. "When Suzy's done typing up that list of revisions Billy Burnett gave me, have her distribute copies to all your people."

"Will do."

Gold got up to leave the office. He was halfway out when he remembered what Howie Simon had jokingly said. "Oh, and one more thing—"

Teddy looked up. "Yeah?"

"Remind everyone to backdate every piece of paper we generate."

Teddy laughed. "That part's easy, my friend. But how the fuck are we going to age the paper?"

CHAPTER 10

(One)

**The Pentagon
Washington, D.C.
16 May 1949**

The office suite where Steven Gold worked was in the basement of the Pentagon. The suite had tan-painted walls and dark brown carpeting. Round milk-glass light fixtures hung from the low ceiling. Steve and the others called it "the bunker," and joked that in the event of an enemy air strike they would be all that would be left of the Air Force in the nation's capital; it would be up to them to represent the Air Force against the commie hordes.

The joke had led Steve and some of the others to while away their time by working on a joint effort: *The USAF Public Relations Counterinsurgency Defense Manual*. Some of the chapters that had already been surreptitiously written, mimeographed, and circulated to selected recipients were: *Sniping with the Hand-held, Elastic-Operated Standard Air Force Issue No. 2 Paper-Clip*; *Enemy Sentry Neutralization/ Immobilization Utilizing the Air Force Regulation Red/Black Manually Operated Typewriter Ribbon*; *Psychological Warfare Utilizing Anonymous Telephone Techniques*; and *The Spitball: Germ Warfare As the Defense of Last Resort*. Steve, thanks to his experience with the Flying Tigers, was working on a chapter outlining some Burmese hand-to-hand combat techniques of inflicting paper cuts.

At the moment, however, Steve's desk was piled high with real work, as it had been for months. A couple of days ago Russia had capitulated, ending the Berlin airlift. That American air-power victory in the skies over Berlin had capped a tremendous half year for the Air Force.

In February a Boeing XB-47 prototype jet bomber had set a coast-to-coast speed record, and in March a B-50 prop-driven bomber had flown nonstop around the world in ninety-four hours, demonstrating, in the words of a press release that had come out of this department, that "the United States could drop atomic bombs at any spot on earth at any time."

A lot of people on the Hill were giving the B-50's achievement the credit for convincing the doubters in Western Europe to join with the United States in a mutual defense treaty—NATO—against the Soviets. As the line of reasoning went, if the Air Force could beat the Soviets in Berlin, it could beat the Soviets anywhere in Western Europe.

The consensus was that the battle of wills against the Reds had been won in April, when the Air Force had been able to announce that it was landing a plane a minute in Berlin every day. In retrospect it was clear that the achievement had struck a tremendous psychological blow against the Reds. It had also handed the Air Force a domestic public relations bonanza. Steve had been up on the Hill almost every day to lobby for more appropriations for the Air Force.

From his desk Steve could see his CO Colonel Stewart talking on the phone in his glass-enclosed office. Steve needed to talk with the colonel. He needed a giant favor, and figured now was as good a time as any to ask for it. He'd already checked with Stewart's secretary and had found out that the colonel had no meetings scheduled for the next couple of hours.

He waited until Colonel Stewart was off the telephone, and then went up and rapped on the door of the colonel's "aquarium." Stewart waved him in.

Steve opened the door. "Colonel, could I talk to you for a few minutes?"

"Come in, Captain." Stewart was a balding, pudgy guy in his forties. He gestured to the red vinyl and chrome chair in front of his green metal desk. "Sit down."

"Thank you, sir." Steve tried to get comfortable, but the stiff plastic acted like a whoopie cushion, making a fart sound every time he shifted his weight.

"What can I do for you?" the colonel asked.

Steve hesitated. He knew what he wanted to say. *How* to say it was the issue. Stewart had made bird colonel during the war, thanks to the outstanding job he'd done holding down a desk in the USAAF's Office of Public Information. The man had a sore spot when it came to those who thought polishing up the Air Force's shiny reputation wasn't every bit as vital to the Air Force as flying airplanes. Steve was about to hit that sore spot with a hammer.

"I'd like to talk to you about my career, sir," Steven began, feeling nervous. He wished that he could smoke, but there were no ashtrays in Stewart's office. "I've been stuck at captain for over three years now—"

"I realize that," Stewart interrupted. "But I want you to know that I'm doing everything I can to get you what I consider to be a long-overdue promotion," he comforted smoothly. "You know that I've written you up as an outstanding officer?"

"Thank you, sir," Steve said.

"The problem is that promotions have been scaled back due to fiscal constraints."

"Begging the colonel's pardon, but the budget has allowed for the promotions of some of the others in the department with less seniority than me."

"Than *I*—" the colonel corrected, sounding miffed.

"Uh, right. . . ."

"The rule is simple, Captain. Just think to yourself: 'less seniority than I *have*—'"

"Pardon me, sir. . . ." Steve murmured.

Stewart's severity abruptly softened. "No, pardon *me*," he apologized, smiling. "I shouldn't have interrupted you, but you know how I *hate* grammatical errors."

"Yes, sir. No problem, sir." Steve thought Stewart was basically okay for a desk jockey, even if he was, at times, chickenshit.

The colonel was drumming his fingers on the desktop. He stared longingly at his telephone. "Well, go on, Captain. What was it you were saying?"

"Well, sir, I think I know why I've been passed over for promotion."

That got Stewart's attention, all right. He leaned back in his chair. "Well, don't keep me in suspense. Fill me in."

"Yes, sir. Well, sir, I think my present career flight path has hit ceiling because the war has been over a long time now," Steve said. "You're the public relations expert, not me, but I do remember that one of the first things you taught me was that in public relations you've got to stay current. Well, if the war is yesterday's news, it stands to reason that my propaganda value to the Air Force has also faded with the passing years."

Stewart looked uncomfortable. "Maybe I agree to a certain extent—"

"Yes, sir."

"But you're still an asset to this department," Stewart said quickly.

"Thanks for saying so, sir," Steve replied. "But that's not really the issue, is it, sir?"

The colonel frowned. "I'm afraid I've lost you."

"I mean, all the other officers in the department have at least some college education," Steve explained. "All I've got is my high school equivalency diploma. I think that when promotions are decided, what's mostly taken into account is how the new rankings will affect the chain of command. If you think about it, Colonel, you'll probably agree that it's not likely the Air Force is going to put a high school dropout in command of a bunch of college men. Leastways, sir, not when the officers in question are doing desk duty during peacetime." Steve shrugged. "These other guys are really good at their specialty. They don't make mistakes in the way they talk or write."

"Everything you've said is true," Stewart admitted. "But there's more to the job than good formal communications skills. In this line of work you've got to know how to handle people, and that's something you've become very good at, Captain. Why do you think I've let you represent us in meetings and at hearings and to the press?"

"Well, sir," Steve hesitated, "I guess I'd always figured it was on account of my war record. . . ."

Stewart shook his head impatiently. "As you said, the war is yesterday's news. I have you as one of the department's front men because you know how to get along with people."

"I do?" Steve asked, unconvinced.

The colonel laughed. "You've been working for me for almost three years, and during that time I've seen you grow tremendously in confidence and maturity. Sure, your lack of an education is increasingly holding you back, but it's a sign of how far you've come that you're finally ready to face that fact, and hopefully make a stab at doing something about it."

Stewart paused. Steve's heart sank. He knew what was coming next.

"Now then," the colonel began, "I've talked to you on many occasions about the educational opportunities that can be enjoyed by Air Force personnel—"

"Begging the colonel's pardon," Steve interrupted, "but

school is hard work, and frankly, I'm not sure that I *want* to work that hard in order to get somewhere I don't think I want to be. . . ." Steve paused. "It's about choices, I guess. And anyway, there's another aspect to the problem of my stalled career, and that's my father."

"What's your father got to do with this?" Stewart asked.

"Sir, the Air Force is buying a lot of my father's Broad-Sword fighters, and procurement has recently authorized preliminary funding to GAT for a jet tanker."

"Yes? So what?" Stewart demanded.

"Well, sir, I've spent a lot of time these last few years nursemaiding the various congressional committees that are always sticking their noses into Air Force business. They're always looking for corruption."

"I know that," Stewart cut him off. "Politicians love publicity, and nothing grabs the headlines like charging that somebody or something's corrupt."

"Yes, sir, you taught me that," Steve replied quickly. "Well, it's occurred to me that maybe it wouldn't look so good if it came out that the Air Force was buying airplanes from Herman Gold while his son was a high-ranking desk jockey in the Pentagon."

The colonel slowly nodded. "Excellent assessment, Captain. I have to admit that I never thought of it that way."

"But maybe the brass has," Steve suggested. "I think the brass is going to go out of its way to keep me from being promoted."

"You mean to say that they're going to be tougher on you than other officers in order to cover themselves, due to who you are."

"Due to who my father is, sir," Steve corrected firmly. "The way I see it, each of my negatives by itself might not be enough to hold me back, but when they get added together . . ." He shrugged. "It seems to me that I'm going to be stuck at a junior level for the rest of my career." Steve paused. "Unless—"

"Unless what?" Stewart asked.

"Sir, unless I get transfered *off* desk duty and into my specialty."

"Which is?"

"Flight duty, sir. Being back in the cockpit of a fighter."

"We've been through all this, Captain," Stewart said tiredly.

"But, Colonel, sir, back during the war they made me a captain because I'd *earned* the promotion."

"You'll earn your promotion here—" Stewart began.

"No, sir!" Steve objected. "With all due respect, sir, I have to differ. You may *suggest* that I be promoted because I've been around a long time or because I've improved or whatever, but when I'm compared to the other guys, there's no way you can say that I've earned it, and that's because I'm simply not as good as the others in this particular assignment."

"Well," Stewart said dryly, "I must say that I see your point. But I *don't* see what I can do to help you. I assume that all this is leading up to the possibility of your being transferred to flight duty?"

"Yes, sir." Steve waited, hopeful. *Now we find out just how much I have learned about public relations,* he thought.

"I'd like to help you out," Stewart said affably. "But I simply don't have that kind of pull."

Gotcha! Steve exalted. As he'd hoped, Stewart was more than willing to make the concession, as long as he was convinced that he couldn't be held to it.

"Well, sir, you see I've been working on something for myself for quite a while," Steve began.

"*You've* been working on something for yourself?" Stewart echoed, sounding startled. "What could you possibly—?"

"Sir, remember what you taught me about how the essence of this job is the art of doing favors and asking favors in return?"

"I do."

"Well, sir, a few months ago Colonel Harris—He works as an aide for the Joint Chiefs—"

"I *know* where Len Harris works," Stewart interrupted.

"Yes, sir. Of course you would, Colonel."

"Get to the point!"

Stewart was beginning to sound angry. Steve guessed that the man was beginning to suspect that he'd been suckered.

"Well, sir, I happened to hear through the grapevine that Colonel Harris was looking to get his son a job as a Senate page. It so happened that during the B-45 Senate hearings I got to be pretty good friends with an aide to Senator Hill. I put in a good word for Harris's son with my buddy, who worked it out for the kid to get the job." Steve allowed himself a smile. "Colonel Harris was pretty happy with the way things turned out, sir. He told me that if there was ever anything he could do for me . . ."

Stewart waved him quiet. "You got Harris to get you your transfer. Is that what you're trying to tell me?"

"Yes, sir," Steve nodded. "Colonel Harris was good enough to use his influence with his boss General Slade to pull the necessary strings to get it done."

"And you said you weren't any good at public relations," Stewart remarked, deadpan.

Steve was worried. Stewart could fuck this up for him if he had a mind to. "You're not mad, are you, Colonel, sir?" Steve asked.

"No, I suppose not," Stewart sighed. "Although I *would* have preferred it if you'd spoken to me before you put your request to Colonel Harris."

"Sorry, sir, but I didn't want to bother you in case it all turned out to be nothing." Steve paused. "My transfer *is* contingent on your approval, Colonel."

"Yes, I know it is." Stewart frowned.

Oh, shit, Steve thought. "You *did* just say that if there was anything you could do to help me. . . ."

"I *know* what I just said," Stewart replied sharply. Suddenly he laughed, shaking his head. "All right. Don't worry about your transfer. I won't stand in your way."

"Thank you, sir!" Steve said, relieved.

"Don't misunderstand me," Stewart warned. "I think you're making the wrong decision—"

"Yes, sir. I appreciate your concern, sir, but I do think it's the right decision for me. I need to feel that I'm the best at what I do, and there's no way I'm going to outclass the competition with a typewriter and a telephone."

"Your promotion to major really *was* on its way—" Stewart said.

"Thank you, sir, but I've been pretty much guaranteed a promotion to major once I go back on flight duty, and depending on where I end up being stationed, there's even the possibility of my taking command of a fighter squadron."

Stewart grunted. "Well, I can see your mind is made up, so I wish you all the best, Captain."

"Thank you, sir. I won't take up any more of your valuable time, sir." Steve stood up.

"You know where you're going to be stationed?" Stewart asked.

"Well, sir, some of it is up to me," Steve replied, shrugging. "I can either go into immediate service with a squadron flying piston-engined Mustangs, or take some time to train to fly a jet. Right now I'm leaning toward the Mustang. I flew one toward the end of the war, and she was a fine plane."

"Steve," Stewart began. "Man to man, can I give you a bit of advice?"

"Uh, yes, sir!" Steve said, startled. "Of course you can, Colonel."

Stewart chuckled ruefully. "You sounded surprised that I might have advice to give someone like you, but I do." He sighed. "I know you don't think much of an old dog desk jockey like myself."

"No, sir, that's not true at all, sir," Steve said earnestly. "Colonel, you're where you want to be in the Air Force, and that's what I want for myself."

Stewart looked amused. "You may find that where you want to be keeps changing relative to where you are."

Steve let that one go by. "Any advice you might give me would be appreciated, sir."

"Okay. If flying is your passion, I strongly urge you to learn to fly jets while the Air Force is willing to teach you. You've already accepted the fact that your lack of an education has severely limited your career options. Don't further limit yourself in your chosen specialty by getting stuck flying an obsolete war machine."

Steve nodded. "I hadn't thought of it that way, sir."

"Let me teach you one last thing, and that's to think before you act. You're not a kid anymore. Now that you're older, and starting to rise up through the ranks, you're going to find that people are going to be far less forgiving of your reckless nature."

"Yes, sir." Steve was anxious to get out of the office. He had to telephone Colonel Harris, and he had a million other things to do.

"Hmm." Stewart, staring at him, seemed to have read his mind. "You're dismissed, Captain." Stewart reached for his telephone. "I've got to start the paperwork to request your replacement."

(Two)

Alexandria, Virginia

It was a warm night for so early in the spring. Steve was lying on his bed, smoking a cigarette and staring up at the ceiling, a scotch and soda within easy reach. He'd been playing Charlie Parker on the record player. The intricate, tortured wail of Bird's alto sax mixed with the street sounds coming in through the open windows, filling the spartan rooms.

He'd had a dinner date with some friends, but he'd canceled out. This evening the music was all the company Steve wanted. He needed to make some decisions and ponder his future.

He'd already come to the conclusion that Colonel Stewart's advice made a lot of sense. Steve had decided to put aside both his sentimentality concerning the Mustang and his anxiousness to get back to active flight duty as soon as possible, and take advantage of this opportunity to get the jet pilot training he was going to need to stay current.

Yeah, jet fighter training was definitely the way to go, as he'd so informed Colonel Harris over the telephone earlier that day.

But his decision to take jet fighter training meant that he now had another decision to make. Colonel Harris had offered him his choice of being assigned to a fighter group flying the F-80 Shooting Star, or an FG being equipped with F-90 BroadSwords.

For most pilots there would be no question about which way to go, Steve thought bitterly. The BroadSword had it all over the Shooting Star. Only the most prestigious fighter groups based stateside, or deployed in Europe to face off with the Soviets, were in line for the first of the swept-wing fighters rolling off the GAT production lines.

Yeah, in terms of prestige and performance, the jet to fly was definitely the BroadSword, but for Steve the choice was a little too complicated to be made merely on the basis of which was the superior machine.

He'd realized he'd been wrong, that he did need company. He needed the advice of someone he trusted and respected. . . .

He got up off the bed and went to the dresser, where his little black book was lying beside the telephone. He dialed the operator and told her he wanted to call California and then read off Linda Forrest's telephone number.

He glanced at his watch while he listened to the clicks and hisses on the telephone as the operator put the call through. It would be a little before seven in Los Angeles. At the other end of the line the telephone began to ring, once, twice, three times. If she was going out for the evening, maybe he'd be lucky and catch her before she left.

"*Hello?*"

"Hello, Baby Blue Eyes," he said, settling down on the floor with the telephone on his lap.

"Well, well, Cap'n, how's Washington since I was there last?"

Every couple of months Linda managed to wrangle her wire service into sending her to Washington. Whenever she was in town they spent their nights together.

"Springlike," Steve said. "I didn't catch you on your way out, did I?"

"Hardly."

Steve smiled. Some dames would hand a guy a line about how they were about to go out on a hot date, just to try and get him jealous, but not Linda. She was beyond all that stuff, which was one of the reasons—nonphysical reasons, at least—why he liked her so much.

"I hate Mondays just on principle," Linda was saying. "But today was particularly rough. Have you called to cheer me up by proposing matrimony?"

"Sounds tempting. . . ."

"Oh, sure," she laughed.

"Actually, I called because I could use some advice," Steve said.

"What's going on?" Linda asked, becoming serious.

Steve filled her in on the details of his transfer. "So there's no question that the BroadSword is the airplane of choice. I'd accept the invitation to join a BroadSword-equipped squadron in a flash, if it hadn't been for Colonel Harris's chance remark . . ."

"Which was?" Linda asked.

"He told me that getting me into a BroadSword outfit would be no problem at all, considering who my father was."

"Uh-oh," Linda sighed. "That spoils it for you, doesn't it?"

"Yeah, it kind of does," Steve replied. "Remember what I

told you about the ribbing I had to take during the war because I was my father's son? I had to prove myself every time I was stationed someplace new."

"And you did," Linda encouraged.

"Yeah, but how would I prove myself in this situation? Remember that only the cream of the crop are getting the first BroadSwords. I can't expect to be welcomed by those pilots when they find out that I haven't flown since the war, that I'd joined their ranks thanks to my daddy's pull."

"Cap'n, you know that you're good enough to fly with the best—" Linda began.

"Sure I am," Steve cut her off. "But that's not the point. I want the satisfaction of getting to *prove* how good I am, not get the benefit of the doubt thanks to my last name."

"Well, it sounds like you've made your decision," Linda remarked. "You'll be flying that other kind of jet you were offered, the *whatsit*—"

"The F-80 Shooting Star," Steve told her. "Yeah, *but*—" He sighed.

"But what?"

"It's a bitter pill for me to swallow, Blue Eyes. You see, I was also told that if I chose a Shooting Star–equipped FG, I would probably get command of a squadron."

"But that's wonderful!" Linda interjected.

"Yeah, but I was also warned that squadron would be part of an FG stationed in a backwater part of the world."

"Steve," Linda whispered, "are you saying that you're upset because you're not going to get to see me so often?"

"Nah, that's not it."

"Oh. . . ."

Shit, Steve thought. "Come on, Blue Eyes," he said impatiently. "Don't go all mushy on me. You know I enjoy seeing you."

"Right."

She sure was sounding funny. *Women,* he thought. Maybe it had been a mistake to call her.

"Okay, Cap'n. I didn't mean to get 'mushy.' Please continue."

"Well, the Berlin airlift confrontation has proven what everybody already knew," Steve began. "That the United States is heading toward a confrontation with the Reds concerning where in Europe the Iron Curtain is going to fall. But I've been warned that if I choose an F-80 equipped organization. I'm going to end up as part of the Far Eastern Air Force, stationed in Japan, and being stuck there is as dull as things could get. I mean, there's no way the Soviets are going to try anything in Asia while they have their hands full in Europe."

"Well, the Russians are in North Korea," Linda pointed out.

"The UN has got the lid on that," Steve countered.

"And China is falling to the communists."

"That backward nation is in no position to threaten the world."

She suddenly broke up laughing.

"What?" Steve demanded.

"This is what I get for becoming involved with a military man," she managed, trying to catch her breath. "I can't believe I'm trying to cheer you up by suggesting possible places for you to go to war."

Steve chuckled. "I guess I am being kind of silly."

"Yes, you are, Cap'n. But don't worry, I have high hopes for you."

"You do, huh? Any chance of you getting to Washington before I ship out?"

"It might be arranged. I'll check my calendar in the office tomorrow and give you a call."

"That's good."

"So," Linda said, "what have you decided?"

"You ever get to Japan?"

"Oh, so *that's* what you decided."

"Hey, what the hell, at least it's flight duty," he told her. "At least nobody will be able to say I'm not my own man trying to make it on my own merits."

"You're an all-right guy, Cap'n."

"You're an all-right girl. Thanks for listening."

"No problem, Cap'n."

Steve hesitated, but he told himself that he might as well say it, or else it would just bother him. "Sorry about hurting your feelings before. I—I really will miss you."

"I know. . . ." She sighed. "I wasn't going to say anything, but, what the hell. I've got that slot in the New York bureau."

"New York? Gee, that's great! It's the promotion you wanted."

"Yeah. . . ." Linda said listlessly.

"You don't sound very happy about it."

"I was a lot happier when I thought it would not only advance my career but also put me that much closer to Washington."

"Oh, right. Gee, you in New York and me in Japan," Steve said. "Couldn't get much farther apart if we tried."

"Nope."

"Well . . ." He suddenly felt terribly awkward. He didn't know what to say, or how to express what he felt. He got all mixed up inside when it came to Linda. "Thanks again for letting me bend your ear."

"Like I said, anytime. I'll do my best to get to Washington before you leave and bend something of yours."

Steve laughed. "That I'm looking forward to."

"Wear you out before those geishas get hold of you," she said lightly.

There, that was better, Steve thought. He could imagine her smile. "'Bye, Blue Eyes."

"'Bye."

He hung up the phone, feeling much better about his decision. Talking it out with Linda had convinced him that he was making the right choice. Nobody could accuse him of engaging in nepotism.

Yeah, it was worth it to his pride, Steve told himself. Even if it meant that as far as seeing some action was concerned, he was definitely going to be in the wrong place at the wrong time.

CHAPTER 11

(One)

Washington National Airport
Virginia
5 September 1949

An Air Force staff sergeant wearing a slate-blue belted overcoat was waiting as Herman Gold exited the Skyworld gate. The sergeant stepped up and saluted smartly.

"Mr. Gold? Would you follow me, sir? There's a car waiting."

Gold nodded, amused. "This is certainly first-class service. I expected to take a cab to the Pentagon."

"Yes, sir," the sergeant said, noncommittal. "If you'd allow me to carry those for you?" He took Gold's carry-on and his briefcase.

"How'd you know who I was?" Gold asked.

"General Simon supplied a photograph of you, sir. Allow me to show you to the car, and then I'll come back for the rest of your luggage."

Gold followed the airman past the long ticket and information desks and the telegraph facility, out through the vestibuled doorway of the busy terminal. It was a blustery cold, gray Monday morning. A light but steady mist slanted down underneath the portico meant to protect car and taxi passengers. Gold cinched his olive trench coat tightly over his charcoal tropical wool suit, and pulled his gray fedora low on his brow to secure it from the wind as the sergeant led him to where a car parked at curbside glistened in the rain. It was a late model, dark blue, unmarked four-door Plymouth with curtained rear windows.

The sergeant opened the rear passenger door for Gold and stood aside. As Gold climbed in, he was surprised to see his old friend from Air Force Procurement, Major General Howard Simon.

"Howie, good to see you," Gold said as he settled into the Plymouth and shook hands with Simon. "Congratulations again on your promotion to two star."

"Sir, may I have your baggage claim ticket?" the sergeant interrupted politely.

"Here you are." Gold handed the claim ticket to the sergeant, who shut the Plymouth's door and then hurried back to the terminal.

"Nasty day, eh?" Simon remarked. "How was it when you left California yesterday?"

"Sunny and mild," Herman boasted.

Simon sighed longingly. "Not supposed to even hit fifty here today. Rain predicted for the rest of the week."

"I can't wait to get back home," Gold laughed. "It's funny, I used to love to travel, but the older I get, the more I hate to leave home."

"I can understand that," Simon replied. "Wonderful place, California."

The sergeant had reappeared with Gold's luggage. He loaded it into the trunk and then came around the car to slide in behind the wheel. He started up the Plymouth, set its heater fan roaring and windshield wipers flapping, and then pulled away.

"Howie, I've got to say I'm surprised to see you here," Gold murmured. "I figured that you'd be meeting me at the Pentagon." He gestured at the stars on Simon's shoulders. "Since when does an Air Force general have the time to come to the airport to pick up visitors?"

For some reason Simon ducked the question. "Herman, you must be exhausted from your flight. Are you sure you're up to a meeting first thing this morning? We could take you to your hotel and put things off."

"Nonsense," Gold laughed. "I traveled in a GAT Monarch GC-7 sleeper. Last night I had a first-class dinner with champagne and then curled up in my berth for a marvelous rest. Slept like a baby." He winked. "Nothing like those purring Rogers & Simpson engines to lull a fellow to sleep."

"Okay, okay," Simon laughed. "You don't have to sell me on your airplanes, right?"

"Right." Gold nodded warmly. "Anyway, Howie, I'm always ready to talk about the AeroTanker."

It had been thirteen months since Gold had challenged his engineers to come up with a jet tanker proposal in forty-eight hours. They'd done the job in spades, finishing the proposal with a few hours to spare. When General Simon and Lieutenant Colonel Billy Burnett had arrived at the airport for their flight back to Dayton, a GAT courier had been waiting to present them with the proposal, which consisted of a detailed three-view drawing of the AT-909, its performance specs, a projected budget, and a delivery schedule.

Less than a month later, Howie Simon had telephoned Gold to congratulate him on pulling off the impossible. The Air Force was very impressed with the AeroTanker proposal and would authorize preliminary funding.

Gold had not been surprised. He'd been in the airplane business long enough to be able to separate the hits from the misses. For example, he'd always had his doubts about the jet bomber project, but he'd felt good about the AeroTanker right from the start.

GAT had been playing an unfamiliar game of poker with a bunch of veteran card sharps when it had pitched its ill-fated long-range jet bomber, but GAT's experience building piston-powered airliners and cargo transports had made coming up with a viable jet tanker a relative snap. All the pieces had been there; the AeroTanker was the result of the right company putting together the right airplane for the right customer for the right job to be done.

Six months ago Gold had presented the Air Force with the results of the 909 model's wind tunnel tests, and the test results from Rogers & Simpson concerning their new SS-60 jet engine. The Air Force liked what it had seen, and had approved further funding, up to a point. The appropriations came far short of the projected twelve million dollars GAT would need to build a full-scale prototype.

Once Gold had been certain of the Air Force's positive evaluation reports, he'd "anonymously" leaked the news to a contact who wrote for *Aviation Trade*. Gold had also pointed out to the reporter that the airline industry could ask for nothing better than having the Air Force put its stamp of approval on the basic design for a commercial carrier.

Pretty soon Gold began getting calls from several of the airline vice presidents in charge of purchasing who were interested in buying into the project. Conspicuously absent was Skyworld Airlines, but then Gold had expected as much, despite the fact that Skyworld had once been a part of GAT. Gold's ex-longtime partner Tim Campbell, who was Skyworld's chairman emeritus and still its chief stockholder, was now heavily involved with Amalgamated-Landis. The rumors had it that A-L had a jet airliner of its own in the works. No doubt Campbell would want to buy A-L's airplane.

Even without Skyworld, GAT had no trouble putting together a consortium on which to lay off the remainder of the project's financial risk during the rest of the development phase and prototype construction. GAT was projecting that a full-scale prototype of the tanker would roll off the assembly lines in 1953, and the commercial version in '54. That would be well after Stoat-Black was expected to be putting its Starstreak airliner into service, but as Gold had hoped, the U.S. airlines had indicated their preference for an American-built product that enjoyed the Air Force's stamp of approval, even if they had to wait for it.

Last week Gold had received a call from General Simon at the Wright-Patterson Research Center, in Dayton, Ohio. The general had wanted Gold to meet him in Washington for briefings with the top brass at the Pentagon on the AT-909. Gold had agreed to come, and had left Los Angeles last night for the eight-hour flight to the nation's capital.

Now Gold was puzzled as he glanced out the Plymouth's rain-streaked window. They were crossing a bridge. Whitecaps were dancing on the wind-rolled surface of the water far below them.

"Howie," Gold murmured. "Isn't this the Potomac we're crossing?"

"It is."

Gold shook his head, confused. "But isn't the Pentagon on the same side of the river as the airport?"

"That's what I wanted to talk to you about," Simon said, sounding uneasy. "We're not going to the Pentagon."

"We're not?"

"Our Pentagon session isn't scheduled until tomorrow," Simon continued. "And the upcoming meeting, for which I got you here a day early, and on false pretenses, isn't about the AeroTanker."

Gold shook his head, confounded. "Howie, what the fuck is going on?"

"You'll see. In the meantime, I wanted to come meet you personally to make it clear to you that I wouldn't have taken part in this subterfuge if I hadn't been convinced that it was absolutely essential to the national interest."

"Holy shit—" Gold laughed weakly. "Will you please tell me what's going on?"

Simon gestured to the driver. "That's all I can say right now. You'll know everything in a few minutes."

Gold, his thoughts in turmoil, nodded mutely as the Plymouth, its tires humming on the wet asphalt, left the river behind and made its way through the crowded Washington streets. Several times when the traffic threatened to slow them up, the driver touched a switch mounted beneath the Plymouth's dash. A siren blared, and the traffic parted to allow them to continue smoothly on their way.

It began to rain more steadily. Thanks to the decreased visibility, Gold, who rarely visited Washington, soon lost his bearings. "Where are we now, Howie?"

"What's called Foggy Bottom," Simon smiled. "See? There's the Lincoln Memorial." He pointed out the white marble building wreathed in mist like some ancient temple on Mount Olympus.

Gold caught a glimpse of the Washington Monument in

the distance, the great spire piercing the fog, and then they were turning onto a narrow side street. Simon pointed out what he said was the rear of the State Department as they drove down a hill and then turned through a gate marked GOVERNMENT PRINTING OFFICE. They came to a stop in an interior, blacktopped courtyard formed by three imposing gray stone buildings.

The sergeant driver got out of the car and came around to open Gold's door. Gold and Simon got out. Simon hurried him through the rain into one of the buildings. A muscular-looking young man in a too-snug suit was seated behind a desk just inside the door.

"General Simon and Herman Gold to see Jack Horton," Simon told the young man, who used the telephone on his desk to relay the news.

"Jack Horton!" Gold echoed. "I haven't seen him since 1945! Howie, what's going on?"

"You'll understand everything soon, Herman," Simon assured him. "Just come with me."

"I'll have to get someone to escort you, General," the young man apologized as he relieved them of their coats and stowed them in a closet. "It's Agency procedure."

"What agency?" Gold whispered to Simon as the young man returned to his telephone.

"Central Intelligence Agency," Simon whispered back.

"What's *that*?" Gold muttered. "Wait, I can probably guess. If Jack Horton is involved with it, it's got to be cloak and dagger."

Simon nodded. "Nobody has publicized it for obvious reasons, but part of the legislation Truman signed back in '47 to create the Department of Defense also authorized a new intelligence-gathering outfit to replace the OSS."

A young woman appeared from a hallway, and led Gold and Simon through several rambling corridors lined with offices to an unmarked, closed door. A secretary seated outside the office smiled and said, "Go right in, gentlemen."

Simon opened the office door and stood aside to let Gold enter. Inside the office, Jack Horton, wearing a gray suit, white shirt, and red tie, stood up from behind his large antique walnut desk. He was as tall and skinny as ever, Gold thought. Horton had grown a rakish bottle-brush mustache, but he still favored a military-style haircut and black horn-rimmed eyeglasses.

"Herman, thank you for coming."

"Jack, don't mention it, but then you never *did* mention it, right?" Gold smiled thinly. "I'll say this for you, you don't look a day older than when I last saw you."

Horton smiled. "It comes from staying single and loving my work." He snapped his fingers. "Oh, and I quit smoking a year ago."

Gold nodded. "Smart. I wish I could get my chief engineer off those coffin nails."

"Who, Teddy?" Simon asked.

Gold nodded. "Teddy's been looking like hell lately." He glanced around the office. "Well, Jack, your work must love you, as well," he remarked. "You certainly seem to have come up in the world since our last meeting."

Horton's large corner office was furnished to suggest a front parlor in a prosperous Georgian town house instead of a place of business. The walls were painted turquoise, and a large rectangular, blue and gold Oriental carpet covered most of the polished wooden floor. A striped Sheraton sofa and a matching armchair were arranged facing Horton's desk, which was swept clean. There wasn't so much as a pen stand on it.

"This is all very nice, indeed," Gold elaborated. "So, Jack, have you gone into the antique business or are you still a spy?"

Horton grimaced. "You're sore at us for fooling you," he mused. "That's okay."

"Thank you for being so understanding," Gold said dryly.

Behind Horton, the tall rain-splattered windows rattled in the wind. Horton moved aside to let Gold see the distant but dramatic view of the Mall.

"On a good day you can see the Washington Monument," Horton said. "But today it's in the fog."

"It's not the only thing in the fog," Gold said pointedly.

"Come on now, seriously—if you wanted to see me, why didn't you just call and say so?"

"You'll understand everything in a little while," Horton replied.

"Everybody keeps telling me that," Gold said sadly. Horton gestured to the armchair, and Gold sat down.

"Herman, Jack figured it would attract a lot less attention at GAT if your people thought you were coming to Washington for a routine get-together with Air Force Procurement," Simon said as he sat down on the sofa. "It's best if nobody back at GAT knows about any of this."

"Leastways, not until you agree to help us," Horton began.

"*Assuming* I agree to help you. . . ." Gold cut him off crossly.

"Fair enough," Horton smiled, settling in behind the desk. "I'll start from the beginning, but first I need your word that no matter what you decide, everything we discuss in this office will remain absolutely confidential. You'll understand why—"

"In a little while." Gold scowled. "*That* I know already. Nothing else do I know, but that has been drummed into me."

"Herman," Jack Horton cut him off, frowning. "Exactly one week ago today—on August twenty-ninth—the Soviets test detonated their first atomic bomb."

Gold stared at Horton a moment, and then he looked at Simon. "Is he kidding?"

"I'm afraid not, Herman," Simon replied. "I'd better add that this is highly classified information. As of yet, not even the President's cabinet has been advised." Simon's blue eyes glinted with sardonic amusement. "The only reason they told *me* was because they needed my cooperation to lure you here."

Gold nodded, trying to come to grips with what he'd just heard. *The Russians had the bomb*— He felt his shoulders hunch, as if to ward off a sudden blow.

"I guess we all knew that it was going to be only a matter of time," Gold muttered. "But it makes life a little bit more complicated now, doesn't it?" He shivered. "The world just got to be a lot smaller, more dangerous place. . . ."

Horton nodded somberly. "Smaller in one sense, but larger in others."

"I'm not sure I follow you," Gold said.

"They don't call it the Iron Curtain for nothing, Herman. We live in an open society, so the commies are having themselves a picnic snooping on us, but Russia is a closed society. We need hard information on them, but we're having a devil of a time getting it."

"Don't you have spies over there?" Gold asked.

"We've got agents in place," Horton nodded. "But what our people are able to send back to us is limited and vague."

"Back before the Berlin airlift, when it became clear that the Cold War was heating up, the CIA came to the Air Force to discuss their problem," General Simon said. "And the matter got kicked over to the research center at Dayton, which was how I got drawn into it. Our lab boys came up with an interim solution: a high-altitude balloon, carrying a powerful camera. We float them from Europe. Over Russia they snap their pictures, and then we hope like hell that they make it to Japan, where a radio signal detaches the camera so it can come down by parachute."

"Sometimes it works and sometimes it doesn't," Horton said, shrugging. "When it doesn't, and the commies get ahold of it, we stiff it out, claiming that it's nothing but a weather balloon. The commies don't believe us, but we don't much care. What really bothers us is that the balloon's routes vary randomly with the wind, and they can only shoot pictures of what happens to be below them. What we need is a way to travel directly to a chosen, specific target."

Gold nodded. "In other words, an airplane."

"An airplane," Horton agreed.

"I can't help thinking back to my own flying days in the military," Gold smiled. "You know, of course, that during World War One, long before airplanes were used as fighters or bombers, they were used as observation and scouting craft—"

"Excuse me, Herman," Horton interrupted, glancing at

his wristwatch. "But getting back to the matter at hand, General Simon has suggested that there might be a way to adapt your BroadSword fighter to high-altitude photographic and electronic reconnaissance."

Gold frowned. "The BroadSword is fast enough, and it wouldn't take much to fit her with a camera pod, but there's a cruising range problem." He brightened. "Howie, I'm sure you're familiar with the work Bell Labs has been doing for the National Advisory Committee for Aeronautics?"

"Sure, the X-series rocket plane," Simon replied.

Gold nodded. "Well, the X-series carries so little fuel and uses it up so rapidly that it has to be air launched—carried up hitched to the belly of a bomber and then released in midair."

"Would that work for a BroadSword, General?" Horton asked eagerly.

Simon grinned. "If Herman says it will."

Gold smiled back. "I see no reason why we can't modify some BroadSwords to carry your photographic and electronic snooping gear and rig them to be air launched along the Russian border. From there, within reason of course, they can dart in and out of the Soviet Union."

"Sounds feasible," Simon decreed. "Herman, I think it would be very helpful if some of your people at GAT worked with us on the modifications. Most have Government security clearances, and nobody knows the Broad-Sword like they do."

"I like that idea," Horton said. "And it's given me one of my own. Herman, you've got some of the best aviation minds in the nation working for you."

"I can't argue with that," Gold shrugged.

"Once you've selected your BroadSword team and have them working with the Air Force's people, why not keep them together?" Horton continued. "What I'm suggesting is an ongoing research and design lab devoted to advancing aerial reconnaissance research. For example, the Broad-Sword's modifications will serve as a stopgap solution to our problem, but we still need a reconnaissance airplane with the range to penetrate the innermost reaches of the Soviet

Union. Your secret team within GAT could begin the R&D on such a plane."

"Look at you!" General Simon laughed. "Jack, you look like a kid dreaming of being let loose in a candy store."

"An exclusive Agency candy store is exactly what I want," Horton grinned. He eyed Gold. "How about it, Herman? You willing to run one for us?"

If I don't do it, somebody else will, Gold thought. That would probably cost GAT essential government goodwill and lucrative government contracts. Besides, Gold found the whole idea intriguing, provided his company did not have to bear the brunt of the cost involved.

"This kind of work gets expensive," Gold cautioned. "You can't expect GAT to pay for it out of its own pocket."

"Of course not," Horton replied. "On the other hand, it would blow security and attract commie agents the way spilled honey pulls flies if we funded you overtly. . . ." He was quiet for a moment. "Try this on for size. What would you say to an arrangement where appropriations were channeled to you from this agency through a cut-out?"

"What's a cut-out?" Gold asked.

"It's a middleman," General Simon replied. "Jack, what about your contacts at the National Advisory Committee for Aeronautics?"

"Yeah," Horton smiled. "I'm owed a favor over there. Howie, we could probably divert some additional funding to the candy store through the Air Force, right?"

When Simon nodded, Gold said, "You two guys work pretty closely, don't you?"

Simon shrugged. "You said it yourself, Herman. Observation and aviation have gone together from the very beginning."

"To put it another way, *we're* the spies, but the *Air Force* owns the skies," Horton said whimsically. "Okay, Herman, if we can solve the appropriations problem, are you willing to build us what we need?"

"I'm willing to try," Gold replied. "Who will I report to?"

"Me," Simon and Horton said in unison.

Gold laughed.

"For now, I guess, you'd best report to both of us," Horton said uneasily.

Simon, looking disgusted, nodded.

This, Gold thought to himself, *is one match that wasn't made in heaven. . . .*

(Two)

Mayflower Hotel
Washington, D.C.

"The thing with Horton and his spooks," Howie Simon explained, "is that they push too hard. They just never know when to quit."

Gold nodded. They were in the coffee shop at the Mayflower. Simon had given Gold a ride to the hotel, and had then accepted Gold's offer to come in for coffee and a chat.

"Back during the war, and just after, when it was still the OSS, these guys were content to come along for the ride," Simon continued irritably. "They needed wings for their observation and spy missions, and they just about kissed our asses when we were willing to lend a hand. Now they're getting pushy," he repeated. "I happen to know that they've successfully recruited some Air Force officers into their fold. Sometimes I think that they're trying to build themselves their own private air force inside the one we've already got."

"On the other hand," Gold said, smiling, "from the little I heard this morning, something tells me Horton and his bunch have on occasion *funded* some Air Force operations."

"Well, maybe once in a while we've gotten them to pay their fair share for projects that were of mutual interest," Simon grumbled.

"There you are, Howie," Gold said. "They pay, so they figure they're entitled to have a say in things."

"Enough about this," Simon said sourly. "Catch me up on what's going on with you. For instance, how's your son doing?"

"At the moment he's in Texas, learning to fly jets," Gold sighed. "Learning all about electronic navigation, principles of flight and gunnery, and so forth. He wrote to me saying that he's finding it exciting but a whole new ball game."

"Well, it *is* a whole new ball game," Simon chuckled. "What else would you call playing follow-the-leader in a mock dogfight at five hundred knots?"

"Ow! Please!" Gold winced. "Erica and I are nervous enough about it."

"Hey, he'll be okay," Simon said.

"At least I can take some comfort in the fact that he'll be flying the finest jet fighter in the sky."

"What do you mean?" Simon asked, puzzled.

"A BroadSword," Gold boasted. "I twisted a few arms, and called in a couple of favors to set it up for Steve to go directly from training school to March Air Force Base in California. The FG at March is probably the best the Air Force has."

"I know that," Simon said, "but—"

"I figure to have some newsreel cameras rolling when my son takes possession of his BroadSword. Pretty good PR idea, huh? Herman Gold builds them, and his son flies them, so they've got to be the best!"

"Herman—"

"And believe me," Gold continued, "the fact that Stevie is going to be stationed only fifty miles from home has made his mother very happy. And if Stevie comes home on leave more often, who knows? Maybe I can expose him a little at a time to what's going on at GAT, and get him to agree to come work with me." He smiled thinly. "Someday. . . . "

"It sounds good, Herman," Simon shrugged. "Did Steve say when he'd changed his assignment?"

"What?" Gold asked. "What assignment?"

"In his letters to you," Simon explained, "didn't he mention when he . . ." He paused. "Herm, you *have* told Steve about all of these plans you've made?"

"Well, no," Gold replied slowly. "I figured it would be a surprise. I didn't think there'd be any problem. I mean, what fighter pilot in his right mind wouldn't want to fly a Broad-Sword?"

Simon looked uneasy. "When I heard from you that your son was returning to flight duty, I asked around about him."

"Yeah? So? What did you find out?"

"That Steve had his choice of assignments. He chose to take command of a squadron flying Lockheed Shooting Stars."

"He chose an F-80?" Gold echoed in disbelief.

"He's going to be stationed in Japan, Herman."

"Japan?" Gold was stunned, but all at once it made sense. "I guess he wants to be as far away from me as he can get," he said softly.

"I'm sorry, Herm."

Gold shrugged. "I'm suddenly feeling tired, Howie." He signaled the waitress for the check. "If you don't mind, I think I'll go up to my room to rest."

Simon looked away, obviously embarrassed. "I—I thought you would have *known* all this."

Gold laughed bitterly. "You would *think* I would have known, given the fact that we're talking about *my son*—"

"Herman," Simon began hurriedly, "maybe I heard wrong."

"But when it comes to my son," Gold continued harshly, "I guess I don't know anything at all."

CHAPTER 12

(One)

North Korea, near the 38th Parallel
11 October 1950

Steven Gold's Lockheed F-80C Shooting Star was over six miles high. His was the lead jet fighter in a finger-four formation that raked white contrails against the curved blue dome of the sky.

Far beneath the combat air patrol the smudged gray clouds moved like ponderous elephants across the ancient Korean landscape. Down on the ground it was a pleasant sixty-eight degrees, but at 36,000 feet the razor-cold air was as thin and clear as fine crystal. The sun beating down through the Shooting Star's teardrop canopy pleasantly heated the cockpit, taking the edge off the air conditioning. The ride was incredibly smooth and peaceful. The only sounds Steve Gold heard were his own raspy breathing, routed from the microphone in his oxygen mask into the radio earphones built into his rigid, visored helmet, and the steady, lulling roar of the airplane's General Electric J-33-A-23 turbojet.

Steve's eyes flicked across the glittering array of instruments to assure himself that all of his systems were in the green, and then slowly twisted his head, surveying the thin sky above. Any physical movement was difficult. Steve was encased in multiple layers of cotton and rubberized fabrics which made up his long underwear, flight overalls, G-suit, and survival gear, and firmly trussed by his safety harness to his ejection seat.

On the ground Steve's movements were slow and cumbersome, like those of a medieval knight in armor. But his ungainliness fell away once he was strapped into and hooked up to his Shooting Star. In the air the steel dart became an extension of his body, and he became its brain—its soul.

Steve punched his mike button. "Bugs Flight, this is Bugs Leader."

"Ehhh, what's up, doc?" Bugs One—Lieutenant Mike DeAngelo—radioed in.

Steve glanced to his starboard side. DeAngelo was Steve's wingman. His fighter, *Miss Mischief,* was flying close by. Viewed from the side, the Lockheed F-80C Shooting Star's fuselage was shaped like a stainless-steel cigar tube. Coming at you, the "Shooter" had a pair of intake air ducts that flared out like a shark's gills. The F-80 had stubby, non-swept wings tipped with teardrop-shaped auxiliary fuel tanks. This particular flight of F-80s wore the three concentric orange nose rings and the tic-tac-toe pattern of orange slashes on their vertical tail fins that identified them as members of the 19th Fighter Interceptor Squadron. The 19th was attached to the Eighth Fighter Bomber Wing, based at Itazuke Air Base on Kyushu, the southernmost of the main Japanese Islands.

Steve clicked his throat mike. "Time to go downstairs and bust up some commie tanks—"

"Talk about 'cwazy wabbits,'" DeAngelo muttered darkly.

"You gonna be okay, Mikey?" Steve asked, concerned.

"Yeah, sure," DeAngelo said in his flat New England accent. "Gonna be a day at the beach. Chowda and clam cakes at Rocky Point. . . ."

No harm in letting DeAngelo run off at the mouth, Steve thought as he led his flight in a spiraling dive down toward the river valley. *Do Mikey good to expend some nervous energy before the flight tackles the dirty job at hand.*

Mike DeAngelo was new. He'd rotated into the squadron a few weeks ago, as the big push against the commies began at Inchon. DeAngelo was in his early thirties, short and stocky, with a round face and eyes as small and black as

California olives. He was an ace who'd flown a P-51 Mustang over Europe during the last war.

DeAngelo was the son of an accountant in Providence, Rhode Island. After the war, he'd finished his education to become a CPA, and had gone into partnership with his father. He was married, and had two kids. When this Korean thing had flared up, DeAngelo was called back by the Air Force to take jet fighter training.

Steve knew that Mike had answered that call grudgingly. During a late night bull session over a bottle of scotch, Mike had bitterly complained that he'd already done his part for his country. Why was he again being asked to risk his life? After all, this was not a *real* war, like the last one. This Korean thing was only a vaguely understood battle of wills between East and West over some obscure patch of ground, a patch that the United States had already pretty much admitted was relatively unimportant in terms of American security.

It was one thing for Steve to be here, DeAngelo had explained. Steve was a professional. War was his job. What DeAngelo could not understand was why he and a few others had again been plucked out of their lives by the military and told to fight to the death for Korea, when so many back home who had never fought for their country were continuing on like nothing was happening.

The CPA from New England didn't much believe in this war, but he was here nonetheless, flying against a savage enemy obsessed with wiping him from the sky. The bottom line was that the Air Force had told him to do the job, so DeAngelo was doing it.

Steve loved Mike like a brother for that.

Steve's radio crackled. "Bugs Flight, Bugs Flight, come in. This is Super Snooper."

Thanks to their morning briefing, Bugs Flight knew that Super Snooper was a captain named Joe Evans. Evans was based at K-32, an advance airfield a bit north of Chongju that was known as Chau-Chau to the Koreans and Cha-Cha to the Americans.

Steve keyed his mike. "Super Snooper, this is Bugs

Leader. Soupie, baby, talk to me. You got any nasty old weeds we can dig out of MacArthur's garden?"

Evans was assigned to Tactical Control Group. He flew a piston-engined T-6 trainer armed with nothing but harmless smoke rockets. It was TCG's job to fly low over enemy-held ground in order to find and pinpoint targets for bombing-strafing runs. TCG usually found such targets by taking ground fire and then coming around for a second pass in order to fire a smoke rocket to mark the spot where the ground fire came from. Not surprisingly, the pilots of TCG were widely considered to be the meanest tigers in the Air Force.

"Oh, I've got a lot of nasty weeds for you to pull," Evans responded. "They're big, tough red ones. I'm looking at six tanks, plus maybe a dozen trucks and a lot of troops. The whole shebang is strung out along the riverbank. Now, you cats gonna plow some dirt or what?" Evans demanded, feigning disgust.

"Coming down through the cloud cover now," Steve responded.

"Kerrist," Evans growled. "Why dontcha wait a little longer? Maybe these commies will die of old age."

Okay by me, Steve thought. This had turned out to be a nasty little war. Not a fighter pilot's kind of war at all, even if it had begun grandly enough. . . .

Back in June, in the days following the commie invasion from the North, Steve's squadron had helped to fly high cover escort during the evacuation of American citizens from Seoul. Steve's F-80 had been among the Shooting Stars flying high above Seoul's Kimpo Airfield on the afternoon of June 27, when a trio of North Korean prop-driven Yak fighters made the mistake of bouncing a flight of P-82, twin-boomed, twin-engined Mustangs. The Twin Mustangs had been flying low for cover for the USAF transports on the ground to pick up American citizens.

The NKAF Yaks had come in low from out of the clouds to shoot up one of the Twin Mustangs. Steve had heard the excited chatter among the Mustangs' pilots, and had descended to get a better view of the action. He'd felt like a spectator watching a sporting event from high up in a stadium's bleachers as beneath him the Mustangs swirled like hungry sharks around the Yaks, blowing the commies out of the sky.

Because of limited fuel capacity—each F-80 Shooting Star had only a short time above Seoul, so Steve had not been present when later that afternoon some F-80s from the 35th Fighter Bomber Squadron had chopped up a gaggle of Russian-built NKAF IL-10 fighters over Kimpo.

That had been the first time that U.S. jets had engaged in combat. Steve had cursed himself for having missed it, and cursed the Reds for not having seen fit to attack when he'd been around.

At the time, Steve and the other pilots who'd missed out had taken some solace from their belief that this was only the beginning of aerial combat in Korea. They'd been sure that commies would give those American pilots who'd racked up high scores in World War Two the opportunity to become aces in *two* wars.

It hadn't turned out that way. The NKAF had folded out of the game early on, leaving the battle to the communist ground forces. Throughout July and August the North Korean People's Army had made a southward push, spearheaded by battalions of Soviet-built T-34 tanks. The commies were well trained, and vastly outnumbered the U.S. and South Korean ROK forces, which lacked the weapons to pierce the thick armor that protected the enemy's tanks. It had quickly become evident that it was going to be up to American air power to slow the commies down long enough for the ROK-U.S. ground forces to regroup and rebuild. If the fly-boys couldn't do it, democratic freedom could kiss its ass good-bye in Korea.

The NKPA needed bridges and railways to move their tanks and men, so air power proceeded to deny the enemy what he needed, despite the miserable flying conditions of the rainy Korean summer. The USAF's B-29 light bombers tore up the bridges and rail tracks. Its F-82 Twin Mustangs and F-80 Shooting Stars, and the Navy's Panther jet squadrons flying from offshore carriers, went after the commie tank and troop carrier convoys that were lined up at those ruined bridges.

Steve had taken part in many of those ground-support missions, and was proud of the job he had done killing tanks and trains, but on-deck strafing missions, no matter how successful, did not earn a pilot ace status. With NKAF combat planes as rare as hen's teeth, it looked like the Korean war was going to be a bust as far as dogfighting was concerned. For Steve, that made it hardly a war at all.

Toward the end of summer, the commie advance bogged down as they were denied their armor, supplies, and communications. The respite allowed the UN the time to rally, and allowed American forces to get their second wind. In September, General MacArthur's daring landing at Inchon took the Reds completely by surprise. Since then, slowly but steadily the UN forces had rolled back the commies.

On the first of October, ROK forces, acting on the orders of US commanders, had crossed the 38th parallel. A few days ago, on the ninth, as B-29s bombed the North Korean capital of Pyongyang and South Korean troops rolled through the mountains of the North, meeting little resistance, MacArthur informed the commies that he expected *all* of North Korea to surrender, not just those Reds still on South Korean soil.

It looked as if the war was almost over, but meanwhile there were still scattered pockets of enemy resistance, such as the tank convoy in the valley below that had been spotted by TCG. Steve and his flight had been dispatched from Itazuke Air Base to destroy this concentration of enemy armor.

As the Shooting Stars descended beneath the cloud cover, the river below became visible: a gunmetal-blue snake wriggling through its rugged valley. The hills were carpeted with scrub oak and pines. Summer was fading into the dry winter season. The terrain was fading as well. The hills had gone from mottled green to several different shades of brown. Sometimes the land was the color of mud, sometimes it was the texture and hue of tobacco leaf, and sometimes it was as deeply burnished as an old leather A-2 flight jacket.

About a mile distant, at twelve-o'clock low, Steve spotted the speck in the sky that was Evans's T-6 trainer.

"Bugs Flight, check your systems," Steve ordered his pilots.

"All green," DeAngelo said.

"All green," echoed Lieutenants Molloy and Brady, who made up the flight's second element.

"Evans," Steve called, his eyes fixed on the tiny prop-driven olive drab painted airplane that was hopping like a flea over the brown-hide hills.

"Super Snooper here," Evans replied.

"We're closing on you."

"About fucking time."

Each pilot would have only enough fuel for two passes if he wanted to make it back home to Japan. The F-80 had been designed as a short-range jet interceptor, not a ground-support airplane. Its internal fuel supply gave it an operating radius of only one hundred miles, and that was when it was flying at the altitudes for which it was designed: above fifteen thousand feet.

Even with its original equipment auxiliary fuel tanks there was no way a Shooting Star could be running a mission like this, but back in July some engineers attached to the 49th Fighter Bomber Wing over at Misawa Air Base had come up with a way to increase the Shooting Stars' range by cutting in half a standard wingtip auxiliary fuel tank and welding in a couple more sections to make an elongated tank. A pair of these overgrown "Misawa" tanks shackled to the F-80's wingtips strained the airplane's structure, but it gave the jet up to an extra hour of flying time. Steve's flight was equipped with "Misawas," but in a situation like this, where the jets were going to be gulping fuel attacking 'on deck,' the extra-large tip tanks only afforded a few extra minutes on target.

"X marks the spot," Evans said as he began to fire off his smoke rockets. "Watch your assess coming through, boys. I count three machine-gun emplacements on the slopes. I'll mark them for you."

It's going to be a rough day's work, all right, Steve

thought. The commies were dug in deep. Evans's T-6 was darting and swooping like a butterfly as it fired off smoke rockets to mark the positions of the machine-gun nests. The smoke plumed off the rocky slopes and swirled like dust devils around the scrub and tall golden weeds that led down to the water's edge. There, scattered in among the slow-moving but powerful Russian-manufactured, canvas-sided GAZ trucks churning up mud on the riverbank, were the six T-34 tanks.

The Soviet-built T-34—Steve and the other pilots had learned all about the monsters at briefings, and through hard experience. It had been the T-34 that had allowed the Russians to beat the Germans back in '45, and it was the T-34 that might still allow the North Koreans to win this war. The tank was twenty feet long and ten feet wide. It carried a crew of five and was specially designed for travel over mud and snow. Its diesel engine could take it hundreds of miles thanks to the auxiliary fuel drums strapped to its rear decking, and its armor plate could deflect a direct hit from a 105-millimeter howitzer, as the American forces had learned to their sorrow this previous summer. When it was time to hit back, the T-34 carried an 85-millimeter antiaircraft gun and two 7.62-millimeter machine guns. The weaponry was quite capable of reaching out to swat an F-80 out of the sky the way an ox might twitch its tail to rid itself of a pesky fly.

The only weapon an F-80 could carry that was capable of killing a T-34 was a five-inch high-velocity aircraft rocket. Each of the F-80s in Bugs Flight had eight such HVARs mounted on racks beneath their wings.

But there was a catch—

The only way an HVAR had a chance against the tank's low, sloped turret or 19-millimeter thick armor was if it was fired from a thirty-degree angle, at a range of about fifteen hundred feet. Any closer and the rocket's engine would not have the time to kick in and increase its velocity, causing the rocket to bounce off the tank. Any farther away from the target and the chances of accuracy were too slim. To further increase the odds of killing the tank, or at least hitting its treads and in that way disabling it, the recommended procedure was to let loose with a salvo, or "ripple," of four HVARs.

As Steve was mulling all of this over, his radio earphones suddenly crackled. "This is a fucking shit-brick run," Steve heard DeAngelo complain.

"Roger that," Steve said. "Fucking Reds are going to be throwing everything including shit bricks at us, and we're going to have to fly low and straight and take it."

The valley was narrow, and its walls were steep, so the strafing runs would have to proceed along the river. That meant that the hills would hem in the Shooting Stars, keeping them from taking evasive action as the Koreans shot up at them. The jets would simply have to endure this gauntlet of defensive fire until they were close enough to launch their HVARs at the tanks.

"Bugs Three and Four will go in first," Steve ordered.

"Chicken, huh, Major?" Bugs Three, Lieutenant Brady, muttered.

Steve laughed. Brady knew as well as the others that he was doing them a favor. The first element would be in and out before the commies could effectively zero in, but the enemy would be ready and waiting when it was Steve and DeAngelo's turn to attack.

"Okay, Bugs Four. Follow me in," Brady told his wingman.

"This is the part I hate," Molloy said as he took up his position a good ways behind and several hundred feet above Brady.

The valley was too narrow for more than one jet to attack at a time, so the two elements of the flight would follow each other's nose to tail to try and keep their attack constant. Molloy's job as Brady's wingman would be to suppress any answering fire directed toward the lead jet, until it was time for him to launch his own rockets. Meanwhile, Steve would watch Molloy's back. DeAngelo would in turn watch his, and then Brady would be coming back in for his second run, hopefully in time to suppress ground fire for DeAngelo as he attacked the tanks. Molloy would again cover for Brady, and so on, until everyone had made his second pass.

"Yeah, I hate this part," Lieutenant Molloy was muttering as Brady's jet dipped low into the valley. "Major Gold, have I ever mentioned that I hated this part?"

"You'll get no sympathy from the major," DeAngelo cut in. "He's still a bitter man from having lost command of his squadron."

Steve clicked on his mike so that the others could hear his laughter. DeAngelo's ribbing was meant in good fun, and Steve took it that way.

Back in April, after successfully completing jet fighter training, he'd received his promotion to major. He'd immediately shipped out to join up with the Eighth, and take command of the 19th Squadron.

His command hadn't lasted very long. Steve served as CO only until the end of July, when squadron command was transferred to a full bird colonel named Billings. Steve had not been much upset about losing the squadron. He'd understood that the change had nothing to do with him personally. FEAF had been considered a backwater post until Korea had turned hot, and then the organization quickly became top-heavy with senior officers wanting a piece of the action. Billings was a good guy, and he'd had experience running a wartime squadron from the last war. Steve had been assured that an outstanding evaluation of his brief tenure as CO would be inserted into his record. Anyway, relinquishing command had allowed him more time to fly. All the tedious paperwork that Steve had been saddled with as CO had kept him pretty much grounded.

Evans's T-6 scout plane had climbed out of the valley as Bugs Three and Four went in fast and low. The commie troops along the riverbank scattered as Brady opened up with his six nose-mounted .50-caliber machine guns. The armor-piercing, phosphorous-loaded incendiary rounds stitched geysers of mud toward a truck, which abruptly exploded in a ball of orange flame. Tendrils of fire reached out to lick another truck, and that one went up as well. A machine-gun nest dug into the hill began to track Brady. Molloy instantly veered toward the muzzle flash, and opened up with his own half-dozen .50s. The machine-gun nest went silent.

"Thanks," Brady muttered.

"No problem," Molloy answered calmly.

Brady fired a ripple of four HVARs at a tank. The rockets seemed to hang in the air, and then abruptly picked up velocity as their own engines kicked in. They streaked down, trailing contrails of gray smoke, impacting to erupt in four terrific explosions that quickly united into a curtain of destructive force around the tank.

"Bugs Three, you all right?" Steve called out. He was just entering the valley as Brady's F-80 streaked past the enemy position and climbed to come around in a wide, banking turn.

"Everything's green," Brady announced. "I think I got a tank."

"Affirmative," Molloy said. "I see it burning. I'm beginning my run now. Jesus Christ! It's a regular shit-brick storm down here, all right! Those machine-gun nests on the slope have me bracketed!"

"I'll suppress," Steve firmly cut him off. He quickly veered toward the slopes to rake the nest with his nose guns. He didn't want Molloy getting distracted. Shit-brick runs could unnerve even the most aggressive of pilots, which, in Steve's opinion, Molloy was not. He was a World War Two fighter pilot veteran, but he wasn't an ace. Like DeAngelo, he'd been called back by the Air Force, and like DeAngelo he was just as pissed off about it. DeAngelo had not let his resentment toward the Air Force blunt his tiger instincts, but Molloy was a pussy by fighter pilots' standards. He had more balls that average, of course, otherwise he wouldn't be in a cockpit, but he was no tiger. Steve had recognized the fact the first time he'd flown with Molloy. He knew that when it got *really* hairy—like now—Molloy would need calm, steady encouragement to keep from losing it.

"Major! Where are you, dammit!" Molloy cursed. "I'm taking small-arms fire!"

"I'm on it," Steve said as he dropped his fighter's nose to

strafe the commie troops who were firing into the sky with rifles and submachine guns.

The small-arms ground fire coming up at them was definitely intense. The commies had to some extent countered last summer's air offensive by developing a devastating technique of putting up a curtainlike pattern of small-arms fire at low-flying attacking planes. They'd even been known to throw stones, sticks, and, for all anybody knew, their own shit into the sky—hence the term "shit-brick run."

Back in July the commies' tactic had seemed funny, but the Air Force stopped laughing when their prop-driven attack bombers began to go down. Rumor had it that the Air Force brass back at the Pentagon were busy conducting a reassessment of the Air Force's capabilities and limitations in a guerilla war. The stopgap solution to the problem had been to restrict the relatively slow prop-driven bombers to high-and-medium-altitude missions, leaving the on-deck action to the jets, which were supposed to be fast enough to get in and out before the commie duck hunters could draw their beads.

Steve had stayed as close as was possible behind Molloy, and had kept hammering away with his nose .50s, scattering bodies and torching another truck. "Okay, Molloy, do your job and get on out."

"Firing rockets now," Molloy said.

Steve watched the HVARs streak down and explode around a tank.

"Watch yourself," Molloy whispered as he came out of the valley. "Down there is one stirred-up hornet's nest."

"Affirmative," Steve said absently. He was concentrating on his flying. Wafting clouds of smoke from the burning trucks were now moving across the valley floor. The smoke hid the enemy, but even worse, obscured the slopes. A slight miscalculation on approach and the Shooting Stars could find themselves cartwheeling against the rocky hillside.

The smoke momentarily lifed from around the tank that Molloy had attacked. "Molloy," Steve radioed, "you got his treads."

"Sorry. . . ."

"Don't be. That was good shooting."

"He's not dead," Molloy pointed out. "He can still bite."

"Yeah, but he can't go anywhere, which makes him almost as good as dead," Steve replied. "Bugs Two," he called as he began his attack dive. "You with me, Bugs Two?"

"I'm here," DeAngelo replied.

The twisting, turbulent ribbon that was the river slid beneath the Shooting Star's nose as Steve careened through the valley. The high slopes on either side whipped past as the smoking target site loomed.

A flicker of fire coming at him from his port side caught Steve's attention.

"I'm pulling heavy machine-gun fire from the hillside—"

"I'm on it for you, Steve," DeAngelo said.

Steve forced himself to concentrate on his run and forget about the machine-gun nests. Suppressing them was his wingman's job. *His* job was to kill a tank.

The commie troops had formed defensive groups around the surviving trucks and tanks and were now steadfastly holding their positions. As Steve looked down at the massed soldiers, a glittering orange winking like that of fireflies flickered in his eyes.

Rifles and submachine guns, Steve thought grimly.

You had to give the Reds credit. Their side definitely had its share of heroes. Not even the Japs in the last war had been so fanatical.

Steve centered his guns on the clustered enemy and thumbed his trigger. A heavy rain of fiery lead peppered the soldiers as they crumpled away, some of the bodies rolled down the bank into the river.

"God, I hate it when they just stand there and take it like that," DeAngelo said weakly as the soldiers went down beneath Steve's chattering guns.

"I hear you," Steve said.

"What kind of political system is it that makes them into human ants like that?"

Steve fired a salvo of rockets at a tank. His Shooting Star shuddered as the HVARs tore loose. Their own engines lit at the very moment their target opened up with its cannon and machine guns. Steve watched his rockets seem to cage the tank with smoky contrails and then explode. As he whipped past, he glimpsed a sudden, fifth explosion, one that sent a column of fire reaching up into the sky.

"How'd I do?" he demanded as he climbed out of the valley and veered to starboard, crossing the river. "I must have hit something?"

"I'll say!" DeAngelo cried. "You cracked him open like he was a bug!"

"All right!" Steve laughed as he came around in a starboard circle. "Your turn, Mike. Go to it!"

As he flew back along the river in the opposite direction, he watched DeAngelo begin his attack dive. Suddenly the two remaining machine-gun nests sparked to life, effectively broadsiding DeAngelo's jet.

"I'm taking hits!" DeAngelo called.

Fuck, Steve thought. "Bugs Three! Where are you?" he demanded savagely.

"I'm on my way—" Brady began.

"Negative!" Steve ordered. "You should have been here! Now there's no time! You hang back, Bugs Three."

"Wilco," Brady replied, sounding affronted.

"Mike!" Steve called as he flung his jet back across the river toward the machine-gun nests. "I'm coming in to fly cover for you."

The diving turn was sharp. Increased gravity tore at him. Steve was on the verge of blacking out, but the bladders sewn into his G-suit mercilessly squeezed his thighs and abdomen, forcing the blood back up into his torso and brain. He got one of the commie gun emplacements in his sights and opened up with his nose guns, pelting it, and then veered to get the other. The nest had moved off DeAngelo and was now firing at Steve in an attempt to defend itself from his attack.

By now Steve was too close to the slopes to use his fixed-mount nose guns. The hills were looming up at him, which meant that he had to get his nose *up* if he was going to clear the crest.

As he streaked past the gun emplacement, he impulsively fired off an HVAR, and had time to glimpse the smoking rocket corkscrew to earth. The HVAR exploded about fifty feet above the machine-gun nest, burying it in an avalanche of debris.

"Great shooting!" crowed Brady, who was just beginning his second run.

Steve gritted his teeth against the increased G's as he wrenched his F-80 out of its dive and climbed, desperate to clear the valley. The G-suit was tightening around him like a vise as he was flattened against the back of his seat. He could hear the engine screaming as his Shooting Star struggled to regain that high perch in the sky for which it had been born.

Steve looked down through the side window of his canopy as his plane scraped past the ridge with less than a hundred feet to spare. Below him he saw a single commie soldier draped in that quilted uniform that they wore, standing at the top of the slope. The commie, his rifle in the crook of his arm, was staring back at Steve. The soldier looked close enough to touch. The Red was likely feeling the scalding buffeting of the Shooting Star's exhaust.

As Steve stared down, time seemed to stand still. The shrill roar of the F-80's engine receded. The smoke and fire from the valley floor dropped away. There was just Steve, strapped into the great six-ton silver bird that was struggling to find purchase in the air.

And there was that lone communist foot soldier who was now shouldering his weapon.

Steve never actually saw the soldier shoot at him, but he felt those three ridiculously puny rifle rounds pelting his jet, and by the third *plink!* the world rushed back with a vengeance. A trembling ran through the aircraft like a dog shaking off water. On the instrument panel warning lights began flashing like rubies.

"Bugs Flight, this is Bugs Leader," Steve began calmly as he left the ridge behind. "I'm hit. I'm hit."

Whatever damage he had sustained seemed minor, so he immediately began to climb, to give himself as much sky as possible to work with should things go radically wrong. He studied his instruments. Everything seemed normal, but his warning lights were still on. He still had some rockets left, so he was tempted to make another run through the valley, but he decided against it. It was more important to get his jet home in one piece than try to kill another tank.

"Brady, I'm on my way home," Steve radioed. "You and Molloy stick around and take your final pass."

"Wilco," Brady replied.

"Major, what do you want me to do?" DeAngelo broke in.

"Keep me company on the way home, will you, Mike?"

"Wilco, I'll chaperon," DeAngelo said genially. "But I'm warning you now, I expect a kiss at the front door."

"If I *get* to the front door," Steve said as he streaked away from the valley on a course for home. "Japan seems a long way off at the moment."

"Do you think you need to bail out?" DeAngelo asked.

Steve studied his instruments. "Negative . . . plane seems to be responding all right. But I've got warning lights flashing all over the place. I just don't know. . . ."

"Bugs One, this is Super Snooper," Evans cut in. "Bugs One, come in please."

"Snooper, this is Bugs One," Steve replied, relaxing a little as his altimeter read twenty thousand feet. "Soupy, you still around?"

"I'm on my way back to Cha-Cha," the TCG pilot said. "Listen now, Bugs Leader. You don't want to be ditching anyplace around here. There's a whole bunch of commie stragglers wandering around these parts, and they don't know they've lost their war. They get hold of you, Bugsy, they're gonna cook themselves up some winged jackrabbit stew in one of their Mongolian hot pots. You read me?"

"Affirmative," Steve said as he leveled off at 25,000 feet. The North Koreans were not known for their kind and merciful treatment of prisoners, and *especially* not pilots. "Some neighborhood you've got here, Evans."

The TCG pilot's deep, melodious laughter filled Steve's

helmet. "Bugsy, this ain't nothing compared to where I grew up in Philly. . . ."

"Steve, I'm coming up behind you," DeAngelo cut in. "Stay level and I'll look you over."

"Affirmative. My hydraulics and fuel readings seem okay," Steve said, and laughed. "Good thing, too. I never would have lived it down if some commie with a squirrel gun had salted my tail."

"Steve, you sure your hydraulic pressure is reading okay?" DeAngelo asked, sounding concerned.

Steve felt his stomach clench. *Shit—shit—shit—* he thought. "What's up, Mikey? What do you see?"

"You're leaking something."

"Hydraulic fluid?"

"Some sort of fluid," DeAngelo replied vaguely. "Fuck, Major, they taught me how to fly'em, not fix'em—"

"That makes two of us," Steve said. "I'll tell you this much—this bird is going into the shop when we get back."

At that moment, as if to perversely contradict him, Steve's engine died. He felt the jet seem to stumble in flight like a fly abruptly hindered by the sticky strands of a spider's web.

"Christ! Steve!" DeAngelo suddenly shouted. "You've got a flameout!"

I kind of know that, Steve thought. In the sudden, sickening silence there was only the mournful keening of the wind against his canopy, mixing with his own harried breathing. The red lights of the instrument panel cast crimson reflections against Steve's visor. The warning lights glowed balefully, as if to say, *"we told you so."*

With his engine out, his hydraulic boost had dropped, making his flight controls feel like they'd been soaked in molasses and then dredged in sawdust. The jet's forward glide speed would keep the engine's turbine blades windmilling at sufficient speed to keep up hydraulic pressure, but Steve would have to keep his use of the controls to a minimum to avoid exhausting the accumulator pressure supply.

"I'm attempting a relight," Steve said, thinking that the windmilling engine should have evaporated the excess fuel by now. He went through the relight procedure, but it didn't work. He switched from his main fuel flow control system to the emergency system and again went through the restart procedure, with no luck.

"Mike, I can't relight her," Steve complained. "Are you clear of me?"

"You bailing out?"

"Negative. I want to blow off my garbage—"

"I'm clear."

Steve rechecked to make sure, then jettisoned the remaining HVARs and the external wingtip tanks. It hurt to see those custom-built Misawas fall away, but since this bird had just turned into a glider, Steve wanted as little drag as possible, and extra fuel weighing him down was the last thing he needed. He began shutting down the airplane's unessential electrical components. The engine would not windmill enough to provide adequate output to the generator. Whatever electrics he used would have to draw power off the battery, which at best could last no more than ten minutes.

"Steve, you sure you don't want to bail out?" DeAngelo asked nervously.

"Negative. You heard what Super Snooper said."

"You sure as hell aren't going to make it to Japan."

"Affirmative," Steve said briskly. There was no sense denying that he was going down someplace far from home. The question was where?

He was now down to about 22,000 feet, and falling, but slowly. He patted himself on the back for having been smart enough to get altitude when he'd had the chance. It also helped that there was no wind. At least the weather, if not luck, was running his way.

"Hey, Steve!" DeAngelo exclaimed. "They've been working on the airfield at Taegu, preparing it for F-80s. Maybe the work's gone far enough along for you to set down there."

"Negative. Taegu's too far away. I've got maybe another twenty miles before this bird goes to ground."

"If not Taegu, where?"

Steve hesitated. "I'm going to try to put her down at

Cha-Cha." *There,* he thought, exhaling a deep sigh of relief. *Saying it out loud was almost as hard as actually doing it.*

"Say again?" DeAngelo requested. "I don't think I read you. . . ."

Steve chuckled. "You heard me, all right. I'm landing at Cha-Cha."

"Major," DeAngelo began patiently, "Cha-Cha is an advance base. Strictly a prop-plane fly-by-night operation. You can't set an F-80 down in the boondocks."

Steve glanced to starboard. DeAngelo had cut his own speed to fly at Steve's side. Steve, looking out through his canopy, could see Mike in his helmet, oxygen mask, and visor staring back at him.

"Since when does a lieutenant tell a major what he can do?" Steve joked.

"Steve, don't be such a jerk."

Steve smiled. "That's 'Don't be such a jerk, *sir.*' I happen to outrank you."

"Yeah? Well, I'm older than you."

"Got me there."

"So you'd better start making some sense," DeAngelo grumbled. "Before I decide to drop back and put an HVAR up that good-for-nothing F-80's ass pipe. That would get you to bail out whether you liked it or not!"

Steve waved to DeAngelo. "Have I ever told you you're beautiful when you're angry?"

"I've also got a few hundred rounds left in my guns," DeAngelo said firmly. "Ought to be enough to chew off your tail."

"Okay, okay," Steve laughed in surrender. "Here's my thinking. I still have control of the airplane, even if she is a glider. That means I still have choices. So I'm choosing to stay with my airplane. If it turns out that I crash in an attempted landing, at least it'll be at my own hands. That's one hell of a lot better way to go than being executed while I'm on my knees by the commies, or even worse, being picked off by a sniper while I'm dangling helplessly in the air from my chute."

"I read you, Major," DeAngelo said quietly. "But you

could also bail out once you're *over* Cha-Cha. That way you won't fall into enemy hands."

But I could still be picked off by a sniper, Steve thought. "You're right, Mike. Maybe I will do that."

"You'd *better* do that!" another voice cut in.

"Evans, is that you?" Steve demanded. "Where are you, Soupie?"

"A couple of miles from Cha-Cha."

"Have you been monitoring the entire time?"

"Affirmative," Evans replied.

"Okay," Steve said. "Then you know my situation."

"You better know *Cha-Cha's* situation. What we have is a thirty-eight-hundred-foot clay and gravel runway."

"Great. . . ." Steve sighed. The F-80 was happy with a little over twice that. "Is it in good shape, at least?"

"If you like potholes," Evans said.

"What the hell kind of operation do you TCG boys run?" Steve complained.

"The kind of operation we like. We got us a genuine cinder-block building, and some Quonsets, and some tar-paper shacks; we've got us some jeeps and trucks, a first-rate radio-radar setup, a couple of T-6s, and a baker's dozen of F-51 Mustangs equipped to fly close support."

"Personnel?" Steve asked.

"There's a hundred of us," Evans said. "Besides me, five other TCG people, and nine USAF instructor pilots to fly those combat missions. Everyone else is Korean. ROK troops are responsible for base security."

"*Is* the base secure?"

"Very. So's the road we're on, thanks to the September offensive," Evans said. "We've had FEAF brass come by for a visit, and currently have a civilian newsreel contingent visiting from Japan. But like I said before, you can still find scattered groups of commies holding out in the hills."

"Hear that last bit, DeAngelo?" Steve demanded. "There's no way I'm bailing out. Evans, who's in command at Cha-Cha?"

"That would be Major Kell."

Steve checked his altitude: seventeen thousand feet and

starting to drop a bit more steadily. Still plenty of glide time to reach Cha-Cha, however.

"Okay, Captain. After you set down, you tell your major to close all traffic and clear the strip of any parked airplanes."

"The major ain't going to like it," Evans warned.

"I'm not concerned about that," Steve said.

"He's going to deny you permission to land."

"He can't deny me," Steve said. "By the time I'm over your base, this Shooting Star will have completed its transition into a *falling* star, and it will be falling on Cha-Cha. It would be in Cha-Cha's best interests to try and catch it. You read me, Captain?"

"Affirmative," Evans chuckled. "I hope you live long enough to meet Kell, Bugsy. The sparks would fly. You boys got our coordinates on your maps?"

"Affirmative," Steve replied. "But I'm not sure about any of my compassess."

"Okay," Evans said. "Bugs Two, your instruments functioning?"

"Affirmative," DeAngelo said.

"Okay, Bugsy. You let your wingman guide you until you see a main road heading toward the west. Then you can just follow that road to Cha-Cha. Meanwhile, I'll do my best to see that the welcome mat, such as it is, is out for you."

"Thanks," Steve said quietly. "Mike?"

"Yeah, Steve," DeAngelo replied instantly.

"First of all, how's your fuel holding out?"

"I've got enough. I never took that second run at the target site, remember?"

"Okay, then," Steve replied, "what I want you to do is get me to that road, and then beat it home. You don't wait around. You get home safe. That is a direct order, Lieutenant. Do you read me?"

"Affirmative," DeAngelo said reluctantly.

DeAngelo moved out ahead to take the lead. A couple of minutes later the road, looking like scar tissue slashed across the leathery Korean landscape, came into view.

"Good-bye, Bugs Two," Steve said firmly.

"I could stick around a little longer. . . ."

Steve heard the concern in DeAngelo's voice. "Appreciate it, but there's nothing more you can do for me, Mikey," he consoled. "Now carry out your orders, Lieutenant."

"Wilco. See you later, Major." DeAngelo paused. "See you *home*," he added fervently.

"See you," Steve murmured. *I hope—*

He watched with longing as DeAngelo's sleek bird pulled away. In an instant the F-80's tailpipe was a distant speck glowing white-orange in the pale blue sky. Then DeAngelo was gone, and Steve was alone.

He steered with feather-light touches to the controls, wanting to conserve as much of his hydraulic boost as possible. He was traveling at a little over two hundred miles an hour. At that rate it would be just a few minutes to Cha-Cha. That was a good thing. He was going to want to radio contact with Cha-Cha's control, and the F-80's battery had to be fading.

Steve took a deep breath and let it out slowly. He felt keyed up and tense with anticipation, but he also felt strangely relaxed. The wind was whistling soothingly. His own breathing reminded him that he was alive and well. The radio white noise whispering inside his helmet reminded him of the sound a seashell made when it was held up to the ear.

He found himself thinking back on jet fighter training school. He'd found the strict discipline an ordeal after his cushy assignment in Washington. The cool, sarcastic instructor pilots hadn't cared that he was a captain and an ace from the last war, that he was on line to become a major. As far as the IPs were concerned, Steve was just another know-nothing cadet who was going to have to prove himself all over again.

And he had proved himself, although it hadn't been easy. Steve had hated all those hours spent in the classroom, and his nights spent studying goddamned mathematical formulas that seemed to go right out of his head as soon as he shut the textbook. He'd just squeaked by the written exams.

He thought about the early morning PT routines, the afternoon marches through the scorchingly hot Texas countryside while chanting, "Every man a tiger!" What a joke that had seemed! He was a goddamned combat veteran, an ace, and as aggressive in the air as any man could be. He didn't need any candy-ass motivation; he needed wings and armament, and then he would get the job—*any job*—done.

And then there had been that first, unsettling time he'd settled into the pilot's chair in the twin-seat cockpit of the T-33 trainer, which was essentially a modified Shooting Star. He'd been dismayed by the multitude of instrument displays, by all the buttons, switches, and levers.

His IP, picking up on Steve's confusion, had laughed at him. Through the intercom, his voice crackling with static and sarcasm, the IP had sneered, *"We don't fly 'em by the seat of our pants anymore, Captain."*

"Bugs Leader, this is K-32—" The officious-sounding voice came crackling over the radio. "Bugs Leader, come in, please."

Steve shook himself alert. "K-32, this is Bugs Leader."

"Bugs Leader, this Major Kell, K-32's CO. We have you on radar. We should be coming into your view anytime now."

The F-80 was at fifteen thousand feet, but now she was dropping fast, silently curving like a spent arrow toward the earth. As Steve crested a line of hills, he saw Cha-Cha just a couple of miles ahead.

"K-32, I have you in sight," Steve said. He closed the distance to the base in under a minute, which was ample time for him to see that Cha-Cha was everything Evans had said, and less.

The ragtag collection of parked vehicles and clustered buildings was just a wide spot in the road. A long, low cinder-block structure, its flat roof tangled with radio and radar gear, hugged the edge of the clay airstrip, which was ridiculously short, and from Steve's vantage looked like a flesh-colored Band-Aid stuck down on the burnt grass. As Steve circled to lose altitude, he saw that the base's fleet of World War Two vintage fighters was still parked on either side of the runway.

"K-32, you were supposed to clear the goddamned field—" he radioed.

"Bugs Leader, as CO of the field I am denying you permission to land. Do you read? Permission to land denied!"

"Major, what do you expect me to do?"

"Abandon your plane. Bail out."

"Negative," Steve said firmly. "I brought her this far. I think I can save her for another day."

"Negative, Bugs Leader. We have no heavy-fire-fighting equipment. What if you crash and the fire somehow ignites our fuel and ammo stores? It's just too risky. We have civilians here—"

"Oh, yeah, that newsreel outing," Steve remarked. "Tell me, Major, how's it going to look to *them* if you turn away a pilot in distress?"

"Dammit, listen to me, Bugs Leader! The runway is only hard-packed clay meant for lighter aircraft. It can't take the weight of your plane."

"I figure it'll be solid enough, provided I grease her in."

"You *figure*," Kell snarled sarcastically.

"Yeah."

"*Provided* you can grease her in. . . ."

This Kell was starting to piss Steve off. The guy reminded Steve of the sarcastic IP he'd been stuck with that first time in the T-33's cockpit. *"You can't fly 'em by the seat of your pants. . . ."* that IP had sneered. Well, Steve was about to find out about that.

"Look, Major," Steve began, "I'll bet you a case of scotch I can land this bird."

There were a few seconds of silence, and then Kell came back on the line. "You're Major Steven Gold, I take it?"

"I am."

"Well, Major Gold, you are one cocky son of a bitch," Kell said thinly.

Steve laughed. "*Well*, Major Kell, you and I finally have something that we agree on. Now you get those fucking Mustangs out of my way," Steve demanded, growing serious. "And you tell those newspeople to make sure they've got plenty of film in their cameras, because I am about to show them something they've never seen before and likely won't see again."

There were a few more seconds of silence. "Wilco," Major Kell finally replied in surrender. "Good luck, Major Gold. I hope you live to collect on your bet."

Steve was now spiraling in a constant, circular rate of descent. As he did so he watched as the personnel down below hurried to push the Mustangs parked along the strip to safety. At six thousand feet he lowered his landing gear, using the emergency procedure. He made sure the main landing gear handle was down and then pulled and held the emergency release. In the emergency mode it took a little time—maybe ten seconds—for all the up-locks to be released. The seconds seemed to stretch into eternity. After fifteen seconds his indicators were still showing that the gear was up.

Oh fuck, Steve thought. *I do not want to belly in.* He was cocky, but he wasn't crazy. If he couldn't get his landing gear down, he would have to bail out after all.

"K-32, come in please."

"Hiya, Bugsy."

"Evans!" Steve exclaimed, pleased not to have to talk to Major Kell. "I think—*I hope*—I've lowered my landing gear, but my indicators are showing that it's still up. Can you visually check?"

"Hold on a second," Evans said. "Okay, we've got binoculars on you, Bugsy. Your gear is down."

"Great," Steve sighed in relief. "My indicators are probably shorting out due to a fault in the system."

"Come on in whenever you think you're ready," Evans said.

Steve yawed the airplane, rocking the main gear to make sure it was locked as he switched to a rectangular flight pattern. Below and ahead of him, the cleared airstrip was waiting. He banked for his straight-on, final approach.

"Evans, this is it."

"Grease her in, Bugsy," Evans said quietly.

The runway was rushing up at Steve. He manually locked his shoulder harness and then jettisoned the F-80's canopy, in case fire did break out and he wanted to get out fast. He used the alternate system in order to get rid of the canopy without arming the ejection seat. The released canopy caught the slipstream and lifted off. The wind clawed at Steve, tearing away his oxygen mask. He gingerly pushed the stick forward to bounce the nose wheel against the clay in a modified touch-and-go in order to insure that his nose gear was locked, and then he went down for real.

He bounced up against the locked harness, feeling the straps bite into his shoulders as the F-80's tires bit the clay, transforming the silky rush of flight into a roaring, vibrating nightmare. Steve pressed the brakes. The jet slowed, but only a little. The windmilling engine was helping by creating drag, but the heavy jet had touched down at over 120 miles an hour. It was now rolling onward like the world's biggest cannonball on wheels. The cinder-block building topped with its radio antennas and radar gear whipped by in a blur.

Not much runway left. Going to overshoot for sure, Steve thought, struggling against panic as the end of the clay hurled toward him—

He stood on the brakes and heard the tortured squeal of his tires above the screaming wind. He imagined the rubber smoking. *If a tire blows and the plane goes over, the fuel left in the internal tanks will ignite. No heavy fire-fighting equipment, Kell said. No way they could get to me in time. . . .*

". . . crazy son of a bitch—" crackled thinly in Steve's ears.

"One crazy son of a bitch. . . ." Major Kell had said.

"You crazy son of a bitch, you did it!" Evans repeated, laughing.

"Huh?" Steve whispered. He clicked his mike button. "Huh . . ." he managed. God, his throat was dry!

"You did it!" Evans crowed. "Congratulations!"

Steve, his muscles trembling, was still pressing with all his might against the brakes. He was trying to get the F-80 to stop, but she couldn't or wouldn't. He wondered what Evans was talking about.

Then he glanced sideways and realized that he wasn't moving after all. He'd thought that he still was, but it must have been some kind of hallucination his keyed-up nervous system had been playing on him.

The F-80 had stopped, all right. Her nose was only a few feet from the end of the runway, but she had stopped.

"Oh, you craz—of a bitc—" Evans was laughing. *"You di—t."*

"You're breaking up," Steve said. "My battery's about dead. I can hardly hear you. Do me a favor, call Itazuke for me, let my people know I'm okay?"

"Wilco," Evans said, almost unintelligible in a burst of static. "Kell's here. He wants to know what brand of scotch?"

"J&B," Steve chuckled. "But whatever he can get will be fine. Nobody expects *him* to work miracles."

A half hour later Steve was in Cha-Cha's mess hut. He had showered and changed into a fresh set of flight overalls.

A flight crew had appeared to help Steve climb down from the cockpit as he was busy unhooking himself from the F-80. Once the crew chief had made sure that Steve did not need medical attention, he explained that Major Kell had spun some bullshit yarn to the press about how they had to remain confined to the pilots' briefing room because the F-80 could still explode. This was in order to give Steve some time to clean up and have something to eat.

Now Steve was alone in the mess hut, seated at a long table. There was no one on duty behind the counter when he'd come in, but there was a coffee urn going. Steve had rummaged around in the food lockers and come up with some bread and ham and mustard.

He was polishing off his second sandwich when he noticed a folded-up newspaper on the floor beneath the table. It was a recent issue of *Stars and Stripes,* one that he hadn't seen. While he ate he thumbed through the paper until he came to the headline across the lower half of the third page:

BROADSWORD BUILDER WARNS AGAINST
SOVIET-BUILT MIGS IN KOREA

LOS ANGELES, Oct. 4—The president and chairman of Gold Aviation and Transport said here today that the Chinese Communists will soon be involved in the Korean conflict, and that his company's F-90 BroadSword jet fighter is the only airplane capable of besting the Chinese Reds' Soviet-built jets.

Herman Gold, in a keynote address to the Greater California Business Council, warned, "Now that the UN Forces have crossed the 38th parallel, it is only a matter of time before the Chinese Reds get into the fighting. Mao Tse-Tung has consistently warned that he will not stand by and allow North Korea to be defeated, and our own government has publicly admitted that thousands of Chinese troops have already entered into battle to shore up the flagging North Koreans.

"Up until now, the United States Air Force has had its own way in Korea," Gold went on to tell his audience, comprised of the most influential leaders of the California business community. "All that will change when the Chinese Reds introduce their Russian-built MiG-15s into the conflict. Our pilots are the best in the world, but we can't expect them to win with inferior equipment. My sources in Washington have told me that recent intelligence reports have appraised the MiG-15 to be a swept-wing, state-of-the-art jet fighter. If that turns out to be the case, I'm certain that the only airplane in the Air Force arsenal capable of besting the MiG and keeping the Korean skies safe for democracy is America's own swept-wing, state-of-the-art jet interceptor, the GAT F-90 BroadSword."

Gold went on to discuss the BroadSword's record-breaking performance specifications. He then mentioned the various subsidiary and independent companies that have subcontracted with GAT to produce components for the BroadSword.

"I say hats off to the American business establishment," Gold concluded to a standing ovation. "It's a testimonial to the American way of life that the free enterprise system has produced an airplane like the BroadSword. God willing, the BroadSword will help our brave boys in Korea keep the communist hordes safely confined behind their Bamboo Curtain."

Steve pushed away his plate. His appetite had been ruined by what he had just read. How dare his father presume to suggest that the Air Force wasn't capable of stopping the commies without GAT-built airplanes!

"Hello, Bugsy—"

Steve looked up. A Negro wearing flight overalls and a sage-green fur-collared flight jacket stood in the doorway, casting a tremendous shadow. The man was huge. He was at least six feet three inches tall, and had to weigh at least 220.

"Evans?—" Steve asked, startled.

"That's me."

Steve nodded. He had, of course, known that there were colored pilots, but he'd never actually met one.

Evans's smile faded. Steve didn't want him to get the wrong idea. He had nothing against colored people. "My God, Evans," he grinned, hoping to hide his astonishment with a joke. "How the hell do they shoehorn a guy your size into a cockpit?"

Evans didn't reply to that. "You sure it's just my size that's taken you by surprise, Major?" he grumbled. "All of a sudden you're looking mighty pale."

"How would *you* know?" Steve grinned, but the joke fell flat. He took out his cigarettes and lit one as Evans went over to the mess counter to help himself to a mug of coffee. "Well, okay," Steve said loudly.

"Okay, what?" Evans demanded, looking over his shoulder as he filled his mug from the urn.

"Okay, so you have a chip on your shoulder because

you're colored. I don't mind," Steve shrugged. "Maybe I got some chips on my shoulder, as well. So let's put this bullshit aside and get back to being friendly."

"You telling me you don't care that I'm colored?" Evans challenged.

"Right."

"That you weren't taken aback to see a colored man wearing wings and captain's bars?"

Steve shrugged. "The Air Force gave them to you. They must know what they're doing."

Evans hesitated a moment, but then smiled thinly. "Leastways, most of the time," he said softly.

Steve smiled back. "Captain, the only color I'm currently hating is red. Today you had the balls to do your job when we were up against those tanks, and that made you okay in my book. Then you stood by me when I was in trouble, and that made you more than okay. If Major Kell ever comes through with that case of scotch he owes me, I'll give you half. What more can I say? I can't fucking *adopt* you."

"You're too fucking irresponsible to be *my* daddy," Evans laughed as he brought over his coffee and sat down. He extended his hand across the table. "Pleased to finally meet you in the flesh, Major."

"Same here," Steve replied, shaking hands. "Did you get through to Itazuke okay?"

"No problem," Evans said as he sipped his coffee. "Everything is taken care of. What we'll do is dismantle your F-80 and truck it to K-2."

"Taegu?" Steve asked.

Evans nodded. "The 822nd Engineers have laid six thousand feet of pierced steel planking for you jet jockeys, and backup facilities are in place. K-2 is now operational for F-80s."

"That takes care of my airplane," Steve remarked. "Now all I have to do is figure out a way home."

"That's no sweat," Evans said. "We've got a transport coming in here tomorrow to take these reporters back to Japan. You can hitch a ride with them."

"That's great," Steve said, relieved.

"Speaking of reporters," Evans continued. "They're still waiting for you in the briefing room."

"Lead me to them," Steve said, standing up.

He followed Evans out of the mess hut. The sky had turned gray and the temperature had dropped, as if to portend the nasty Korean winter around the corner. One of the Mustang pilots had been willing to lend Steve a leather jacket, since the flight personnel at Cha-Cha had just been issued their cold-climate gear. Steve now zipped up the A-2, turning up its collar against the knife-edged wind that was gusting from the east.

"Good thing you landed when you did," Evans remarked as they crossed the compound toward the cinder-block building along the airstrip.

Steve nodded in agreement. "I doubt I would have even tried to land if I'd had to contend with this wind. Where's the briefing room?" Steve asked as they entered the building.

"This way, but first we have to stop at Major Kell's office," Evans said.

"How come?"

"Kell handed the reporters a line about what a big hero he was in helping you to land."

"Kell told them he *helped* me?" Steve scoffed. "I half expected the son of a bitch to scramble his F-51s to shoot me down."

"Well, anyway, the Major wants to make an entrance with you in front of those reporters." Evans shrugged, rolling his eyes. "You'll understand when you meet him.'"

He led Steve past the clerk-typist seated outside Kell's office. "Just try to keep a straight face," he whispered as he knocked on Kell's door, and then opened it.

"Sir, Captain Evans reporting with Major Gold, as ordered, sir." He came to attention and saluted as Steve edged past him into the office.

"Ah! There you are, Major Gold," Kell said briskly, standing up from behind his desk.

"Here I am," Steve agreed.

Kell was a very short man of slight build. He stood

ramrod straight, with his chin jutting, either to make the most of his diminutive height or to dare somebody else to make something out of it. He had a pencil-thin mustache and wispy, dark brown hair parted and slicked down across his high-domed forehead. He wore his khaki trousers tucked into high black boots, and had a dark blue ascot around his throat, tucked into his shirt collar.

"How you doing, Major?" Steve said, shaking hands with Kell. "Nice office you've got here," he added, his eye caught by the well-stocked, glass-fronted liquor cabinet taking up the corner of the room behind Kell's desk.

Kell must have seen him looking longingly at the booze. "Would you care for a drink?"

"You bet! Is that a bottle of Chivas I see peeking out from the back of that bottom shelf?"

"You have good eyes, Major," Kell said lightly, but his smile was colder than the Korean wind.

"Fighter pilots need good eyes," Steve replied. He watched as Kell took a ring of keys out of his pocket and unlocked the cabinet, then removed the bottle of Chivas, but only two glasses.

You dumb bastard, Steve thought. *You've got Evans standing right here and you don't intend to offer him a drink?*

Steve glanced at Evans, who seemed to sense what Steve was about to do. Evans began to shake his head no in warning.

"Captain Evans," Steve said heartily. "What are you having? Chivas as well?"

"Captain, you're dismissed," Kell interrupted.

You cheap bum, Steve thought as Evans crisply saluted and left the office. *Here you're the CO of a combat outfit, and you deny one of your best pilots a drink.*

It wasn't as if Kell was on short rations. The cabinet held plenty more bottles of booze, and like everything else in the office, the labels on those bottles were first-rate.

Kell had plenty of comforts, all right. Despite the cold weather outside, the office was warm, thanks to the potbelly coal stove. How Kell had managed to get wall-to-wall carpeting out here in the middle of nowhere, Steve couldn't imagine. And where had that black leather swivel chair come from, or the pair of brass desk lamps with green glass shades that flanked the pink marble pen stand? The only standard-issue furnishings were the folding canvas chairs meant for visitors.

The wall behind Kell's desk was entirely taken up with a huge silk embroidered reproduction of the FEAF insignia. Steve gazed at it as Kell poured the drinks.

The wall hanging was as big as a double bedspread. It was a beautifully and accurately done insignia rendition. The Air Force wing and star were sewn against the diamond-shaped dark blue background. Crowning the five-pointed star was the gold sunburst that represented the Philippine sun. The United States Army Air Force had been chased out of the Philippines by the Japanese back in '41, but history would forever show that the USAAF had more than paid Tojo back for that slap in the face. Beneath the wing and star were five smaller silver stars arranged in a curve somewhat like a shepherd's crook. The five stars represented the Southern Cross constellation; it had been beneath that constellation that General Kenney had activated FEAF in Australia back in '44.

"Here we are," Kell said. He carefully stowed away his Chivas, relocking the cabinet before handing Steve a glass.

Steve stared glumly. Kell had poured them both a stingy finger's worth of scotch. "Major Kell, where did you get that hanging?"

"Ah, that," Kell said, turning to admire it. "Something, isn't it? I hired some Korean women to sew it for me." He winked at Steve. "It cost next to nothing."

Steve nodded. "And what about this building? Pretty unusual for a post like this to have such luxurious digs. . . ."

"ROK Command was kind enough to put a labor force at my disposal," Kell explained. "But never mind about the building. Here's to our press conference." He raised his glass. "May it advance both our careers."

"Sure thing, Major," Steve said. He knocked back his drink. "That hit the spot."

"Glad you enjoyed it," Kell said, still sipping his drink.

"I don't suppose you'd come across with a case of Chivas to make good on our bet," Steve joked.

Kell finished his scotch and set down the empty glass. "Surely you don't expect me to honor that silly wager?" he demanded.

"A bet's a bet," Steve said, putting his glass on Kell's desk. "Anyway, what's the beef?" He gestured around the office. "With your obvious connections, getting a case of scotch should be easy.

"I was only humoring you when I made that bet," Kell said, shaking his head. "What I did was ascertain that you were on a very *thin edge* psychologically. Accordingly, I merely agreed to your unorthodox wager in order to relax you, thereby giving you the best possible chance of landing your fighter in one piece. Do you read me, Major?"

"Oh, you've come through loud and clear," Steve said evenly. *You welsher.*

"Very good," Kell nodded as he went to the closet and opened it. Steve watched, fascinated, as Kell took out a dark blue visored crush cap and a swagger stick.

That figures, Steve thought, glancing in amusement at the stick. He waited as Kell carefully centered his cap on his head as he stared at his reflection in the full-length mirror on the inside of the closet door.

"Now then, Major," Kell declared, "the press awaits."

"Well, hell," Steve said pleasantly. "Let's not keep them a-waiting any longer than a-necessary. . . ."

The briefing room was next to the radio room, which was at the far end of the building from Kell's office. They entered through a side entrance that led directly onto the raised platform at the front of the room.

The newsreel camera people switched on their bright floodlights as soon as Steve entered onto the platform. The lights made it impossible for him to see who was seated out there. Up on the platform there were a couple of folding chairs in front of a blackboard, and a map of Korea on an easel. Steve grabbed a chair and sat down. Kell, who remained standing, gave him a dirty look. Steve ignored it and enjoyed seeing the CO's face turn red as he began to slap his swagger stick against the side of his leg.

"Major Gold!" a disembodied voice called out from behind the wall of bright lights and whirring movie cameras. "Do you have a statement?"

Steve hesitated. He hadn't much liked public speaking the times he'd been forced into it back when he was working in public relations, but then he thought about that article in *Stars and Stripes*. If his father had seen fit to bad-mouth the Air Force, suggesting that it would be destroyed by the enemy if GAT didn't save it, Steve would just have to set the record straight.

"Yes, I do have a statement to make," Steve began, leaning forward in his chair and planting his elbows on his knees. "I'd like to begin by recounting the purpose of my flight's mission, and how my airplane happened to sustain damage. . . ."

He quickly filled the reporters in on what had happened during the mission, and then said, "Now, I don't want you guys making too much out of how my fighter was disabled. I wouldn't want the American people to get the wrong idea about their Air Force—either its personnel or its equipment."

"Come on, Major!" a reporter challenged. "You telling us it's not news when one commie rifleman can knock down a six-hundred-thousand-dollar airplane?"

"First of all, my plane wasn't knocked down," Steve said firmly. "She's damaged, sure, but she's also right here, safe and relatively sound and in American hands. I don't want to get into a war of words with you guys." Steve paused and smiled. "I know when I'm outgunned."

He waited for the reporters' appreciative chuckles to die away. "Seriously, what you have to understand is that the fault here does not lie with the Shooting Star. The 'Shooter' is a magnificent airplane. You ask any jet jockey, and they'll tell you that she is doing an outstanding job flying long-range operations in the kinds of weather that a year ago would have made the Air Force or Lockheed fall down laughing with disbelief.

"Take it from me—and I've flown just about every fighter the Air Force has come up with—the Shooting Star is one tough airplane. I've seen them make it back to Japan after sustaining the kind of damage that would have knocked a Mustang right out of the sky. We F-80 pilots wouldn't want to fly anything else.

"Now let's examine what happened to me today. First let me make it clear that the incident took place while the F-80 was successfully doing a job that she had never been designed to do. The Shooter belongs up around thirty thousand feet, where it can intercept enemy jets, not down on-deck doing the Triple-T Shuffle."

"What's the Triple-T Shuffle, Major?" a reporter interrupted.

"Shooting up trains, tanks, and trucks."

Steve again waited out the laughter, and then said, "The biggest problem the F-80 has faced has been the fact that she's had to fly from Japan, but now that K-2—Taegu Air Base—is F-80 operational, that problem is licked. You can tell the folks back home that the F-80 and the men who fly her have the situation in Korea well in hand." He paused. "Okay, now I'll take questions, if there are any."

"You think the F-80 can stand up to the commies' MiGs?" a reporter called out.

"Absolutely," Steven said.

"Major Gold," another correspondent, this one a woman, began. "What you've just told us seems to be in direct contradiction to what your father has said about the F-80."

"First of all, let me say that I'm surprised but pleased to hear a woman's voice. I think it's testimony to our fighting forces that what was once disputed territory is now safe enough for women civilians. Now getting back to your question, I *know* what my father said about the F-80's capabilities," Steve said coldly. "I happen to disagree with him when he says that the Shooting Star is inferior to the Broad-Sword." He paused. "I guess the BroadSword will prove to be a capable fighter, but that's *all* I can do: *guess* about it. At least the F-80 has been combat tested. Ask any veteran fighter pilot, and he'll tell you that the confidence that comes from your own and other pilots' accumulated experience with a particular airplane can make all the difference in whether a dogfight is won or lost. Despite what *Herman* Gold has said, *Steven* Gold believes that the F-80 has already sufficiently proven itself to be more than a match for anything the commies can put into the sky. We can only wait and see about the BroadSword. Next question?"

"Major Gold," a reporter began, "Major Kell has already filled us in on how he was able to talk you down."

Steve looked inquiringly at Kell.

"The correspondent is referring to the fact that my radioed instructions to you helped you to make a safe landing," Kell said hastily.

"Oh. . . ." Steve nodded, smiling as he leaned back in his chair. *This one's for you, Evans,* he thought. "Yeah, sure, the major here talked me down. You know how this old tiger did it? He realized that I was *psychologically on edge,* so he made me a *promise* in order to get my mind off my troubles." Steve glanced at Kell. "Didn't you, Major?"

"I'm not sure to what you're referring. . . ." Kell began to sweat.

"How about it, Major Kell?" a different woman reporter called out. "What did you promise him?"

"It—uh—seems to have slipped my mind, exactly." Kell looked beseechingly at Steve.

"Don't be modest, Kell," Steve coaxed. "Tell them how you promised me the scotch—"

"Yes!" Kell exclaimed, sounding relieved. "The scotch!" He confidently turned to face the reporters. "I promised the major a bottle—"

"A case," Steve corrected meaningfully.

"A . . . *case* of scotch," Kell echoed, glaring at Steve.

"I'll let you fellows know when he delivers," Steve said, and heard Evans's deep and sustained laughter coming from the back of the room.

"I have a question," yet another female voice announced. *Holy shit, that sounds like—*Steve sat bolt upright.

"Linda? Linda Forrest?" he called out uncertainly. "Is that you?" He shielded his eyes, trying to see through the bright lights. "Come on, fellas, shut those spots off for a second, would you?"

The lights died. Steve tried to blink away the specks in front of his eyes as he scanned the twenty-odd people sitting with their heads bent, jotting notes or winding up their hand-held movie cameras.

"Linda?" Steve called.

She stood up. She'd been sitting near Evans, toward the back of the room. "My question, Cap'n, is how do you manage to get yourself into and out of such tight scrapes?"

Steve laughed. "What the hell are you doing here?"

"Covering the war for my wire service. What else, Cap'n?"

She had her hair tucked under a duck-billed airman's cap, and was wearing a too-big set of fatigues that hid her lush figure. Steve, wondering what she had on under the fatigues, felt himself beginning to get hard.

"Uh, pardon me, Miss Forrest," Kell patronized, "but that's *Major* Gold, not Captain—"

"The Air Force may have promoted him," Linda said, winking at Steve, "but *I* haven't."

(Two)

It was early evening, and cold, but the wind blowing out of the east had chased away the clouds, revealing a starry sky. Steve was standing out on the far end of the runway, looking at his F-80 in the deepening twilight.

The day's events had caught up with Steve by the time the press conference had ended. Exhausted, he'd asked Linda if they could get together after he'd had a couple of hours of sleep. That had suited her; she'd needed some time to prepare and radio her dispatch to the Japanese mainland, where it would be cabled to the States.

As tired as he'd felt, once Steve had stretched out on a

bunk in the pilots' barracks he'd been unable to sleep. Every time he'd closed his eyes he'd found himself back in the cockpit of his F-80, reliving the mission, and that moment when he'd locked eyes with that lone communist soldier, seeing the expression on the commie's face as he brought his rifle to his shoulder. . . .

It was like that a lot after a CAP. So much was happening at the time that you had to do the best job you could without really thinking about what you were doing at the time. It was well afterward, usually at night when you were trying to get some shut-eye, that one random incident from the mission would rise up in your mind and suddenly the whole damned experience came vividly alive in your fevered brain.

When that happened, Steve was helpless to do anything but give in. A little while ago he'd spent a fidgety couple of hours lying on his back, staring into the darkness and chain-smoking as he relived over and over again the day's mission, including that hellish landing. Finally he gave up trying to sleep, and left the barracks, thinking the cool night air would clear his brain.

The Korean sentries initially challenged him, but then left him alone as he prowled the compound, finally walking the length of the deserted airstrip to gaze at his airplane. Now, as he stared at the F-80, he couldn't help feeling that it was weird that he seemed to take some comfort from being near the jet. Hell, you'd think that he'd had his fill of the big hunk of metal by now.

"I knew I'd find you here," Linda said, coming up behind him.

Steve turned. "Hi, Blue Eyes."

She was all bundled up in a cold-weather insulated parka. Like her other military-issue garments, the parka was way too big for her. In the starlight the hood trimmed with gray-tipped rabbit fur was gathered up around her face like the petals of a silvery flower.

She stood on tiptoe to kiss him on the cheek. He put his arm around her, and with his free hand reached out to pat the side of the jet. "I'm in heaven," he joked. "Surrounded by my two best girls."

She playfully nudged him in the ribs. "Just don't get us mixed up and go sticking your thingie in the wrong tail-pipe...."

"Oh, don't worry," Steve told her. "I know how to tell them apart. Yours is much hotter."

"You'd better believe it," she laughed. "But what are you doing up? You were supposed to be sleeping," she scolded mildly.

"Couldn't," he shrugged. "I was too restless. I guess my nerves are still kind of keyed up from what happened today."

Linda nodded. "That's understandable."

Steve gestured to the shadowy F-80. Even earthbound, its graceful form seemed the evocation of flight.

"I keep thinking about what happened today," Steve murmured, and then he chuckled. "You'll probably think I'm crazy—"

"I already know you're crazy," Linda said.

Steve nodded indulgently. "As scared as I was today, I really enjoyed myself. Especially the glide from the target area to here. I was all alone. It was just me and the airplane, and somehow I *knew* she wouldn't let me down."

Linda nodded. "And she *didn't* let you down."

"That's right," Steve replied adamantly.

"Is that why you felt the need to defend your airplane to the press?" she asked softly.

Steve just shrugged.

"And attack your father?"

"I *never* attacked my father."

She shook her head. "Shall I read you my notes from the press conference?"

"Ah, hell," Steve sighed. He looked at her. "I guess I did get somewhat carried away. Was it that obvious?"

"Let me put it to you this way. Most of the other correspondents used the fact that you disagreed with your father as their leads."

"But not you?"

"I stressed the valiant-pilot-saves-his-airplane-in-emergency-landing angle." She moved away from him, turning her back to stare at the lights of the compound. "I liked your father that time I interviewed him, and I'm sort of fond of you, you big lug. I'm sorry you two don't get along, and I'm not going to add fuel to the fire by immortalizing your dumb, rash provocations issued in the heat of the moment."

"Okay, so maybe I went a little too far this afternoon," Steve sighed. "I can't explain it, but somehow my father always manages to get under my skin. He always seems to know how to say the wrong thing—like that speech he made suggesting that the F-80 was a piece of shit, and that if GAT wasn't ready to save the day with that damned BroadSword the United States Air Force would have to turn tail and run from the commies."

"He didn't exactly say that, Steve...."

"Yeah, he did."

"Come on, Cap'n," she coaxed. "You know as well as I do that all your father was trying to do was promote his company. He never came out and said that the F-80 was a bad airplane."

"Okay," he admitted grudgingly. "Maybe not in so many words, but take it from me, my old man knows how to make a speech. He knew very well that everyone would read between the lines."

"Well, no one is going to have to read between *your* lines concerning what you think of your father's new airplane."

"You mean that crack I made about how the BroadSword hasn't yet met the test of combat?" he asked, troubled.

"Uh-huh."

"Yeah, I guess I do kind of regret that part of what I said." He patted the patch pockets of his A-2 jacket. "You got any smokes? I seem to be out."

Linda produced a pack of Chesterfields, took one for herself, and then gave the pack to Steve. "Hold on to them," she said. "I've got a carton in my bag."

"Thanks." He took out his lighter, cupping the flame while Linda lit her smoke, then lit his own. "Here, hold it like this," he said, showing Linda how to cup her cigarette so that its glowing tip was hidden.

"You think there're snipers?" she asked worriedly, glancing toward the dark hills.

"Nah, the compound isn't blacked out, but why take the chance? I wouldn't want anything to happen to you."

"You wouldn't?" she asked, suddenly shy.

Steve looked away, unable to deal with the sudden rush of emotion he was feeling. "Anyway, now you've got a trick to use to impress all your journalist friends when you get stateside," he said lightly.

Linda laughed softly. They were both quiet for a few moments as they smoked. Finally she said, "You want to know what I think?"

"About what?"

"About you and your father."

Steve shrugged noncommittally.

"I'll take that as an affirmative response," Linda said. "I think that your father never considered the fact that his speech advancing his company's airplane would rile you."

"Oh, sure!" Steve exclaimed. "It's okay for *him* to be thoughtless, but not me, is that it?"

"Let me finish," Linda said. "No, it's not okay for him to forget your feelings, but two wrongs don't make a right."

"I thought you journalists were taught to avoid clichés?" he asked coolly, but she seemed to ignore, or excuse, his sarcasm.

"Sometimes clichés are true." She ground her cigarette out against the sole of her shoe. Steve was amused to see her then field-shred the butt. "You know how badly you felt when you saw your father's published comments?" she asked.

"So?"

"So think how he's going to feel when *he* sees *yours*."

Steve nodded. "He's going to feel pretty bad, I guess."

"I guess. . . ." Linda agreed quietly.

Steve laughed ruefully. "You know what the funny part of all this is? I've got nothing against the BroadSword. It's a damned fine airplane."

"Did you ever tell your father that?" she asked. "Have you ever complimented him on any of his achievements?"

"Not since I was a kid," he admitted. "It's so hard, Linda," he elaborated, shaking his head. "I'm always in the hole with him. Always a day late and a dollar short. *Always!*

As far as he's concerned, I'm always making the wrong decisions, and that's because they're *my* decisions, not his." He dropped what remained of his cigarette to the clay and angrily ground it out beneath his shoe.

Linda put her arms around him and hugged him close. "I think that you're a very brave man willing to fight any war on behalf of your country, but there's one war you're fighting on behalf of yourself, and it's a war you've got to end."

"You mean the war with my father." He nodded and then kissed her on the forehead. "Thanks."

"For what?" she demanded gruffly.

"For making me feel better."

"I wish you could make me feel better," she whispered. "Do you know how horny I am for you?"

"I got horny as soon as I saw you," Steve chuckled. "There I was, sitting up on that stage with all those lights on me. I wondered how the hell I was ever going to get out of there without everyone seeing my boner. I'm hard as a rock right now."

She laughed.

"Maybe that's why I couldn't sleep," he continued. "It wasn't the day's ordeal, or my father at all—it was you!"

"You're a slow thinker, but you *do* draw the right conclusions eventually."

Steve gently tilted up her chin and kissed her. "It's been a long time. . . ."

"Umm. . . . The last time was that weekend in San Francisco, right before you headed off to Japan."

"'Like I said, a long time to go without you." Steve kissed her again.

"Are you telling me you haven't been with those very pretty, very *willing* Japanese girls?" she demanded skeptically.

"I didn't say that at all," Steve said between kisses. "What I said was, it's been so very long . . . since I was with *you*."

"Good answer," Linda murmured, and then she sighed. "Too bad we can't do anything about it. . . ."

"We can't?" Steve asked, frowning.

"Well, I mean, your bunk is in the pilots' barracks, and I'm quartered with the other women correspondents. Where could we go that's private?"

Steve smiled.

The door to Major Kell's office was locked.

"Now what?" Linda whispered, casting anxious glances over her shoulder down the dimly lit corridor.

"Relax," Steve coaxed, trying the door knob a final time.

"I can't," she complained. "I keep thinking that I hear somebody coming."

"No way," Steve promised. "It's just your nerves." He sauntered over to the clerk's desk and tried the middle drawer, which slid open. In it was a ring of keys. "Never knew a clerk who didn't have the keys to his superior's office," he said triumphantly. Out of curiosity he tried some of the other drawers. In the bottom left-hand one he found a two-cell flashlight. "This will come in handy. We don't want to draw attention by switching on lights."

Linda nodded. "But then shouldn't we also be keeping our voices down?" she asked, concerned.

"What for?" Steve asked as he began to try keys in Kell's door. "There's nothing at this end of the building but the briefing room and this office."

"But aren't there guards?" she persisted.

"Outside, patrolling the perimeter. Trust me. Besides us, the only other person in this building is the TCG guy on duty in the radio room, and that's at the opposite end of the building, and to top it off, he's probably wearing a headset."

The third key on the ring clicked in the lock. Steve tried the knob and the door swung open. "Step into my parlor, said the spider to the fly."

Linda hurried in. Steve followed her, shutting and locking the door behind him. He checked to see that the shades were drawn, and then switched on the flashlight. It had a red plastic rim around the lens. By standing it upright, facedown on Kell's desk, the flashlight cast a diffused red glow that was enough to dimly illuminate the office.

"Umm, romantic," Linda smiled, unzipping her parka. "Is this wall-to-wall carpeting?"

Steve nodded. "Nice, huh? I figured we could spread out your parka on the carpet, and then—"

"Steve," Linda interrupted, shivering. "It's cold in here."

"Not much we can do about that, I'm afraid. If I lit the coal stove the smoke would attract attention." He went to the closet and opened it. "No blankets, unfortunately." He pointed to the liquor cabinet. "How about a drink to warm you up?"

"I wouldn't say no."

Steve went to the cabinet. "He's got some Chivas in here."

"That'd be wonderful."

Steve tried the door. "Locked," he frowned.

"Have you got the key to it?"

Steve shook his head. "Not likely the clerk would have need of a key to the major's liquor cabinet."

"Oh, well. . . ." Linda sighed, sounding disappointed.

"Hey, no problem," Steve told her, going over to Kell's desk, where he picked up a stilettolike letter opener from the blotter. He took the letter opener over to the liquor cabinet, carefully inserted its point into the cabinet's lock, and began to jiggle it around. Nothing happened, so he jiggled it a little harder. There was a loud clicking noise. "Ah-hah!" Steve announced.

"You picked the lock?"

"I broke the lock."

"Kell is going to be furious," Linda worried.

"Probably, but what's he going to do about it?" Steve shrugged, opening the cabinet and taking out the bottle of Chivas and two glasses. "I played along with him this afternoon at the press conference. Thanks to me he came off a hero. He told me he expects a commendation. He's not going to want to screw that up."

"If you say so. . . ." Linda replied, sounding unconvinced.

"I know so." Steve poured two generous drinks and

handed one to her. "To us—" he toasted as they clinked glasses.

"Umm, wonderful stuff," Linda said as she sipped the scotch. "But I'm still cold. If we spread my parka out on the carpet, what will we use to cover us once we're undressed?"

Steve looked around the room. His eyes fell on the wall-sized FEAF tapestry. "You shall be covered in silk," he told Linda, and then went over to the wall hanging and gave it an experimental yank. It was attached by only a couple of tacks, and came down easily.

"You are clever!" Linda applauded as Steve bundled up the woven silk and carried it over. She took another swallow of her drink, and then set aside the glass. "And cleverness should be rewarded," she whispered.

She shrugged off her parka and spread it out on the carpet with its quilted lining facing up. Now she kept her eyes on him as she began to unbutton her shirt, letting it drop to the floor. She undid the brass slide of her canvas belt, unzipped her trousers, and stepped out of them.

Steve laughed giddily. What a kick to see her shed her tomboy's fatigues to reveal that she was wearing a lacy chemise.

"These military things are so drab and unflattering," she smiled. "I felt the need to wear something feminine underneath. Do you like?"

"I like," Steve said as she pirouetted for him, looking like an angel in her silky lace, and more than a little devilish in the red light.

Steve finished his drink and quickly shed his own clothes. As he went to her, she put one arm around his neck and with the other hand reached down to gently encircle his erection. Steve sighed as he pressed his face into her dark, tousled hair. Her hand was still on him as she laughingly sank to the floor, gently tugging him down. He disengaged himself in order to grab the wall hanging and spread it out over them so that the FEAF insignia made a silken canopy under which they burrowed.

"Make love to me right now," she whispered urgently as

he glided his hands over her smooth, curvy ass and kissed and sucked her nipples. She pulled him down on top of her and spread her legs, all the while fondling him until he had to stop her or else risk coming too soon.

He was just about to enter her when he abruptly stopped, groaning, realizing that he had no condom. "Linda, we've got no protection for you—"

"I don't care!" she hissed, clawing at him.

"You could get pregnant—"

"Don't worry! It's just before my time of the month!"

She grabbed him and pulled. It was either go along or else risk her breaking it off. They rocked and squirmed beneath the silk, and both climaxed in less than a minute.

Once the initial edge was off, they were able to settle down for a long, leisurely go-around. Forty-five minutes and another round of Chivas later, they were still under the wall hanging, nicely sheened with sweat and just beginning third-round preliminaries when the lights in the office abruptly snapped on.

Steve quickly scuttled halfway out from beneath the now damp and wrinkled tapestry to see Major Kell standing in the doorway. The major was smoking a pipe and wearing a parka over striped pajamas. He had bedroom slippers on his feet and a bundle of manila folders under his arm.

In dogfighting it was best to take the offensive. "What are you doing here?" Steve demanded.

"What am I . . .?" Kell trailed off. "My beautiful wall hanging!" he gasped.

"It's none the worse for wear," Steve said, looking at it, and then shrugged. "A little stained maybe . . ."

"Dammit, Gold! You'd better have a good explanation! You—you—" Kell paused, sniffing and then wrinkling up his nose. "What's that awful *smell*?"

Linda stuck her head out from under the silk. Her blue eyes looked dreamy, and her dark hair hung in damp ringlets around her flushed face. "You were right, Kell, He *is* a major."

CHAPTER THIRTEEN

(One)

**Gold Household,
Bel-Air, California
28 August 1951**

The ringing telephone tore Herman Gold from a deep sleep. He reached out in the darkness of the bedroom to fumble for the receiver in its cradle, found it, and brought it to his ear.

"Yeah?" he mumbled, not yet really awake. "Hello?"

"Herman, it's me."

"Teddy?" Gold yarned. "God, what time is it?"

"It's a little after four A.M."

"What the hell—?" Gold began.

Beside him, Erica stirred in her sleep. "What is it?" she murmured. "Has something happened?" She switched on the lamp on her side of the bed.

Gold, squinting against the light, waved her quiet. "Teddy, where are you?"

"I'm in the design lab."

"Has he worked all night again?" Erica demanded.

Gold shrugged irritably. "Teddy," he began, "I thought that we'd agreed that you were going to take things a little bit easier?" he asked carefully.

"These problems we've got with the GC-909 aren't going to solve themselves."

That's the truth, Gold thought. The AT-909 AreoTanker project for the Air Force was proceeding along according to schedule, but the design team working on the commercial version of the jet transport, the GC-909, had hit some snags. The most serious problem was the commercial jetliner's projected runway requirements. Fully loaded, in warm weather, the GC-909 was going to need too much runway to operate from most of the nation's airports.

I told you that I plan to retire once the GC-909 is operational," Teddy said. "I'll have plenty of time to rest then."

Gold scowled as he heard the double click of Teddy's cigarette lighter.

"Anyway, Herman, I didn't wake you up to chat about the 909," Teddy said, noisily exhaling smoke. "I've been listening to the radio while I was working. They've just broadcast a news bulletin. Another SB has gone down."

"Oh, Christ," Gold sighed. He glanced at Erica. "A fourth Stoat-Black Starstreak has crashed," Gold told her.

"She went down over the Mediterranean, off the coast of Italy," Teddy continued. "The radio says there was a full crew aboard, and capacity passengers."

"They say what they think happened? I mean, can they pin it on a storm or something?"

"Nope. Not yet, anyway. She went down in daylight. There were witnesses on the ground who claim the weather was perfect. They reported that one minute the plane was soaring and the next she just broke up. She was carrying a full crew of six and twenty-five passengers. No survivors, of course."

"It sounds just like the last one," Gold muttered. "That's four crashes in a little over a year. They've got to ground them all now."

"Already have, according to the radio," Teddy said. "Anyway, I'm sorry about waking you up, but I thought you'd want to know."

"I appreciate the call," Gold said. "Now I wish you'd go home and get some rest," he added.

"I'll stretch out here for a few hours," Teddy promised.

"Please see that you do," Gold implored. "I'll see you in the office at the regular time."

"If I'm asleep, don't wake me," Teddy joked, and hung up.

Gold hung up the telephone. He felt wide awake. He sat up and swung his feet out of the bed, sliding them into his slippers.

"Where are you going?" Erica asked.

"Downstairs," Gold said, pulling on a burgundy velour robe. "I'm up, but I don't want to disturb you."

Erica, looking at him, shrugged and began getting out of bed. "I'll make us some coffee."

"It's been one hell of a month for the aircraft industry," Gold said as he sipped his coffee.

He was sitting at the marble-topped, wrought-iron table in the tiled kitchen. The kitchen was dimly lit. The only light was from the recessed fixture above the double sink.

"First Circle Airline is grounded due to its pilots going on strike," he muttered. "And then that Trans-Way airliner goes down over Africa. . . ."

"And now this," Erica sighed. She had her back to Gold as she rummaged through the cabinets. "I know there are some cookies somewhere if I can just figure out where Ramona put them."

Gold watched as Erica took down a tin, opened it, and began to put some cookies on a plate. She was wearing a short-sleeved ivory-colored silk robe over her nightgown. For a while now she'd been wearing her blonde hair cut into a mass of short curls that she said was called a poodle clip. The youthful haircut, combined with her trim figure, made her look a decade younger than her fifty-one years.

"What will Stoat-Black do?" Erica asked as she brought the plate of cookies over to the table and sat down.

"The only thing they can," Gold said. He began nibbling on a cookie. "They've got to cooperate fully with the British government and the European airlines in an investigation."

"Do you think there's something intrinsically wrong with the SB-100?" she asked as she added a dollop of cream to her coffee.

"A few months ago I would have said no," Gold replied,

taking another cookie. "I would have told you that it had to be pilot error. Now I just don't know what to think. Neither do the European airlines, nor Stoat-Black, I would imagine, and that's why they've moved so quickly to ground the Starstreaks." He shrugged. "When you look at the total picture, it's just overwhelming. The first Starstreaks went into service in Europe in April of last year. Within six months there were two serious accidents, but both of them occurred on takeoff and were attributable to pilot error. Takeoff procedures were modified, and everything seemed back to normal. Then, a couple of months later, while supposedly flying high *above* a storm, a Starstreak went down over the North Atlantic. That was considered a mysterious but not totally implausible accident."

"Because of the storm," Erica said.

"Right," Gold nodded. "All airplanes are vulnerable in bad weather, but now there's *this* accident," Gold said. "From what Teddy told me, it suspiciously resembles the last one, except that this time there's no bad weather to blame. This has got to cast doubt on wheather bad weather was truly responsible for knocking down that Starstreak over the North Atlantic." He shook his head in anger and disgust. "Whatever the hell is happening, until the authorities can nail it down, they've got to keep those planes on the ground."

"Don't become so upset about it," Erica said. "It's not your problem—"

"I'm in the airplane business," Gold cut her off impatiently, grabbing another cookie and stuffing it into his mouth. "So it *is* my problem," he managed with his mouth full. "In this business, whenever something terrible happens —to me or one of my competitors—it only serves to undermine the public's confidence in aviation, and that hurts everyone in the industry!"

"But—" Erica tried to interrupt.

"But, nothing!" Gold snapped at her. "You asked me so I'm *telling* you. Be quiet and *listen*. Jets are new to the public, and when something is new people are naturally wary of it. Stoat-Black anticipated that problem by marketing their jetliner as the most safety-tested airplane in history, and the public—in Europe, at least—believed it. Now that the supposedly fail-safe Starstreak has been taken out of service due to its annoying habit of falling out of the sky, how do you think the public is going to react when GAT eventually unveils the GC-909?"

"I understand all that," Erica said coolly. "What I don't understand is why you're yelling at me."

Gold leaned back in his chair, his shoulders sagging. "I'm sorry," he said softly. "I guess I'm upset, and you know me. . . ."

"That I do," she said wryly.

"When I get this way I need to blow off steam."

"And eat," Erica added, eyeing the empty cookie plate.

"And eat," Gold acknowledged as Erica got up to refill the plate.

"I accept your apology," she smiled. "But *I'm* a little upset, too."

"About what?" he asked as she sat back down.

"About *you*," she declared firmly. "I hate to see you get this worked up. You've only just started to calm down since that incident concerning Steven."

Gold held up his hand in warning. "Don't even bring that up now," he grumbled. "It's been months since he made me a laughing stock, and the needling I've had to take on account of it has just begun to die down."

"Oh, Herman—"

"Don't 'Oh, Herman' me," he frowned, reaching for a cookie. "About Steven I have a right to be upset! I still can't believe how my own son could stab me in the back. It was in the newspapers and newsmagazines, on the radio and the television: 'Fighter pilot voices lack of confidence in father's aircraft design.'"

"Herman, you know very well that you started it with that speech."

"I started it, all right. But not with the speech," he said sourly. "I started it twenty-seven years ago, when I didn't wear a rubber."

"Herman!" Erica gasped, looking appalled. Gold winked at her, and she giggled.

Gold, smirking, reached for another cookie. Erica smacked his hand away.

"No more for you," she said, sliding the plate to her side of the table. "You're cut off. I think all that sugar has affected your brain."

"Oh, you know I was just kidding," he said. "Anyway, I've got nothing to be upset about anymore," he grinned broadly. "I've been proven right. *Stevie's* the one who's got egg on his face now."

Back in November the Red Chinese had gotten into the fighting in Korea, just as Gold had predicted. That same month MiG-15s had appeared in the sky. The F-80 Shooting Star pilots who had tangled with the MiGs had scored some kills, but they were quick to admit that their airplanes were outclassed by the Soviet-built swept-wing fighters.

And then, in December, the first BroadSwords had gone into action against the MiGs, with excellent results. Now, according to Gold's contacts in Washington, the biggest news out of Korea—next to the fact that the Soviets had called for negotiations on a cease-fire—was that all F-80–equipped squadrons had been pretty much relegated to ground support and bombing missions. Unless they were attacked, they were to leave the dogfighting to the Broad-Swords.

"You know what bothers me almost more than Stevie's betrayal?" Gold began. "Since December he's written home many times. He even called us from Japan that weekend he was on leave. He had all those chances, and not once did he mention his betrayal of GAT, let alone apologize. I don't mind that my son should disagree with me, but I am disappointed that he's not man enough to admit when he's wrong."

"Oh, Herman," Erica laughed affectionately, "that's the biggest crock you've handed me in years."

"No, it isn't," Gold said sincerely.

"I just don't believe you have the gall to look me in the eye and lie like that, Herman Gold! You claiming that you don't mind that your son disagrees with you. What a crock!"

He glanced at the clock on the wall above the stove. It

was almost six; time to get ready for the office. He stood and stretched. "Erica, I don't know whether you'll believe it or not, but I think something's changed inside of me. I don't want to fight with Stevie anymore. I can't. It's his life, I'm ready to admit that. He can and *should* lead it the way he wants."

"I believe we have a breakthrough here," Erica teased. "That almost sounded emotionally mature."

Gold made a face. "I just wish my son could be as mature. Honey, he should have apologized to me for what he did."

"You'll pardon me for pointing this out to you," Erica said gently, "but it's taken you fifty-three years to become this mature. Your son is only twenty-seven. However, I'm still gratified concerning your progress." She slid the cookie plate toward him. "You may have a cookie."

(Two)

GAT
Burbank

Gold got into the office a little before nine, before any of his secretaries were due in, and immediately telephoned downstairs to check in with Teddy.

The telephone rang several times before it was picked up. "R&D," answered a male voice.

"This is Herman Gold—"

"Yes, sir! This is Renolds, sir."

Gold vaguely remembered that Renolds was an engineer, but he couldn't picture the man. Not surprising. Renolds was a junior member of the team, and for some years now the weekly R&D progress meeting that Gold attended had been restricted to personnel at the project-manager level or higher.

"Mr. Quinn's secretary isn't at her desk yet."

Gold knew as much. His daughter was taking her own car

to work these days because she had to leave later in order to have time to get her son, Robert, now nine years old, ready for school.

"Shall I have Mrs. Greene call your office when she gets in?" Renolds asked.

Gold remembered that Suzy wasn't going to be in at all today. She had some sort of parents-teachers conference to attend at Robert's school. The personnel department would be assigning Teddy a floater for the day.

Gold wondered if Renolds knew who Suzy really was? Likely not. Suzy used her married name, and while Erica had suggested to Teddy that he spread it around that Suzy was widowed, and hence available, she had also warned him against intimidating any possible suitors by revealing that she was the boss's daughter. Suzy liked going along with the pretense, even going so far as to call him 'Mr. Gold' when others could hear. Like Stevie, she clearly wanted people to accept her on her own terms, not because of who her father was.

"Is Mr. Quinn available?" Gold asked.

"Sir, I think he's in his office," Renolds began reluctantly. "But he's got his sign up."

Gold smiled. More then one young engineer had been blistered for ignoring Teddy's hand-lettered "Do *Not* Disturb" sign when it was taped to his office door. It meant that Teddy was either working or sleeping. Gold hoped it was the latter, but either way he knew better than to send poor Renolds into the dragon's lair.

"Well, then we'd better leave Mr. Quinn be," Gold said.

"Yes, sir," Renolds replied, sounding extremely relieved.

"Leave a message for Mr. Quinn's secretary to have him call me when he can."

That morning things got busy very quickly, and it was close to eleven before Gold remembered that he'd not yet heard from Teddy.

That was unusual, Gold thought. He and his chief engineer routinely touched bases several times a day.

He was about to call downstairs again when a secretary buzzed him to say, "Mr. Campbell on line three, sir."

"Tim Campbell?" Gold asked, surprised.

"I don't know, sir. I'll check——"

"No, that's all right," Gold stopped her. "I'll take it." He picked up the receiver and stabbed the flickering button. "Tim?"

"Hello, Herman," Campbell said. "How are you?"

"Uh . . . fine, Tim," Gold said.

Campbell laughed. "Surprised to hear from me, huh?"

"Well, it has been some time since we've talked," Gold replied.

He occasionally ran into Campbell socially, but couldn't remember the last time either man had intentionally looked up the other.

"I don't want to beat around the bush, Herman," Campbell said. "Amalgamated-Landis is going to issue a press release today. I felt that in consideration of our prior history together I should telephone to give you the news personally."

In other words, you want to gloat, Gold thought, smiling. "Okay, Tim," he said indulgently. "What's your news?"

"Just that Amalgamated is offering up to the airlines a commercial jetliner of its own: the AL-12."

Son of a bitch, Gold thought.

"Kind of an unfortunate day to be announcing a new airplane, Timmy," Gold said pleasantly. "Or haven't you heard about the SB-100 crash?"

"Sure, I heard about it," Campbell said. "But as far as I'm concerned it's good news. I'm no hypocrite, Herman. You won't find me crying alligator tears over the fact that the guy ahead of me in a road race just tripped and broke his leg."

"The public——" Gold began.

"I know what you're going to say," Campbell interrupted. "That the public's confidence has been shaken. Well, fuck the public," he said. "Since when did John Q. Public go shopping for a fucking airliner? The public doesn't buy airplanes, *airlines do,* and now that Stoat-Black's wings have been clipped, the airlines have nowhere else to turn but to Amalgamated-Landis."

"Excuse me, Tim, but there is the slight matter of the GC-909."

"'Slight matter' is right," Campbell scoffed.

Gold forced himself to control his temper. "Laugh if you want, Tim, but the airlines are behind my project."

"Yeah? Then how come three months ago every airline who'd seen your presentation sent a representative to Amalgamated's offices to beg *us* to take a crack at designing a jetliner?"

Gold felt sick to his stomach.

"Speechless, huh?" Campbell chuckled.

Gold savagely punched the intercom button.

"Yes, sir?" the secretary responded.

Gold put his hand over the telephone's mouthpiece. "Get Mr. Quinn up here on the double," he whispered into the intercom.

"The airlines made quite a strong case for us to get into the race," Campbell was boasting. "They pointed out how it was unhealthy for the industry for one company to have a monopoly on supplying jetliners. Competition in quality *and* price is what the American way is all about."

"I hope you've got deep pockets," Gold warned.

"Raising money has never been the problem for me that it's been for you, Herm."

Gold grimaced. Some thirty years ago Campbell had joined GAT to keep track of the company's finances, back when the fledgling company had been long on ideas but short on cash. Campbell, to his credit, had worked financial miracles for GAT, but Gold wondered if the son of a bitch was ever going to let him forget it.

"Tim, I know that you can come up with the money," Gold said. "But you're going to need a viable jetliner design to spend it on. You've got to admit that you've never in your life had a creative idea that didn't involve a decimal point."

"It so happens A-L already has its design," Campbell replied. "Don't forget I have Don Harrison working for me as my chief engineer."

"Oh, yeah, young Harrison," Gold acknowledged. "I think I've met him a few times at industry conferences. Yeah, I do remember him. He struck me as being very bright. I'm surprised you're willing to let your ace in the hole get out and around."

"Calling him 'bright' is like calling the ocean deep, Herman," Campbell said. What other thirty-two-year-old guy is running the R&D department of a major aviation concern?"

"He's that good, huh?" Gold said as his secretary stuck her head into the office.

"Mr. Quinn's door is still locked, and his sign is still up," she whispered. "His secretary says he's taken his telephone off the hook."

Gold nodded to dismiss the secretary. That business with the telephone off the hook was Teddy's favorite trick when he was brainstorming and wanted to be left alone.

"Harrison may be a wunderkind, all right," Gold told Campbell, "but you're still going to find it very expensive getting past the trial and error phase to come up with something the airlines are going to like."

"We already have, Herm," Campbell said smugly. "We've previewed our proposal to the airlines, and they've endorsed it."

"But," Gold began, astonished, "how *could* you? You said you've only been at it for a few months."

"Righto."

"But it took us—" Gold paused as all the pieces in the puzzle finally fell into place. "You have our proposal, don't you?" he demanded softly. "That's how you were able to streamline your preliminary design phase. *Answer me*, you fucking crook! You have our proposal."

"Now, Herman," Campbell patronized, "you *know* there's no sense asking me such a dumb question. If I admitted that you were right you could cause A-L all kinds of legal trouble."

But that's what happened, all right, Gold thought. The airlines— at least one of them, at any rate—had leaked GAT's proposal.

"Why did you call to tell me this?" Gold demanded harshly.

"Remember, Herman?" Campbell spat into the phone, his voice cutting. "I always said I'd get even. It looks like pay-back day is at hand."

Gold, cursing, slammed down the phone. Campbell's laughter was still ringing in his ears as he rushed out of his office.

"I'll be in the design department," he told his secretaries as he passed them on his way to the elevators. "I'll be in conference with Mr. Quinn," he shouted over his shoulder. "Hold all my calls. I don't want to be disturbed."

The issue was not that A-L would try to copy the 909, Gold thought as he rang for the elevator. Campbell was not stupid; he would know that a direct steal of even some minor detail of the 909 would give GAT all the opening it needed to nail A-L in court.

Where the fuck is that elevator? he fumed, and then gave up on it and headed for the stairs.

No, he didn't need to lose any sleep over the likelihood of A-L building a duplicate of the GC-909. His fear was exactly the opposite: that the A-L's jetliner was going to be *different*.

Any complex design had drawbacks, and airplanes were no exception. A-L, by getting to examine the GC-909's design, and also hearing the airlines' criticisms of the airplane, could design out all of those sticking points in their own jetliner while it was still on the drawing board. Meanwhile, GAT was stuck with what it had: the production lines were already being tooled to produce a full-scale prototype of the military AreoTanker version, and GAT was in too deep financially to try and counter Amalgamated-Landis's advantage by modifying its basic design.

Gold began hurrying down the stairs a little faster toward Teddy's office. There had to be *something* he could do to counter Campbell, but what?

Panicking wasn't going to help, that was for sure, even *if* he'd worked so hard to make the GC-909 happen. Even *if* the 909 was meant to be GAT's replacement for its piston-engined Monarch series, its ticket into the future of commercial aviation.

Even *if* the airlines played follow the leader and deserted the 909 for whatever Amalgamated-Landis came up with, and GAT was ruined.

"*Remember, Herman?*" Campbell had laughed. "*Payback day is at hand.*"

Back in '33 Campbell had waged a stock battle against Gold to seize control of Skyworld Airlines. Campbell had ultimately ended up with Skyworld, but not before Gold had forced him to pay dearly for the privilege. Campbell had never talked much about it, but Gold had always suspected that Tim was holding a grudge, and now his suspicions were confirmed.

Gold needed to talk with Teddy, to tell him what had happened. Screw Campbell's boy genius of a chief engineer. *His* chief engineer had been with him from the beginning. Together, there was no problem that the two of them couldn't solve.

The temporary replacement was not at her desk outside Teddy's office as Gold barged into the design studio and hurried down the center aisle to Teddy's office. The door was still closed. That childishly scribbled "Do *Not* Disturb" sign was still taped to it.

Gold knocked on the door, but there was no answer. "Teddy! It's me!" he called out, but he got no response at all, not even the usual one, Teddy's crotchety "*Go 'way, Herman! I'm busy in here making you money!*"

Gold tried the doorknob. It was locked.

"He's been in there all morning, Mr. Gold," one of the engineers volunteered. "Haven't seen him once today."

Gold felt a chill travel down his spine. *Now don't be stupid,* he lectured himself. *He's all right in there. He's just working, or better yet, sleeping.*

He went to the vacant desk. There was no intercom. Teddy refused to have one, calling it just one more distraction from his work.

Gold dialed Teddy's number on the telephone. He got the

busy signal he'd expected due to Teddy's having taken the telephone off the hook.

Gold hung up the phone and stared at the door. At that silly sign. "Oh, Jesus Christ. . . ." he murmured.

He abruptly raced toward the locked door and slammed his shoulder against it, but all he got was a tingling shoulder for his effort.

He looked around at the engineers, who were staring at him, shocked.

"Break this door open!" he ordered. They kept staring. "Move!" he yelled.

Two of them did, slamming their shoulders against the door in unison. It still held.

Of course the door is holding, Gold swore to himself. It was steel and fire-resistant, with a dead-bolt lock. Now that GAT had set up its Toy Shop project and begun doing work for the CIA, Gold himself had specified that all the doors to offices where sensitive files were kept be replaced with high-security units.

He glanced at Suzy's desk. He had also issued a memo to his project managers and senior executives, forbidding them for security reasons from giving office keys to their secretaries, but Teddy had never obeyed a rule in his life—

Please don't let him have started now, Gold thought as he pulled out the desk's center drawer and dumped its contents on the carpet. The engineers were still throwing themselves against the door, and Gold was on his hands and knees, rummaging through the spilled paper clips, pencils, and memo pads for that fucking key when the temporary secretary finally appeared.

Gold looked up as she stood there, an appalled expression on her face.

"Who are you?" she demanded. "What do you think you're doing?"

It was so ludicrous that Gold burst out laughing. "I'm Herman Gold," he managed finally. "Where's the key to this office?"

"I don't know," the woman shrugged. "I'm only here for today." Her eyes widened. "Say, if you were *really* Herman

Gold you'd know that it's against the rules to leave office keys lying around." She hurried to the telephone. "I'm calling security," she said.

"Of course! A pass key!" Gold jumped to his feet and hurried to the desk, where he snatched the receiver from her hand.

"You're in big trouble now, *whoever* you are," the secretary squawked in outrage.

Gold dialed the number for security. It was busy.

He threw the phone down, looked around wildly, and then collared one of the engineers. "You get somebody from security with a pass key to this office," he ordered. "Tell them it's an emergency."

"Yes, sir!" The engineer went racing off.

"And somebody call the infirmary!" Gold shouted. "Tell them I think Mr. Quinn is sick, and that we'd better have a nurse—"

"Mr. Gold!" One of the other engineers was sitting on the carpet, grinning as he removed the key that had been cellophane-taped to the underside of the desk's center drawer.

Gold snatched the key and fumbled it into the lock. He twisted it, and the door swung open. He went into the office, while several others stayed bunched up in the doorway.

Teddy in his white lab coat, his shoes off, and his glasses pushed up on his head, was perched on his stool, bent over his drafting table with his head resting on his folded arms.

He's just sleeping, Gold thought. He went over to Teddy and gently prodded the man's shoulder.

"Wake up," he murmured. "Teddy, wake up!"

Teddy began to move. Gold could feel his tension draining. "You old bastard," he laughed, turning away. "What a scare you gave me—"

From the doorway the secretary shrilly screamed as Teddy's head and shoulders slid off the drafting table and he began to topple from his stool.

Gold spun around and lunged, just managing to catch Teddy. Together thay sank slowly to the carpet, where Gold sat cross-legged, cradling him in his arms.

"Hell of a way to treat your best friend," Gold murmured.

He pressed his lips to Teddy's forehead. His own tears felt shockingly warm against Teddy's flesh, which was cold and pale as marble. "After all we've been through, how can you leave me in a bind like this? Tim Campbell just called me, you know. It looks like we're up against it again, old friend. Like that time back in '25, remember? When the government wanted to take our mail routes away?"

He held Teddy in his arms, talking to him while the nurse came and went, until the ambulance attendants appeared to gently pry the body from his embrace and take it away.

CHAPTER 14

(One)

Over Kumch'ong Airfield
NKAF Air Base, North Korea
30 August 1951

Steve and his wingman Mike DeAngelo brought their Shooting Stars in low in a surprise attack upon the commie airfield. As they crested the hills overlooking Kumch'ong, Steve was braced for automatic antiaircraft-weapons fire. He was surprised that there seemed to be no ground defenses in place. There seemed to be nothing down there but construction equipment and supplies, and the hundreds of laborers who were now scattering from the bomb-cratered strip littered with the charred remains of airplanes and ground-support vehicles.

Last week Kumch'ong and the commie airfields like it in northwestern Korea had been savagely hit by B-29s. Today's attack was meant to stop the Reds from putting the facility back into operation, and to cost them their precious Soviet-built construction equipment.

Close to the airstrip, near what was left of the burned-out compound, a large tent city had been erected to house the laborers. The smoke from the myriad cookfires and charcoal braziers scattered amid the tenementlike cluster of canvas structures rose to form a gray haze over the area.

"You take the tents, I've got the airstrip," Steve told DeAngelo.

"Wilco." DeAngelo's silver and orange bird banked off toward its prey.

The laborers out in the open on the airstrip had dropped their picks and shovels and were scattering, but Steve did not bother to strafe. He'd let the napalm canisters shackled beneath his wings do the dirty work. As he dived on the airstrip, he released the canisters and then pulled up and away as the napalm hit the ground and detonated into a thunderous, rolling fog of crimson fire and oily black smoke. The bulldozers, steamrollers, trucks, and other heavy equipment, the piles and barrels of construction material all vanished beneath that high tide of flames.

As Steve came around, he saw DeAngelo drop his canisters on the tent city, obliterating it. The tents burned like paper. The two fires spawned by the F-80s quickly united to turn Kumch'ong into hell on earth.

"Let's go home," Steve radioed as he gained altitude and banked his Shooting Star onto a southward course.

"Hard to remember where home is," DeAngelo remarked as he took up his position a little above and behind Steve.

"I know what you mean."

The 19th Squadron had been one traveling medicine show these past few months. The Air Force had only been able to keep its F-80 groups at Taegu Airfield for a short while before the pierced steel strip that had been laid over the rice paddies broke down under constant use. When Eight Fighter-Bomber Wing went looking for a new home, it found the no-vacancy signs up everywhere. With Seoul's Kimpo field cratered by enemy bombs, and Suwon and Kawon fields both bogs due to a combination of poor drainage and the summer rains, there was no room, so back the Eighth had to go to the Japanese mainland. That sucked eggs, because nobody liked flying over water, and the great distance from Japan to North Korea meant that the F-80s could spend no more than five minutes over a target.

Meanwhile, Air Force and Army engineer units were working overtime to get Kimpo's strip patched up. In June, the Eighth moved there. It didn't take more than a couple of months to realize that Kimpo's roughly paved, short runways just weren't suitable for use by F-80s carrying heavy bomb loads. Tire failures became commonplace, and the F-80s' engines were suffering wear and tear due to the water and alcohol injection procedures being used to give the heavily loaded jets the extra boost they needed to get airborne so rapidly.

In August, when construction of the long concrete runways at Kawon had been completed, somebody had the bright idea that the BroadSwords based there could make do with shorter runways because the F-90s were lighter and carried no external ordnance. By summer's end, the F-80 Shooting Star and F-90 BroadSword groups had exchanged places, and Steve and the rest of the 19th Squadron was settled in at Kawon, twenty-five miles south of Seoul.

"I didn't notice any defensive fire back there at all, did you?" DeAngelo asked.

"Nope, that was nice and easy," Steve replied. "Just the way you like it, huh, Mikey?"

"Affirmative," DeAngelo replied. "A good ending to a mission that started out like shit."

"I'll say," Steve chuckled.

Four Shooting Stars had started out from Kawon, but malfunctions had forced one airplane to return immediately to base and another to make an emergency landing at nearby Suwon. Steve had been upset, but he hadn't been surprised. These days a fifty percent down rate wasn't unusual within the Shooting Star squadrons. With all the moving around, Maintenance and Supply never had the chance to set up decent workshop facilities. Meanwhile, dust, rust, and just plain old age were catching up with the hardworking F-80s. What compounded the problem was that no more Shooting Stars were being built. The Air Force was switching over to Broad-Swords for fighter duty, and to the F-84 Thunderjets built by Republic Aircraft for the fighter-bomber work which was currently being handled by the Shooting Stars.

With half of his flight down, Steve had briefly considered scrubbing the mission, but he'd radioed DeAngelo to talk it over and Mike had been game to push on. Like Steve, Mike had realized that it was important to deliver today's second punch in the one-two combination FEAF had initiated against Kumch'ong and the other enemy airfields. Stomping the enemy had become a matter of psychological, as well as strategic importance.

The peace talks that had been halfheartedly stuttering along might just as well have been about some other war for all the good they were doing the armies slugging it out in Korea. The newspaper editorials had begun calling it "The Seasaw War" because the commies and the UN-American forces seemed doomed to keep trading the same stretches of ground back and forth.

New Year's Eve, 1950, had seen the commies launch a successful push toward Seoul that was barely stopped at Wonju. A counteroffensive against the Reds had been launched in February, and by April Seoul had been retaken, and the UN was once again north of the 38th parallel. April also saw a new Supreme Commander of UN Forces as Truman sacked MacArthur for publicly suggesting that Asia had replaced Europe as the likely arena where all future contests between the East and West would be fought. The new commander, General Ridgeway, had barely eased into his post when the communists launched another ferocious offensive, taking back the 38th parallel in an onward-rolling series of "banzai" attacks. It didn't seem to matter how many commies were killed; more just kept on coming. Finally, the enemy's human wave began to falter and the UN forces managed to once again cross the 38th.

Meanwhile, back home the editorial writers who had grown sick of writing about seasaws, began lamenting Korea as the "Battle of the Hills."

Throughout the months of fighting American air power had continued to fly ground support and strategic bombing missions, but things had changed. FEAF no longer owned the skies, now that the commies were pouring in MiGs. Latest intelligence counts had it that over five hundred MiGs had been thrown into the battle. The brass felt that there was only one fighter that had any hope of wresting away the sky from all of those MiGs, but there were less than one hundred BroadSwords in all of Korea.

Outnumbered so badly, there was no way the Broad-Sword patrols could be everywhere at once, so the MiGs found it easy to evade the BroadSwords in order to attack the B-29 formations and Shooting Star fighter-bombers. By late summer the MiG situation had gotten so bad that the area along the Chinese–North Korean border—dubbed "MiG Alley"—had been put off limits to all airplanes lacking BroadSword escort.

A lot of the F-80 jockeys had grumbled about the restriction. For Steve, the turn of events was doubly humiliating. Not only had he been proven wrong about his father's BroadSwords, but now he had no chance at all of becoming an ace in this war, since Shooting Stars had been relegated to flying strategically important, but nevertheless pussy missions like today's wienie roast at Kumch'ong.

It boggled Steve's mind that he'd been warned off engaging the enemy. He was a fighter pilot, dammit. A jet jockey in the cockpit of an F-80, not a little boy in a soapbox racer who needed to be told by his mama that he couldn't cross the big, bad, busy street unless he had his older brother, Mr. BroadSword, looking out for him.

Sure he'd heard all the stories about what a super airplane the MiG was, but what those stories left out was that, the few times when an F-80 was being piloted by somebody who knew what he was doing, the Shooting Star had managed to draw blood against its adversary.

It was the first lesson of fighter piloting, and Steve had learned it when he'd been a Flying Tiger, up against the Japs over Rangoon: *It's not the machine, but the man who makes the difference in a dogfight.*

So what if the MiG was a state-of-the-art machine? Everyone knew that the commies were putting poorly trained Koreans into the cockpits. Through the grapevine he'd heard all about the pussy NKAF pilots. When they bounced from behind, they would huddle in their MiGs' armored cockpits, unwilling to break either way because that would expose their canopies to gunfire. He'd heard about the North Koreans who'd bailed out of their airplanes at the first hint of trouble, who'd demonstrated inept gunnery, inability to manuever their airplanes, and a total lack of cooperation between the pilots in a flight.

Steve was ready to turn in his wings if he couldn't knock such pilots out of the sky, no matter what the capabilities of their respective machines.

If only he got the chance. He'd been brooding about it since November, when the first MiGs had appeared. For ten months he'd been listening enviously to the stories of F-80 pilots who'd happened to run into stray MiGs.

If only it could happen to him. . . .

They were at twenty thousand feet, flying over the Ye-song River and approaching the 39th Parallel, when Steve spotted the twin contrails high above, like thin white scars against the blue hide of the sky. "Mike!" he called excitedly. "We've got company!"

"I see them," DeAngelo said as the sun glinted off the two silver specks drawing the parallel contrails. "What do you think? We're awful far south," he added nervously. "They must be BroadSwords, right?"

"Dunno. Could be MiGs," Steve said slowly. "We're not too far from Sariwon or Simak."

"Come on," DeAngelo laughed derisively. "We pulverized them a long time ago."

"Maybe the Reds got one or both back into operation."

"Bullshit!"

"They might have," Steve protested.

"Christ, you sound positively wistful," DeAngelo said.

Steve just laughed. "They can't have seen us yet. We're in their blind spot." He paused. "Let's *take* them!"

"No way! They might be MiGs."

"You just said they couldn't be," Steve pointed out.

"I've been wrong before."

"Mikey, listen to me. If they are MiGs—and I hope like hell they are—there's a pair of them. One each. We could each nab a kill."

"If they're drawing contrails, they must be at 45,000 or better," DeAngelo said. "We don't belong up there, Steve."

"That's bullshit, Mikey. I say we *can* take them."

"It's against current Far East Command regs to engage them."

"We can say that *they* bounced *us*," Steve replied. "There's no reg against defending yourself. And who knows, maybe after we get these two FEC will rescind that bullshit rule about how us Shooting Star squadrons are supposed to run away and leave all the fun to the BroadSword jockeys."

"I just don't like the idea of going looking for trouble," DeAngelo muttered.

"Come *on*, Mike! We've got all the advantages in this setup. We've got the drop on them, and we're experienced pilots while they're probably just a couple of NKAF trainees."

"I'd like to get home to my wife and kids in one piece."

Steve paused. "You've been laying eggs too long. You've forgotten that you're a fighter ace!"

"I haven't forgotten, Steve. It's just not that important to me anymore. I've got my family to think about."

"Look," Steve began crisply, "I'm going after them. If they're BroadSwords, no harm done. I'll just wax their tails to show them who's boss, but if they're MiGs..."

"Fuck you, Major!" DeAngelo exploded savagely. "I'm your wingman, and that means I go where you go."

"Well, okay!" Steve said, gratified. "Friends stick together."

"Right, friend. And when we get home, I'm going to punch your fucking face in for making me do this!"

"That's a deal," Steve laughed. "But for now, you'd better punch tanks."

"Tanks jettisoned," DeAngelo announced.

Steve watched his own wing tanks fall away, and increased his throttle. As he pulled up, heading for those two silvery specks in the bright blue sky, he felt an anticipatory tingling in his groin.

He had to laugh. *This is better than sex.*

His prey—either MiGs or BroadSwords; the two swept-wing jets looked so much alike that Steve wouldn't know until the last moment—were traveling above and directly ahead of him. That set them up perfectly for a yo-yo attack. Steve would climb as rapidly as he could and then go into a shallow dive to gain extra speed. When the distance between himself and his target had closed, he would pull up into his attack, and if everything went smoothly, the enemy's belly would be in his gun sights.

As Steve leveled off and then began to angle down into his dive, he noticed that DeAngelo had come right along with him. The consummate wingman, DeAngelo hadn't needed to be told what tactic Steve was using. Mikey had merely watched and then played follow the leader.

As Steve came out of his dive and began to pull up toward his adversary, he saw on its wings the red five-pointed star outlined in white that told him that this fight was for real. He armed his guns as he stared up at the MiG, his gloved fingers itching in anticipation of firing that first burst. The Soviet-built fighter was a burnished gray aluminum color, except for its nose and tail, which were painted blue.

He was two thousand feet below the MiG; still too far away. On his port side, DeAngelo had moved off a bit in order to execute his own attack. Steve noticed that DeAngelo's MiG had the same blue nose and tail, but in addition, had a jagged blue lightning bolt stretching the length of its fuselage.

Steve had closed to one thousand feet. *The NKAF pilots*

are afraid to break, he thought, grinning wolfishly. *They're just crouching and taking it.* This was going to be like shooting fish in a barrel. *Pop,* he thought, *get ready to eat your words about F-80s versus MiGs—*

Six hundred feet. His sights were planted on the MiG's gut.

Now. The F-80 shuddered as he loosed a burst of armor-piercing incendiary from his six nose-mounted .50s.

Above him his MiG abruptly raised its nose and rolled to starboard down Steve's vector fighter in a steep descending turn that put the MiG below and behind Steve.

Out of sight—

Cursing, Steve broke to port as DeAngelo's panicked voice filled his helmet.

"Steve, I lost mine! Do you see him?"

Before Steve could reply he felt his F-80 taking a jarring hit from his MiG's cannons. The fucking commie had used his superior speed and climbing ability to come around and lock on to *his* tail.

"Steve. He's on my six!" DeAngelo cried out. "Get him off me!"

"I've got my own troubles, Mikey," Steve muttered as he abruptly attempted a high-speed variation on the yo-yo, pulling up sharply to reduce his speed. The sickeningly abrupt move pushed his stomach up into his rib cage, but the maneuver worked. The streaking MiG overshot beneath him. Steve immediately mashed down the F-80s nose and cobbed his throttle, centering his guns on the MiG's tailpipe and holding down the firing button. His guns raised sparks off the MiG's tail and wings.

"Steve, I can't shake mine—" DeAngelo said.

Mikey's voice was sounding reedy; he was scared. Like he was near crying. *He never wanted in on this,* Steve thought, feeling guilty.

"Dive!" Steve called to DeAngelo. "Get low, where you've got the advantage!"

"I can't! I'd give him a clear shot at me. He's real close, this son of a bitch. I haven't seen aerial combat maneuvers like this since I was up against the Luftwaffe. Oh, he's good, whoever he is. *North Korean trainees, huh?*" Steve could hear DeAngelo's sarcastic sneer.

"Oh, shit! He's on my six again. He's sticking to me like he's glued there! I'm taking hits!"

Steve desperately wanted to look around for Mikey, but he didn't dare take his eyes off his own MiG, which was jinking around in a series of random turns and skids, trying to spoil Steve's aim long enough for it to get some altitude, where the MiG's superior speed might get it out of gun range. It might have worked, Steve thought, but all dog-fights cost altitude, and this one had dropped down to 15,000 feet. Down here the heavier F-80 had the speed advantage, and Steve was too good a shot. As the F-80's guns continued to hammer sparks off the MiG, Steve guessed that the commie pilot must have concluded that the way things were going, he was not going to last long enough to get back up to 25,000, where he could have things his way.

Abruptly the MiG broke to port and went into a spiral dive. Steve put himself in the commie's shoes and immediately guessed what the MiG pilot had in mind. The Red was hoping that Steve would try to stay on his tail, forgetting that in a dive the heavier Shooting Star would automatically increase its velocity and, hopefully, overshoot.

Nice try, pal, Steve thought as he abandoned his position on the MiG's six, and threw his heavier Shooting Star into an even steeper angle of descent. The negative G-force drove the blood up into his brain, and his vision began to go red-out, but the punishing dive allowed him to gain on the MiG. He pulled up for another try at the MiG's belly and managed to stitch holes along its silvery gut from nose to tail. He finally must have hit something important, because the aircraft began to flounder, leaking black smoke from its tailpipe. The MiG pilot blew his canopy and bailed out.

Steve came up and around in a vertical climb aileron turn, spinning 360 degrees like a top in order to look for DeAngelo. At twenty thousand feet Steve saw his wingman maybe two miles away, still being pursued by the MiG.

"Hang on, Mike! I'm coming!"

Steve pulled out of his climb and cobbed the throttle for

maximum speed. Behind him the MiG he'd killed had brushed a bold slash of smoke diagonally across the sky as it fell. Its pilot was wafting down beneath his deployed chute.

As Steve streaked toward DeAngelo, he saw Mike roll into a spiral dive.

"Good move, Mikey!" Steve radioed. "Be ready to wax him."

As the MiG overshot the F-80, DeAngelo reversed his direction with a roll, pulling up in perfect position to lock on to the climbing MiG's tail.

"Nice flying!" Steve roared, relieved and elated. "Now get him, Mikey!"

But DeAngelo broke away from the MiG. He was trying to run.

He never wanted any part of this fight, Steve reminded himself sadly. *He hasn't got the killer instinct anymore.*

Within moments the MiG had come around to again lock on to DeAngelo's six-o'clock position.

DeAngelo may have lost his killer instinct, but he's up against a born killer, Steve realized as he watched the MiG begin to squeeze off rounds from its nose-mounted trio of one 37-millimeter cannon and twin 23-millimeter guns. The MiG's cannons had a slower rate of fire than machine guns, but each hit counted more, especially when its target had lost its nerve and refused to take any evasive maneuvers as it tried to escape.

The irony of the situation was not lost on Steve. It was DeAngelo who had reverted to a trainee's behavior of crouching within his armored cockpit and hoping for the best as a clearly superior enemy ravaged him.

I got Mikey into this, damn me, Steve thought. *I've got to get him out—*

But the MiG was still too far away. Steve began firing anyway, in the hope that he might remind the commie that it was two against one, and in that way scare him off. At the very least, Steve figured his shooting would distract the MiG pilot long enough for Mike to get some relief.

It didn't happen. That damned commie in his blue lightning bolt MiG showed steely concentration, taking his time lining up his shots as he attacked DeAngelo.

Steve saw the cannon rounds striking Mikey's Shooting Star. Pieces of the airplane were flying off. It began to leak smoke.

"Hang on, Mike, I'm almost there—"

"No good. She's hurt bad, and so am I. . . . Shrapnel or something. . . . I can't control her. I'm bailing out!"

Steve saw the Shooting Star's canopy blow off. The commie, to his credit, immediately broke off the attack.

Come on, Mikey, do it! Eject!

The F-80 abruptly vanished in a blossom of flame. Steve stared, horrified, as the fiery rain of wreckage that had been Mike DeAngelo's airplane plummeted to earth from out of the oily smudge of smoke that hung in the sky.

There was no sign of Mike.

Steve flew toward the MiG, intent upon killing it. The MiG took the time to do an insolent, eight-point roll in celebration of its victory, and then it streaked off toward home.

Steve poured it on, but as the commie quickly shrank down to a speck on the horizon he bitterly had to accept the fact that there was no way he could catch a MiG in a Shooting Star.

He broke off the chase as his low fuel indicator came on. It was now or never to start home if he wanted to land with something more than fumes in his tank.

As Steve came around, he began broadcasting a Mayday. A Tactical Air Direction station answered the call. Steve identified himself and his flight, and explained what had happened. He was asked for the coordinates where DeAngelo had gone down. Steve wearily gave them.

"Did you see a chute?" the TAD operator asked.

"Negative chute," Steve replied.

"Well, we've got Search and Rescue on the horn, Major. They'll put out a chopper anyway."

"It's a waste of SAR's time," Steve said.

"There's always hope," the TAD man protested.

No, sometimes there isn't, Steve thought. "Yeah, sure," he said. "Over and out."

(Two)

Officers' Club
Kawon Airfield, South Korea
2 September 1951

At eleven A.M. on a Sunday morning Steve was the only customer in the officers' club at Kawon, which was a badly deteriorating tarpaper shack built on low stilts to protect against flooding during the summer months. Inside, there was a rickety bar and a bunch of card tables and folding chairs. The windows were covered with cheese-cloth curtains, which let in the breeze but still kept the joint dimly lit. The plywood walls were papered over with pinups and a series of posterboard renditions of the colors of the various squadrons based at Kawon. The 19th's orange markings were prominently displayed.

There were no bar stools. Steve stood at the bar, contemplating his bourbon. The Korean national behind the bar was polishing glasses and steadfastly ignoring him. The Korean had the radio on the shelf behind the bar tuned to a U.S. Army–run station broadcasting out of Seoul. "Tennessee Waltz" was being sung by Patti Page. The Korean crooned along with Patti whenever she got to the refrain part about remembering the night. The rest of the lyrics evidently stumped him. He just whistled through his teeth along with the tune.

Steve knocked back his bourbon, and for the third time gestured to the Korean to fill his glass. While he was waiting, he lit a Pall Mall off the butt of the one that lay smoldering in the ashtray. The ashtray was made out of pine-green plastic and in bold white lettering strongly recommended to Steve that he guard against bad breath by chewing "Fresh-OH!" chlorophyll gum.

The music ended, and the radio announcer came on and began to murmur unintelligibly. Behind Steve a lance of daylight stabbed into the club and receded as the door closed again.

"Thought I'd find you here, Major."

Steve looked over his shoulder as his CO, Colonel Billings, came over to the bar. Billings was a barrel-chested, middle-aged man with pale blue eyes. He had a thick neck that overflowed his shirt collar, a shaved head, and a waxed, handlebar mustache.

Billings slapped a thin manila folder on the bar in front of Steve.

"What's that? Paperwork, Colonel?"

"Open it and see," Billings replied.

Steve pulled the folder toward him and opened it, remembering that in his brief stint as squadron CO he'd been saddled with paperwork. At the time, he'd hated it, but at the moment it didn't seem all that bad to be stuck behind a desk where the worst mistake you could make was a typo in a memo. Typos didn't cost lives. . . .

Steve squinted in the dim light to read the first paragraphs, and then he looked up at Billings. "Sir, this looks like your report on the incident with the MiGs. . . ."

"It is. Search and Rescue found the remains of DeAngelo's F-80, and the wreckage of the MiG that you shot down. You've got yourself your first confirmed kill."

Steve skipped to the last page and quickly skimmed it. "Colonel, I strongly portest the conclusions you've reached."

Billings frowned. "But I've totally absolved you concerning the matter of Lieutenant DeAngelo's death."

"That's just it, sir." Steve, unable to meet Billings's gaze, stared at his drink, then picked it up and knocked it back. "It *was* my fault. I killed Mikey. I'm more to blame for his death than that commie."

The radio began playing "Come On-A My House" by Rosemary Clooney. The Korean broke into a wide grin and hurried to turn up the volume.

Colonel Billings signaled the bartender. "You got any coffee, son?"

"No coffee," the Korean said, sounding peeved at the interruption.

"Then how about Coca-Cola?" When the Korean nodded, Billings said, "Two Coca-Colas, then. *Cold* ones, son. And turn down that goddamned radio."

Sulking, the Korean did as he was told, slamming down the two bottles of pop and stalking away to the far corner of the bar.

Billings threw down some coins. He gathered up the manila folder and the sodas, and said, "Come on, Major, let's you and me sit down and discuss this." He led Steve to a table, and after they were seated, slid a Coca-Cola toward him. "Drink that. The caffeine will help sober you up."

"I'm sober, Colonel," Steve said.

Billings stared at him and then nodded. "Yes, I believe you are. . . ."

"I've been trying to get drunk for a couple of days now, but every time I get close, I think about Mikey, and I sober right up."

"Okay, Major," Billings said. "I want you to consider the fact that trying to lay blame on yourself for what happened a couple of days ago is about as profitable an endeavor as shoveling horse shit into the wind." He sniffed. "Which you smell like you've been doing. Tell me, Major, when was the last time you took a bath, or had a shave, for that matter?"

"Not since I killed Mikey, I guess," Steve replied.

Billings scowled. "You keep saying things like that and I'm going to lose my temper, Major, in which case I will have to take you outside this shithole and boot your ass up and down the airstrip."

Steve tapped the manila folder. "There's something in there that's wrong," he said. "There's something you don't know."

"What would that be, Major?" Billings demanded skeptically.

"I lied to you. Those MiGs didn't bounce us. We bounced *them*."

Billings smiled sadly. "I knew that, son."

Steve stared. "But how could you have?"

"Two things tipped me off," Billings began. "First of all, taking into account the coordinates of the dogfight, there was no way a pair of MiGs would have dropped down into Shooting Star cruising altitude looking for trouble. Those two Reds were already pretty far south. No way would they have risked their skins chasing you very far at low altitudes, where they would have been gulping the fuel they would have needed to get home." He shook his head. "No, the only scenario that held water was that you and DeAngelo *went looking* for trouble."

Steve nodded ruefully. "You said two things tipped you off, Colonel. What was the second?"

Billings smiled. "I know *you*, Major. I've heard you complain about how unfair it was that F-80s have been restricted from MiG Alley without BroadSword escort." Billings smiled. "No way would you have passed up engaging the enemy if the situation presented itself."

"Okay, then," Steve shrugged. "If you know that I lied to you, that should make it worse for me."

"Nah, it doesn't. You're not the first F-80 jockey who's used the old *they*-bounced-*us* dodge."

"Come on, Colonel!" Steve complained. "I've been going nuts about what happened to Mikey. I deserve some kind of punishment."

"It's no use, son. You want me to crucify you because that might make the guilt you're feeling somehow easier to bear. Well, I'm not going to do it. You're a good pilot. You *got* your MiG. You fought him on his terms, but you got him." Billings shook his head. "You're much too valuable to be thrown away over this one mistake in judgment on your part."

"Some 'mistake in judgment,'" Steve sneered. "I cost a man his life!"

"Nobody forced DeAngelo to follow you."

"Come on, Colonel!" Steve's voice rose. "You *know* better than that. Mike was my wingman! He was honor bound to go where I led him, even if his best instincts were against it."

"He might still be alive today if he hadn't lost his nerve up there," Billings said. He hesitated, his eyes narrowing. "I presume you *were* telling me the truth when you reported that DeAngelo managed to break free of his MiG, and then passed up the opportunity to press his own attack."

"That part is true," Steve said earnestly. "I think he got shook when he saw how good those commie pilots were." Steve frowned. "I've got to say, Colonel, I got a little shook over that, as well. I'd heard that the North Korean pilots were green. But those guys knew all the tricks of the trade."

"Yeah, well . . ." Billings trailed off, looking hesitant.

"What?" Steve demanded, perking up. "Come on, Colonel. You look like you know something."

"I do."

"Then spill—"

"Ah, what the hell, Billings began, lowering his voice. "You came clean with me, and now I'll return the favor. You weren't flying against North Koreans; you were flying against Russians."

"Holy shit—" Steve gasped. "How do you know that?"

"This is still restricted info, Major," Billings warned.

"I'll keep my trap shut, sir, no problem," Steve swore. "But please, I need to know."

"Okay. CIA reports have it that the Soviets have started to use this war as a training school for their fighter pilots."

"And so you think those two we tangled with were Russians?"

"I don't think," Billings replied. "I *know*. When you told me how well those two MiGs handled themselves, I got suspicious, so I sent along your description of their markings to a friend of mine who's in a position to know about such matters. He confirmed to me that those markings belong to a crack squadron made up of Soviet aces from the last war."

"Damn, that explains a lot," Steve said. He thought back on how the pilot in that lightning bolt MiG had shown such determined concentration, refusing to be distracted as he finished off DeAngelo.

"You and Mike were up against the best the commies have got," Billings said. "You bested your opponent, and DeAngelo might have, if only he hadn't lost his nerve."

"That's being too hard on Mike," Steve protested.

"Here's how I see it," Billings said, cutting him off. "There are two separate issues here. Yes, you were wrong to engage those MiGs in the first place, but once you had, DeAngelo was wrong to cut and run the way he did. He was a trained fighter pilot, and losing his nerve like that, well . . ." he trailed off, shaking his head. "A fighter jock who turns pussy in a dogfight has got to be considered responsible for his own death."

"I still got him into that mess, Colonel."

Billings nodded. "Like I said, two separate issues. Yes, you broke a reg, but there's precedent for me to look the other way if one of my tigers shows a little too much initiative. No other F-80 pilot has been disciplined for tangling with a MiG, so neither will you be. As far as the Air Force is concerned, the matter is closed."

"And I get off scot-free," Steve said softly.

"No, you don't," Billings said.

"How's that?"

"Just look at yourself," Billings demanded. "You're putting yourself through worse hell than anything the Air Force could do to you. You've got your own conscience to deal with, son. Something tells me that no matter where you go, or what you do, Lieutenant Mike DeAngelo will be flying off your wing for some time to come."

Steve, nodding, put his hand up to his eyes. "What am I going to do?" he implored softly. "I can't sleep. I close my eyes and I see him. I see him in that photo he used to carry around. The one where he's with his wife and kids."

"Listen now, Major," Billings said. "Just remember that you're human, and that you're allowed to make a mistake now and then, just like anyone else. It isn't your fault that circumstances have put you in a place where those mistakes can cost lives." He paused. "As for what happened concerning DeAngelo, that'll ease some over time." He sighed. "That much I can tell you from personal experience. As far as DeAngelo's family is concerned, I think that it would be appropriate if you wrote them—"

"I couldn't!" Steve protested, shaking his head.

"You can, and will," Billings said sharply. "As a matter of fact, I'm ordering you to do it. I expect you to show some of the same guts you showed against that MiG, and carry out that order."

"What could I possibly say to them?" Steve began.

"Off the record, I suggest you lie to DeAngelo's wife, Major. Make up some bullshit about how her husband died a hero. Give her something she can hold on to, something she can maybe show his kids someday."

"Yeah," Steve nodded slowly. "I can do that." He looked up at Billings. "He was a hero," he said defiantly. "He could have licked that MiG, but he just . . ." he trailed off. "He just got tired, I guess."

"Yeah, you'll put the right things into that letter," Billings said. His stern expression softened. "And although you may find this hard to believe, Major, writing that letter might even make *you* feel a little better."

"I don't care about me," Steve said. "But that letter will go out today, sir."

"All right, then." Billings stood up.

"Wait a minute, Colonel," Steve began. "There's something *else* I can do to try and somehow make amends to Mikey. I can *kill MiGs* for him."

"Look here, now," Billings glowered, "I've kept your ass out of the fire this time, but from now on I expect you to leave the MiGs to the BroadSword jockeys."

"That's what I'm getting at," Steve said. "I need to be flying a BroadSword."

Groaning, Billings sat back down. "You're just going to have to be patient about that, Major. Chances are we'll be switching over to BroadSwords sooner or later."

"Begging the colonel's pardon, but the 19th has already earned itself a reputation as a crack fighter-bomber outfit, so chances are we'll get switched over to Thunderjets."

"Possible, but—"

Steve shuddered. "Hell, they might even take away our F-80s and issue us refurbished Mustangs and new orders to fly ground-support missions for the rest of the war!"

"That could happen, all right," Billings admitted.

"Even if it doesn't, even if the 19th is put on line for F-90s, it could take forever to get them. You know as well as I do that we're not getting all the BroadSwords we need due to our government's commitment to NATO. The F-90s that *ought* to be here are being sent to Europe!"

"Careful, Major," Billings smiled. "You're starting to sound like MacArthur, and you *know* what happened to him."

Steve smiled politely, but he was in no mood for jokes. "Sir, I respectfully request that you approve my request for a transfer into an existing BroadSword unit, or a squadron immediately on line for the airplane."

"It won't happen," Billings replied. "You're not even trained to fly an F-90."

"Training is no problem," Steve said. "They've got mobile training units that can check out a pilot in less than a month."

"This is certainly a turnaround for you, son," Billings scowled. "I seem to remember that you made a few headlines when you bad-mouthed your daddy's airplane. I seem to remember that in your opinion the F-80 squadrons were going to single-handedly keep Korea safe for democracy. Aren't you sort of putting yourself in the position of eating crow?"

"I don't care about me. All I care about is evening up the score for Mikey," Steve said firmly. "If it takes flying a BroadSword to do it, so be it." He smiled thinly. "Who knows, Major? If I get to patrol MiG Alley, I might even be lucky enough to run into a certain pilot who favors blue lightning bolts."

"Major, I sympathize with you," Billings said. "I really do. To be frank, I think you *ought* to be flying a Broad-Sword. Hell, any F-80 jockey who can knock down a MiG being flown by a Russian hotshot has got to be a *born* fighter jock."

"Then what's the problem, Colonel?"

"The thing of it is, son, I'll be glad to approve your request for a transfer, but I don't think it's going to cut much mustard one way or the other. The bottom line is that every damned fighter jock and *his mother* wants to fly a Broad-Sword. I just don't have the *clout* to get you transferred."

Steve nodded, more to himself than to Billings. "That's okay, Colonel. I know somebody who *does*. . . ."

CHAPTER 15

(one)

GAT
Burbank
8 January 1952

Gold was meeting in his office with the two engineers he'd come to rely on since Teddy Quinn's death. The meeting was not progressing smoothly.

It's mostly my fault there's so much tension between us, Gold thought, feeling guilty. He knew that he was behaving impossibly toward the men he'd tapped to run things. He knew it, but he couldn't help it. He was just too filled with grief over losing Teddy, and could barely supress his rage toward his old friend for deserting him.

There'd been a special chemistry from a friendship that had stretched over thirty years. They'd known each other's quirks and had been able to finish each other's thoughts so that together they'd been more than the sum of their parts; together there had been nothing they couldn't make happen, and no problem that they couldn't lick. Except for Erica, Gold couldn't think of anyone he needed more in this world.

But now Teddy was gone, and Gold felt lost.

"Herman, are you listening?" Ken Wilcox suddenly demanded, like a teacher zeroing in on an inattentive student.

"Um, pardon me?" Gold blinked away his dark reveries as he stared at Wilcox.

Wilcox was in his fifties. He had a long, thin face with a hawk's beak of a nose and a brush cut and mustache the color of iron filings. Wilcox was a first-rate engineer. He had a string of degrees from MIT, and had been Teddy's departmental administrative assistant, as well as the Broad-Sword project manager. He was also the most senior member of the R&D department, so he'd pretty much expected to take over Teddy's spot. At the time, Gold, who had been distraught and hadn't any better ideas about filling the vacancy, had been willing to oblige.

"I think you were a thousand miles away, Herman," Wilcox declared hotly.

"Sorry about that," Gold muttered, thinking that Wilcox had been exactly right, but was nevertheless a fool for saying it.

Gold had never really liked Wilcox. He thought he had, but these days Wilcox was definitely rubbing him the wrong way. Gold disliked the way Wilcox sat perched on the edge of his chair, the way he kept his charcoal flannel–clad knees pressed together and his report file on his lap like some old spinster. Wilcox was so compact and tidy, his necktie always perfectly knotted, his shirts and suits and shoes all just so. He made Gold feel large and sloppy by comparison.

"The topic currently under discussion was the Air Force's requested design modifications to the BroadSword," Wilcox said crossly.

"Yes, of course," Gold forced a smile. *Wilcox,* he thought, *you've got a face like a hatchet.* He picked up a pencil and began to doodle a hatchet on a legal pad.

"The Air Force wants a more powerful engine for the fighter, but Rogers & Simpson has said that will have to wait for a while," Wilcox continued. "Meanwhile, the Air Force has come up with a way to modify the BroadSword's wing to improve its performance."

Gold nodded. "I've already spoken to General Simon about it." He glanced up at Wilcox and then added a brush cut and mustache to the hatchet. "Howie's R&D people in Dayton think that the new wing slat will reduce drag and increase high-altitude performance?"

"Our test evaluations concur," Wilcox replied. "The modifications will make the BroadSword superior to the MiG in every way."

"Howie also said that the Air Force has begun to retrofit the F-90s they already have," Gold said.

"That's correct."

"All right, then," Gold said. He scribbled over the doodle, and then tossed aside his pencil. "I want to get the specs on the new wing design to all the companies who have subcontracted with us to build BroadSwords."

Wilcox looked horrified. "Excuse me, but you don't mean you want to make this new wing design a *running* modification?"

"That's exactly what I mean."

"Herman"—Wilcox shook his head in the manner of a man about to explain something to an idiot—"it'll cost GAT a fortune if they have to halt their production lines to retool."

"I appreciate your concern about the budget," Gold said, thinking that Wilcox lacked Teddy's creative spark, but that he was a good administrator and always careful with a dollar, like now. "Normally I would agree with you, Ken, but in this specific instance there's more at stake than profits. This is GAT's finest hour. For the first time in history—maybe the *only* time—our country is in a war where our airmen are almost exclusively flying GAT-produced fighters."

"That's no reason to throw money away," Wilcox began.

"Our boys in Korea are depending on us to supply them with the finest airplanes possible," Gold said. "I don't intend to let them down."

"Nevertheless, Herman, as chief engineer—"

"Excuse me, Ken, but you're only *acting* chief engineer," Gold snapped, and immediately regretted his harsh tone. Before he could say anything further, Wilcox had jumped to his feet.

"These past five months I've taken a lot from you, Herman—"

Oh, shit. Gold thought wearily. "Just sit down, Ken—"

"No! I've had it! I've taken all the insults I'm going to take! It's been almost five months since Teddy died, and since I took over there hasn't been one thing I've done right as far as you're concerned. You don't want a replacement for Teddy, you want a whipping boy. Well, I'm not it! I'm resigning from GAT, effective immediately."

Gold watched, bemused, as Wilcox stormed out of the office.

"Feeling relieved?" Calvin Jennings suddenly asked, startling Gold. Jennings had been so quiet the last few minutes that Gold had almost forgotten he was there.

Now Gold stared at him. Jennings was in his early forties. He was a dark-haired, dark-skinned native Californian with a bushy black beard.

"You have something to add to this, Cal?" Gold demanded belligerently.

Jennings held up both hands in mock surrender. "You know, nobody *killed* Teddy Quinn," he said quietly. "Teddy just up and died."

"What's that supposed to mean?"

Jennings only shrugged. He reached into the inside pocket of his herringbone sports jacket for a curved-stem bulldog briar pipe. There was no tobacco in it. Jennings didn't smoke. He just liked to chew on the pipe.

Gold took a deep breath and let it out. "You think I've been too tough on Wilcox, is that it? He was only in the job temporarily. I never figured on making him Teddy's replacement permanently—"

"I don't think you much liked Wilcox in the first place," Jennings interrupted.

"That's true."

"But even if you had liked him at first, you would have

ended up disenchanted with him. It's the mama's-cooking syndrome."

"What?"

"You know why I never got married, Herman?" Jennings asked, chewing on his pipe. "I came close a number of times, but I always backed out after the woman cooked me a meal, because it just didn't taste like mama's cooking. You get it?"

"Yeah, I guess," Gold sighed. "Wilcox didn't do things the way Teddy did, which meant that as far as I was concerned, he was doing things wrong."

"You got it," Jennings nodded. "Between us, I never much liked Wilcox either, but he was right on the money when he said that you've been treating him like a whipping boy. You know, filling Teddy's shoes on technical expertise alone is going to be a tall order. It's going to be next to impossible if you also insist on that person *being* Teddy."

"Yeah, I guess I know that," Gold admitted. "I was thinking of bringing in somebody from outside the company." He paused. "Cal, you've been with us, what, five years?"

"A little more," Jennings said.

"Okay," Gold nodded. "How do you think the department would react if I did bring in somebody new? Do you think there'd be any animosity if I didn't pick a successor from in-house?"

"I think that the staff will have trouble getting used to anyone new who replaces Teddy, but we've come to the real-ization that the adjustment will be necessary. The question is, Herman, have you?"

Gold hesitated before answering. "Yeah, I guess I have, finally." He nodded. "For the longest time I guess I was denying to myself that Teddy was gone. I was digging in my heels, as if I held out long enough, death would ac-quiese and send back Teddy. I know that won't happen and that I owe it to the company to deal with my personal grief on a separate basis and get on with filling Teddy's position. As a matter of fact, I'm having lunch today with someone I've been thinking of offering the job to." He grinned. "Unless, of course, you'd like a crack at it, Cal?"

"Not a chance!" Jennings said quickly. "I'm an excellent engineer, but a lousy administrator. I can't even keep track of my own checkbook. No way do I want to take on running a department."

"Okay, okay," Gold chuckled. "Just kidding."

"Anyway," Jennings smiled, "if I became chief engineer I'd have to deal with you a lot more often."

Gold didn't think that was so funny. "We'd just better get on with our meeting," he said evenly. "What's the latest on the SB-100?"

Jennings was just back from the Royal Aircraft Establishment laboratories in Farnborough, England, headquarters for the investigative team searching for the cause or causes of the SB-100s' mysterious crashes. As one of the world's foremost authorities on high-altitude aerodynamics, Jennings had been Stoat-Black's first choice when Sir Hugh Luddy had contacted Gold to ask for personnel to assist in the British-government sponsored investigation.

Gold had been glad to lend Jennings, because he sincerely wanted to help Stoat-Black, but also because having Jennings at the RAE labs meant that GAT now had an inside track on where the investigation was leading. Gold was hopeful that as the possible causes of the crash became known his company could discover and engineer out any similar design flaws in the AeroTanker/GC-909 project. For that reason Gold was holding up construction of the AeroTanker prototype, but he couldn't postpone the construction start date forever. The Air Force was getting antsy.

Now Gold listened as Jennings outlined the lengthy underseas search for the wreckage, and the time-consuming examination of what had been salvaged from the ocean floor. Jennings explained that the investigative team had eliminated from blame both the SB-100's engines, and its fuel delivery system.

"We're starting to take a closer look at the question of metal fatigue," Jennings concluded.

"That theory creates more questions than it answers," Gold scowled.

"Nevertheless, we do have those witness reports claiming that the SB just came apart in the air," Jennings said, gesturing with his pipe. "If we eliminate the engines and the fuel system and sabotage, there's not a hell of a lot left beyond metal fatigue that could cause an airplane to come down the way the SBs did."

"So you're thinking the explosion was actually rapid decompression due to metal fatigue?" Gold asked.

"It's basically a question of isolating what structural component failed," Jennings nodded.

"It could be any number of things," Gold sighed. "Anything and everything, from the interior framework to the rivets." He studied Jennings. "I don't suppose you'd care to hazard a guess?—"

"A guess?" Jennings looked pained.

"Yeah, you know. What's your gut reaction?"

"Herman, I'm a scientist. I couldn't possibly issue an informed opinion until all the test results are in."

"Right." *Christ, I miss you, Teddy.* "Okay, Cal. You'll be going back to England at the end of the week?"

"Yes, after a short visit with my mother."

"What's next on the agenda over there?"

"Well, we'll be trying a number of things. We're going to run pressure chamber tests on structurally accurate scale models of the SB-100, and we'll be building a water pressure tank in order to subject a full-scale Starstreak fuselage to repeated sudden pressure changes, and some of us have volunteered to monitor changes in an SB-100 while it's in flight—"

"Whoa!" Gold interrupted. "Slow up there a minute. You mean to say that some of you intend to actually go up in a Starstreak and try to duplicate the conditions that led to the previous crashes?"

Jennings nodded.

"Nah, that's out of the question for you, Cal. I'm ordering you not to take part in that particular experiment, and that's final. I'll cable Luddy and tell him as much. I admire your courage, Cal, really I do, but I don't want to risk losing any more of my best engineers."

"Well, if you say so, Herman," Jennings shrugged.

"I say so," Gold said firmly. "Anyway, I can't have you off flying around, because I want you at Farnborough. I want you to cable daily reports."

"Things don't happen that quickly in this sort of work," Jennings smiled.

"*I'll* be the judge of that," Gold insisted.

Jennings was frowning. "I thought you were ready to begin learning to trust others?"

"Now you just listen to me—" Gold began, his temper flaring, but the amused expression on Jennings's face stopped him. "You're right, Cal," he admitted. "You're the best there is. Even better than Teddy in your particular specialty, which is why Stoat-Black begged me to send you. If I don't hear from you, I'll assume that there's nothing to report."

Gold's intercom buzzed. He pressed the talk button. "Yes, what is it?"

"Your son is on the line."

"What? Steve?" Gold blurted, startled. He glanced at Jennings. "It's my boy. He's in Korea."

"I'll let you take your call in private." Jennings got up to leave.

"Thanks for your report, Cal," Gold called after him. "And for the advice."

Jennings smiled over his shoulder as he stepped out of the office, closing the door behind him.

Gold snatched up the telephone. "Stevie? Hello, Stevie?"

"Hi, Pop. Happy New Year!" Steve said, his voice faint against the crackling long-distance connection.

"Happy New Year to you, son. Are you all right? Nothing's happened, has it?"

"I'm fine," Steve assured him. "At the moment I'm sitting here in a beautiful hotel in Tokyo, where I'm on leave for three wonderful days, so I thought I'd call."

"Of course I'm glad to hear from you," Gold said. "But

you should have called when you could catch me at home so that your mother could speak with you as well."

"I'm planning to, Pop, but I wanted the chance to talk to you about something without Mom listening."

"Yes, what is it?"

"It's been on my mind since September, but I've waited until now because I knew I was scheduled for some leave time. I wanted to be able to telephone, to discuss it with you personally."

"Okay," Gold said. "What is it?"

Steve seemed to hesitate. "But first let me tell you how sorry I was to hear about Teddy. I wrote you as soon as I heard."

"Yes, I got your letter," Gold said softly. "It was a very nice letter, too. Thank you for sending it."

"Well, Teddy meant a lot to me, too, Pop," Steve said.

"I know."

"He was like an uncle. You wrote that it was a heart attack?"

"Yes."

"I wish I could have been at the funeral. I still can't believe he's gone."

"I know what you mean," Gold said, and then forced lightness into his voice. "Anyway, it's about eight P.M. in Tokyo, so whatever you want to discuss with me must be pretty important if it's got you cooped up in your hotel room talking to your old man when you could be out and around."

"It is, Pop. . . ." Steve said reluctantly. "Okay," he sighed. "I might as well just say it. I want a favor. I want you to pull some strings to get me transferred into a Broad-Sword fighter outfit."

Gold laughed coldly. "You're kidding, right?"

"Pop . . ."

"You've got a lot of balls, Stevie, I'll say that much for you," Gold began, growing angry. "Back in '49 I begged you to join a BroadSword outfit, and you spit in my eye. Then you proceeded to humiliate me by going public with your doubts about the BroadSword. You were proven wrong and I was proven right, but did I ever get an apology from you? No!"

"Pop—"

"Never mind a *public* apology," Gold said. "All I'm talking about is a private admission from you that you were wrong, but I never got it. Now you expect me to call in favors to put you at the top of the list to be assigned an airplane everybody in the Air Force wants to fly!"

"Pop, I've never asked you for anything—"

"Wrong, Steve!" Gold exploded. "That's wrong! You've *constantly* been asking me for something, and do you know what it's been? It's been *my indulgence*, while you've treated me like dirt."

"Okay, Pop, you're right and I'm wrong," Steve said quietly. "Is that what you want to hear? I apologize to you."

"Don't patronize me."

"I mean it, Pop! No more bullshit. This is on the level! I was wrong not to have apologized before. I've always been wrong."

He paused, and when he began again Gold could hear his desperate urgency. "Look, I don't want to—I *can't*—negotiate with you about this. It's something I *need*, and you can do it for me. I'll do anything—pay the price—if you'll do it, but I'm begging you."

"What's happened?" Gold asked sharply. "What's going on?"

"Ah, Pop..." Steve's voice broke. "You always said I was selfish. Well, maybe it's caught up with me."

"Dammit, Stevie, what's got you so upset?" Gold demanded, his own anger forgotten in his worry concerning his son.

"I—I think I got somebody *killed*, Pop."

"Talk to me," Gold said calmly. "Just talk to me. Start from the beginning."

Gold kept asking questions until he'd managed to coax out of his son the whole story concerning the pilot who'd died during the dogfight Steve had initiated against the MiGs. When Steve was done, Gold said, "So you want to get into a BroadSword fighter unit in order to try and avenge your friend's death, is that it?"

"Yes."

"Your CO was right, you know. This wasn't your fault."

"Yes."

"It won't bring your friend back," Gold said, realizing as he said it that it was a banal remark, just like the supposedly comforting platitudes offered up to him concerning Teddy.

"I know all that stuff, Pop. But it doesn't make any difference to the way I feel."

"But hunting MiGs will?"

"If Mikey knew what I was up to, he'd approve. I feel that, Pop. Right now I have to go with my feelings."

"I'll get you into a BroadSword unit."

"Thanks, Pop," Steve said, and then hesitated. "I really am sorry about the way I've been acting for so long. I guess I had a chip on my shoulder, but it's gone now."

"Forget it. It's yesterday's news," Gold replied, and then laughed. "I guess my chip's gone as well. It's a good feeling, huh, Stevie?"

"Yeah. Thanks again, Pop. For everything."

"I miss you, son."

"We've both been missing each other for a long time," Steve said softly. "Maybe sometime pretty soon we can do something about that."

(Two)

The Top Hat Grill
Los Angeles

Gold got to the restaurant ten minutes late. The maître d' told him that his luncheon guest hadn't yet arrived.

Nice move, Gold thought. He couldn't help smiling as he made his way through the crowded dining room to his customary corner booth. The waiter instantly appeared to take his drink order. Gold asked for a Bloody Mary.

Nice move, indeed. Positively ballsy. If the situation were reversed, I'm not sure I'd have the balls to keep me waiting.

He waited another few minutes, sipping at his drink, before Don Harrison appeared in the doorway.

Gold nodded in satisfaction as the maître d' showed the tall, broad-shouldered young engineer to the booth. Harrison's thinning blond hair was slicked back. It looked wet, as if he'd just finished combing it. He was dressed to the nines in a three-piece, gray pinstripe suit, white shirt, and somber tie. The conservative attire made him look older than thirty-two.

Yeah, the lateness bit is cute, Gold thought. But appearances don't lie. The kid was here to make an impression and talk business.

"I'm so sorry, Mr. Gold," Harrison apologized as Gold stood up to shake hands. "We were in meetings all morning, and then the traffic—"

"Was awful, yeah, I know, Don," Gold nodded indulgently as they sat down. "Forget about it. What would you like to drink?"

"Well . . ." Harrison nervously glanced at Gold's half-finished Bloody Mary. "I think just a club soda."

The waiter came to present them with menus.

"You know, I've never been here before, Mr. Gold."

"Call me Herman."

Harrison smiled brightly. He put on a pair of tan, round-framed eyeglasses to scan the menu and then set it aside. "You seem to know what you're having, Herman. What do you recommend?"

"The lobster salad is out of this world."

As the lunch progressed, they chatted amiably about the latest news concerning the Korean peace talks, with both agreeing that it made sense for the UN forces to reject any possibility of an armistice as long as the communists insisted upon building air bases in the North.

The conversation shifted to politics. The man of the hour was General Eisenhower, Supreme Commander of Allied Forces in Europe. A few months ago Ike had been in the headlines when Truman had publicly offered to sponsor him as President on the Democratic ticket. The other day Eisenhower had announced that he would run for President, but as a Republican. Both Gold and Harrison agreed that Ike was pretty much a shoe-in come November.

They talked sports. Harrison, a Stanford graduate, was disappointed when his team got trounced by Illinois in last week's Rose Bowl.

Gold waited for their coffee to be served before he finally brought up the reason that he'd invited Harrison to lunch. "Well, Don, we've met several times before, and I've always been impressed with you. It goes without saying that you're highly regarded in the industry. I wanted this opportunity to get to know you a little better, and I must say, I like what I've heard from you so far. I like the way you think. I guess you know that I'm looking for someone to fill a very important position at GAT."

"I kind of suspected we'd be talking about that," Harrison began. "I mean, when you called last week to invite me to lunch . . ."

Gold nodded. "We're in for some exciting times at GAT. We've got a number of projects on the back burner. One program we're working on is very special," Gold added, thinking about GAT's work for the CIA, "but I can't tell you about that until you're officially signed on."

"You're offering me a job?" Harrison asked.

"Not a job. The job," Gold emphasized, pausing to look Harrison in the eye. "I'm taking about chief engineer."

"Whew," Harrison laughed. "Like I said, I can't pretend that this is a complete surprise, but to actually be offered the job . . ." he trailed off, shaking his head. "I'm leaning toward accepting your offer, Mr. Gold. How could I not be? But I have some reservations."

Gold gestured expansively. "Whatever they are, we can work them out," he said. "For instance, let me say right now that I intend to double the salary."

"Twice as much as I'm making at A-L?" Harrison echoed in disbelief. "That's extremely generous."

"Don't worry. You'll earn it. You'll be shouldering double your work load and responsibilities. Like I said before, we've got a lot of irons in the fire. I think you'll find that GAT is in another league compared to A-L."

"There's something else on my mind," Harrison began.

"Sure there is, Donnie," Gold nodded "You want to talk about profit sharing, stock options, all that stuff. We'll work it out to your satisfaction. Don't worry, Donnie—"

"Don," Harrison said forthrightly.

"Huh?"

"Excuse me for interrupting you," Harrison said. "But my name's Donald, or Don, but not Donnie." He shrugged, frowning slightly. "Donnie's a kid's name. I'm no kid."

"Okay, Don," Gold chuckled. "You surprise me. It took balls to correct me the way you just did. I like ballsy behavior." Gold paused. "When it's appropriate."

"There are a few other points I'd need to get straight between us."

Gold nodded. "For instance?"

"For instance, are you offering me this job because you want me, or because you want to get back at Tim Campbell?"

Gold chuckled. "Now I *am* surprised. Just how much do you know, Don?"

"When Tim told me he wanted to build a jetliner to compete with what GAT had in the works, I could tell that there was more to the competition than just business," Harrison replied. "The way Tim was talking, I got the feeling that there was something personal between you two. I know you two were partners back in '33, but then you split up."

"Old history," Gold grimaced. "You were, what, thirteen years old in 1933?"

"I was twelve, growing up in Hartford, Connecticut," Harrison smiled. "Anyway, from the way Tim was talking about you, I could guess that from his point of view, whatever had happened between you two was still eating at him."

"Okay," Gold said. "I don't want to go into the whole story today. Someday, maybe, I'll tell you about it, but not today. Getting back to your question—sure, I wouldn't mind hamstringing Amalgamated-Landis by stealing you away, but I'm not about to turn over my R&D department to anyone but the best. I think *you're* the best, and that's why we're having this conversation, okay?"

"Yes," Harrison said. "Thank you."

"Now *I've* got a question for *you*. How did Campbell get his hands on the specs to the GC-909?"

Harrison hesitated. "Through an airline," he said vaguely.

"I know *that* much," Gold scowled. "But *which* airline? Who betrayed my confidence?"

"I'm not ready to answer that yet. Not until I'm officially hired. If I told you what you wanted to know right now, I'd be betraying my current employer. Do you understand?"

"Sure," Gold said impatiently. "So I'm officially offering you the job. Do you accept?"

"Not yet," Harrison said quietly. "There are a couple more things. A-L is a big company, Herman."

"Not as big as GAT," Gold interrupted.

"Granted, but big nonetheless," Harrison smiled. "As A-L's chief engineer I've got total control of R&D."

"You can have the same thing at GAT—"

"Not good enough, Herman," Harrison cut him off. "I want more."

"More what?" Gold asked cautiously.

"I'm ready to leave A-L because I can't learn anything form Campbell."

Gold shook his head. "I've got to say that you're wrong there. I've known Tim a long time. He's a genius, in his way."

"Yeah," Harrison acknowledged, "but his genius doesn't do me any good, because he won't share it. He's the most secretive man I've ever met," he complained. "He doesn't trust anybody."

Gold thought about his conversation earlier that day with Cal Jennings. "Trust is hard to come by," he said quietly.

"I think you'd better listen to me very carefully, Herman," Harrison began. "You can't lure me away from A-L with money. I have enough money now, and there are any number of companies who'd be willing to give me more anytime I hinted that I was available. I want something even more valuable from you."

"Which is?" Gold asked, intrigued.

"I want a promise from you to involve me in every aspect of your business. Right now, GAT is one of the biggest and best. That's because of you. I'll be your chief engineer, Herman, if I can *also* be your partner."

"You're talking about being my partner?" Gold frowned. "You said you knew a little something about what happened between me and Tim Campbell."

"I do."

"Then you must realize that the last time I had a partner it didn't work out too well." Gold shook his head. "I don't know about this, Don. Not even Teddy Quinn was my partner."

"I'm *not* Teddy Quinn," Harrison said firmly. "You'd better get *that* straight first thing. You're not hiring another Teddy Quinn. You're hiring *me*."

Gold thought it over. Harrison was an interesting kid. He wasn't at all like Teddy, but that was probably a good thing. Still, the kid was asking a lot.

Gold glanced at Harrison, who was watching him intently. The kid wasn't bluffing, Gold realized. If he rufused Harrison's request, he'd have to continue his search for a new chief engineer.

"Okay," Gold nodded. "You want to learn all facets of the aviation business, you've got it, but let me warn you now. You can kiss your personal life good-bye. You have a family?"

"I'm single."

"Good thing, because now you're married to GAT." Gold extended his hand across the table. "If you're finally ready to accept my offer?"

"I am," Harrison smiled back, suddenly shy as he shook

hands with Gold. "I guess I better get back to the office to break the news to Tim."

"A word of advice about that," Gold said. "You move everything that's meaningful to you out of your office *before* you tell him. If I know Tim Campbell—and boy, do I ever know him—he's going to have a security guard escort you directly off the premises once you give him the good news."

"Okay," Harrison chuckled. "Thanks."

"One more thing," Gold said. "Now that you're *officially* an employee . . ."

"Oh, yeah . . . how'd Campbell get his mitts on your GC proposal?"

"Yeah."

Harrison laughed. "He did pretty much the same thing that you're doing now. He got the info through Skyworld Airlines—"

"But Tim controls Skyworld. It was the only airline to turn down GAT's invitation to invest in the 909. Skyworld wouldn't have had access to the Niner's specs."

"That's why Tim figured that you'd never suspect Skyworld," Harrison said gleefully. "And it looks like he was right. You see, Tim had Skyworld hire an upper management type away from Nationwide Air Transport, which *did* buy into the 909. Skyworld made the guy a tremendous offer. No way he could refuse it. There was just one condition. He had to bring with him copies of the 909's specs, and minutes from all the meetings between GAT and the airlines."

Gold nodded ruefully. "And once Skyworld had the information, Campbell had it."

"Simple as that," Harrison nodded.

"That son of a bitch," Gold said, shaking his head. "So that's how he screwed me." He began to laugh. "You have to admire him. He's so pure in his way."

Now it was Harrison's turn to laugh. "Like you, you mean?"

"Huh?"

"After all, you're stealing *me* from *him*."

Gold, grinning, leaned back against the red leather upholstery of the restaurant booth. "Don't let anyone tell you different. Two wrongs *do* make a right."

CHAPTER 16

(One)

MiG Alley, Korea
4 August 1952

There were gray rain clouds blanketing the North Korean terrain between the Yalu and Chongchon rivers, but at thirty thousand feet the sky was clear and blue. Steve's BroadSword flight was on its third sweep of the Yalu's southern bank when his flight leader, Major Larsen, called "Bingo!" the code word that meant he was low on fuel.

The flight made a wide, lazy turn toward home, which was about two hundred miles away. Five minutes later Larsen announced that the MiGs were springing their ambush.

"Steel Fist Three, this is Fist Lead," Major Larsen called, his voice betraying his excitement. Larsen was flying with his wingman about a quarter mile ahead and a thousand feet below Steve's element. "Come in, Fist Three—"

Steve punched his mike button. "This is Steel Fist Three."

"Fist Three, GCI out of Cho-Do has bandit tracks."

"Affirmative, I've been monitoring the channel," Steve said.

GCI stood for Ground Control Interception, and Cho-Do was a small island in the Yellow Sea about eight miles off the Korean mainland. GCI was part of Tactical Air Control. It was GCI's job to guide the Combat Air Patrols to the MiGs, warn the CAPs if they were about to get ambushed, and coordinate pilot rescue operations.

"Cho-Do says they have eight bandits on their screen," Larsen chattered. "The bandits crossed at Sui-ho. They're closing on us fast."

Larsen liked to talk, and since he was flight leader, Steve liked to let him. He was an okay guy who'd flown a Jug over the Pacific in the last war when he'd missed becoming an ace by one kill. He was making up for that this time around. He already had six kills: four MiGs and two prop-driven IL-10s.

"We stick with our original plan, Fist Lead?" Steve asked.

"Affirmative," Larsen replied. "We're still the 'worm.' Head on home, but not too fast. We don't want them to get discouraged."

The idea had come down from FEAF Command, in response to pilots' complaints that something was needed to shake up the status quo. Lately trying to catch MiGs had become even more infuriating than usual. The commie jets would go up in force, and begin a leisurely orbit over the Yalu River, the natural boundary between North Korea and Manchuria. Like Indians around a wagon train the MiGs would circle, flying at fifty thousand feet, too high up for BroadSwords to go and get them, but every now and then a handful of MiGs would swoop down to bounce the F-90s. The BroadSwords would jockey for position and invariably end up on the MiGs' tails, but before they had time to get a kill, the MiGs would hightail it across the Yalu into Manchuria, where the BroadSwords were not allowed to follow.

Today's plan was simple, but it depended on split-second timing. Steel Fist Flight was the "worm"—the bait meant to lure the MiGs away from the Yalu. FEAFcom hoped that the MiGs would be willing to follow because they thought Steel Fist Flight would be easy pickings: four BroadSwords all alone, and after a half hour spent on Patrol, obviously low on fuel. What the MiGs didn't know was that eight fresh, fully fueled BroadSwords, flying low in flights of two to avoid detection by enemy radar, were closing on the scene. Like cavalry riding to the rescue, the double flight of BroadSwords were the "hook" that would snare the MiGs, hopefully *before* they had a chance to chew on the "worm."

"The bandits should be closing on you anytime now, Fist Three," Larsen radioed. "Better punch your tanks, to get them all hot and bothered."

The plan was for Steve and his wingman to appear as if they were preparing to engage the MiGs, but they would not do so unless the plan somehow went wrong, and they had to save their skins. The lopsided odds were not the issue. The problem was that their airplanes did not have enough fuel left to engage in combat maneuvers.

"You heard Fist Lead," Steve told his wingman, Lieutenant Garret. "It's time to look tough."

"Might as well drop my tanks," Garret chuckled. "They're as dry as my mouth was this morning."

Steve laughed. There'd been quite a bash last night at the officers' club to celebrate the Helsinki Summer Olympics, which had ended with the good old U.S.A. having whipped the Soviet Union.

Steve, with Garret sticking close by, banked his F-90 in a wide turn meant to entice the MiGs to come on ahead; that the two lone BroadSwords wearing the 44th's bright green, diagonal double slash on their aft fuselages, tail rudders, and wings were foolishly willing to stay and do battle.

"Heads up, Fist Four," Steve radioed Garret. "When they come, it'll probably be from up high."

"Affirmative. I just hope the hook gets here when it's supposed to."

"Wouldn't you like a chance at these bandits?" Steve joked.

"Normally, sure. But not when I'm running on fumes. And not with this hangover."

Yeah, it had been some party last night, Steve thought as he searched the sky for signs of the enemy. It had done everyone good to blow off a little steam. There had been so much pent-up frustration over the way things were going.

In Panmunjom the peace talks were stalled on the question of whether the commie POWs who wanted to stay in the South would be forced to return behind the Bamboo Curtain when the war was over. Out on the battlefield fighting had entered into a morale-sapping series of bloody skirmishes like the one at that aptly named hellhole, Heartbreak Ridge. Meanwhile, the stalemate on the ground had reached up into the sky. The BroadSword pilots were far superior to their commie counterparts, but their prowess was blunted by the enemy's superior numbers. Not only weren't there enough BroadSwords, but maintenance of what was available was continuing to be a problem. The commies, meanwhile, seemed to have an endless supply of fresh MiGs.

When all that bad news was taken into account, it was no wonder that the news that the Americans had whipped the commies' asses at Helsinki had been cause for celebration at Chusan. Sure it was just sports, but at least it had been a *decisive* victory, and that was something that was so far sadly lacking in the Korean War. . . .

"Heads up, Fist Three," Garret said. "Bandits at two o'clock. . . . Coming in low for a change."

"I've got them, Fist Four."

There were eight of them, flying in a line abreast. Eight specks glinting in the sun and closing fast, like a pack of wolves falling on a pair of lambs.

"Fist Lead, come in," Steve radioed Larsen. "We're about to be engaged. No sign of hook."

"Hook's on the way," Larsen replied.

"Maybe so," Steve said, arming his guns. "But if hook don't get here soon, this worm is going to have to *turn*."

"Here comes our guys!" Garret broke in. "They're coming in at four o'clock."

"Beautiful!" Steve laughed as the eight MiGs were intercepted by six BroadSwords. The MiG battle line fell apart as the commie pilots scattered in confusion. A BroadSword locked on to a MiG's six o'clock and began firing. Steve watched the sparks rise up off the MiG and the BroadSword chewed a big bite off the commie's starboard wing. The MiG's canopy blew, and the pilot ejected.

Oh, it's turning out to be a lovely day, after all, Steve thought, supremely happy to be where he was.

There were times when being a VIP's son came in handy, he had to admit. It had been only a couple of weeks after his telephone conversation with his father that his new orders had been cut, instructing him to join up with the 44th Fighter Interceptor Squadron operating out of Chusan Airfield, near Seoul. He'd settled in by the middle of February, and had trained in his F-90 eight hours a day, seven days a week. On April 2, he'd been deemed ready for full combat duty.

Throughout that spring, Steve and the rest of the 44th, and the FI squadrons like them, flew high-cover escort missions and CAPs over the 6,500 square miles of Interdiction Zone A, the area surrounding the North Korean–Chinese border, better known as MiG Alley. He'd scored his first BroadSword kill in April, when he'd downed a MiG near Sinaju. In May he got his second and third kills on the same patrol, over the southern bank of the Yalu, near the Suiho dam. That double score had given him four kills overall, counting the MiG that he'd dropped back in September '51 in his Shooting Star.

At that point Steve had figured that he'd be a jet ace before he knew it, but it hadn't turned out that way. The MiGs became shy, playing their new, favorite game of pee-kaboo over the Yalu. Steve hadn't gotten the opportunity to fire his guns all summer.

Now Steve and his wingman loitered on the battle scene at high altitude in order to conserve fuel, making great spiral passes at close to five hundred miles an hour in order to watch the battle.

If only I had the gas to get into this brawl, he thought enviously as another two MiGs fell before the BroadSword's guns.

The remaining five MiGs had decided to run. Four of them split up into two elements, and then each pair made a wide, 180-degree turn back toward the Yalu, climbing all the while in hopes of getting away from the Broad-Swords.

"Fist Three, remember we're on bingo fuel," Garret said nervously.

"Affirmative," Steve replied. "Let's go—"

The words died in his throat as Steve stared at the fifth MiG: it had a blue nose and tail, and a jagged, blue lightning bolt running the length of its fuselage. Steve was able to get a good look at it because it wasn't running away. Like a mama hen prepared to sacrifice herself in order to keep a predator off her departing brook of chicks, the blue lightning MiG was hanging back to engage the BroadSwords.

"Fist Three. We've got to break for home," Garret said.

Steve didn't reply. He couldn't. He was too busy staring, thinking that he was hallucinating, that the blue lightning MiG was a vision brought on by his own desire, the way a desperately thirsty man will think he sees water in the desert. How many times had Steve *dreamed* about getting another crack at that son of a bitch who had blown Mikey DeAngelo out of the sky, and now here it was.

He blinked his eyes, looked away, and looked back, giving the MiG every opportunity to disappear like the mirage he half believed it was.

It didn't disappear. Instead, he watched the MiG come around incredibly fast, to drop down on the six o'clock of a BroadSword. The blue lightning MiG peppered the F-90 with gunfire. Steve watched the cannon rounds roll like fiery baseballs from the MiG's chin pod of guns until it scored a hit, and when you were blasting away with 37- and 23-millimeter projectiles, one hit was all it took.

Steve monitored the panicked exchange between the wounded BroadSword and its flight.

"This is Lance Three! I'm hit! Mayday! Mayday! I'm hit! Get him off me!"

"Lance Lead on the way."

"Arrow Three and Four on the way."

"Diamond Flight on the way."

The shot-up BroadSword, leaking smoke, headed for

home as the other F-90s broke off their pursuit of the fleeing MiGs to close in on blue lightning.

That's just what he wants you to do, Steve thought, watching in admiration as the canny MiG pilot led the BroadSwords on a merry zigzag chase. As Steve had expected, not one of the F-90 jockeys was able to draw a bead on him long enough to fire.

"Oh, I gotta get in on this," Steve muttered.

"Negative, Fist Three," Garret yelled. "We're bingo fuel!"

"But—" Steve watched in frustration as the pilot of the blue lightning MiG did his signature eight-point victory roll before banking away. *Yes, I do remember your little dance,* Steve thought savagely.

"This is Lance Lead," Steve heard one of the attacking BroadSword pilots call. "Break off chase. I repeat, break off. It looks like Yalu Charlie has outfoxed again . . ."

Yalu who? Steve wondered.

"Fist Three! *Damn* you," Garret swore. "We've got to go home."

His wingman's desperate tone jolted Steve out of his preoccupation. *Garret is sounding just the way Mickey did before I got him killed.*

No way was Steve going to let that blue lightning MiG make him responsible for another wingman's life.

"Affirmative, Fist Four," Steve said, bringing his Broad-Sword around. "No problem, Lieutenant. We're going home right now."

(Two)

Officers' Club
Chusan Airfield, near Seoul

That evening Steve barged into the club with more on his mind than drinking. He elbowed his way up to the bar and got himself a beer, then turned to survey the joint. It was crowded, dark, and smoky, so it took Steve a moment to find Larsen, but then he spotted the flight leader sitting at a corner table, a shot of whiskey and a long-necked beer in front of him.

"Hey, pull up a chair," Larsen said in welcome as Steve came over.

Larsen was in his late thirties. He was dark complexioned, with shiny black hair, bushy eyebrows, and a thick mustache. Given a cigar and enough whiskey, he could do a creditable imitation of Groucho Marx.

"Things went pretty well today, huh?" Larsen said as Steve sat down. "Three MiGs killed, while only one Broad-Sword got a little shot up, and it made it home okay."

Steve nodded impatiently. "Who's Yalu Charlie?"

"Yeah, I heard you ran into him today."

"Why didn't anybody tell me about him?" Steve demanded.

"Why didn't you ask?" Larsen launched into his Groucho act, rolling his eyes and flicking the ash off a non-existent cigar.

"Cut the horseplay!" Steve fumed. "This is important."

"What's your big concern about YC?" Larsen asked, his smile fading. "He's just another honcho MiG driver. . . ."

Honcho, Steve thought grimly. *I haven't heard that word for a while.*

"Honcho" was Japanese for "boss." It was a term of respect the BroadSword jockeys reserved for those MiG pilots who could handle themselves in a dogfight.

"This Yalu Charlie son of a bitch is not just another honcho as far as I'm concerned," Steve began. He quickly filled Larsen in on what had happened back in August '51 when he and Mike DeAngelo had tangled with the blue lightning bolt MiG.

"Okay," Larsen muttered. He paused to sip his whiskey, and then chased it with a swallow of beer. "Here's what I know about Yalu Charlie. Number one, like most commie honcho pilots, he's Russian."

"That much I knew," Steve said, lighting a cigarette.

"An instructor pilot," Larsen added.

"Right," Steve agreed. "Part of some kind of crack Russian squadron?"

"I never heard that," Larsen shrugged. "Anyway, like I said, Charlie's an IP. Those MiGs you saw him shepherding today were obviously his latest class. They must be close to graduating if Charlie was willing to bring them across the Yalu."

"If those were student pilots, they've got some homework to do," Steve said. "The hook flights were tearing them up until Charlie decided to send his students home and hold the fort all by himself."

"And he did, didn't he?" Larsen chuckled. "He can pull shit like that because he's that good. There's no way to know, of course, but my feeling is that Charlie's got to be an ace."

"I heard he was one, in the last war."

"I mean *this* war," Larsen said flatly.

"Someday we'll have to ask him," Steve said, smiling thinly.

"Yeah, right," Larsen muttered into his whiskey.

"I've been here since February," Steve said. "If the Yalu is Charlie's territory, how come I haven't seen him before?"

"I guess you just missed him." Larsen paused. "Yeah, now that I think back on it, you did just miss Charlie's finals week and graduation ceremony. And then you missed him again in the spring, because we were flying about a hundred miles south of the Yalu, mopping up some MiG activity near Sinanju, remember?"

"Sure I remember," Steve said. "But what are you talking about concerning all this 'finals' and 'graduation' stuff?"

"Okay," Larsen grinned. "I said that Charlie was an instructor pilot. Here's his MO. When he begins training a new class of MiG jockeys he keeps them well behind enemy lines. Then he gradually brings them closer to the Yalu— and us—all the while practicing high-altitude combat maneuvers with them."

Steve grimaced. "So that we can't touch them."

"Right," Larsen replied. "When they come close to graduating, he starts to let them dart across the river, but still at high altitude. That's when we know it's 'finals week.' Finally he lets them come down and engage in combat. That's the 'graduation ceremony.'"

"And then Charlie disappears for a while," Steve said.

"You got it," Larsen nodded. "And when he does disappear, we know that he's once again deep behind the lines, starting a new class."

"So, if this is 'finals,' the chances are that we won't be seeing him again for a few months."

"Maybe some CAP will spot him again, but yeah, basically you're right," Larsen acknowledged. "He's winding down this time around. We likely won't get another good look at him until around October or November—for all the good it will do us," he added wryly.

"What do you mean?"

"Come on, Steve." Larsen looked down at his drink. "You've seen Charlie in action," he moped. "Nobody can touch him."

"I'm going to do more than *touch* him," Steve said firmly.

Larsen shook his head. "Believe me, a lot of us have tried and failed."

"I'm not going to fail."

"Steve, he ain't called *Yalu* Charlie for nothing," Larsen chided. "Today was an exception. Usually he sticks to the vicinity of the river like glue. You know what that means. He's so good that it's next to impossible to get him into trouble, but even if you could lock on to his six o'clock, all he's got to do is cob the throttle and zip back across the river, and after today you can bet that he's going to be *extra particular* about straying far from home."

"Then that's the key," Steve said.

"What is?" Larsen asked, frowning.

"It's simple. Yalu Charlie thinks he's safe on the north side of the river. That's where he lets his guard down."

Larsen shrugged. "He probably lets his guard down back in Moscow as well, but big shit, you can't touch him there, either."

"No, not in Moscow," Steve said softly. "It's too far away. But the Yalu is right here. All I have to do is fly across it."

"You listen to me." Larsen leveled his index finger like a gun at Steve. "Before your time, I guess it was a year ago, a couple of the 44th's pilots got carried away and went across the Yalu. They claimed navigational error, but that didn't cut any ice with the CO. He had their balls for breakfast. Do you read me, Steve?"

"You're pulling my leg," Steve began.

"Negative!"

Steve was still skeptical. Colonel Gleason was in his fifties. He was a small, bald-headed man with thick wire-rimmed spectacles. The pilots didn't see too much of Gleason; he preferred to leave the daily briefings to his staff so that he would have more time to hunt bugs. It was said that he had an extensive collection and that some of his finds were in museums. In good weather you could find him with his butterfly net creeping around in the brush on the outskirts of the base.

"Gleason put those two pilots up for a court-martial," Larsen continued. "They were found not guilty, but he wasn't satisfied. He found some excuse to have them grounded for good."

"Get out of here," Steve laughed uneasily.

"You think I'm kidding?" Larsen demanded.

Steve stared. "You're telling me that Gleason actually was vindictive enough to permanently clip their wings?"

"Like they were a couple of his butterflies pinned to a blotter," Larsen nodded vigorously.

"I guess I believe you," Steve said dubiously.

"I'm just telling you," Larsen shrugged. "Believe it or not, Gleason's the kind of officer who does not believe in anybody rocking the boat. He's a stickler for the rules, he likes to hold a grudge, and he knows how to get even. You cross that river, and you'd better enjoy your flight, because that'll be your last."

"Okay," Steve said. "I hear you. Thanks for the warning. But I still intend to avenge my buddy, and I think I know a way to do it. The problem is that if it's going to work, I'm going to need the flight's cooperation."

"You just hold on! You leave us out of it! You want to go up against Gleason, that's your business, but—"

"Listen to me," Steve implored.

"No way!" Larsen cut him off emphatically. "And that's final!"

Nodding, Steve leaned back in his chair to study Larsen. *Maybe a little reverse psychology,* he thought. "Ah, hell, I guess you're right."

"I *know* I'm right!"

"Anyway," Steve began, "even if you *did* go along, the other guys would probably veto my idea."

"What do you mean?" Larsen demanded, sounding affronted. "I'm flight leader," he smugly thumbed his chest. "If I like the idea, the other guys will string along, don't you worry."

"Okay," Steve said quickly, leaning in close to Larsen to confide in him. "What I have in mind will leave the rest of the flight in the clear. I don't want *you* guys to cross the river. I only need you to cover for me. No way will Gleason be able to nail you." He paused. "But if you don't think you can get the other guys to go along, that's okay."

"Nah, nah . . . don't worry."

Steve pretended to hesitate. "Maybe I *should* wait for a time when the entire flight is together."

"I *told* you there'd be no problem!"

"Well, if you say so. . . ." Steve grinned. "Okay, then, next time Yalu Charlie begins finals week, here's what I want to do. . . ."

CHAPTER 17

(One)

GAT
R&D Department
14 May 1952

Don Harrison stared longingly out the conference room's windows, only half listening to the cost analysis report on a new fighter design. It was a warm, sunny day, and Harrison was suffering from spring fever.

The conference room overlooked the parking lot. Harrison's new white Hudson Commodore Eight convertible was parked out there. He'd bought the car to celebrate landing this job. If he craned his neck, he could see it gleaming in the sun.

It would be grand to put the top down on the Commodore and go for a drive along the coast. Or maybe go hiking in the nearby California foothills. Or even be working at his drafting table in his office.

It was a good day to be anywhere but here, sitting at the head of this conference table, trying to ignore the stony expressions on the faces of his senior engineers and project managers.

But he had to correct himself. These were not his people. To say that they swore their allegiance to GAT, not to him, would be a supreme understatement. There wasn't one of them who wouldn't gladly plant a dagger between his shoulder blades if given half a chance.

I've been here four months now, Harrison thought.

Since then these guys have gone from mildly resenting my usurping Teddy Quinn's authority to completely hating my guts.

Sitting at the far end of the conference table was Susan Greene, his personal secretary. She attended all the conferences to take the minutes.

She had been Teddy Quinn's secretary, so ironically Harrison had initially thought that she would be the only one in the department who would have trouble making the adjustment to his work style. It had turned out exactly the opposite of what he had expected. Susan had been the only one to sincerely welcome him with an open mind.

Now Harrison watched her as she busily took down in shorthand what the project manager was saying. She was an extraordinarily efficient secretary. He didn't know how he would ever get along without her. She was a damned fine-looking woman, as well. She was built big but shapely, with lovely skin, gleaming blonde hair, and big brown eyes. She had an easy, feline way of moving, like a tigress.

He wondered, as he had many times, if she was a tigress in bed.

Susan must have felt his eyes on her. She suddenly glanced up at him and smiled in the oddest way, as if she'd read his mind.

Harrison, flustered and feeling himself blushing, quickly looked away. "Forgive me," he interrupted the project manager. "I'd like to hear more, but we're running short on time, Mr. Randall—"

"Randolph," the man said evenly. "My name's Randolph."

"Yes, of course, Mr. Randolph," he stammered, off balance. *Shit! he thought. They'll be snickering about this behind my back.*

Randolph was in his forties. His pug nose was too small for his broad, round face, but Harrison envied the man's thick head of salt-and-pepper curls. His own, baby-fine blonde hair was making a quick retreat to the back of his head. He had to wear a hat when riding in his new convertible to avoid a sunburned scalp.

"Anyway, Mr. Randolph," Harrison said, "if you'll just route a copy of your analysis to Miss Greene—"

"Sure, I'll drop a copy onto Suzy's desk," Randolph interrupted. He looked at Suzy and winked. The others chuckled.

He's making fun of me, damn him. Harrison swallowed his anger. *I'm always odd man out,* he brooded. *They treat me like a barely tolerated guest, not the head of this department.*

"We need to talk about the GC-909," he said. He looked toward Cal Jennings, the 909 project manager.

"Everything is under control, now that we know what caused the Stoat-Black Starstreak breakups," Jennings announced.

Harrison nodded. Jennings had co-authored the final report submitted by the British panel that had solved the mystery of the SB-100's repeated high-altitude breakups. In March of this year the panel had discovered that the Starstreak's Achilles heel had been the cutouts in the hull to accommodate the jetliner's windows. Repeated pressurizings and depressurizings had weakened the joinngs where the frames met the hull. At high altitudes, the frame could pop out, causing a split in the hull that would destroy the plane.

"We've made running changes in the 909's fuselage to avoid this problem situation," Jennings said. "We've designed reinforcements into the fuselage. Tear-stoppers, if you will."

"Have you routed a memo on that to public relations?" Harrison interrupted.

"Well, no. . . ." Jennings said. "What we've done is very technical. I doubt those flacks upstairs would understand the engineering aspects. The public sure as hell wouldn't."

"If the PR department can't understand well enough to explain it to the public, it's your job as project manager to make them understand," Harrison said.

"That's not the way we've usually done it—" Jennings began.

"It's how I want it done, *now,* however," Harrison replied firmly, and paused. "Miss Greene?"

"Sir?" she asked, looking up.

"Take a memo to PR: I want a promotional film made," he continued, thinking out loud. "We'll build a mock-up of the SB-100 and 909's cabins. We'll pressurize them, and then, somehow, dramatically puncture both. It should be very impressive to the public when it sees the SB-100 peel open like a sardine can, while our jetliner—thanks to its tear-stoppers—stays intact." Harrison paused and smiled. "Suggest to the PR department that we call our film 'The Gauntlet of the Sky.' Mr. Jennings, I know you're busy," Harrison said apologetically, "but after your stint on that panel, you know the SB-100 as well as any Stoat-Black engineer. I'd like you to supervise the building of the mock-ups."

Jennings was scowling through his bushy black beard. "I think I'll wait until I hear from Herman about this."

"That won't be necessary, Mr. Jennings," Harrison said icily.

"He usually authorizes such expenditures."

"I'm sick of this insubordination!" Harrison exploded.

"Sir," Susan quickly interrupted, her voice calmly steady against the shocked silence. "I'll route a copy of this memo to the top floor right away, adding a note asking Mr. Gold to initial his approval of the idea."

"Thank you for that suggestion, Miss Greene," Harrison nodded. "The rest of you had better realize that when Amalgamated-Landis committed to entering into this competition to build a jetliner, they decided to play for keeps. They knew that they were risking a lot by throwing down the gauntlet of challenge, but they have a lot going for them."

"They've also suffered a terrible setback," Randolph observed.

"What?" Harrison asked, distracted. "Pardon?"

"They've lost *you*, right?"

Harrison struggled to keep control of his temper amid the laughter; he knew that he'd made a serious tactical error by losing it a few moments before. *It's not necessary that they like me*, he told himself, *as long as they accept the logic of what I have to say.*

"Listen to me," he said loudly. "Because I've only recently come from A-L, I know a few things about what's going on there. For instance, A-L salesmen have been telling their prospective customer airlines that although GAT will have earlier deliveries, if the airlines are willing to wait another year, A-L will supply them with a better airplane."

That got their attention, he thought as the laughter subsided.

"That's a lot of crap," Randolph said.

"Why?" Harrison shrugged. "Think about it; *all of you* think about it! A-L has been stressing the fact that its jetliner has all the features of the 909, plus none of the drawbacks. The A-L sales slogan has been that the AL12 'puts the icing on the cake.' "

"That can't be working," Jennings said nervously.

"Oh, no?" Harrison countered. "Then how come A-L is now ahead of us on advance orders?" The room was silent. "We've got a prototype almost ready to go," he continued, "and all they've got is a paper airline, *and yet their orders outnumber ours.*"

He waited a beat to let that last bit sink in and hopefully shake up these complacent bastards. "Gentlemen, Amalgamated-Landis may be the tortoise and GAT may be the hare, but as in the fable, the hare now has to scramble to catch up. That's why I want to do this promotional film, and why we have to work overtime to solve the problems that continue to plague the 909. We've got to exploit every advantage if the 909 is going to beat out the AL-12 as the world's foremost jetliner."

He paused again, and then nodded. "Meeting adjourned."

He watched from his place at the head of the table as the others collected their papers and filed out, murmuring to each other. Down at the opposite end of the table Susan Greene was still seated, finishing up her note taking.

When they were the only two still in the room, he broke the silence, asking, "They hate me, don't they?"

She looked up at him. He could tell that she was forcing a lie. "No, of course they don't."

"Oh, come on," he said plaintively. "I *know* they do." He shrugged. "I just don't know what to *do* about it."

She closed her steno book and looked at him. "Are you asking for my advice?"

"Yes," he nodded. His heart rate increased and it was suddenly difficult to catch his breath, the way it always was when he found himself in a personal conversation with an attractive woman.

"Okay," she said briskly. "First of all, you need to drop your formality. You should be on a first-name basis with your staff. You should have been on a first-name basis since day one."

"Really. . ." Harrison hesitated. "Susan?"

She laughed. "Yes, *Don*." She shook her head. "Were you like this at A-L?"

"No," he admitted, "but things were different there. It was smaller, and I'd been there for ages. Worked my way up, if you know what I mean."

"Sure, I do," she shrugged. "At A-L you earned everyone's respect, but it's tougher here. My—" she paused, remembering that with Teddy gone, nobody in the department knew that she was Herman Gold's daughter. "I mean, *our* boss, Mr. Gold, has made you chief engineer, and a lot of people around here are a little resentful of that fact."

"I know *that much* Susan, but what should I do about it?" he demanded. "Besides calling people by their first names, I mean?"

"Well," she said, and paused thoughtfully. "I think you should ask for their help."

"Huh?" he asked, puzzled. "But I don't need any help."

She shook her head, sighing. "That's *precisely* why you should ask for some. People don't feel threatened by someone who asks them for help."

"I bet Teddy never asked for help," he muttered.

"He didn't have to," she said. "But he hired all of these people. Also, you've got to take into account the age factor. Teddy was much older than you. He was sort of—" She paused. "Avuncular."

"A father figure, you mean?"

She nodded. "People felt comforted by his presence. But now he's gone and here you are, threatening the hierarchy like some upstart young bull."

Harrison burst out laughing. "I don't think *any woman* has ever referred to me as *a bull* before."

Susan blushed, and his heartbeat quickened further still. He began to wonder if he could ask her out.

"You know what I meant," she said softly.

Harrison nodded. "How'd you get to be so smart?"

Susan grinned wryly. "Life, I guess."

"Oh, yes," he said. "You're a widow, aren't you? You lost your husband in the war?"

Susan nodded. "That's not what I was referring to, but yes, since you brought it up. It is true that I'm a widow. I have a son."

"Oh, really?" Harrison replied. "How old?"

"He's ten."

"Oh. . . ." He sensed an awkward silence rising between them, as was always the case sooner or later when it came to women.

"Well!" Susan said crisply, gathering up her notebooks and folders. "I've got work to do."

"So you really think I should ask the others for help?" Harrison began quickly, unwilling to let their conversation end. "To get them to like me, I mean," he prodded.

"Yes," she smiled. "It doesn't matter if you really need help. Ask for it anyway, and act impressed with its quality when it's given to you. Then, while you're chatting, why not suggest getting together for lunch?"

"Try that with all the senior people, is that the idea?"

"Sure!" she enthused. "Before you know it, you'll be wondering what all today's fuss was about."

"You really think so? That I can win them over, I mean?"

"Why not?" she laughed. "Why ever couldn't you?"

"I've never been very good with people."

"Well, I think you're a very nice guy," she told him.

"Really—in that case would you like to have dinner with me?" he blurted out abruptly.

His heart sank as she began to laugh. *She thought I was joking.*

She must have read his reaction in his expression. "Oh, Don... I'm sorry. You were serious? I thought you were ...Oh, never mind," she trailed off, shaking her head. "The point is that you don't have to take me out to persuade me to like you. I already do!"

"Yes, of course," he muttered, pretending to be busy shuffling the folders in front of him. *Never should have asked her,* he thought. *Never, never should have.*

"Well, I'll get started on that memo to the PR department," she said, getting up.

"Yes, thank you." He watched her leave the room, feeling like a total ass for asking her out. He should have known better; known that he was being too forward. *Damn, damn, damn.* Now he was going to feel uncomfortable with her for who knew how long?

He decided to wait a few minutes before leaving. Give her a head start so that he wouldn't have to try to come up with conversation while they were walking back to their desks.

(Two)

He was just trying to be nice to me, wasn't he? Susan wondered. *He wasn't really asking me out to dinner, was he?*

She was back at her desk. She'd been preparing to type up that memo when she'd paused.

Had he asked her out intending to be polite, or was he really interested?

It had been so long since she'd been out with a man that his invitation had shocked her. She'd automatically said no without really considering the idea, assuming it was just his way of being cordial, but then again, if he'd only wanted to be cordial, he would have invited her to lunch, not dinner.

She pushed away from her typewriter. She needed to think about this.

He was cute in his way. Certainly not classically handsome, as her husband, Blaize, had been, but certainly attractive with his broad shoulders and pretty hazel eyes.

She watched him come out of the conference room at the far end of the department and walk toward her on his way to his office. He was very *definitely* going bald, she thought. The overhead light fixtures were reflecting off his high forehead.

So what if he's going bald? she scolded herself angrily. She wasn't perfect. She was almost thirty-one years old, for God's sake, and starting to show a few signs of wear and tear of her own.

Yes, she thought, Don Harrison had a lot going for him. He had a sweet grin and a good laugh. He'd seemed not the least put off the way some men were when she brought up the fact that she had a son. And Don was clearly brilliant, and he was most certainly a gentleman.

And she'd *enjoyed* talking to him. That was the most important thing. For the first time in a long time, she'd made small talk with a man and if had been *fun*, not a *chore*. She wouldn't mind talking to him some more.

He kept his eyes averted as he passed by her desk.

"Don?" she heard herself murmur.

He paused in his office doorway. He looked distraught. "Yes?"

"Do you . . . ?" She hesitated. "Do you like Italian food? There's a place in Santa Monica I used to go to quite a lot. I could meet you there for a bite some evening."

"Why not tonight?" he asked.

She took a deep breath. *It's been so long. Am I really ready to try again?* "Why not?" she agreed lightly.

CHAPTER 18

(One)

MiG Alley, Over Manchuria
5 October 1952

Steve was flying at 47,000 feet: operational ceiling for the BroadSword. He had his wing tanks in place, and was throttled down for maximum conservation of fuel.

At this altitude the sky was an endless, crystalline blue. The earth below looked like a crinkled expanse of chocolate furred with green mold. Off to the south, *very far south,* was a thin, tangled quicksilver cord: the Yalu River.

Where all good BroadSword pilots are supposed to be, Steve idly thought as he checked his instruments and maps to ascertain his position and heading. Somewhere to his east was Bao Kung Cheng Airfield, the commie base where the MiG drivers were trained for combat. Somewhere to his south, on the safe side of the Yalu, was the rest of Steel Fist Flight.

"Back Door, come in," Larsen called. "Come in, Back Door."

"This is Black Door," Steve replied.

"We've got a double flight of MiGs orbiting the river."

Steve's heartbeat quickened. "That's got to be blueballs?"

"Now don't be getting antsy," Larsen responded. "We'll check it out and let you know. We've got to be sure that this isn't a false alarm before you shoot your wad."

"Affirmative," Steve said.

"Fist Lead, out," Larsen replied.

Nothing to do now but wait, Steve thought.

It had been an anxious couple of months since his reunion last August with Yalu Charlie. Since then Steve had obsessed on his scheme to bring down the Russian. Nothing else mattered to him: not becoming a jet ace, and not his big fight and the ensuing break-off with Linda Forrest.

He'd downed that fifth MiG back in September, but it had seemed like small potatoes. As far as Steve was concerned, he could single-handedly bring down the entire Red air force, but he still wouldn't be satisfied until he'd had the blue lightning MiG in his gun sight.

The fight with Linda had also taken place in September, oddly enough. She'd come to Chusan Airfield along with a contingent of newspeople on a tour of the front. Steve had bribed an airman a couple of bucks to get the key to an out-of-the-way storeroom in Operations Center so they could have themselves a good time in it for a couple of nights, but then Linda had gotten all mushy, starting in about how she loved him and how maybe they should be thinking about marriage.

In hindsight, Steve guessed that with his mind on Yalu Charlie's imminent reappearance, he'd been a mite too emphatic about how marriage wasn't in the cards for him right now, and not likely in the future.

Well, telling her that had sure as hell been a mistake, because for the rest of the visit she had been as cold to him as the air temperature at fifty thousand feet, and letting that storeroom go to waste had been a damn shame because the sex between them had always been outstanding.

She and the rest of the contingent of news hounds had left a couple of days later, and that had been the last Steve had seen or heard from her.

Oh, yeah. The last except for that card, postmarked Japan. On it was a brief, scrawled message:

> You want to be JUST FRIENDS? That's fine with me. But that's ALL we're going to be from now on. Get it? (NOT ANYMORE YOU AREN'T!!!)
>
> YOUR *PAL*,
> L.

Yeah, Steve had gotten the message, all right. It was too bad. Linda had been the only woman friend that he'd ever had. In hindsight he guessed that the question of marriage inevitably had to come along sooner or later to louse things up.

A couple of weeks after that, Steve had traded a couple of fifths of booze to a file clerk assigned to base Operations Center in return for the opportunity to scan the reports the flight leaders filed after each CAP. The first mention of Yalu Charlie sightings had appeared in yesterday's reports.

Today Steve had initiated "Operation Back Door."

It wasn't much of a plan, but it was the best that Steve could come up with. The first part of it called for Steel Fist Flight to keep mum concerning the fact that Steve wasn't with them. This was for the benefit of any GCI operators who might me monitoring their chatter. Of course, Steve wasn't showing up on GCI's screens, but he was hoping that the busy radar jockeys wouldn't notice.

Meanwhile, Steve was flying above forbidden Chinese territory at maximum ceiling to conserve fuel. If commie radar picked him, Steve hoped that they would figure that he was one of their own, maybe with radio trouble, which would explain why he wasn't answering their calls. Along that line of wishful thinking, Steve was hoping that the GCI radar jockeys surveying enemy air space would also assume from his position and altitude that he was a MiG.

Steve glanced at the clock in the upper right-hand corner of the BroadSword's instrument panel. Larsen was certainly taking his time calling back.

It's got to be Charlie, Steve thought. *I feel it. Come on, Charlie. It's today, or maybe tomorrow.*

Or never. . . .

He knew that he could only pull a jury-rigged dodge like this once or twice before it fell apart and he was caught and hung out to dry for disobeying orders not to cross the Yalu . . .

"Back Door, Back Door, come in." It was Larsen, and

from his excited tone Steve knew what he was going to say before he said it.

"Back Door here," Steve said, already bringing his BroadSword around toward Bao Kung Cheng field before he'd even heard Larsen say:

"You're a go, Back Door. Repeat, *you are a go*."

It was the prearranged signal that meant that the Yalu had been sighted, and that he and his flock of fledgling pilots were on their way home to Bao Kung Cheng.

"Affirmative. Thanks."

"Don't thank me," Larsen said dryly. "It's your funeral."

"Back Door out," Steve said, smiling as he remembered what Larsen had said to him this morning on the ready line:

"I'm not worried about you getting past Bao Kung Cheng's guns or beating Charlie. I'm worried that you won't survive the drubbing our own side is going to give you when you get home."

Steve guessed that he was breaking just about every rule in the book this time around. Back in November 1950, the Air Force had briefly entertained the idea of allowing its pilots the right of hot pursuit across the Yalu, but the outcry from America's allies in Korea had forced the brass to drop the idea.

And all that ruckus had only been over the issue of hot pursuit: a few moments' flying time over Manchuria while in the heat of a dogfight. What the hell was the UN going to say when it found out a USAF pilot had intentionally invaded Chinese airspace for an extended time period in order to carry out a premeditated, illegal attack on a Soviet pilot?

The second half of the plan was as cunningly simple (or foolishly naive; take your pick) as the first part. The idea was to intercept Charlie as he was coming in for a landing at his home airfield.

The tactic had a couple of advantages, Steve reassured himself as he pushed the stick forward and the Broad-Sword began to lose altitude. First and foremost was the element of surprise. Steve was gambling that the commies would never expect a BroadSword to attack their heavily fortified base from deep within their own territory. Hopefully he could get in and out before the commies would have time to bring their antiaircraft defenses to bear, or scramble their jets. The second advantage came from the fact that Steve was planning on bouncing Charlie as the Russian was preparing to land; at low altitude his Broad-Sword had superior performance capabilities over Charlie's MiG.

The gray-green, tobacco-brown terrain was rising up at Steve. He punched his tanks, checked his guns, and began his approach toward the Red airfield. He was now in the enemy's backyard, so he went down on deck to avoid being picked up on their radar. There were no trees—the commies had likely chopped them all for firewood. Steve concentrated on his flying as he got *real low*. His screaming Broad-Sword rose and fell with the hills and dips of the North Korean terrain as he flew at four hundred knots toward the enemy airfield, his jet wash throwing up rocks and dirt in his wake as the bramble tickled his fighter's silvery belly.

The scruffy hills dropped away, and then he was traveling down a broad slope, toward Bao Kung Cheng's airdrome and complex of runways. Dead-on, Charlie's flock of MiGs were raising dust as they taxied along the concrete airstrips toward their revetments. The blue lightning MiG was still in the air. As Steve had hoped, Charlie had waited to land last. He was just committing to his landing approach.

Steve pulled up to get the altitude he would need to bounce Charlie. The commie maintenance workers and other base personnel were all staring up at Steve in what he guessed was disbelief at seeing the red, white, and blue over their heads. He had no time to think about them, however. He cobbed the throttle to come around fast and hard, sustaining punishing G's through the 180-degree turn that put him on Charlie's six-o'clock high.

Evidently Charlie hadn't noticed Steve, and clearly nobody had radioed the Russian to warn him of what was coming. The blue lightning MiG was still settling down toward the runway as Steve dived, then chopped his throttle and popped his speed brakes. His shoulder harness strained to keep him from bashing his visor against his gun sight as he centered the cherry-red circle of his gun sight on the MiG's spine and squeezed off a burst.

Armor-piercing incendiaries spilled out from the Broad-Sword's six .50-caliber nose guns. The APIs raised dust spouts and chips off the concrete runway, and blindingly white sparks off the blue lightning MiG's dirty aluminum wings and fuselage. Charlie's airplane began to yaw as Steve's tracer rounds caged it in bars of fire.

Steve held down his trigger, spraying Charlie with APIs. *It's all over,* he thought. *You're one cooked commie goose. With the runway a few feet below you, and me point-blank above, you've got nowhere to go.*

He was gently bringing up the BroadSword's nose in order to dance the APIs along the MiG's fuselage toward its canopy, when the Russian pilot touched down on the concrete runway.

Beautiful move, Steve thought, even as he cursed Charlie for outsmarting him. As the Russian's tires hit the runway, the suddenly earthbound MiG experienced an abrupt drop in speed which caused the BroadSword to overshoot.

Steve was suddenly looking at empty runway. He pulled up to execute a hard starboard chandelle to try to once again come around behind Charlie, who had only bounced the concrete and was now airborne again. Steve watched as Charlie retracted his landing gear and came around in a chandelle of his own.

Airborne, Yalu Charlie was one wet hornet, shaking off water and spoiling for a fight.

And I'm the guy to give it to you, Steve thought.

The MiG might have been faster at high altitude, but at any altitude the BroadSword could make the tighter turns. As Charlie did his best to come around, Steve rolled his BroadSword inside of Charlie's wide turn and again locked on to the commie's six o'clock. He centered the gun sight's red circle on the MiG's glowing tailpipe and squeezed off a burst. Once again the MiG began sparkling with hits. Charlie pitched and yawed, trying to throw off Steve's aim as he led his tormentor back over the field.

Steve guessed that the Russian was hoping that Bao

Kung Cheng's antiaircraft batteries might put the Broad-Sword on his tail out of business, so he stayed close to the MiG, just outside the turbulent reach of Charlie's jet wash. As the two jets streaked the field at great speed and low altitude, there was no way the commie gunners could fire without the risk of hitting their own airplane.

Charlie made a climbing turn away from the field, avoiding the hills to the north and heading out toward the lower ground approaching the Yalu.

Steve grinned. Charlie had obviously realized that the ground defenses couldn't help him, and had probably decided that the smart thing for him to do was clear the airspace over the field so that other MiGs could take off to join the fight. Whatever Charlie's motives, taking the chase toward the Yalu suited Steve as well. For one thing it took him closer to home. For another, it gave them some privacy—at least five minutes' worth—in which to conduct their business.

"Now you get the idea, Charles," Steve muttered. "This little dance is just between you and me."

The MiG's desperate attempt to gain altitude exposed its upper fuselage and canopy to Steve's guns. There was no time to aim. Steve just led the MiG with his own jet's snout and held down the firing button.

It was Charlie who flew into Steve's hose spray of tracers. The APIs shattered the MiG's canopy, sending sparkling shards of plexiglass spinning away. As Charlie banked away from the gunfire, Steve saw the wind tear away the Russian's oxygen mask.

Steve laughed in triumph. Without a canopy or mask there was no way Charlie could take the fight up into the cold, thin higher reaches, where the MiG had the performance advantage.

Charlie leveled off at five hundred feet and began to really pour on the speed, but Steve was able to stay right on his six o'clock, firing bursts whenever he could get the gun sight's red pipper on target. The MiG began smoking as Steve repeatedly raised sparks off its pocked aluminum hide.

But Steve was beginning to worry about his ammo supply. The BroadSword carried 1,602 rounds, which translated into only 276 shots per gun, and the nose-mounted .50s spat them out fast. *What if I run out of bullets before I can knock Charlie down?*

The chase had taken them farther south. They were coming up on the Yalu. Steve once again centered the red circle on Charlie's tailpipe and mashed his trigger. This time bits and pieces of the MiG began spinning off.

He's got to go down any time now—Steve reassured himself.

The MiG banked out over the river and then *dropped down* to *skim* the turbulent waters.

You are one fucking expert pilot, Charles, Steve thought in admiration. *But if you can do it, so can I.*

He nevertheless found himself gritting his teeth in apprehension as he dipped toward the Yalu's rushing silver waters. BroadSwords did not come equipped with pontoons.

It immediately became clear just what Charlie was up to. He was flying so close to the surface of the river that the watery wake he was throwing up was splashing Steve's canopy, obscuring his vision. He couldn't see to *steer*, never mind *shoot*.

Steve pulled up. The river was a glinting metal ribbon giddily unspooling fifty feet below his wings. Charlie was flying about twenty-five feet above the water, less than one hundred feet ahead. Steve dropped his nose a bit to align his guns on the MiG. He intended to hammer Charlie into the river.

Charlie must have read his mind. The commie chose that moment to climb to starboard, leaving the river and heading out over North Korean territory.

Steve wrenched back his stick to stay with the MiG. Both jets were screaming as they clawed their way into the sky. At twelve hundred feet Steve managed to once again get his gun sight on Charlie and fired.

His guns spat out a handful of rounds and then went dead.

Nothing left—godammit! Momentarily distracted, Steve didn't notice Charlie popping his own speed brakes.

As his BroadSword overshot the MiG Steve turned his head to watch in despair as Charlie raised his MiG's nose and began firing from point-blank range.

The first flurry of crimson fireballs from the MiG's trio of cannon lobbed past Steve's canopy, but then Charlie adjusted his aim.

Steve felt the jarring impact, and the BroadSword skidded and yawed out of control as the MiG's cannon rounds clipped off the BroadSword's port-side horizontal stabilizer, and the tip of its port wing.

No question about it, Steve thought. *This baby is going down.* He was sending out a breathless, speedy SOS when he saw the MiG fly past him and falter in midair before Charlie ejected.

Evidently Charlie must have been so close behind the BroadSword that some of the whirling debris that he'd shot off the F-90 had gotten sucked into his air intake, totally destroying the MiG's already ravaged engine.

Time for me to get out as well, Steve thought.

He hunched down and pulled up the hand grips on both sides of his seat. His shoulder harness automatically locked as his canopy blew off, exposing him to the shrill wind which bit at him like something rabid. He rocked his body back into the seat, bringing up his knees tight against his chest as he placed his boots in the footrests. He pressed his helmet back against the headrest and tucked in his chin.

He squeezed the seat-ejection triggers.

He cried out as the explosive charge brutally booted him up and out of the cockpit. His shoulder harness released, and Steve kicked away from the seat to fall, tumbling in space. The ground was hungrily reaching up to embrace him—

And then the automatic chute deployed, and Steve's belly went out through the top of his head as his downward tumble was joltingly checked. As he swung beneath the chute he could see the oily black smoke that marked the spots where his BroadSword and Charlie's MiG had gone down. The smoke was a mixed blessing. It would act as a beacon to Search and Rescue, but also bring the North Koreans. Their jets must have scrambled by now. They'd be here any moment. The NKPA ground forces would take a little longer.

First things first, he reminded himself. *I've got to land in one piece.* He worked the suspension shrouds the way he'd been taught at jet fighter training school, keeping his eyes on the horizon, resisting the urge to look down at the ground rushing up between his legs.

Keep loose, he reminded himself. *Knees bent, fall and roll when you hit, then move fast to get out of the harness before the wind catches the silk and it begins to drag you.*

A couple of hundred feet away Charlie was also preparing to land. Charlie had tried to work his chute to carry him across to the northern, Manchurian side of the Yalu, but he hadn't the altitude to make it. He was coming down on the North Korean side, just like Steve.

Steve just had time to glimpse Charlie hitting the ground, and then it was his turn. He made an awful splattering noise, like what you'd hear at a butcher shop, as he hit the muddy riverbank, and rolled like a rag doll to absorb the impact. Dripping mud, he jumped to his feet, astounded that he hadn't broken anything, and slipped out of his harness. He disregarded his helmet, Mae West, and the rest of his flight gear, and then looked around for Charlie, fearful that the Red might try to ambush him. He saw the Russian about sixty yards away, still trying to get out of his own harness.

It must be jammed on him, Steve thought. *Hey, my luck's still holding. If I play my cards right, I can go home with a Russian POW.*

He began to run toward Charlie along the boggy, weed-strewn riverbank. As he closed on the Russian he drew his four-inch-barrel, Smith & Wesson .38-caliber revolver from his waist holster.

Charlie had finally gotten out of his chute harness. He was wearing a dark blue flight suit and a quilted jacket. He wore no G-suit. The commies didn't have them.

The Russian removed his helmet. He had short-cut blond hair. As Charlie threw the helmet aside, he caught sight of Steve. His right hand began to claw at the flapped holster on his hip.

Steve was less than twenty-five feet away when he yelled, "Stop!" at Charlie, and then fired a shot in the air.

Charlie ignored Steve's shout, but froze at the sound of the gunshot. His hand moved away from his holster. Then both of his hands went up above his head as Steve approached, his .38 leveled at the Russian.

As Steve got closer he saw that Charlie looked to be in his thirties. He was clean-shaven, with high cheekbones and dark eyes that were spaced wide apart.

"You speak English?" Steve called out over the sound of the rushing river splashing against its banks.

"*Da*—yes," Charlie said.

"You're my prisoner!" Steve declared. "Do you understand?"

Charlie smiled.

"What's so funny?" Steve demanded.

"NKPA forces will soon be here," the Russian said in heavily accented English. "I think you would be well advised to place yourself in my hands."

"Listen, Charlie, I want you to—" Steve paused. "What's your name?"

"Vladimir," the Russian said, and then smiled. "What is your name, might I ask?"

"Steve."

"You are an excellent pilot, Steve."

"Same goes for you, Vladimir." Steve gestured with his revolver. "I've got to ask you to get rid of your gun. Take it out slowly and throw it in the river."

He watched as the Russian did as he was told, drawing a nasty-looking, flat black automatic out of his holster. Both men watched it splash into the Yalu.

Just then Steve heard the roar of jet engines and looked overhead. The sun glinted off three MiGs high in the sky to the north. Steve watched them begin to drop down toward the river.

"You see?" the Russian said gently. "It is useless. Ground forces will soon be here as well."

"Shut up, and let me think," Steve demanded. He anxiously scanned the sky to the south. *Where the fuck is the Search and Rescue whirlybird?*

He looked around for some decent cover from which to make a stand, but there was nothing but a low jumble of rocks and some brush about twenty feet away from the riverbank.

"If you surrender to me, I will guarantee that you receive humane treatment," the Russian said.

"I will guarantee that I'll blow your head off if you don't do exactly as I tell you," Steve said, approaching him. "If I'm close to you, those MiGs can't strafe."

"As you wish, but it is useless—"

"Shut up! Get down on the ground and lie on your stomach."

"Why?"

"I'm going to tie your hands behind your back with one of your boot laces," Steve said.

"That is not necessary."

"Do as I tell you, or I'll shoot."

"No. And you will not shoot," the Russian said, shouting to be heard over the roar of the MiGs orbiting them. "If you shoot me, those MiGs will strafe you. It is not necessary to tie my hands. I give you my word as a fellow officer and pilot that I will remain your prisoner until such time that you might surrender to me."

Steve stared at him. "And if I should say that's not acceptable?"

The Russian shrugged. "Then I suppose you *will* have to shoot me."

Steve, glaring at the Russian, finally shrugged and sighed. "Okay, Valdimir. I'll accept your word."

The Russian nodded. "Thank you."

Both men glanced into the sky as the MiGs suddenly veered off, seeming to head back north.

"What?" the Russian frowned as the MiGs left.

"Look there!" Steve laughed, pointing to the south, where the sun was glinting off eight specks in the sky. "Those are BroadSwords, Vladimir. Your MiGs beat it because they didn't want to be caught low. If the BroadSwords have made it here, the chopper can't be far behind." He laughed again as the droning *whap-whap-whap* of the whirlybird became audible and quickly increased in volume.

The olive drab Sikorsky H-19 helicopter, looking like a pregnant dragonfly, appeared low in the eastern sky. Steve realized that the chopper, unsure of where he had gone down, had been slowly traveling the river, looking for survivors. Now, as the H-19's pilot saw Steve and his prisoner, the chopper picked up speed, to hover about thirty feet above their heads. Far overhead, the BroadSwords orbited to provide top cover.

"No place to land here," Steve yelled to the Russian over the helicopter's roaring motor. "They'll have to lower a sling. Remember, you gave your word that you accept that you're my prisoner."

The Russian nodded as a crewman standing in the H-19's opened sliding door began lowering a sling.

"You first, Vlaldimir." The Russian slid his head and shoulders into the sling, and then said, "Ready."

"Go!" Steve yelled. He watched the chopper's winch hoist the Russian into the air, and then waited anxiously, looking around for signs of the NKPA as the sling came down for him. When it did he holstered his gun, slid into the sling, and yelled, "Okay!"

The winch hauled him up, and then the crewman was hauling him inside the chopper, which was already coming around to get the hell back to safety on the other side of the 38th parallel.

The Russian was sitting on the floor in the corner of the noisy chopper. Another crewman was keeping him covered with a carbine.

"He's okay," Steve shouted above the engine racket. "He's my prisoner."

"If you say so, sir," the crewman nodded. He lowered his carbine but still kept a wary eye on the Russian as Steve sat down next to him.

"I've got to say you're taking this pretty well, Vladimir."

The Russian smiled. "It will be all right for me. You will see."

Steve shrugged.

"Can I ask you," the Russian began, "why did you hunt me as you did?"

"You shot down and killed my friend," Steve replied, watching the man for his reaction.

The Russian shrugged apologetically. "Forgive me, but I have shot down so many. Was he a BroadSword pilot?"

"No. He flew an F-80. A Shooting Star."

"I am sorry . . . I don't remember."

"You shot him down after he and I bounced you and a buddy over the Yesong River, near Sariwon, in September 1951."

The Russian's dark eyes widened.

Steve nodded. "I got your buddy. You got mine."

"That was you?" He laughed ruefully. "Even *then* I thought that you were a fine pilot. Now I know that for a fact."

"We're okay now, sir," the winch operator called out. He was still standing in the doorway, but had swung back the winch, replacing it with a fixed-mounted .30-caliber machine gun. "We've got the BroadSwords flying high cover, and we've just picked up an escort of Mustangs that'll stick with us until we're over friendly territory. We should have you back home in a half hour. The pilot's radioing to find out what we're supposed to do with your Russky prisoner, there. We've picked up some North Korean POWs in our time, but this is the first Russian we've ever had the privilege of delivering."

(Two)

Chusan Airfield

A burly-looking MP and several Air Force officers who Steve had never seen before were waiting at Chusan field as the chopper set down. The officers stepped up to Steve and saluted as he climbed down out of the chopper.

"Major Gold? I'm Major Donald, from FEAFcom Intelligence," the officer said.

"Boy, you guys got here fast," Steve laughed.

"Yes, well," Donald smiled thinly. "Is it true you have a Russian POW?"

Steve nodded. He jerked his thumb over his shoulder as he glanced at the MP. "He's in the copter."

The MP looked uncomfortable. "Sorry, sir," he said as he relieved Steve of his .38, and then pulled Steve's wrists behind his back and snapped on a pair of handcuffs.

"These officers here are for the prisoner," the MP continued. "Colonel Gleason sent me for *you*."

"You will stand at attention, Major Gold," Colonel Claude Gleason, CO of the 44th said. He was seated behind his desk as Steve was escorted into the office by the MP.

"Just let me get the circulation back into my wrists, Colonel," Steve muttered, shaking his hands. "They just came off after being on for the last three hours."

Colonel Claude Gleason, CO of the 44th Squadron, glared at Steve from behind his desk. "You've got a lot of balls talking back to me, considering what you've done!" Gleason snapped. "You," he addressed the MP. "Wait outside."

Steve looked around. The walls of Gleason's office were lined with framed specimens from his entomological collection. Steve was surrounded by flattened, multicolored butterflies stuck to their pale blue blotter backgrounds by pins shoved through their wings.

Fitting audience, Steve couldn't help thinking. *Don't worry, you poor bastards. I'm about to join you. Gleason's probably got a spot on the wall all reserved for me.*

"Colonel, may I speak frankly?"

"You may not!" Gleason spat.

"Well, I think I will anyway," Steve said, too angry to be concerned about his insolence. "Sure I broke some rules, but I don't deserve this sort of treatment."

"Oh, you don't?" Gleason demanded. He was scarlet with anger. The flushed crimson went up past his ears to suffuse his balding scalp. His hands were trembling with fury as he whipped off his wire-rimmed spectacles and began to polish them with the tip of his dark blue necktie.

"You didn't need to send an MP for me," Steve continued. "And you didn't need to have him handcuff me. And *then* you didn't need to keep me sitting outside your office for the past three hours with those goddamned cuffs on."

"Don't you dare use profanity in this office—" Gleason began.

"Goddamned cuffs!" Steve yelled out, cutting him off. "There! I had my say! Now you can do your worst, Colonel! I'm glad I did what I did! I swore I'd get Yalu Charlie to avenge my friend's death and I did it. Now I don't care what happens to me. Understand?"

"Quite," Gleason nodded. "Are you finished now, Major?"

"I'm finished."

"'Good. Now let me tell you something," Gleason said coldly as he replaced his glasses. "First of all, I know all about what happened to you and your friend a year ago August. While you were waiting outside my office, I looked into the matter. Now then, I won't even bring up the questionable circumstances which led to the engagement between your Shooting Stars, and those MiGs. The bottom line is that your friend died in combat. Unfortunate? Yes. But when a country is at war, such things happen."

Steve opened his mouth to speak.

"Shut up!" Gleason slammed the desktop with the flat of his hand. "Not another word out of you, or I *swear* I'll call in the MP and have you recuffed and *gagged*."

Probably do it, too, Steve thought. He kept his mouth shut.

"What you did today, Major Gold, was unaccountably irresponsible. Do you think that FEAFcom has posted China off-limits to aggravate you pilots? Do you think that FEAFcom is rooting for the commies? That it wants *them* to win, and that's why we've agreed to allow them sanctuary in Manchuria?"

I think I'll assume that these are rhetorical questions, Steve decided.

"Wake up and smell the coffee, Major Gold! We have nuclear weapons, and so do the Russians, but thankfully, neither side is insane enough to want to use them. Accordingly, what we have here in Korea by mutual agreement of both sides is a 'limited' war. That agreement came within a hairbreadth of being abrogated by you, thanks to your deciding to invade China and ambush a Soviet military advisor."

"Military advisor!" Steve exploded. "How can you call Yalu Charlie a fucking military advisor?"

Gleason leapt to his feet. He came around from behind his desk, to stand toe to toe with Steve, except that the colonel was a half foot shorter, so he had to tilt back his head to stare into Steve's eyes.

"You want to know what's been happening for the three hours I've kept you waiting, Major Gold?" Gleason's breath thudded into Steve's face. "I've been on the horn with the brass in Japan, who have been on the horn with the brass in Washington, which has been on the horn with Moscow. President Truman has shown great interest in this matter, as well."

"I said that I was prepared to accept the consequences of my actions," Steve said quietly.

"You are?" Gleason nodded, smiling coldly.

"Yes, sir."

"I suppose you expect a court-martial?"

Steve couldn't resist. "I don't expect a medal, sir."

Gleason, shaking his head, walked back to his desk and sat down in his chair. "It's too bad you don't expect that, you miserable son of a bitch, because a medal is just what you're getting."

"Sir?" Steve asked, totally confused.

"Sir?" Gleason mimicked, looking at Steve in disgust. "You know what you are, you son of a bitch? You are *born lucky.*"

Oh, no, Steve thought, appalled. *Pop's somehow found out, used his influence to get me out of this. I can't let him. Not this time. I played, and now I should have to pay. Otherwise I'll never be able to look anyone in the eye again for the rest of my life.* "Sir," he began. "I—"

"It so happens," Gleason continued, ignoring him, "that your prisoner, Vladimir Sergeyevich Volkov, is the son of some VIP in Moscow. The Russians want him back. Desperately. They are so anxious to retrieve him, as a matter of fact, that they have hinted that upon his return they will persuade the North Koreans to be a bit more flexible about some of the logjams tying up the progress of the peace talks."

Steve bit hard on his lower lip in a desperate attempt to keep from smiling. He lost.

"*Yesss,*" Gleason hissed from between clenched teeth. "It *is-s-s* funny in its way, *is-s-s-n't* it?"

"If you only knew, sir . . ."

"To further cloud the issue, the press has somehow gotten hold of the story. You're already being touted as a hero by the wire services. Since the news out of Korea has been downbeat for so long, the brass has decided that putting a heroic slant on what you've done may be just what the doctor ordered." Gleason paused. "By all rights, you should be court-martialed and sentenced to ten years hard labor, but that's not going to happen. Instead, you're being turned into a hero."

"Thank you, sir!" Steve said brightly.

Gleason looked like he was about to say something nasty, but he stopped and just shook his head. "Number one," he said briskly, "you are being relieved of flight duty, effective immediately, and being sent back to the States. You've had more than your share of combat tours, and in any event, it's too risky to allow you to remain in Korea. Imagine the propaganda value to the Reds if they managed to get hold of *you.*"

"Number two, once you're stateside, you will be receiving the Medal of Honor and a promotion in rank to—oh, how it *galls* me to say this—lieutenant colonel."

"Thank you, sir."

"Get out of here, Major," Gleason scowled. "And on your way out ask the MP if you can have those handcuffs as a souvenir." Gleason looked wistful. "Of what might have been."

CHAPTER 19

(One)

GAT
Burbank
31 December 1952

Susan Greene was busy typing a report for Don Harrison. As usual, his writing style left a lot to be desired, so Susan was doing a little revision work as she typed; just smoothing out the sentences as she worked.

The clacking of her typewriter's keys was the only sound in the department. It was only four o'clock in the afternoon, but it was New Year's Eve. Most of the designers had never come back from lunch, and that handful who had returned had left early.

The department's telephones had been pretty quiet during the morning, and absolutely mute all afternoon. The lack of interruptions had allowed Susan to become engrossed in her work, so that when the telephone on her desk began to ring, it startled her.

"Mr. Harrison's office," she answered.

"Yes, is he in?" a familiar woman's voice began. "It's . . ."

"Yes, I know who it is," Susan said, doing her best to sound pleasant and businesslike. Just a moment, please." She buzzed Don on the intercom. "Your lady friend on line one. . . ."

"Thanks, Suzy," Don said.

Susan heard Don say, *"Hi, honey. Is the champagne chilling?"* And then she resolutely went back to her typing to drown out his voice.

She'd thought that her first date with Don back in May had boded well. They'd had dinner at Donde's, a romantic Italian seafood place in Santa Monica. Donde's had been her choice because it had been her and Blaize's favorite neighborhood place back when they were living in that little walk-up by the pier. Going there with Don on their first date had been an exorcism of sorts for Susan. She'd meant to exorcise Blaize from her immediate thoughts so that she could see this man Don Harrison with eyes unclouded by her late husband's image.

Of course she would always love Blaize. Just as she would always eat and breathe and sleep, loving Blaize was a condition of her existence. But she'd come to the conclusion that she could also love another man. Maybe this new love would not be as pure as her first. Maybe it would never penetrate into the marrow of her bones, but it would be a real love, in any case.

So she'd taken Don Harrison to Donde's, and that first night, over pasta with shrimp and white wine, she'd talked about her husband the English test pilot, the RAF fighter ace, the war hero posthumously awarded his own country's Victoria Cross, and a Distinguished Flying Cross from the United States.

Don was a good listener. He asked the right questions to keep her talking, and pretty soon they were laughing together over the latest antics of her ten-year-old son, and then, miraculously, the talk about the past was exhausted, and there she was, sitting across from a man and talking to him about herself, and enjoying it.

Susan realized that she'd been typing the same line over and over again, and quit in disgust. Her mind was no longer on her work. The walls of Don's office were so thin, and the department was so quiet. She could clearly hear his laughter, even if his words did remain an unintelligible murmur.

Thinking back on that first date at Donde's, she now supposed that it had been inevitable and probably for the best that she'd had too much wine and let slip who her parents were.

Don had laughed and laughed. He'd said that he didn't mind dating the boss's daughter, and then he'd asked if she and Robert might like to go for a drive along the shore the following Sunday afternoon.

Maybe that's the problem: that I let my son intrude on the relationship too soon. Susan now brooded. *Or maybe the fact that I'm the boss's daughter matters to Don, after all.*

Or maybe she had just wanted this relationship too much; queered it somehow by pushing too hard. Don was a bit too much the repressed gentleman for that (as Blaize had been, but without Blaize's wildly romantic streak).

Whatever the reason, or reasons, their burgeoning romantic relationship was soon stalled. Susan had thought that maybe she could get things back on track, but then this woman from out of Don's past had called. Evidently this Linda Forrest knew just how to go about ensnaring a man.

Or maybe the chemistry was just right between them? Susan thought. *But what's the point of wondering on the why of it? Some people hit it off together and others don't, and that's that.*

She tried her best to ignore Don's laughter as he chatted with his new flame. For the past few weeks the two love-birds had been giggling on the telephone together half a dozen times a day.

She quickly resumed typing as she heard Don hang up the telephone. A few moments later he came out of his office wearing his hat and carrying his briefcase.

"Suzy," he scolded her good-naturedly. "It's New Year's Eve, for Godsakes—"

"I just want to finish this report, Don," she said, keeping her eyes trained on her typewriter.

"Don't you have plans for this evening?" he asked.

"Yes," she said evenly, glancing up at him. "I have a date." *With my son,* she added silently.

"Good!" he nodded.

He didn't seem the least bit jealous. It was clearly hopeless, and what did she care? Leave him to Linda Forrest and good riddance, she thought. He was losing his hair anyway.

"I want you to go home early, and that's an order, got it?"

"Got it," she smiled sweetly.

"Oh, and Suzy—" He came close and bent toward her to give her a kiss on the forehead. "Happy New Year," he murmured.

And why the hell this stodgy, bumbling, balding man's touch should affect her so, she had no idea.

"Happy New Year to you, too, Don," she said brightly.

She watched him as he walked away from her and out of the department. And then she slid a fresh sheet of paper into her machine and went back to her typing.

(Two)

The Reginald Hotel
Chicago
23 April 1953

It was a little after nine on Thursday morning. Steven Gold, nude, was lying on his back, his head propped up with pillows in the big double bed of his tastefully furnished, moderately expensive hotel room. The room was exactly like the endless series of other moderately expensive hotel rooms he'd been in over the last few months. When he'd first opened his eyes a half hour ago, he'd had no idea where he was.

But now he knew he was in Chicago, he thought as he sipped the tepid room-service coffee, and smoked a Pall Mall. The cigarette tasted terrible. He hadn't even brushed his teeth yet. He reached over to the bedside nightstand and dropped the smoke into last night's ice bucket, which stood next to last night's empty scotch bottle.

In a couple of hours he had to be cleaned up and in his dress uniform. He had his speech to give to the Greater Chicago Federated Boys' Society. After the speech, it was over to city hall to receive the key to the city from the mayor, and say a few words.

Then the press conference for the local papers. The reporters would shout the same old questions: *"What do you think about Ike being the President-elect?"* and *"How do you think the war's going?"*

Pretending never to have heard those questions before was bad, but trying to sound fresh giving the speech was the worst. The speech was titled, "How I Captured Yalu Charlie." It was one part truth and all the rest bullshit; scripted for him by the Air Force's Office of Public Information.

He'd already given the speech twenty-two times; first as an exclusive to *PhotoWeek* magazine, and then in front of civic and church organizations all across the country. He would probably give it another fifty times before he was done.

The speech was full of stuff about how he'd knocked down the blue lightning MiG on behalf of the Flag, and Liberty, and Mom's Apple Pie. Now, he wasn't a dummy. He knew why it had to be that way. Hell, he couldn't get up there and tell the audience the whole grisly mess concerning Mikey DeAngelo,—that Lieutenant Colonel Steven Gold was in reality a maverick fighter jock who had blithely broken the rules in order to avenge his buddy's death and in the process almost turned the world into one big Hiroshima.

The same way he knew all that, he knew he was damned lucky not to have been court-martialed and imprisoned. Hell, he *would* have ended up breaking big rocks into little ones if good old Vladimir—AKA Yalu Charlie—hadn't gone and knocked himself out of the sky by flying into the BroadSword's debris.

Yeah, I'm lucky, Steve thought, staring at the ceiling cracks as he lit another smoke. But it still got to him, having to say that phony speech over and over. At some point during the intervening months since he'd been reassigned from Korea to Washington, D.C., what had really happened that day in the sky over Bao Kung Cheng had faded from his own mind, to be replaced by the contents of the speech.

That had made Steve feel all hollow inside. It had

made him feel like maybe the commendation he *should* have received was not the Medal of Honor, but the Academy Award for Best Actor in a film called "The Korean War."

But the war, and your popularity on the rubber-chicken circuit ain't going to last forever, Stevie boy. So then what?

He knew that he had his present slot for as long as he wanted it, but the problem was he didn't want it at all. It had been a kick at first to be back in Washington with the title of Special Spokesman for the Air Force of Public Information, but what it entailed was hanging around the Hill waiting to have his picture taken with influential politicians, just like the last time. He sure as hell didn't want to do that for the rest of his career, assuming the Air Force wanted to let him. But then what else *was* there for a twenty-nine-year-old light colonel with a high school equivalency diploma?

This war isn't going to last forever, Steve thought again, and had to grin. It was probably too much to hope for *another* one to come along anytime soon.

He kicked out of bed, heading for the shower.

He had some extended leave time coming once his speaking engagements were fulfilled. Maybe he'd spend it at home in California, he mused. It would be good to get to know his father again, Steve thought. God, they'd been close when he was just a kid.

And then, who knew? If things worked out, maybe he wouldn't make a career out of the Air Force after all.

Steve had always resisted the notion of going to work at GAT, in part because he didn't want his father to take him for granted, and in part because he didn't want the world to think that he'd gotten his job through nepotism. But now he was beginning to think that maybe he *could* make a niche for himself at GAT. Maybe he could do some kind of spokesman job for GAT the way he'd been doing for the Air Force.

It was worth thinking about, Steve decided. Maybe he'd end up working with Pop, after all. . . .

ALSO BY T. E. CRUISE

Wings of Gold: The Aces
Wings of Gold Book III: The Hot Pilots*

Published by
POPULAR LIBRARY   *forthcoming

A new world brought fresh challenge. They rose to meet both.

HERMAN GOLD

He had a fine son, but a reluctant heir—and feared that Gold Aviation was destined to die with him.

STEVEN GOLD

Record-setting World War II flying ace and Medal of Honor winner, he knew the button-down world of his father's company could never be his.

BENNY DETKIN

He wanted to kill Nazis, but when they sent him to the Pacific theater instead of Europe, he shot those Zeros right out of the sky.

SUZY GOLD

Still stunningly attractive, she sought the men who wouldn't threaten her loyalty to the memory of her heroic husband.

DONALD HARRISON

A Gold only by marriage, he felt like the bastard son, challenged by both the brother-in-law and stepson who bore the stratospheric standards set by the . . .

WINGS of GOLD

BOOK II
THE FLYBOYS